BAD GIRLS, BAD GIRLS,

— WHATCHA GONNA DO? —

BAD GIRLS, BAD GIRLS,
— WHATCHA GONNA DO? —

CYNTHIA VOIGT

Atheneum Books for Young Readers
New York   London   Toronto   Sydney

Mostly, this book is dedicated to the people who work to make
this world a better place for its inhabitants
(Betsy and Joe spring to mind),
And also to the folks at Ovenworks,
who opened my eyes to the joys of dishwashing—
Ken and Pete and Emily.

Atheneum Books for Young Readers
An imprint of Simon & Schuster Children's Publishing Division
1230 Avenue of the Americas, New York, New York 10020
Book design by Ann Zeak
The text for this book is set in Janson Text.
Manufactured in the United States of America
First Edition
2 4 6 8 10 9 7 5 3
Library of Congress Cataloging-in-Publication Data
Voigt, Cynthia.
Bad girls, bad girls, whatcha gonna do? / Cynthia Voigt.—1st ed.
p. cm.
Summary: As new ninth graders eager only to survive high school,
Mikey and Margalo must deal creatively with stolen money
and cheating on the tennis courts.
ISBN-13: 978-0-689-82474-6
ISBN-10: 0-689-82474-2
[1. High schools—Fiction. 2. Schools—Fiction.
3. Bullies–Fiction. 4. Tennis–Fiction. 5. Sports—Corrupt
practices—Fiction.] I. Titles.
PZ7.V874Wgm 2006
[Fic]—dc22   2005005547

Contents

I

Hadrian's Fall

— 1 —

At the Bottom of the Food Chain

Ninth grade stinks," said Mikey. "Big-time."

Margalo agreed. "Stinkius, stinkior, stinkissimus," she said, partly for the fun of trying out her new Latin skills and partly for the fun of irritating Mikey.

"It's overloud and overcomplicated and overpopulated. And it's taking a long time."

It was the third Friday of ninth grade. The ME twins, Mikey Elsinger and Margalo Epps, best friends since fifth grade, sat at their usual table at the rear of the high school cafeteria. The tables farthest back—back from the entryway, back from the cafeteria lines—were, socially speaking, the least desirable, the social cellar of high school.

Keeping up her side of the disagreement Mikey reminded Margalo, "Gazillions of people speak Spanish."

"As if you care about communicating with people," Margalo said, and bit into her sandwich.

"Latin's a dead language," Mikey recited, separating each line of the poem into its own sentence to increase the annoyance value. "It's dead as dead can be. First it killed the Romans."

"I told you in June I was taking Latin. You could have signed up for it too."

"And now it's killing me," Mikey concluded. She unwrapped her own sandwich triumphantly.

They both brought lunch from home, Margalo for financial reasons, Mikey from culinary concerns, so for the moment they were alone at the back of the room and could take advantage of the relative privacy to have a nice little quarrel.

In contrast to Margalo's peanut-butter-and-grape-jelly sandwich on lightly toasted supermarket whole wheat bread, Mikey had thick slices of leftover roasted chicken on thick slices of homemade multigrain bread. Between them they also had six Oreo cookies, a banana, an apple, and—torn between her desire to show off her baking and her disinclination to share, Mikey had brought a double serving—two generous slabs of chocolate cake with chocolate frosting.

"Thanks," Margalo said, accepting the piece of cake, setting aside her sandwich. When you were hungry, the thing that was going to taste best was the thing to eat first. That was one of the few things she and Mikey absolutely agreed

4

on. After the first bite she offered her usual style of compliment, "Pretty good, Mikey," and waited for Mikey's usual style of acceptance, "I know."

But, "Uh-oh," Mikey said.

Margalo had her eye on the cake in her hands. "Uh-oh what?"

"Uh-oh that."

By now the tables were filling up. Students from all four grades shared each of the three lunch periods, so that all sizes and ages were represented in the cafeteria, all types and both genders, not to mention the usual variety of teenage humanity: blonde and brunette and redhead, both natural and artificial, the hair short, shorter, and shortest or, conversely, long, longer, and longest. (Blondest and longest being considered the best for the female gender.) There were tall students and short students, ranging from skinny to overweight, buff to totally unexercised, and a large mass of regularly sized and normally muscled. (Tallest and buffest being the most desirable for boys, in general.) Although the majority of students were standard Caucasians of one style or another, they were not an overwhelming majority; more than a third of the school was the usual mix of Asian, African American and Hispanic, and by senior year of high school there were as many mixed-up groups seated together as self-segregated groups seated separately. But even in that big, crowded room, the ninth graders were recognizable. They stood out by standing shorter and scrawnier and fewer.

Margalo scanned the room. "Uh-oh, there," Mikey pointed and then Margalo saw.

It was Hadrian Klenk, of course. Somebody—a big, stocky boy wearing a *Star Wars* t-shirt (bright red, with an image of the *Millennium Falcon*, under which was printed HAN SOLO RULES)—held a full lunch tray up over Hadrian's head, and Hadrian was reaching up to try to reclaim it. The tray passed over to a pair of raised hands behind Hadrian, another boy in another *Star Wars* t-shirt (black, with an image of the *Death Star*, and written under it, DARTH VADER RULES) who continued the game of keep-away by passing the tray—which dropped a fork and knife onto Hadrian's head as it went by—to a third boy (blue, no image, just YODA FOR PRESIDENT).

As Hadrian turned, still reaching, he was tripped by the first boy which caused him to stumble—arms outstretched to break his fall—into a passing girl who was trying to ignore the little scene taking place between her and her table. The girl's plate of salad greens slid off of her tray and bounced onto the floor, spraying her shoes with lettuce and oily dressing. She glared at Hadrian. Hadrian ducked his head and backed away.

People watched this, some amused, some pitying, some irritated, and some just relieved that whatever was happening was happening to Hadrian Klenk, not to them. The general opinion about Hadrian seemed to be *Poor kid, but you'd think he'd figure it out.*

(Figure what out wasn't clear. Things? Life? High School?

And what, having figured out whatever it was, Hadrian was supposed to do about it also remained an unanswered question.)

After three Fridays, however, Hadrian had figured out what he *could* do. He scurried across to the side of the room, making his circuitous way to where Mikey and Margalo sat.

"Who are those guys?" Mikey wondered, watching Hadrian creep along beside the walls.

"I think they're juniors. Or maybe oversized sophomores?"

They kept their eyes on Hadrian, who had reached a corner of the big room.

"I think if Hadrian can just get a part in the fall play," Margalo predicted, "then people will start accepting him. At least some people. At least sort of."

"It didn't happen after last year's play," Mikey pointed out.

"But the part he had in that wasn't—and besides, last year everybody was all excited about Shawn, who can't even act. He's just handsome."

This opinion Margalo presented with a sideways glance at Mikey, who assured her, "He'd have to be a lot handsomer than he is to justify being such a total twithead."

"Anyway," Margalo continued, reassured that Mikey was still over her big eighth-grade crush on Shawn Macavity, "nobody even noticed how good Hadrian was. Except me. Not even the director. Shawn was all anybody talked about, you remember."

Mikey smiled. *I remember that and I remember more, too.* "Not after the dance. Not me."

They watched Hadrian negotiate the back of a table.

"I'm going to make Hadrian come to Drama Club with me today," Margalo said. "Now that they've got someone to teach Drama, Drama Club is starting. What do you think?"

"You know I'm playing tennis. Coach Sandy plans to make the regionals again next spring."

"We were talking about Hadrian," Margalo reminded her. "And Drama. And the way—I don't much like the way people are treating Hadrian in high school."

"I wish he'd just mace those guys," Mikey said.

"Or you could do it," Margalo suggested.

"Or you could think of some way to get at them," Mikey countered.

"Like what?" Margalo asked, sarcastic. "Like, beat them up? Sic Rhonda Ransom on them?" But then once she'd given voice to that sarcastic idea, she couldn't help thinking about it, wondering if it would work and how she would fool Rhonda into going along with it.

"Where do you buy Mace, anyway?" Mikey asked.

"And someone else would just step up to take their places," Margalo realized. "Besides, I bet Mace is illegal at school."

"Or pepper. They can't make a rule against pepper, can they? He could just throw pepper in their faces."

"I can't picture Hadrian doing anything that aggressive," Margalo said.

"Does that mean *we* have to do it for him?" Mikey asked.

They had determined on the first day of ninth grade to stick together, and they had shaken hands on the deal—as if they needed to, as if they hadn't been sticking together through thick and thin (a lot of thick, and a lot of thin, too) for four years already, and not a one of those years any easier than its predecessor. On the first day of ninth grade, after the opening assembly and before splitting up for most of the day (they had only Earth Science and Lunch A together), Mikey and Margalo had stood facing each other in the middle of the hall, ignoring the people moving around them. They had faced each other and reached out right hands to shake on it, and they shook, two World War II pilots about to take off on a two-plane mission where they were going to have to be at each other's shoulder—to guard and defend, also to lead the way—if they wanted to have any hope of coming back alive.

"I don't know that we *have* to," Margalo answered thoughtfully, then—seeing that people were arriving to sit at their table—she finished hastily—"but I don't see anybody else doing anything. Of course, they may know something we don't."

"They just think they do," Mikey muttered.

"Yeah, but they may be right," Margalo said as she turned to greet Hadrian. "Hey."

"I'm sorry, Mikey," he greeted them. It was Mikey who loaned him lunch money every day. He repaid her on Monday mornings, before anybody could take it off of him.

Hadrian was an under-age ninth grader, the victim of not merely one but two grade skippings. He had a big, square head and he moved his scrawny seventh-grade-boy's body with its narrow shoulders hunched forward under his heavy knapsack—totally dorky looking. No ninth grader should be wearing that kind of shirt, and if a ninth grader for some reason had to, he should have the sense not to tuck the shirt into his pants, and if he didn't even have that much style sense he should at least know enough not to wear a belt. No ninth grader should look like he couldn't wait to turn fifty.

Hadrian sat in a chair facing them, which put his back to the room. Probably he was hoping that no one would notice he was there.

Who knew what might happen to someone like Hadrian in high school? The most visible potential victim in the ninth grade, in a system where everybody took it for granted that ninth graders were the natural prey of every upper class? Anything could happen, and none of it much fun for him.

"I'm sorry that I couldn't—," he said, indicating the room behind him and the people in it with a short, jabbing gesture of his head.

"I'm not sharing," Mikey told him.

"That would be out of character. I'll get a banana on my way out. I still have a quarter, and they put out enough fruit for all three lunches. But can I stay even if I'm not eating?"

"Be my guest," said Mikey, waving her hand at the table. As far as she and Margalo were concerned, Hadrian made up for his various and several personal deficiencies by being incredibly intelligent and also interested in a wide variety of subjects. There was nothing Hadrian didn't know something about, and he never pretended to know something when he didn't. But that didn't seem to be a recipe for success in high school, any more than it had been in middle school. The only real difference was that before high school Hadrian had had only one real tormenter—Louis Caselli, class clown, class idiot, long-time sworn enemy of Mikey, and therefore Margalo. But in high school every grade had its share of bullies. From about the first day of school this *Star Wars* trio had singled out Hadrian. Everybody knew that.

The Who's Who of ninth graders was pretty short. There was Ronnie Caselli, of course, immediately one of the most popular girls in the school, and her cousin Louis Caselli, known as the biggest goof-off in the class. Rhonda Ransom got noticed as the big blonde, Mikey Elsinger as supposedly an ace tennis player, Hadrian Klenk as the perfect nerd, big brain and all—the kid was taking Calculus, a junior advanced-level class! And Chemistry for his elective! of all the jerkwater choices. Ira Pliotes was famous as the kid whose father owned a movie theater, Shawn Macavity as planning to be on TV he was so handsome (and didn't he know it), Cassie Davis as the urban nightmare artist bad-attitude chick. Those were the ninth graders the whole school knew. The rest, well, maybe you ran into a couple in an activity or a non-Varsity sport, or one of the mixed-grade classes, like Creative Writing, Band, or Art. But it was hard to tell one ninth grader from another this early in the year. They all looked alike. Except for the ones like Hadrian Klenk who went around looking so weird, it was no wonder he got picked on.

"We don't mind having you here," Mikey assured Hadrian.

"Drama starts today," Margalo reminded him.

Hadrian said, "I didn't tell my mother—"

"You can call her."

"Tennis started right off, like football," Mikey told them, not for the first time.

They ignored her. "You said you would," Margalo reminded Hadrian.

"We're already playing on tennis ladders, separate for boys and girls, and my guess is the top six players on each will be the varsity squad."

Hadrian shrugged, then looked at Margalo out of big brown eyes, like some spaniel asking for mercy or food.

She was unmoved. "I don't know why—since we both know what a good actor you are—you don't do a tough-guy act."

"My Arnold Schwarzenegger imitation?" Hadrian asked with a high-pitched laugh. He made his hands into fists and began assuming body-builder poses in his chair.

They laughed too, but Margalo insisted, "You know what I mean. You *could*."

"Yeah, but I *am* acting. I'm acting invisible. It's just that I'm not successful."

"You'd do better to act tough," Mikey advised.

"I couldn't do much worse," Hadrian admitted. "But once I really learn the layout, I'll be able to keep out of harm's way."

"You're coming to Drama," Margalo repeated. Giving him a chance to become a star onstage was the only thing she could think of that might help Hadrian out. She knew it wasn't much of an idea and there wasn't much of a chance. After all, they were just ninth graders. But since it was the only idea and chance around, she stuck with it.

"I've already won two matches," Mikey reported. "That makes me number eighteen on the girls' ladder."

Cassie Davis cut this non-conversation short. She ruffled Hadrian's hair as she sat down beside him. "You're like some friendly little animal," she told him, "all brown and bushy. I can't resist." She reached out again and he drew back, as far away as he could get without leaving the table. For a long moment, Cassie held her pose, forcing him to hold his.

With her long-fingered hands, the nails kept short so they wouldn't interfere with her artwork but painted maroon to make her fashion statement, and her artificially black hair cropped short and then tipped with bright blue, Cassie looked like a witch. In ninth grade she had given up wearing any makeup except heavy mascara and had taken up wearing Dickies work trousers, which were white and stained with many colors in oil and acrylic, pastels and india ink. Her black tank top showed splotches of the brightest slices of the color wheel, white and yellow and red, pea green and aqua. Cassie settled down to her cafeteria lunch of two bowls of fruit salad and a grilled cheese sandwich, plus a container of milk and a basket of fries. "Say hey, Hay, what's new?" she asked.

Hadrian shook his head, Nothing, you already know that. He folded his hands on the table in front of him, studying his own fingers.

Casey Wolsowski joined them at that point, at about the same time as Jace, but not together with him. Jace was together with Cassie, and had been for most of eighth grade, despite her complaints about him and his about her. He sat beside Cassie and reached over to take a couple of french fries, before picking up a spoon to begin on one of the bowls of fruit. "Got you a banana," he told her.

"I took two fruit bowls because that's what I want for my own lunch."

"You like bananas," Jace said, setting the fruit down on her tray and removing one of the fruit bowls to his own.

Casey meanwhile circled the table, to sit with her back to the wall next to Margalo, with whom she shared an interest in reading and the most advanced freshman English class. Round little Casey seemed to spend her life in hiding, behind big glasses, behind shapeless denim, behind a book. Seated, her knapsack at her feet, her tray beside her, she pulled a paperback book out of the big pocket on the front of her jumper. To read, Casey took *off* her glasses. She opened the book flat on the table in front of her and picked up her fork.

Margalo was always impressed by Casey's ability to eat without looking. She was also curious about the book. It looked old, and often read, and it seemed to be poetry. *John Brown's Body*?

"Art Club meets today," Cassie told them. "Peter Paul's the advisor. Did you know he shows at a gallery in New York? You should have signed up for it," she told Jace.

He protested. "You hate activities." She shrugged. "You hate clubs." She shrugged again. "Outings," he reminded her. "Outings on buses."

"An artist can't be a hermit. Not if she wants to be relevant to her time."

"Yeah, but I didn't even try out for the soccer team because of you. And now it's too late."

"Hey, man, don't blame me. That was your choice."

"So I guess I'll try Art Club, since we have until the thirtieth to pick activities."

"I'm playing tennis," Mikey told this new audience. They already knew, or would have guessed, and were not interested.

"What's the book?" Margalo asked Casey.

"My grandmother gave it to me."

"Is it good?"

"It won the Pulitzer," Hadrian reported.

"I wouldn't mind winning a Pulitzer," Cassie announced. "But they don't give one for Art. Peter Paul says I've got talent."

"And here I was busting my brain to solve the mystery of

your sudden interest in Art Club," said Jace. "While I should really be trying to figure out who walked off with my Oakleys. Those glasses cost my mom a *fortune*."

"Have you looked in the Lost and Found?" Casey suggested.

He snorted, disgusted. "Get real."

Casey returned to reading while she ate, or eating while she read.

"I wanna show you all something," Cassie said, and reached down into the knapsack at her feet.

"Not this again," Jace grumbled.

Cassie pulled out her eight-by-ten sketchbook, telling them, "If Peter Paul can stick around for all four years, I might just graduate high school."

As if in response to Cassie's declaration, the cafeteria loudspeakers blared out their Attention! signal, a long whistle call. It silenced all but the most talkative students in the big room, and even those were reduced to whispering. People stared up at the two loudspeakers, one on each side of the entryway, as if they were faces with expressions that could be read. Even ninth graders, by the third Friday of the school year, were accustomed to the crackle and buzz and then the long whistle that halted a class in its tracks. (Announcements were never made during the four-minute changeover times between classes because the hallways were so crowded and noisy nobody would hear them. Also, there were no loudspeakers in the halls.)

A woman's voice reeled off five names in rapid succession,

four boys—Bill Somebody, Walter Somebody Else, a Daniel, and a Martin—and one girl, Janice Timmer. "Report to Mr. Robredo's office at the end of Lunch A," the voice instructed the five.

"Way to go Janice!" someone cheered, and a few people applauded and whistled, causing the faculty members on lunch duty to move closer, like a flock of birds gathering in the sky, ready to fly towards trouble.

After a reminder about where the Late Activities buses departed from, the loudspeakers gave a closing whistle and fell silent.

Immediately, conversations roared back to life. The noise of trays being stacked and utensils and plates being tossed onto the conveyor belt added to the confusion.

"Like any ninth grader is going to get to do anything in any activity," Cassie told them. "Or club, either, unless maybe something like the Community Aid Club."

Casey disagreed from behind her book. "On the literary magazine everyone gets to help with proofreading. In pairs. And we all vote on every submission."

"The magazine comes out, what? Twice a year? Art Club is actually an open studio. It's really just extra studio time. Peter Paul sets up subjects, still lifes, problems to solve, and he's talking about live models in the spring. He only wants people who are serious about art," she warned Jace, before saying to the rest of them, "Look at this." She opened the sketchbook to show them three small sketches, all on one page: one of an ear and the hair around it, one of a braid, and one of a hand.

They passed the sketchbook around, and Cassie watched their reactions as she explained, "The assignment was a portrait, in pencil."

"*She*—what else, right?—she did something entirely different from everybody else," Jace remarked, but whether it was pride or irritation in his voice wasn't clear. When, like Jace, a person has become a cynic by osmosis, not nature, it isn't always clear what his sarcasm means. "Like this," and he pulled out his own sketch pad, opening it to a drawing of Cassie's face—a lot like her in the eyes and hair. You'd recognize her easily if you knew she was the one Jace was likely to want to draw. Nobody said anything.

"That's Mikey," Hadrian said, turning back to Cassie's sketches and indicating an ear you could barely see behind a section of thick braid. Although it wasn't shown in the picture, there was probably a hand pulling the braid forward, but the braid was the star of the sketch. That braid knew its own mind. That braid knew where it was going and how to get there. "It *is* Mikey, isn't it?"

"And that's me," Margalo said of the ear with hair tucked smoothly behind it, everything neat and orderly, except that the whorls of ear seemed to curl into secret places and disappear there.

"See?" Cassie asked Jace.

"But who's that, the one with the finger like God's finger

on the Sistine Chapel?" asked Casey, and then she guessed, "Peter Paul?"

"You should have done the top of his head," Jace said. "With that bald spot he tries to hide."

"Those are really good drawings," Hadrian said.

Cassie nodded, agreeing. She folded the sketchbook closed.

Not to be outdone, Mikey reminded them, "Coach Sandy wants the team to get to the regionals this year. We might even win and go to the statewides. Because this year I'll be on the team."

"Right," said Cassie. "I'm sure she won't notice that you're a ninth grader."

"Sports are about how you play, not what grade you're in," Mikey told them, not mentioning the speech Coach Sandy had made to the people who came to sign up for tennis on the second day of school. About learning the game and doing the drills. About serving your time on the bench to earn your position on the team. Once the coach saw the kind of tennis Mikey played, she'd change her tune. "Coach Sandy knows how to win. She played pro tennis."

Cassie was the cynic by nature. "If she's so good, what's she doing coaching a high school sports team?"

"A person might ask the same about Peter Paul," said Jace.

Cassie shook her head pityingly at him. "Art's different. Art's harder."

Casey looked up from her book to ask, "What's easy?"

Responses surged at her from both sides, and from across

the table, too. "Cheerleading." "Computers." "Cooking." "Football." "Business." "Teaching." "Politics, once you're elected." "Math." "Science."

Everyone named things they had no interest in trying to do or talent for doing.

Casey didn't add anything. She put on her glasses and looked at them all, letting the variety of responses speak for themselves.

They were speaking to deaf ears. "Reading," Mikey concluded, glaring at Casey.

— 2 —

All the World's a Stage

Drama Club met in the Drama classroom, which was as large as one of the labs, but instead of being filled with high tables, tall stools and locked cupboards, the room was mostly empty space. Beside the door was a big wooden teacher's desk, and benches were stacked up along the opposite wall, ready to be set out in rows. A triangle-shaped wooden platform built out from one corner covered about a quarter of the floor space, making a low stage. On the walls hung framed posters advertising famous plays—*Death of a Salesman, King Lear, Hedda Gabler, Our Town, Carousel, Into the Woods, Blithe Spirit.* Some of these Margalo had heard of, but most not. She studied the posters while she waited just inside the doorway for Hadrian.

People moved past her, upperclassmen mostly, old hands at Drama. They dropped their knapsacks behind and beside and in front of the teacher's desk before settling themselves down on the carpeted floor, facing the stage. When it became apparent that Hadrian was not going to arrive, Margalo sat down alone at the back of the room. The only other ninth graders there were not people who wanted to be seen sitting with her—Shawn Macavity and Heather McGinty, one of the few girls who still had a leftover hopeless crush on him.

As they waited to begin, the people in the room were talking, entirely relaxed, planning to enjoy themselves. Drama had the reputation of being a lot of fun. The last teacher, Mr. Maxwell, had been young, and single, and he drove an old MGB sports car with the top down, winter or summer, as long as the skies were clear. But Mr. Maxwell had handed in his resignation the day after Labor Day, the last day before the first day of school, causing something of an uproar. After a frantic search, the school had found someone new to town, just out of college with a drama degree. People were curious about her. But she wasn't in the room, so there was a brief exchange of information while they waited, for the teacher to arrive and let them find out for themselves about her, for the bell to ring. "Young, pretty, engaged," were the basic bits of information they knew about her, plus, "This is her first teaching job."

It was that last that made her such a big question mark for everyone. Nobody wanted to take part in someone's bad play, a play that people might make jokes about afterwards, or think you were a jerk to be in. Most of the people in the room were in wait-and-see mode, ready to check out of the activity if it looked to be un-cool.

It was a good sign that the teacher arrived at the center of a small group of seniors, probably from the acting class, one of them carrying a big cardboard box. The box was taken up to the platform while the knapsacks were dropped on top of the pile, and then the four students came to sit at the front of the room, while the teacher stepped up onto the stage and they could all get a good look at her.

For once rumor was accurate. She *was* young and pretty, with soft, wavy brown hair and big eyes. A diamond flashed on her left hand, so that, too, was accurate. But what rumor had not mentioned was that she shone with happiness. In loose-fitting slacks and one of those styled t-shirts that adults wore, she was certainly easy to look at, but it was the smile on her face that captured you. It lit up the whole room. You wanted to smile right back. You thought that at any minute you were going to start having a really good time, and even if you didn't, you were going to be happier than before. Because this teacher was really glad to see them, and really glad to be there in class with them.

Her cheeks were a little pink, so they knew she was nervous, and she jammed her hands down into her pant pockets the way a nervous person does. But her voice was strong and confident, and happy, too.

"Hello. Good afternoon. Let's see—my name is Jeanette Hendriks and I prefer to be called Ms. Hendriks, if you would, please." She grinned then, as if suspecting that the title was too dignified but still, she hoped they would try using it. "And this as you know is Drama. Drama Club. Out of which we will put on the three productions of the year— one of which I promise you will be a musical. Okay, that's the really important and interesting thing to cover today, our plans for the year, but if I remember high school correctly, you'll want to hear a little about me before we settle down to work. Yes?" and she smiled approvingly at them.

They smiled approvingly back.

Ms. Hendriks was just finishing up telling them about the course requirements, and thesis requirements, for a drama major when Hadrian Klenk scuttled into the room, keeping low as he took a place beside Margalo. Margalo glanced at him, not paying much attention, thinking about the chances of getting any kind of a role in a play, and about the chances of anybody else wanting to be assistant director.

Then she looked again. Hadrian was tucking his shirt into his khakis, awkwardly. It isn't easy to tuck in your shirt when you're sitting on the floor, and it's even harder if you are trying at the same time to unobtrusively wipe tears from your cheeks. "What happened?" Margalo whispered.

Hadrian shook his head. "Nothing." Then he shrugged. "Nothing new."

"You okay?" Margalo whispered.

He nodded.

Ms. Hendriks was looking in their direction as she told her

story about moving to town because it was where her fiancé lived—and here she took her left hand out of her pocket to show them the ring. Margalo met the teacher's gaze with a bright, attentive face. Probably Hadrian did the same, since her attention moved on, away, as she reported to those who hadn't heard the news, "Mr. Maxwell has taken a job in California."

This was explained by Richard Carstairs, the senior who had played every male lead for the last couple of years, usually with Sally King (who happened also to be his girlfriend) getting the female leads. "He wants to act. He wants to be in movies, but the job's not acting. It's just another teaching job. But it's in L.A. He'll be on the spot."

Ms. Hendriks reclaimed their attention. "I myself always wanted to direct. For my senior thesis I directed—entirely on my own, casting, costumes, sets, everything, which I guess makes me a producer, too. I did have an advisor, for when I had doubts, which," she admitted with another happy smile, "*did* happen, and not infrequently. Anyway, the play I chose was *The Lady's Not for Burning*, which I understand some of this year's ninth graders were in a production of last spring? Were any of you involved in that production?"

Four hands went up and she nodded. This was good news.

"So I am not without experience in producing and directing a play," Ms. Hendriks went on. "And I am especially not without . . . I guess you have to call it enthusiasm." For some reason this made them all laugh. "As I see it, the director

25

takes all the different ingredients—script and actors primarily, but also sets and staging, lighting . . . The director gets all of these component parts to work together to bring her vision of the play alive, onstage, and it's . . . It's wonderful," she told them, her eyes glowing, "to see a play come alive. To be part of that."

Every student in the room was smiling back at her, and at the possibility and excitement of working on a play with her. She went on. "The first thing you need to do for Drama Club, then, is pick up your copies of *A Midsummer Night's Dream*. That's Shakespeare, of course." She indicated the box beside her. "Some of these are the Folger edition, some the Cambridge University Press. Both have good notes," she reassured them, misunderstanding the sudden silence in the room. "For the first few weeks in here we'll study each scene and talk over the characters and their motivations to be sure we understand the lines. Shakespeare can be difficult," she explained, in case they didn't know this. She smiled around at all of them, to include everyone in the excitement of it all.

"So if you'll each come up to get a book, and sign the book assignment sheet? Then, if there is any time left, I'll give you the historical background of the play. Do you know the layout of Shakespeare's theater? The Globe?"

Only one hand went up, Hadrian's. This puzzled the teacher, but she went on to ask, "Does anyone have any questions?" at which Hadrian's hand went down and Richard Carstair's hand went up. "Yes, Richard?" she asked.

"Mr. Maxwell promised we'd do comedy this year."

"*Midsummer Night's Dream* is a comedy."

"We did *Romeo and Juliet* last year and *Macbeth* the year before," Richard tried to explain, and a few sympathetic groans greeted the memory. "Macbeth, that was"—"Grim." "But the witches were fun."—"dumb."

Ms. Hendriks considered this for a long moment, while they watched her. Then she made her own explanation. "You know, Shakespeare is a real actor's writer. Anyone who is serious about acting studies Shakespeare. Anyone who wants to learn about theater. His characters, his language, his . . . the drama of his works. I wouldn't feel right not giving you this opportunity," she concluded happily.

"I get enough Shakespeare in English class," somebody protested.

"He's not relevant," someone added.

"He's not funny."

"Mr. Maxwell said."

Ms. Hendrik's smile didn't fade. She was entirely sympathetic to this point of view. "Then probably there's no point in your staying in Drama, is there? If you feel that way."

At that a lot of people stood up and left, maybe half of the crowded room. Shawn Macavity explained to Heather as they left that it would be a better career move for him to take Martial Arts, no matter what the teacher said. "These days you have to know karate moves, you know? To get work," he added, in case she didn't follow his reasoning.

27

Only thirty-four people remained in the room. Ms. Hendriks looked around at them eagerly, saying, "Before you come to get your books, we should get acquainted." She came to the edge of the platform and sat down on it, making everyone almost equal.

Margalo and Hadrian were the only ninth graders in the group.

"You already know my name and my theatrical experience," Ms. Hendriks said. "It's your turn now to tell me about yourselves. Who wants to start off?"

Neither Margalo nor Hadrian volunteered.

— 3 —

At the Bottom of the Pecking Order

"Where's Hadrian?" Casey looked up from a copy of *Murder Must Advertise*. "Lunch is half over and—have any of you seen Hadrian?"

It was the fourth Friday of ninth grade, and certain concerns were beginning to establish themselves, like seedlings taking root. Hadrian was just such an established concern, right up there with grades and boy/girl-friends. Less major were: Louis Caselli's chances of passing any of his courses in the first marking period; what was wrong with Tanisha Harris; Rhonda Ransom's mother refusing to let her daughter take sex education because that was something a child should learn at home ("And we all know what *that* means," Cassie remarked); whether Ralph had really copied his History report off the Internet and, then, if he'd get caught; and—back to sex, many things got back to sex—why the school thought ninth grade needed to start off the year with sex ed. But nobody wanted to talk about that.

Nobody, also, knew where Hadrian was. They had all been looking up occasionally at the door, or glancing around at the edges of the room for a scurrying figure in case they had missed his entry. All now included not only the usual—Mikey and Margalo, Casey, Cassie and Jace— but also two new lunch companions. Tenth graders. Boys. Tim had joined Casey one lunch to continue his attempts to talk her into changing her mind about accepting one of the submissions to the literary magazine (he had succeeded in this) and then had fallen into a ridiculous and, he claimed, useful discussion with Margalo about the "Dear Stella" advice column in the school newspaper, which he wrote, along with occasional op-ed pieces. The next day he had been back, and with him his friend Felix—one of those skinny, long-haired boys whose shoelaces are often untied. Felix claimed to be a photographer, although he never had a camera with him at school because he didn't want it ripped off and he didn't take Photography or any other Art course because he didn't want anybody messing with his talent.

Not one of them, for all the looking, had seen Hadrian Klenk that lunch period.

Margalo gave voice to their concern. "He's taking a long time getting here today."

"Everything in ninth grade is taking a long time," Mikey

pointed out. The tennis coach hadn't spoken to her except to assign her to one court or another for drills.

"Probably he's spooking around somewhere—in the library?—waiting for a chance to bolt for the cafeteria," Jace suggested.

"Who are those goons anyway?" Margalo asked Tim and Felix. "Do you know them? Are they in your class?"

"No, they're eleventh graders, they did the same kind of things to some of us last year. It's—"

He was interrupted by the arrival of Ronnie Caselli at their table. In the surprised silence that greeted her she pulled out a chair opposite Mikey and Margalo, Hadrian's usual chair if she had known it.

"Hey everybody," she said, dividing her smile equally between the girls and the boys. "Am I interrupting?" she asked, aware that, for this lunch table, to have Ronnie Caselli sitting and talking with them would cause a big boost in their ratings. But Ronnie wasn't one of those stuck-up popular high school girls; she also managed to be a pretty nice person, at least a lot of the time, especially when there wasn't any boyfriend situation in question. Now she asked them, but looked to Margalo to answer, "You know, I haven't had a chance to catch up with you since . . ." She hesitated, figuring out how long it had been.

"Sixth grade?" Mikey suggested.

Ronnie laughed. "Come on, Mikey, it hasn't been that long. But how was your summer? Did you play a lot of tennis?" and then she asked Margalo, "Did you have time to do anything besides baby-sit? Because that savings account of yours must be getting sort of fat by now, even without any Café ME money. But why *did* you decide to close it down?" she asked them both.

"When we were in Texas—," Margalo began.

"That's right! You went to see Mikey's mother and her new husband. I forgot all about that." Ronnie turned to explain to Tim and Felix, "I get distracted because in August a whole lot of Italian boys come over to work for a month at a restaurant—the owner's a friend of my dad's. They come to improve their English, and Sophie—she's my cousin, she graduated last year—she and I sort of have to show them around." Ronnie grimaced, not unhappily and turned back to Mikey. "Is your new stepfather as rich as they say?"

"I don't know. How rich do they say he is?" Mikey asked, and Ronnie laughed again. Ronnie had a good laugh, as warm and quiet as soup bubbling on the stove. It made you want to join in on enjoying whatever was so funny. That Mikey hadn't meant to crack a joke never entered anybody's mind when Ronnie laughed.

"He's a businessman," Margalo went resolutely on, even though she suspected Ronnie's attention wasn't on her own question.

"Venture capitalist," Mikey specified.

"—and he advised us," Margalo said, "to either drop out of school and really concentrate on making Café ME a success—"

32

"Which he said it could well be," Mikey added.

"—or close it down," Margalo concluded. "If we weren't ready to take it as far as we could make it go. Which we aren't because we have to go to school."

"But what will you do instead?" asked Ronnie, who got Mikey and Margalo in a way most people didn't.

"That's it, exactly," Mikey agreed.

"Concentrate on getting out of ninth grade alive?" Margalo suggested.

Ronnie seemed to think that, of the two of them, it was Mikey who made jokes. Margalo she had labeled The Serious One, so she reassured her, "Ninth grade's not all that bad."

"I guess, as long as you're not Hadrian Klenk," Margalo said.

"I know," Ronnie agreed immediately. "He has lunch with you, doesn't he? Where is he?"

"He's gone missing," Cassie reported.

As if Ronnie hadn't noticed Cassie sitting there between Jace and Tim, "Cassie, hey," she said. Then she asked, "You're Mr. Paul's prize pupil, you'd know—does he realize how people are ripping off his art room supplies? Not me, but . . . I can see them doing it. They think it's a joke."

"He thinks it's a joke too. But the joke's on them because it's the school that pays for the supplies and it's their parents who pay the taxes that pay for the school. Peter Paul doesn't care what they do."

This puzzled Ronnie. It pleased Cassie and irritated

Mikey, and it made Margalo wonder what supplies and for what purposes, other than art, they might be taken, and further whether, if they were taken for art purposes it was really stealing. It confirmed Jace's opinion that Cassie paid entirely too much attention to things Peter Paul said, it worried Casey, it made Tim consider an editorial on teacher attitudes, and it didn't interest Felix in the slightest, but Ronnie was simply puzzled to hear this.

After a brief silence, "We were actually talking about those three eleventh graders who . . . follow Hadrian around," Casey said.

"Do you think they'd stop if I asked them?" Ronnie wondered. "Like Louis last year. Although, Louis likes doing things for me and these guys aren't my cousins, and . . . so I guess I can't, and I don't know who I'd ask to do it for me. But I'll think about it," she promised them. "They're just stupid anyway," she assured the table. "I'd never date any of them, even if they are upperclassmen." She glanced at Tim and Felix and added, in case they were getting their hopes up, "I don't date underclassmen anymore."

Since they had each privately been thinking of maybe getting their hopes up about Ronnie Caselli, it was actually sort of kind of her to say that straight out. She knew how pretty she was, with her heavy dark hair and big brown eyes and that great body. She knew how most boys reacted to her.

"Poor Shawn," remarked Cassie, not sincerely.

"Shawn's way over me," Ronnie told her, then realized, "I

know who they are, those three. The red-haired one, he's sort of their leader, he's Sven. And one of the others, I don't know which one, is Toby, and the third I think is maybe Harold? I'm not sure about him."

"I'm not sure about any of them," said Margalo.

"I am," Mikey said. "And I'm sure I'd like to punch them out."

"I'd like to see you try," Cassie agreed. "Then we'd all go with you to the emergency room, wouldn't we?"

"But you know," Tim said, with an apologetic smile that crinkled up the skin beside his bright blue eyes, his usual expression when he was being entirely sincere but didn't want to appear uncoolly earnest, "this kind of thing happens in high school. It's part of the experience. It's not just Hadrian, and it's not just boys who do it either. Girls do it too, although in different ways. And it's not just high school, either. It's just worse in high school."

"Yeah, but where *is* Hadrian?" Mikey insisted.

Ronnie said, "I have to get going, but I wanted to ask you, Margalo? If you've talked to Tan, if she's mad at me or something. Because she dropped out of fall Track, did you know that?"

They didn't.

"And when I asked her about it, she just . . . she brushes me off. You know?"

They didn't know that, either.

"So could you ask her?" Ronnie asked them. "Because you

guys always got along all right, and if she's mad at me, if I've done something? Would you tell her I'm sorry? I'd be real grateful if you will," Ronnie concluded, rising, pulling her scoop-necked t-shirt down over her slim hips, brushing back her long hair, heading towards her usual lunch table among upperclassmen, particularly the athletic upperclassmen. "See you."

Only Tim and Felix were attending to this because that was the moment that Hadrian Klenk materialized without warning at the table, like some teleported character on *Star Trek*.

"You're late," Mikey accused him, reaching into her jeans pocket to pull out a couple of dollar bills for him.

"I can pick up a grilled cheese sandwich on my way out," he told them, sitting in the chair Ronnie had just vacated.

"Yeah, but where were you?"

"What happened?"

"Where's your knapsack?"

Hadrian said, "It doesn't matter. I've got copies of all the homework for my afternoon classes in my locker, and I can get tonight's assignments again from people. You have the English assignment, don't you, Margalo?"

"But what about your books? And your notebooks?"

"I've got a good memory and more notebooks in my locker. I always have a spare notebook, and I have a full copy of class notes at home, on my computer. I bring it up to date every day," he assured them.

"But Hadrian," Casey insisted gently, "what happened?"

He blushed, pink spreading up to stain his high cheekbones, spreading down his skinny neck into his shirt collar. "I was in the bathroom, alone. And they—So I locked myself in a stall, but they waited. So I told them, if they broke down the door they'd leave fingerprints and get in trouble for vandalism. I knew that only one of them at a time could crawl under, and they don't like doing things one at a time. So all I had to do was wait," Hadrian told them, still red in the face. "After a while people came in after lunch, so—You know, they mostly don't like to do anything to me when there are people around. So all they did was take my knapsack, which I had dropped by the sinks when—"

"Doesn't that mean you have to keep replacing books?" Felix asked. "Don't the teachers, like, notice? It's got to be expensive, all those books."

"I usually leave the textbooks at home, except Calculus, and that one he lets me keep in the classroom," Hadrian explained.

"Usually," Tim told him, "after a few months Sven moves on to someone new."

"*That's* a relief," Cassie responded in her most sarcastic tone.

"And after sophomore year, once you're an upperclassman," Tim continued, "I don't know why, really, but this kind of bullying almost never happens among upperclassmen."

"No," Hadrian agreed. "By then everybody just hates you. And ignores you."

"Not hate," Tim said.

"Okay, despise," Hadrian agreed. He also agreed, "That would be better. But I'm mostly concerned about making it from Monday to Friday. Today's Friday," he reminded them more cheerfully.

"Yeah, but it's only the fourth Friday, and look at you already," Mikey pointed out. Then, as was her way, she continued on with her own line of thought. "There are thirty-six weeks in the school year—six six-week marking periods—and if today's the fourth, that means we have thirty-two weeks to go."

"It also means there's only a couple of weeks until this marking period ends," Felix said. "Which means a whole bunch of unit tests coming up so teachers can get some grades on us," he explained.

"Hard times for Louis Caselli," Cassie announced happily.

Margalo stuck with Mikey. "You're forgetting that the first week of school was really only half."

"Thanksgiving week fills that out," Mikey answered.

"Thanksgiving's not until the end of next month," Margalo pointed out.

"Okay, Thanksgiving week *will* fill out the first week, when I don't count it, at the end of next month," Mikey said, ever reasonable.

"You're going to keep count?" Jace asked.

"It's not like it's some massive mathematical project requiring dozens of computers all linked up together," Mikey told him. "And it's not like I have too much to do, without Café ME to work on."

"And it's not like I care," added Cassie, getting up from her seat. "C'mon, Hay. Come with me. I'll be your bodyguard."

Hadrian looked a little doubtful at this offer.

"Just to the cafeteria doorway," Cassie told him. "Unless you want to come to Art with me?"

"I have Calculus," Hadrian explained, rising to go with her. "Don't forget I want to get my lunch."

Tim and Felix and Casey left together, as did Mikey and Margalo, who didn't have to bother with trays so they could make a quick exit. They dropped their crumpled-up brown paper bags into the waiting receptacle and joined the throng streaming out of the big room. Mikey was chewing her bottom lip in an *I'm thinking* way, so Margalo just waited for her to start talking.

Finally it burst out. "What are all those people doing at our lunch table?"

Margalo smirked. "It's your magnetic personality."

"Right." Mikey smiled right back at her, with teeth.

"Okay, it's *my* magnetic personality."

Mikey kept smiling.

"Besides, there aren't that many of them," Margalo said. They had just stepped out into the hallway when they were joined by Tanisha Harris. "Hey, you two, so what takes you so long at lunch?"

"We were waiting for Hadrian," Mikey said.

"You should do something about Hadrian," Tan told her. "You really should. Hey, Margalo."

"Ronnie thinks you're mad at her," Mikey said. "Are you?"

"Not particularly. No more than at anybody else."

Mikey looked at Margalo, eyebrows raised. Was Tan joking? "Does that include me? Why would you be mad at me?"

For her part, Margalo observed, "You're wearing a skirt again. And that's a great-looking top."

Tan smiled, a secret, satisfied smile. She knew how good she looked. Her long gold skirt swished around her legs. The square-necked top was striped on the diagonal in rich oranges, bright yellows, turquoise blues, and the occasional thin black line, for contrast and emphasis.

"When did you turn into a skirt wearer?" Now that she noticed it, Mikey was a little outraged.

"Nothing wrong with growing up," said Tan.

That was the difference, Margalo realized. That was the right name for the change. Tan was in their class, a ninth grader, but this year she looked much older than the rest of them. Tan was tall anyway, with long, strong legs, and she wore her dark, curly hair cut short. Tan held herself straight, a natural athlete, confident in her body. She walked along the high school hallways like she should be a queen approaching her throne, or a movie star ignoring her fans. Her dark eyes and high cheekbones, her silky, dark skin— somehow Tan was giving the impression this year of being different, from the rest of them and from who she had been before. Maybe it was her sandals? They weren't Tevas or Birkenstocks or flip-flops or jellies. They were lady sandals, a broad brown leather band across the foot, a ring into which she had slipped her big toes.

"But mad why?" asked Margalo.

"Not exactly mad," Tan said. "I just wish you'd do something for Hadrian."

"We are," Mikey said.

"Why us? Why not you?" Margalo asked.

Tan stopped, with a little swirl of skirt, and looked at them. "Think about what would happen if a black kid attacked a white kid."

"Yeah, but you're a girl, *and* you're wearing a skirt," Margalo pointed out.

"You think there wouldn't be some getting even? You think being female is any protection? What century are you living in, girl? Because I can promise you, even in that century being a girl wasn't much protection. Maybe even the opposite," and Tan turned away, started walking again, but faster and angrier. They speeded up beside her.

"Yeah, but we're in school," Margalo argued. "School's not exactly a normal social environment."

"It's normal enough," Tan promised her.

"Is that why you're not taking Track?" Mikey asked. "Because of the bad social environment? Because what about college? What about your athletic scholarship?" Both Tan and Margalo had longer legs than she did so she was almost jogging.

"What about not kidding myself," Tan countered. "Ask Margalo. She knows what I'm talking about."

"What's she talking about, Margalo?"

"She's talking about how it can be really hard—for some people especially, people who aren't white, people who aren't male or rich or somehow influential—to get where you want to go. And that's if you have somewhere you want to get to. It's almost worse if you do have somewhere you want to get to. Am I right?"

Tan grinned. "Yes, ma'am. Yes indeedy. You are about one hundred percent correct."

Mikey explained patiently, "But that doesn't have anything to do with Track."

"You tell her," Tan said to Margalo, then didn't give Margalo a chance. "Why do you think Margalo works at all those baby-sitting jobs all the time—to buy designer jeans?"

Still patiently, Mikey said, "She's saving her money. For college."

"I don't wear jeans," Margalo said. She didn't need anybody's pity.

"Whatever," Tan said. "All I'm saying is, that road looks too long and too uphill to me."

"But you could still run the hundred meters," Mikey pointed out. People were always veering off from the topic.

Tan just shook her head and increased her pace. "See you in class," she said over her shoulder.

Mikey slowed down to let her pull ahead and then disappear into the crowd. "What's happened to her?" she asked Margalo.

"High school?" Margalo guessed. "Getting older?"

"I thought she *liked* sports," Mikey said.

— 4 —

All the World's a Tennis Court

That afternoon, which was overcast and cool, Mikey took on the last ninth grader on the girls' tennis ladder. After this win, she had to make her way through the sophomores before she could start challenging the juniors, and after them the seniors, to take her place on the tennis team next spring. It was pretty irritating the number of warm bodies Mikey had to climb over, when all she wanted was to play her best tennis against good opponents under the watchful eye of a good coach.

So far the coach hadn't noticed Mikey, which told you how overcrowded the tennis classes were, because—as Coach Sandy had assured them at the first meeting—her plan was to find the best players, and train them, and have a winning team in the spring.

Mikey's plan was to be on that winning team with Coach

Sandy. This meant that she was going to have to keep working her way up the tennis ladder, which meant waiting for her chances to play matches until a court fell empty and she was next in line to use it. Often, that also meant trying to get her set finished in the last twenty minutes of the practice time. But that Mikey could do easily. This Tammy player, for example, couldn't handle the kind of power Mikey could produce off her forehand, and her backhand, too, not to mention her serve. On the few occasions that Tammy managed to return Mikey's serve, Mikey had been at the net, waiting to put it away. She hadn't lost a single point on serve. When Tammy was serving, Mikey returned with a hard topspin drive, backhand or forehand, into a corner, backhand or forehand, and charged the net to put away whatever weak defensive shot Tammy managed to make, on those occasions when she managed to make one. As the games went along, Mikey noticed that when her shots landed close to the line, they were usually called out. Some of them she would have sworn were in for sure. She wondered if Tammy knew the unwritten tennis rule, that you call a shot good unless you're *sure* it's out. But since most of the time Mikey could place her shots unarguably in, that was what she did. It wasn't placement that was beating Tammy, it was power. Mikey took the final point of the set at the net, so she waited there for her opponent to come up and shake hands.

"They said you were good," Tammy reported. She didn't seem to mind losing, which was okay with Mikey. "I guess they weren't kidding."

Mikey nodded, and they shook hands to end the match. Her first coach had told them always to say something good about an opponent's game after the handshake, so Mikey—after some thought—said, "That's a nice forehand cross-court you're working on."

"Not so nice that you didn't bagel me."

"But they're right about me," Mikey explained. "I really am good."

Tammy's smile stiffened. "Anyway, who do you play next?"

They were talking as they walked off, exiting through the gate in the high wire fence that surrounded the courts. They went up to the bench where they had dropped their tennis bags and knapsacks.

"Karen Hooper," Mikey said.

"Wouldn't it be something if a ninth grader got to the top half of the ladder? Or even, what if a ninth grader made the tennis team?" Tammy sounded genuinely excited by the thought. If Mikey had been her, she'd have chopped her tennis racket up into little pieces, or hung it by the neck until it was dead, but maybe Tammy just liked playing and didn't mind losing.

"Well," Mikey said, "I'm good enough."

Tammy stared at Mikey until—nobody would say something like that seriously, would they?—she grinned and remarked, "You're certainly confident enough."

Why shouldn't I be? Mikey was about to ask, when she heard her name being called. "Elsinger!" So she had no chance to remind Tammy about the unwritten rule.

"Elsinger! Over here!"

Coach Sandy was standing by Court One. She wore her usual pleated skirt and Windbreaker, and she held her hand out behind her. "Somebody pass me a racket." Somebody did. "We've got five minutes, Elsinger. I want to show you something."

About time, Mikey said to herself, but kept her face expressionless as she followed the coach out onto the court.

Coach Sandy had tennis balls in the pocket of her Windbreaker. "I'll serve first," she told Mikey, and jogged to the opposite side of the court to get into position.

Mikey prepared to receive serve. She didn't know what to expect. She'd never seen the coach actually playing, so she didn't know what kind of a serve she'd be looking at. She went on full alert.

The coach tossed the ball up into the air, then sent it into the center of the service box. *Not much of a serve*, was Mikey's reaction as she pounded a backhand return, cross-court, into the coach's backhand corner and made her approach to the net.

The coach floated a lob, up, over Mikey's head and out of reach, but low enough so that Mikey didn't have time to realize what was happening and turn to run it down before it bounced in.

"Fifteen–love," Coach Sandy said, and crossed back to the center to take her second serve, with the same smooth, easy motion, no effort to it.

The ease of the motion distracted Mikey, who admired it and tried to figure out how it worked. Perhaps that was why she was a little late on the return, sending the ball closer to the center than she'd planned, which meant she could expect a better shot from the coach, as she waited, poised behind the net, ready to put the ball away.

But the ball floated over her head, again, and landed just inside the baseline, again.

"Thirty–love," said Coach Sandy.

The people watching stopped talking among themselves to laugh.

When Coach Sandy served for the third time, Mikey whipped a backhand down the center, right at her, and as she moved towards the net kept a careful eye on the coach's racket so that when she turned its face to lob, Mikey would have enough time to race back and put that lob away with an over-head from the baseline, another one of her killer shots.

But this time the ball went whizzing past her, a line drive into her forehand corner. "Forty–love," said the coach.

On the next serve, determined to win at least one point in the game, Mikey was ready for anything. The coach served with the same easy motion, only this time the ball whipped into the T at the center of the court, and for all of her fast reflexes, Mikey couldn't even get the rim of her racket on it. *Where did that come from?*

"Let's not waste time changing sides," Coach Sandy told her. "Your serve."

Mikey served one of her best, as much power as she could get into it.

It came back at her feet as she was approaching the net. At her feet and unreturnable.

"Love–fifteen," she said, returning to the baseline, to fire another serve into the ad court and get herself to the net so fast that the coach's return wouldn't have time to be too low to return. But this one looped up over her head, a lob again! Although she raced off to run it down, all she could do was shove the ball back over her shoulder, then—wheeling around to get back in position—see Coach Sandy put it away with a backhand overhead shot that sliced the ball sideways and short, across the court.

"Love–thirty."

For her third serve Mikey took a little power off and directed it right into the body, but the coach side-stepped neatly, and her racket sliced swiftly, and the service return barely made it over the net before it sank to the ground—a drop shot. Although Mikey, who had decided to stay back, pelted for the net at top speed, she couldn't lift the ball back over into play. "Love–forty," she announced.

"Let's play out the next point, shall we?" the coach called.

As if Mikey hadn't been trying to play out all the previous seven.

Mikey served, down the middle to reduce the angle of the return, and when the ball came back deep to her forehand, she got into position and waited, racket back, to step into her cross-court winner.

Except that winner came back, also cross-court. Mikey set up and sent a forehand winner down the line.

This one also came back, bouncing at mid court, drawing her forward for a shot she kept deep but couldn't get much angle on, and then she went on forward to the net to cut off the slice backhand, sending the ball short and cross-court, but that one too came back, looping high on her forehand so that she could barely get to it, and then the next return shot went into her own backhand corner. That one she ran down with a wild swing that, if she'd been intending a lob, would have satisfied her, but she never lobbed.

Coach Sandy got ready for an overhead.

Mikey got ready to try to block it back, which she did, so Coach Sandy lined up for another overhead, this time taken halfway to the net. This Mikey once again blocked back.

The next overhead Coach Sandy swung down on from close to the net, so the ball bounced close to the service line, then up, up, and out over the fence, out of the court. That overhead was unblockable, ungettable. "That's game," Coach Sandy said. She grinned at Mikey, pleased with herself, her eyes alight with the satisfactions of an easy victory.

Mikey had been entirely outplayed, which made her feel like sort of a jerk. Even during the last point Mikey had known that even while the coach was playing shot after shot, she could have won the point any time she decided to.

"Has that taken you down a peg or two?" Coach Sandy asked as they walked off the court, adding, "You've got a lot to learn, Elsinger."

"Okay."

"Like, some variety in your strokes," the coach went on.

She didn't need to go on, in Mikey's opinion. Mikey was still taking in how weak her defenses had been.

"Like, having a game plan," the coach said.

As usual, none of the other tennis players paid any attention to Mikey as they went off to catch the Activities buses. They were all busy with their own friends and their own plans, none of which included Mikey. The coach had returned to her office in the cellar of the gym, and through the big window the players could see her talking on the phone as they filed past. She didn't look up to wave, or come to the door to chat with them. That wasn't the kind of coach she was. The kind of coach she was was exacting and strict and ambitious—a winning coach.

Mikey looked at her through the window, and half of her wanted to say, *Next time, you'll see,* while half wanted to ask, *Can't we start right now?* And half wanted to just go into that office and pop the short, blond woman on the snoot, for making Mikey feel clumsy and inept on the tennis court. The tennis court was Mikey's native habitat and Coach Sandy seemed to want to take that confidence away from her.

In fact, ninth grade seemed designed to make her wonder about herself. If she was as good a tennis player as she thought.

Or as smart a person. Or as able to look out for herself.

Mikey had a sudden—and deeply unpleasant—thought: What if ninth grade was right? What if she had peaked in eighth grade? What if there was never going to be anything she could do about anything, in ninth grade or ever again?

What if ninth grade was what the rest of her life was going to be like?

Mikey started to run for the late bus. She needed to talk to Margalo and hear what Margalo had to say about people making bad tennis calls and a coach who wanted to undermine a player's confidence.

— 5 —

A Little Hope Can't Hurt, Can It?

Mikey had to wait until the end of the day, when there were fifteen minutes between the end of the last class and whatever you were doing next—taking a bus, reporting for some sport or an activity, just hanging out or heading to work, to the library, heading for home, heading for trouble, whatever. She had to wait from lunch and through three afternoon classes, each separated by a four-minute change-over, which was much too short a time to, first, run Margalo down and then, second, be told what was up before they separated for their next classes.

Mikey wanted as much time as she could get to ask about the two bombshells Margalo had dropped onto their lunch table. Mikey couldn't even decide which she wanted to check up on first, not to mention which part of which one she most wanted to get clear. As soon as Margalo got to her locker,

Mikey—who had been waiting there, not patiently—demanded, "When did you decide to get a job?"

Margalo seemed surprised by the question, as if she didn't quite know what Mikey was talking about. "What?"

"What's *wrong* with you?" Mikey demanded. "You jabbered away all during lunch, chitter-chatter nonstop, like some talking machine. And now . . ."

The hallway was loud with the sounds of falling books and clanging locker doors, of people calling to one another— "Wait up!"—and footsteps thumping. "Look out!" was the most frequently overheard phrase in that hallway at that time on a Friday afternoon in the middle of October. The sixth Friday of ninth grade, Mikey could have told Margalo. Thirty to go.

Margalo looked over her shoulder beyond Mikey to the crowded hallway. "Have you seen Hadrian?"

"Why would I see Hadrian? You're the one who's in Drama with him."

"He's supposed to try out today so he'll get a part, so—"

"We know, we know."

"I'm reading too, but just for one of the fairies, but maybe I won't."

Mikey got Margalo back on topic. "Job. Aurora. What's going on?"

"Oh, that. She always said I could get a real job when I was fourteen, and I'm fourteen."

"But why do you want one?"

"For a regular income, and so when I look for my next job I can say I have experience. And for my résumé."

"You have a résumé? What are you doing with a résumé? You're fourteen, Margalo. You're in ninth grade."

"To put on college applications, to show I'm a worker."

Well, that sounded like Margalo's usual long-range thinking. Mikey relaxed. "So what kind of a job are you looking for?" She wondered if she wanted to look for a job too, and, if she did look for a job, if she would get one. She wondered if she could get a better job than Margalo could get.

"I have to go," Margalo said. "Really. Because Hadrian—"

"Are you having a crush on Hadrian Klenk?" Mikey demanded. She had to go too, but you didn't see her rushing off, and she had tennis to go to, not just a club. Tennis was a varsity sport.

"Don't be stupid. You know my plan for Hadrian, and the first step is—"

Mikey had heard all this before. "And what's this about Aurora—"

"Tell you later. I'll tell you about that on the bus." Margalo was already walking away, her olive green knapsack hanging off of one shoulder, pushing her way into the crowd of students, looking back to tell Mikey this before hurrying off.

Mikey finished her question anyway. "—and a GED?"

Nobody wanted to be late for this meeting of Drama Club. A lot would get decided that day. Everybody was a little

55

jittery, as if before an exam, nervous about how their readings would go, nervous about their chances of being selected for a role, hoping to be chosen, and if they were chosen, hoping to do well. Being in a play was good for your social life, and being in a Shakespeare play was good not only for your social life but also for your academic standing. Whatever else you could say about Shakespeare, he was smart, and everybody—even teachers, who maybe should know better—assumed that you had to be smart yourself to be in a Shakespeare play.

Margalo set her knapsack down on top of a pile beside the teacher's desk. The knapsacks were in almost all colors, each one differentiated from others of the same color by some kind of marking, a drawing, lettering, logo, name or initials, or sometimes even a miniature stuffed animal clipped onto the zipper. Margalo had her own initials in white painted in lowercase letters on the front of her olive green knapsack, *me*. On the back, like a mirror image, she had painted *em*.

She waited just inside the door for Hadrian. Ms. Hendriks had asked them to prepare a short reading from the character that they would most like to play. That was no problem for Margalo, whose minor character said about two words altogether. Hadrian, on the other hand, had decided to try for the part of Bottom, and he had asked Margalo to help him prepare. But her family's telephone restriction rule (no conversation to last more than five minutes) made that impossible. Also impossible was getting together during school hours, since Hadrian spent his non-class time trying to avoid Sven and his two goons, keeping an eye out, keeping to the side, not staying in any one place long enough to go rehearse lines for a play.

Margalo didn't know if she was more nervous and excited for Hadrian or for herself. Although, when she thought about it, for herself she was just nervous.

The clock ticked off the final moments. Ms. Hendriks arrived. She dropped her books and purse on top of the desk and went immediately to the platform stage, on which she had already set up two chairs, facing each other. She seated herself on one of them and set her clipboard on her lap, pen at the ready. The room filled up. Even Shawn Macavity was there, confident that people would overlook his not being a club member for the sake of his star power. He greeted people, although not Margalo, "Some fun, hunh?" They humphed and ignored him.

Because Sven and the goons had gotten bored with taking Hadrian's knapsack from him, hiding or destroying his homework papers, sometimes tossing the knapsack into a cafeteria garbage can, sometimes putting it behind a toilet in one of the girls' bathrooms. . . .

But who did they get to help them with that? Margalo wondered now. She didn't like to think of all the possible answers to that question. She was just relieved that they seemed to have stopped pulling that particular trick, so she could be pretty sure that if Hadrian's green knapsack, with his initials stenciled on it in big black letters, wasn't there by the desk, he hadn't yet arrived.

But she wasn't sure what the tardiness meant. She was pretty sure he wouldn't lose his nerve, not about acting.

When the bell rang, and people had fallen silent, Ms. Hendriks looked up from her clipboard and said, "All right, then. Seniors first. Who . . ."

She stopped speaking. She stared at the doorway. Different expressions crossed over her face so quickly that the people watching could barely identify one expression and figure out how to react to it before another had replaced it. Irritation was replaced by laughter was replaced by pity was replaced by confusion was replaced by decision, and Ms. Hendriks stood up to ask, "What is going on here?"

By then everybody in the room had turned to look, and seeing, many had shifted themselves around to face the door, and the hallway beyond, so they could really see.

Margalo looked too, and she didn't know what to do. She couldn't even think of anything to say.

Nobody answered Ms. Hendriks' question, not anyone in Drama Club, nor any of the three juniors standing in the doorway, looking even larger than usual compared to the short, slight figure that stood in their midst, as if they were the military guard and he was their captive, brought in for questioning. He wore belted khakis and a plaid short-sleeved shirt. His hair stood up in thick, short spikes all over his head, making him look like a plastic hedgehog toy for some baby's bathtub. A knapsack hung beside his knees and his face was bright red. Hadrian Klenk.

Why that picture struck them as funny, nobody could have said. Maybe it was because the guards were so big, so tall and broad and thick-limbed, and their prisoner so much littler. It was ridiculous to see all of those great big guards for that one little prisoner, like using three German shepherds to herd a Chihuahua.

Or maybe it was Hadrian's hair, which looked like some moth-eaten hairbrush. Or a cartoon bomb. Or one of those designer fruits their mothers sometimes brought home from the store and tried to convince them to eat.

Or maybe it was how bright red Hadrian's face was, like some teacher about to explode into anger.

For whatever reason—and Ms. Hendriks could have told them that comedy works in a variety of different ways— almost everybody in the room started to laugh. Not Margalo and not Ms. Hendriks, but they were about the only ones left out. Of course everybody knew they shouldn't want to laugh, and shouldn't be laughing, so everybody tried to muffle it, which of course made it even funnier.

Equally of course, when the three comedians saw how successful they were being, they went further. Sven took his big hand off of Hadrian's thin shoulder and beat both fists on his chest, making Tarzan noises.

But when Ms. Hendriks took a step towards the front of the platform and then stepped down onto the floor, they fled.

This left Hadrian alone in the doorway. Then he saw Margalo and scuttled over to sit down beside her. Ms. Hendriks stood staring at the empty doorway. Everyone could see that she didn't know what to do next.

Margalo didn't blame her. Even she, sitting beside Hadrian, a person who was known to be on his side and not even smiling at the way he looked, didn't know which would make it worse for him—to be noticed or to be ignored, to make a big to-do about it or to pretend nothing had happened and there was nothing at all odd about him.

Ms. Hendriks apparently decided on pretending. She stepped up onto the platform and sat back down. "Which senior wants to go first?" she asked, as if the last two minutes had taken place in a time warp that aliens had erased from her memory.

It took a few seconds for everybody to turn around again and face her, and by that time Sally King had already stepped up onto the platform to read for the unisex part of Puck, the mischief-making sprite who was the personal servant of Oberon, king of the fairies. Puck was the one single stand-out part in the play, and even that wasn't a particularly starring role. Puck had a lot of lines and appeared in a lot of scenes, and then—at the very end—he got to speak directly to the audience and claim credit for the whole performance. Puck was the part you remembered, after the play. Well, Puck and Bottom. But Bottom was a jerk, like an old-fashioned redneck hillbilly type, so nobody thought of asking to play Bottom. Nobody except Hadrian, that is.

"When she hears you read," Margalo murmured to Hadrian. "When they all hear you." She was sort of excited for him and impatient to get to the turnaround-surprise ending of this scene. Hadrian didn't say anything, but she didn't look at him. If she were Hadrian, she wouldn't want anyone looking at her right now. Instead she listened to Sally King's tryout.

Sally read Puck well, with her usual mischievious *I can get away with anything, just watch* expression. She would make a good Puck, Margalo thought; it was typecasting, one egocentric and self-satisfied character played by another. She thought Sally *should* get the part—even though Sally was the kind of person who you wanted *not* to get what she wanted. She had a slim, boyish build and a bold smile; with her hair in two short ponytails, one on each side of her head, she already looked like Puck.

Margalo had an unexpected thought: What if Sally King really was talented? Just because you didn't like someone, that didn't mean they couldn't be talented. Just because you didn't want them to be, that didn't mean they *wouldn't* be. She wished it was Mikey sitting beside her, not Hadrian, because then she could tell Mikey that idea, and at the end she could add, "And vice versa," to irritate Mikey, who—irritated on schedule—would respond, "No Latin."

After Sally came Richard, no surprise. By that time, Margalo dared to sneak a look across at Hadrian, who sat so quiet and lifeless it was almost as if he wasn't there. It was like sitting next to a pile of mashed potatoes, and no fun at all. And he looked, with his hair like that—it was grotesque, really funny. She wasn't surprised to hear occasional whispers, followed by muffled snorts of laughter, scattered around the room.

Richard took the seat Sally had vacated and told Ms. Hendriks, "First I thought me and Sally could be the Duke and his bride, but those aren't big parts, so then I thought Oberon and his queen. But she wants to be Puck."

"You could still play Oberon," Ms. Hendriks offered.

Richard scratched at the back of his neck, where his brown hair curled up a little. "Yeah, but, you know? Like Sally says, who wants to be the King of the Fairies?" He grinned at her and at the gathered students.

Ms. Hendriks didn't grin back, but many people in the room choked back laughter.

"Then what part will you be reading for us today?" Ms. Hendriks asked.

"Demetrius, because the other guy is sort of a noodle, you know?" Richard looked at the teacher's expression and added, "I'll play Oberon, though, if you want me to. I mean, all of Shakespeare's parts are pretty good ones," he explained to his audience.

"Hadrian should play Oberon," someone suggested, to increasingly out-loud laughter.

Hadrian sat invisible. Margalo's brain was frozen. It would all get better when they heard him read, she repeated to herself.

"But he's gotta keep that hairdo," someone else said.

"Hadrian's a natural for fairy king," someone added, and the whole room—still with the same two exceptions—burst into uncontrolled laughter. Ms. Hendriks, standing again, said, "Patrick. That's more than enough. You're excused from the room."

"But I haven't read."

"You heard me," she said.

"But everybody was—"

"You're excused from Drama, too," she told him. "I will inform Mr. Robredo of the change in your schedule."

The room was now completely silent.

"It wasn't just me," Patrick protested, but he knew nobody would stand up for him. He rose to his feet and looked resentfully around the room, his gaze finally settling on Hadrian Klenk, the invisible boy, who had caused him to be thrown out of Drama. "It was just a joke," Patrick said, turning back to the teacher. "Can't you tell a joke when you hear it?"

Ms. Hendriks did not bend. "Yes," she said. "But I didn't hear one. Go."

For a really nice person, and young, and female, and in love, and pretty, too, Ms. Hendriks was being awfully strict. His friends felt they should stick up for Patrick, so they, too, snuck dirty looks at Hadrian, who shrank back into himself to let that wave of blame and anger flow over him.

In fact, probably the only person who still felt sorry for

Hadrian was Ms. Hendriks. Margalo didn't have to feel sorry for him because as soon as he read for a part in the play, Hadrian's school life would be on the road to recovery.

The tryout readings continued, students one after the other going up to sit in the chair facing Ms. Hendriks and read—or occasionally recite from memory—the lines they had prepared. After the last junior had read, Margalo said, without looking at Hadrian, "I don't have a chance."

Out of the corner of her eye she saw his spiky head nodding agreement.

"But *you* do," she told him.

However, when the last tenth grader had read, Ms. Hendriks stood up. "Thank you all very much," she told them. "You've worked hard for this, and it shows. These were good auditions."

"What about me?" Shawn Macavity asked. He raised his hand, then stood up so she could see him better. "What about my part?"

"And you are?"

"Shawn Macavity," he answered, with an unspoken *of course* and a wide smile on his handsome face.

"You're not a member of Drama Club, are you?"

"Not a member, but I'm going to be an actor. I didn't want to do all that Shakespeare study," he reminded her, "but I do want a part."

"What speech did you prepare?"

"I didn't know I was supposed to," he explained, and offered, "I can still read."

"And what grade are you in, Shawn?" she asked.

"Ninth."

The teacher relaxed. "Oh. Well. In that case, you see, you couldn't be in the play anyway. I've been told that it's school policy not to give ninth graders roles in the plays, unless there are extenuating circumstances. Which there aren't," she added before he could say anything. "So I'll be casting especially seniors, since this is their last year in Drama."

"Good," said Richard and Sally, John Lawrence and Carl Dane, almost in unison.

"In any case, I would always want to offer a part first to someone who is a member of Drama Club," she told Shawn. "Who has shown interest. Who understands our ideas about the play."

"But I told you. I want to act, not talk about plays."

"And I can sympathize with that," she told him.

This left Shawn standing there looking foolish— handsome, but foolish. Margalo decided that rather than standing up right then to object to Hadrian's not getting a chance, she would wait until the teacher was alone. When teachers weren't worried about looking and acting like authority figures, sometimes they would change their mind.

Ms. Hendriks announced then, "Now, I need to have the names of people interested in working behind the scenes." With a humorous smile she added, "We accept workers from all classes for behind-the-scenes jobs. Mr. Paul and some of his Advanced Art students will be making sets for us, so that's taken care of, but we need a stage manager and people to work backstage moving flats, changing furniture, making sure the right props are ready." She turned to the senior who had read for the Duke, but not at all well, although he had clearly made a real effort, even memorizing his lines. "Carl? I'd like you to take that responsibility. You'll have a couple of assistants, of course—"

"Do I have to?"

"No, of course not. But it is the part I'm offering you in this production," Ms. Hendriks told him firmly.

She was having an unusually firm day.

The bell rang then, and people got up to retrieve their belongings, although Ms. Hendriks wasn't quite finished.

"Let me know what you'd like to do backstage," she called over the increasing noise. "I'll post the cast list Monday, first thing," she promised them. "Remember, we have only seven weeks until performance. We'll also need people to go over lines with the actors, people to help with the costumes, the stage manager usually cues lines during the performance, but we'll need ushers . . ."

They weren't listening. They were talking among themselves. "You were really good, you're sure to get Helena." "So were you, and Sally didn't want either Helena or Hermia, so you're sure to get Hermia, and we'll be in it together."

"If I don't get any lines, I'm not sure I want to commit the

time. I might drop Drama and concentrate on Spanish Club."
"Drama's my only activity so I can't drop it. My college applications will look totally lame with *no* activity. I guess I could help Carl."

Ms. Hendriks called out, "We'll need understudies!"

"*There's* a real waste of time. Maybe in movies, and I guess sometimes in a real play, some understudy gets to go on, but not in a school production. People in school plays really want their chance at the spotlight. Even if they're sick and throwing up." "Remember Sally whispering Lady MacBeth last year? I could barely keep from laughing."

"And we need general dogsbodies!" called Ms. Hendriks.

The room had emptied out, and Ms. Hendriks noticed that Hadrian and Margalo were still standing there, still paying attention, apparently waiting to say something.

"Yes?" she asked, stepping off the platform to join them. "What is it, Hadrian?" Like many of the teachers, Ms. Hendriks was especially nice to Hadrian Klenk. "And you are . . . Margalo," she remembered. "Margalo Epps."

"Hadrian is ready to read for Bottom," Margalo said as if she was deciding it. She was as tall as the teacher and could look directly into her hazel eyes, as an equal.

"But I explained—"

Hadrian interrupted. "Actually, I wouldn't mind being an understudy. Because I memorize really well so I could do more than one part. I could do a lot, easily. I mean, what if someone can't perform, I mean, like, in a rehearsal?"

Ms. Hendriks wanted to say yes. She was nodding, thinking about the suggestion, smiling sympathetically. "You could help with lines, too, couldn't you? I'll see who else signs up, Hadrian, but I don't think there'll be a big rush. Most people don't want to be an underling."

They agreed with her. It was only natural, like not wanting to be a ninth grader.

"Or a groundling," said Hadrian.

Ms. Hendriks looked carefully at him. "Like in the Elizabethan theater? Are you some kind of a theater nut?"

He nodded, almost as if he was embarrassed at her question. Or flattered.

She ran her left hand through her hair, with a glinting of diamond. "I'd have guessed you for a gamer."

"I never got into games. They're not . . ."

"Real," the teacher supplied.

Margalo had had enough of being an underling or groundling or just plain peanut-butter-and-jelly nobody in the conversation. With a little edge of sarcasm in her voice she asked, "Real like the stage?" to let them know that she had ideas too and was worth not-ignoring.

Ms. Hendriks turned to her with a happy expression. "You don't think the stage is real? Then what art is? Because it's not television or most films." The teacher seemed to be enjoying the talk, which was pretty unusual, a teacher enjoying just talking ideas with students. But this was her first year teaching.

"I didn't say the stage *wasn't* real," Margalo pointed out. "I just raised the question, because . . . theater isn't common reality, not what most people mean. It's the kind of reality . . . like fairy tales have, psychological reality, sociological."

Ms. Hendriks nodded, but instead of continuing with that interesting topic, she said, "I want to ask you something. Because I gather you were the assistant director last year for—"

"How do you know that?"

"I read your folder."

What did that mean? Did every teacher read every student's folder? Did they have to read them? What was in Margalo's school folder for Ms. Hendriks, or any teacher, to read?

Ms. Hendriks seemed to be backtracking, apologizing. "I looked at all of them, to help me understand the people I'm teaching and working with. I probably won't do it again, if I'm asked back for next year."

Margalo set aside the folder question, temporarily, and said, "Is that the same thing as what you called a dogsbody? I read a book called—"

"A dogsbody does everything. Whatever anybody tells him to do, or her, whatever needs doing."

Margalo continued stubbornly. "—called *Dogsbody*, and he's one of the stars, I mean the celestial stars, Sirius."

Ms. Hendriks had been re-distracted and interrupted again. "I know it. I always thought that book would make an interesting script, for animation—for the old Disney studios, you know?"

"I never read it," Hadrian said, now inserting himself into *their* conversation.

"It's good," Margalo told him. "If you don't mind fantasy."

"I don't mind anything good," he told her.

"I'll probably be able to use both of you," Ms. Hendriks told them then, and seemed pleased at the prospect. "After all, it's the underclassmen who are the bedrock of a Drama department, the building blocks, getting trained. But Hadrian? Can I say something about your hair? Because . . . well, you saw how people . . ."

Hadrian seemed to fold back into himself. It was as if, for a few minutes, talking, he had forgotten what he looked like.

And that reminded Margalo. "You should let us read, I mean, let Hadrian, because—"

Ms. Hendriks shook her head definitely. "There just aren't enough parts, and there's policy, too. But . . . Hadrian? The hair?"

He nodded without looking up, then turned away and Margalo followed him, with an apologetic look back over her shoulder at Ms. Hendriks, who for once didn't look cheerful. She looked like someone who thought she hadn't done a good enough job at something.

"I've got a comb," Margalo said to Hadrian's back as he bent over to pick up his knapsack. She reached down for her own, adding, "I can loan it to you."

Hadrian said, "I just don't want my mother . . ." He didn't have to finish that sentence.

She accompanied him out into the emptying corridor. Hadrian kept his eyes lowered, but Margalo looked around, looking for trouble, where it might come from. Anybody knew that you could get in trouble being alone with just Hadrian Klenk. Sven and his friend Toby and their friend Harold played football, she thought, so they probably wouldn't be in the building at that hour. As far as she knew, only those three had nothing better to think about than how to torment Hadrian Klenk; so maybe they were temporarily safe. Or Hadrian was safe for the time being. She herself was pretty much safe pretty much most of the time.

As safe, at least, as anybody was, at just about any time. Or anyway, she *felt* safe enough. Maybe safety was like intelligence? Margalo thought, and almost laughed. If you acted like you were smart, most people believed you. So what *was* real?

Thinking about reality, and what was true, and how the real danger of lying was not that you might get caught but that you might start believing your own lies, somehow led Margalo right to an idea. She grabbed Hadrian's arm. "Tell your mother it's a new style you're trying."

"What?" He pulled his arm away.

"Tell her you and some friends all moussed your hair this way. Tell her everyone did it."

"But it looks ridiculous."

"Tell her it was a style experiment. Think about it, Hadrian."

He did, and she could see relief grow in him as he imagined himself telling his mother this, and what she would say, and what he would say then. His head came up and he was smiling. It was a weak and wavery smile, but still a smile. "She'll hate it," he predicted. "I can tell her I don't like it much myself. That'll make her happy."

"She won't ask any questions," Margalo added.

"Thank you," Hadrian said then. "You saved my life."

"I saved your mother's life," Margalo corrected.

Mikey and Margalo didn't need to consult each other. They moved down the length of the school bus to a rear seat. Not *the* rear seat, which was a long bench where others might join them, or at least adjoin them, and not the seats right in front of that bench, either. They took a two-person seat far enough back in the center section of the bus so a private conversation would be buried in all the noise and confusion.

Mikey started off as Margalo was just sitting down in her aisle seat. "I'm half-way up the sophomore section of the ladder and she actually paid me a compliment today." Misunderstanding Margalo's expression, she explained, "Coach Sandy."

As soon as she was settled into her seat, Margalo started off her own topic. "He didn't get to read. No ninth grader did."

"She said I had a good drop shot."

"There was never any chance he'd get a part. I should have known."

They were ninth-grade girls, best friends since fifth grade, and they could carry on two conversations at one time, listening to both and talking about both almost simultaneously. Two was about Mikey's outside limit, but Margalo could carry on as many as four different conversations on different topics before she lost her way.

"I'd have thought it would have been my backhand crosscourt," Mikey said.

"They moussed his hair into—a whole headful of spikes. Then they frog-marched him to Drama," Margalo reported. "They got off on people laughing. It's going to just make them worse."

"At least," Mikey said, "they've stopped taking his knapsack. So, what's Hadrian going to do?"

"Understudy some parts probably. Which means he won't appear onstage, which means . . ." She got distracted by another dismal thought. "Probably, if they've given up taking his knapsack, they'll move on to something more. As we just saw."

Mikey turned to look right into Margalo's face, as if it was Margalo she was angry at. "I don't like it one bit."

"And the rest of us do?"

But Mikey had returned to her own dismal thoughts. "I don't even have a good drop shot."

The bus motor rumbled to life, the long iron arm closed

73

the front doors, and the bus pulled out, swaying a little as it made the turn onto the main road. Margalo and Mikey clutched at the knapsacks they held on their laps. ME was stenciled in big red letters on the front of Mikey's bright hunter's orange knapsack, the color that kept you from being shot at, if you happened to be carrying your knapsack through the woods during hunting season. She had bought it last summer in Texas, where hunter's orange was a common color. When the bus lurched forward into traffic, a few girls gave little screams and a few boys cheered the driver. "Rock on!"

After things had settled down—at least, settled down as much as a busload of high school students could—Mikey remembered to ask Margalo, "What *about* Aurora and a GED? Is she really going to try to do it? Why?"

"Lily's in school all day, and Aurora would like a job. She's already taking a class, two classes in fact, English and History. She wants to work with little children so she might even take college courses, after."

"I thought she wanted to be a stay-at-home mom."

"That's what Esther says. Esther says if Aurora is going to go to school, she's going to run away and live with her father, because she wants a mother who stays at home to be a mother."

"But Aurora's not Esther's mother, she's her stepmother," Mikey reminded her.

"I know."

"And, her father doesn't want her living with him anyway. He's got a whole new family."

"She knows."

"What does Aurora say?"

"She says she wants Esther to let her try it, to see how much difference it actually makes."

"Aurora doesn't stick up for herself enough," Mikey announced, then asked, "What does Esther say to that?"

"She says she'll go live with you."

That shut Mikey up.

Margalo enjoyed being one up for just a couple of minutes before she introduced her own concern. "I know we all have folders, records, but do you think all of our teachers have read them?"

"I don't think they're that interested," Mikey said, offering as proof, "Coach Sandy wouldn't have ignored me."

"You think not?"

"Why would she?" Mikey asked, and answered herself, "There's no possible reason."

Margalo could think of at least two possible reasons, but she was concerned about something else. "Don't you think that's an invasion of privacy?"

Put that way, Mikey got it immediately. "Do you want me to ask Jackson?" Jackson was someone who knew a lot about almost everything. They guessed that you couldn't be a successful venture capitalist for all the years he'd been one without being pretty smart, and learning a whole lot too.

"No, not unless you want to. School records are open, I think. Even to students. At least, our own records."

"What about teachers' records? Are they open too? Can we read *their* folders? That would be fair, and administrators too."

"But maybe I'll take a look at mine, to make sure it's only about, like, having the required shots, and grades."

"Disciplinary measures will be in there too," Mikey said, and she smiled. "I hope mine is a really fat folder."

"You could work on that." Seeing it from that new point of view, Margalo relaxed. Let the folder-keepers keep themselves busy keeping folders, and that would keep them out of her hair. "We could both work on it."

"Yeah, but Louis Caselli is way ahead."

"We could try to catch up."

They were both laughing now, just like any other high school students going home on the late bus after a long school day. This was the kind of idea they liked to think about, figuring out how to do it—get a fatter student record folder than Louis Caselli—without getting into real trouble themselves with the school authorities or into real trouble with grades.

"Or maybe, maybe we should work on helping Louis increase his," Margalo suggested.

"Louis can always use help," Mikey agreed.

Margalo admitted, "I wish we could help Hadrian."

"Yeah, but how? That Sven and his two friends—"

"Toby and Harold."

"They're . . ."

Neither of them knew the best way to end that thought. Upperclassmen? Really mean? Much bigger than we are? Unstoppable—even by the school authorities? Too smart to get caught in the act?

No, probably not that last one. They weren't too smart for anything, in Margalo and Mikey's opinion.

"But Mikey," Margalo said, the unexpected comparison causing her to turn in her seat and face her friend and cohort, as if having a friend and cohort made the idea easier to have. "Are they acting all that different from the way we . . . I mean, remember getting Louis thrown out of our fifth-grade class?" she reminded Mikey, and herself, and then remembered too, "And getting him brought back in?"

"Rhonda and the roadkill," Mikey agreed happily. She was untroubled by the comparison. "But we were getting even," she pointed out. At all the memories she added, "I miss fifth grade. I wouldn't mind being back in fifth grade."

"Yes you would," Margalo said crisply. "Think about it. Fifth grade is eight years from graduation, and ninth is only four."

"Actually, it'll be only three and five-sixths years when this marking period ends next week," Mikey said.

"But are we really any different?" Margalo asked again. "When we were getting even, like—remember seventh grade?"

"They were picking on us," Mikey reminded her, and

smiled at the memories. *Those were the days.* "We were just picking back."

"They thought we were weak. Powerless."

"We weren't."

"But Hadrian is. I really hoped he'd get a part. And so did he, I think. That just makes it all the worse that she wouldn't even let him read for one, when you hope for something and don't get it."

"Hoping's pointless," Mikey told Margalo.

"You sound like Cassie," Margalo said, not as a compliment.

Mikey just went on. "The point is to *do* something."

"The only thing I can think of to do is murder them."

Mikey was willing to consider that option. "All three? How would we do it?"

"In books people use rat poison."

"We've got the rats," Mikey observed. "Now all we need is the poison."

Mikey was giving this idea such serious consideration that Margalo felt the need to point out its obvious drawback. "I'm not about to go to jail for those three."

"Yeah, but we might not get caught."

"Unless," Margalo said, "we could be like the seven-at-one-blow little tailor? Who got the ogres fighting among themselves?"

"You're having a nervous breakdown," Mikey told her. "I can't even sew."

Looking out the window, she saw that the bus was nearing Margalo's stop. "Are you baby-sitting tonight?"

"And tomorrow night too."

"In the morning, then," Mikey told her. "I'll be over tomorrow morning then. Tell Aurora I'll make breakfast." Mikey and her divorced father, with whom she lived, had organized their weekends. Saturday afternoons they did something together, which these days meant doing something with his girlfriend and her two little boys; Sunday mornings they cleaned house; and Sunday afternoons Mikey had league tennis practice. So Saturday morning was about the only time she and Margalo had for getting together. "Maybe I'll make omelets. Will Lily and Stevie eat omelets, do you think?"

Margalo was getting ready to stand up. "As long as there's nothing weird in them."

"For the rest of us I'll make cheese omelets with herbs," and Mikey was off, planning a meal.

Margalo followed her, suggesting, "Chives and parsley."

"Plus biscuits." Mikey liked getting the last word, even if they were in total agreement.

Rising from her seat, her knapsack held against her stomach, Margalo turned to join the others lining up in the aisle. She was almost at the door when Mikey remembered, and stood up to shout down the length of the half-empty bus, "What do *you* think about Aurora's GED? Margalo!"

But Margalo didn't hear her. Mikey groaned. Now either she was going to have to telephone Margalo's house, and risk being talked at by Margalo's adoring stepsister, Esther, or she was going to have to wait until tomorrow morning to find out. She couldn't decide which would be worse, waiting or Esther.

— 6 —

There's Bad, and Also There's Worse

That year Halloween fell on a Saturday, and it was on Friday the thirtieth of October—week eight, by Mikey's count; twenty-eight weeks left—that the homeroom teachers handed out to the students their report cards for the first marking period, first thing in the morning. Perhaps it was the combination of pre-Halloween excitement with hot news of bad grades, or good grades, or good-enough grades, that caused Hadrian's catastrophe. Grade news certainly exacerbated the usual high school nerviness, and everyone knew that Sven had been caught copying answers on the History unit test, so he was flunking History for sure and his parents required him to get at least a C in everything, so he was going to get it when he got home. On the whole, people were pleased that Sven was going to get it from someone. Also, people—especially the Varsity players—were nervous about

81

Saturday's football game against Benjamin Franklin High School, a team with a 5–0 record. Nobody liked to be wiped out, not even by a really good team. Also, there was the usual weekend excitement and anxiety about who was going out with whom, what parties were being given, who was being invited to which, and if they were going to continue getting away with the things that they had—so far—been getting away with.

By the time Mikey sat down beside Margalo for Lunch A, slowed down as she had been by students clustering in the halls to discuss their grades, or celebrate them, or bemoan them, Casey was already there and Cassie was approaching, with Tim, Felix and Jace close behind.

Margalo looked up from her bologna sandwich and opened her mouth to say something, but Mikey didn't give her a chance. "She gave me an A minus in Spanish." To Margalo's inquiring expression, *There's something wrong with an A minus?* Mikey said, "I shouldn't get over a B. You know I haven't gotten anything better than a B on any of the tests."

"Does she give a lot of credit for homework? Or weight class discussion grades?" Margalo suggested.

Mikey shook her head. "It's a bad A, Margalo."

What Margalo thought about the concept of a bad A (could there be good Ds?) Mikey never found out because Cassie had news to tell, news so important that she didn't even sit down before she announced it. "Did you hear about Hadrian?"

"Where is he anyway?" Mikey asked. "He wasn't in Math and he's never absent. Was he in English?"

"What's happened?" Margalo asked, shaking her head, No, to answer Mikey's second question.

Tim slammed his tray down on the table, announcing, "It's just not right." But Cassie wanted to be the one to tell them, it being something that revealed once again what rotters human beings could be, so she told the story.

"Those guys—I don't even *want* to know their names—Eenie, Meenie and Minie—Larry, Curly and Moe—Tom, Dick and Harry—"

"Mean, Stupid and Immature," Casey suggested. She had looked up from *Crime and Punishment* and her lunch; she had even closed the book, although she kept a finger in it to mark her place. "I heard about it."

"The juniors," Margalo guessed. She did know their names, but that wasn't the point. "What did they do to him now?"

Cassie said, "The story is they broke his arm."

"They *what*?"

"That's not what I heard."

"I thought it was his leg."

"I heard his wrist."

Cassie raised her voice to drown them out. "Whichever limb it was, there was an ambulance."

This caused a silence.

Margalo broke it. "Is he all right?"

"Well, he walked to the ambulance."

"Some girls found him in the hallway," Tim reported. "It was a couple of seniors."

"But why didn't someone stop them?" Mikey asked.

"There's never anyone around. That's their MO," Felix explained.

Cassie continued. "Mr. Robredo had them in his office for two hours—before he suspended them."

"Had them in his office all three? Or one at a time?" Mikey wanted to know. She had not personally met up with the legendary Mr. Robredo, but she had heard about him. Even Louis Caselli didn't want to mix it up with Mr. Robredo, even Louis Caselli on his most foolhardy, suicidal, delusional days.

The worrisome thing about Mr. Robredo was that he was absolutely serious about his job, and absolutely straight. He wouldn't cut you any slack, even if he thought you were funny, even if your parents knew him socially. He wouldn't cut anybody any slack, he didn't take any lip off anybody, he was happy to consider expelling people, and he did what he said he'd do. Nobody wanted to be taken in to see Mr. Robredo. With somebody that fair, you couldn't be sure how it would turn out for you.

Cassie reported, "One at a time. Then the police came. Casey, ask your father what happened."

"No," Casey said.

"Don't be such a priss. I didn't mean go ask him now. We

all know that at school you pretend not to be related. I mean, this weekend. I mean, tell us Monday."

"I don't *believe* this," Mikey announced, although she did.

On Monday, however, there was no need for Casey to report anything, or for rumors to be sifted and sorted to get at their kernels of truth. On Monday, Hadrian was back in school. His left arm was in a sling—"Luckily, I'm right-handed," he said—because his collarbone had been broken. "They were shoving me. It's what they do. It's *one* of the things they do," he reported, in case they wanted the whole picture.

Cassie demanded, "What are you going to do about it?"

"I just have to keep it immobilized. I don't have to return to gym until after New Year's," Hadrian told them happily.

Cassie insisted, "Aren't you furious?"

"More likely frightened," said Felix. "That's what I'd be."

Cassie ignored him, asking, "Don't you want to go after them?"

"Him and what army?" Tim asked.

"Can you sue?" Margalo wondered. She suggested, "Aggravated personal assault."

Hadrian shook his head. "Besides, they're out of school for three weeks. I can relax."

At lunch that day many people stopped off to tell Hadrian "Hey."

What was that supposed to mean? That now they were

85

going to be his friends? That they felt sorry for him? That it would never happen again?

Ronnie came by, said, "Hey, Hadrian," and slipped away. Derrie and Annaliese also lingered long enough to say "Hey," and "Hey." Jason said "Hey," and added, with feeling, "*man*," while Shawn just put a hand on Hadrian's thin shoulder as he walked by behind him.

The hand made Hadrian jump up from his chair, but once he saw who it was, he sat down again.

Tan said "Hey" to Hadrian, then turned on Mikey and Margalo. "What are you going to do about this?"

"What can *we* do?" Mikey demanded right back, while Hadrian pointed out pacifically, "They're suspended for three weeks."

"That doesn't change anything. What about after that?" Tan asked. But she answered herself. "Never mind. I know. It's not anybody's fault."

"Of course it's not my fault," Mikey agreed.

"It's not Hadrian's fault either," Margalo said.

"That's what I mean," said Tan.

"It's just the way things are," said Cassie. "It's high school."

"And *that*," declared Tanisha Harris, "is *why* they're this way. Nobody ever does anything and it's never anybody's fault. The people that can do something don't want to, and the rest of us don't dare. Or don't care."

"We *care*," argued Tim.

"Right," said Cassie, cramming as much sarcasm into one

word as most people needed a sentence to use up. "I can tell. So can Hadrian. Can't you, Hadrian?"

Hadrian shrank down into his seat, suddenly deaf from birth, and Tan walked away, her skirt swishing a little.

"What's wrong with *her*?" asked Casey, looking up from her reading, which that day was *Pride and Prejudice*.

"You have to ask?" Cassie answered.

"Has anyone ever put a restraining order on your mouth?" asked Felix unexpectedly.

Margalo looked at Mikey to comment silently on this leaping-to-Casey's-defense: Did Felix want to be Casey's boyfriend?

"Besides me, I mean," said Felix.

"Ha, ha," Cassie countered.

A couple more people swooped by, hesitating only long enough to say, "Hey, Hadrian," and "Hey," as they went on to their destination tables. Ira Pliotes added a little more. "Good to see you back," he said, and waited until Hadrian had looked up and answered, "Thanks."

It was almost a pleasure to have Louis Caselli come strutting up to their table and *not* say "Hey." Louis was so pleased with himself that he was dancing from one foot to the other. "I guess you aren't the only smart people around here," he announced, as if it was just the three of them—him and Mikey and Margalo—in the room.

At his news Margalo glanced in wide-eyed mock surprise at

Mikey, then back at Louis. "I'm sorry," she said insincerely, adding dishonestly, "I couldn't hear you."

Louis strutted a step closer. "I said," he practically yelled, "that you aren't the only smart people around here. Because I got a B in wood shop. Not a B minus, a straight B. That's an honors grade," he told them, in case they had forgotten.

"Good going, man," said Tim. "Congratulations." Then he asked politely, since Louis lingered, "How were the rest?"

"English and Math don't mean anything, not in the real world," Louis informed him. He noticed Hadrian Klenk. "Klenk," he began, decided against it, and strutted off away, stopping to announce his good grade at another table.

"That's gotta be Louis Caselli," Tim said to Margalo. He turned to his best friend, sitting beside him, "D'you know who that was?"

Felix had no interest in Louis Caselli. "At the movies on Friday?" he asked the table. "You know who I saw? You'll never guess."

"Just tell us," Cassie advised him.

"Chet Parker." He looked around expectantly.

Mikey and Margalo weren't sure who Chet Parker was, although they thought they'd heard the name. Mikey was sure she could take Felix's way of telling news for only about one half second longer.

"He's a senior, Mister Cool. He's got great facial bones, photogenic, you know? He's on all three varsities, drives an '88 BMW," Felix said. "He's got everything. And he's smart, too, or anyway, he gets the grades. He's applied early admission to Duke, and he'll probably get in."

"The girls are all over him," Tim added. "He can have anybody he wants."

Cassie snorted a *Not me* snort.

"He was at the movies with that long-haired blonde. Rhonda?" Felix said. He grinned an *I'm in the know* grin and said, "Her Mommy's going to be sorry she didn't take Sex Ed. But that makes me think, we should all go to the movies next Saturday. Anybody want to? Tim? What do you say, Mikey? Jace?"

"You'd probably pick something with subtitles," Mikey objected. "Or aliens."

"I'll hold your hand if you get scared," Felix offered.

"I don't get scared," Mikey told him.

"Then you can hold my hand, because I do. Or we could go the week after. That one's animated. Japanese."

Nobody, including Hadrian, made the mistake of thinking he was part of the general invitation. Mikey declined on account of her regular Saturday-afternoon father-commitment, or more precisely, father-and-girlfriend, or most precisely, father-and-girlfriend-and-girlfriend's-two-little-boys. Margalo had a job interview, although she was pretty sure they wouldn't give it to her, since the ad specified cash register experience. "You lied?" asked Tim, and she reassured him, "I just didn't say what kind of experience I have on what kind of cash register."

❖

89

Margalo had a good time telling them about the interview the next Monday, and she didn't mind a bit their knowing that she didn't get the job. "They had a test. I was supposed to ring out a basket of groceries, so they figured out right away that I didn't know what I was doing."

"Didn't they even think of teaching you?" asked Tim. "That's pretty shortsighted of them."

"Too bad" and "Tough" and "Better luck next time" were the general opinions on her failure, but it was Mikey who said, "So probably there's no sense in lying on job applications because it's pretty sure you'll get found out. Were you embarrassed?" she asked.

It had never crossed Margalo's mind to be embarrassed. "No, why should I be?"

It was interesting—to Margalo, at least—that the thing she didn't like talking about was Drama. She wasn't like Mikey, who didn't care how bored you got with her obsessive interests, tennis mostly, with her day-by-day reporting of progress up the tennis ladder. "I'll be halfway through the juniors, at least, by the end of the fall season," Mikey promised them, until Cassie finally groaned, "Who *cares*?" and asked Mikey— who of course didn't get it—"What are you going to have to talk about in the winter, without tennis?" "Basketball. Why?" asked Mikey.

In this respect Margalo considered herself about the exact opposite of Mikey. The more something mattered to her, the less able—and willing—she was to talk about it. She could never find the right words for the really important things, things she had a lot of hope attached to, or a lot of pride attached to. Or things that, if she lost them, her whole life would be different, every day of it. When she tried to talk about those things, feelings swelled up inside of her—big, unmanageable feelings, the kinds of feelings words couldn't convey.

Whereas Mikey thought the only things worth talking about, and thinking about, were whatever was really important to her. About the exact opposite of Margalo.

Except, of course, that Margalo *could* talk to Mikey about those important things, and Mikey, when she and Margalo were just talking, didn't mind what the subject was. So even while they were opposite to one another, they were also opposite to their usual selves when they were with each other. (*People are so interesting!* Margalo thought, the kind of thing people say to themselves when what they also mean is, *I am so interesting!*)

A couple of days later Margalo could tell them about an interview for a job at a veterinarian's boarding kennel—"This is for that college account of yours, right?" asked Tim, impressed—and Hadrian's arm was out of its sling and he had enjoyed ten days of leisurely lunches. It was the second-to-last Friday before Thanksgiving, by Mikey's count the tenth Friday of the school year. Also, it was Friday the thirteenth. "Are you superstitious?" Casey asked Felix and Tim, and

Mikey reminded them, "Remember, we can't count Friday of Thanksgiving week," and Cassie said, "Whadda you mean *we*?" while Hadrian told them all, as if it was an announcement of the utmost importance, "There's only one more week."

The table paid no attention, except for Mikey, who corrected him, "Two until Thanksgiving," and then corrected herself, "Two weeks minus one day. Thanksgiving's always a Thursday," she explained, in case anyone at the table hadn't grasped this fact.

Nobody paid much attention to Mikey, either. Including Hadrian.

He said, "I mean until they come back. Until the suspension is up. I've been thinking, and I think I'm going to need some help, at least at first, and maybe for a while after, so I was wondering—Will you help me?" He looked around at all of their faces, one after the other.

Casey had her nose buried in *Gone with the Wind*, but the others returned his glance, wondering what he was talking about.

Hadrian clarified it. "They come back to school next Friday."

"Who they?" Mikey demanded impatiently until she realized just as Margalo said it, "The Three Stooges."

"And they're going to be really angry. At me."

None of the people at the table had thought of this, but as soon as Hadrian mentioned it they all fell silent, thinking unhappy thoughts. Even Casey looked up from her book to join in, silently.

He was right. He was right, and they were sorry, but what could they do?

"Would you like me to write an editorial?" Tim asked Hadrian. "Raise public awareness? Most people—I mean the vast majority—they don't like this kind of bullying."

"I know, but what difference does that make?" Hadrian asked, an entirely reasonable question.

"It's pretty dumb of them to be mad at *you*," Mikey observed.

"Pretty dumb just about describes them," Cassie observed. "So that's no surprise."

"But will you help me?" Hadrian asked again.

"Help you do what?" Margalo asked him. "What do you want to do? Can you . . . for example, can you get a restraining order to keep them—what is it?—two hundred yards away from you?"

"I don't think so," Hadrian said. "I'd have had to have filed complaints all along to do that. And if I'd filed complaints . . ." He didn't need to finish that idea. They knew what would have happened to Hadrian if he had had the courage—or the foolhardiness—to complain to the school authorities.

"What do you want *us* to do?" Mikey asked.

"I was thinking, if you were my bodyguards? You and Margalo."

"We don't have the time. Besides, I have tennis until

93

Thanksgiving, and we're in mostly different classes. What about Louis Caselli? Could you hire him? He's probably going to have to repeat the year, so he won't care about cutting classes."

"I could ask," said Hadrian in a voice so full of doubt they knew he'd never do it. "But it would be three against one, and Louis isn't exactly big."

"Louis is bad at Math," Mikey observed. "He might not figure out the odds, and you'd have time to get away while they were dealing with him."

"It's more likely that Louis would manage to make everything worse," Margalo predicted.

"Can you afford to transfer to a private school?" Casey wondered. "Or you could probably get a scholarship to one, with your grades."

"You're telling him to run away?" Mikey asked.

"There's Drama," Hadrian argued. "And if they send me to private school, what about my sisters?"

"I thought you were an only child."

"They're both younger," Hadrian said.

Margalo had been thinking. "What if you get people in each one of your classes to stick close to you? I will in English, and Casey will too, won't you?"

"I'll do Math," Mikey offered.

Hadrian reminded them, "It's the hallways not the classrooms where things happen. And bathrooms. And outside."

They *knew* that. They didn't need Hadrian Klenk reminding them. Sometimes, they wished he'd just keep his mouth shut and disappear. They felt sorry for him and all, and they knew it wasn't fair at all, but still . . .

Bad feelings—irritated, annoyed, impatient feelings, feelings that blamed Hadrian for their existence, that suspected it was somehow his fault, that just wanted not to have to deal with this—all of those feelings started to rise up, invisible, yes, but they felt like a flooding river rising slowly up over its banks and lapping up around their feet.

Hadrian pulled his feet up onto the rung of his seat. He hunched his skinny shoulders and dug with his spoon into the bowl of pudding on his lunch tray.

That was when Margalo had her idea.

— 7 —

A Few Happy Moments

"A restraining order!"

"But I told you—," Hadrian started to say.

"No," Margalo interrupted him. "I mean, if you can't get a restraining order from the police, what if you got one from the ninth grade? No, listen. Think," she said, raising her voice over Cassie's "Right, like . . ." and Casey's "No one has ever . . . " "What if the ninth grade, or a lot of us, anyway—I bet a lot of people would, never mind their motives. What if we put our own restraining order on the three of them? To keep away from Hadrian."

"But we don't have the right to do that," Hadrian pointed out.

Felix asked, "Why just the ninth grade? Why not include tenth graders too? I mean, those three guys used to go after me sometimes, last year, and not just me. I didn't even get it all that badly, but it was no fun, I can tell you, so you can count me in. What about you, Tim?"

"Why would they bully *you*?" Casey wondered but Tim was saying, "They never went for me personally, but I wouldn't mind. I mean, in a democracy it's up to the majority to control the bad elements itself."

"Those aren't bad elements," Mikey said. "They're stupid elements. If there's a restraining order posted, they'll believe it," she told Hadrian. "You write one, Margalo," she said, giving the order, then explaining to the others, "She'll know how to make it sound official."

Margalo hastened to modify Mikey's bossiness. She turned to Casey. "Would you be willing to advise me? Would you look at a draft? Or I can call you and read it to you."

"Exactly when are they coming back to school?" Tim asked.

"Friday."

"The eleventh Friday," said Mikey. "Only twenty-five to go."

They ignored her.

Tim said, "We can post copies on the bulletin board outside of the library and by the gym entrance."

"One at the main entrance too," Casey suggested.

"Like one of those Most Wanted posters in the post office?" Jace suggested.

"If most people in our two grades enforce it, it'll be a de facto restraining order," Tim announced with pleasure.

"You're taking Latin too?" Mikey demanded.

"I can print out as many copies as we want. I've got some good heavy paper," Tim offered. "But we'll need some kind of images, don't you think? Felix?"

"What *is* it with Latin?" Mikey demanded.

"Give me negatives and I'll print pictures," Felix offered.

"I can draw pictures," Jace said while Cassie announced, "Just give me a couple of minutes."

Then Tim was having second thoughts. "What do you think the school will say about doing this?"

"Like I care," Cassie answered.

Quietly Casey told them, "My dad would get it, and he's not the only one on the faculty who would. They mean well, you know. Really, they do."

"All we can do is try it and see what happens," Margalo suggested.

"Well," Mikey announced, "I don't care what the school says, and neither should any of us."

Tim pointed out, "But some of us do."

Hadrian said then, "I don't want to get anyone in trouble. You don't have to do this."

Margalo disagreed. "You know? I think I do. Not for you," she said, and then added quickly, "Not *just* for you. Okay. If we have images, we can put names under them. I'm for the Three Stooges, Moe and Curly and Larry, and I think Sven should be Moe. We should do it that way," she explained, "because if we make it a joke on them, then people will really do it. People like doing the right thing for a while, but a joke lasts much longer."

They argued happily about that for a few minutes, who should be Larry, if it was more of a joke if Curly had a crew cut or actually had curly hair, because Toby wore his hair in a short crew cut. Then there was a less happy argument, between Felix and Cassie and Jace, about who was going to make the pictures and what the pictures should look like. It was the *should* that got them into trouble.

Finally Tim suggested, "How about one by each of you? That would work pretty well, visually, don't you think? Three different images, wouldn't that be more interesting? You guys decide among yourselves who's going to do which one, but can you have them for me by Monday morning? Because we'll want to put the notices up on Wednesday."

"Will we need signatures?" Casey wondered.

"We'll tell people what we're doing," they answered. "That, plus the actual restraining orders posted all over the school will do it. I can't wait for those three to get back to school and see what we've got waiting for them. Can you, Hadrian?"

They all turned to look at Hadrian. He looked both hopeful and worried. "Are you sure it'll work?"

"Of course not," Margalo told him.

"Because it could just make things worse," he said.

"How much worse can they get?" asked Mikey.

"Things can always get worse," Hadrian assured her.

By waiting until Wednesday to post their notices, they gave rumors about what the ninth grade was up to two and a half days to be planted and to grow fat and weedy, fed by curiosity and a sense of injustice. On Wednesday they waited until Lunch A, hoping that the school—by which they meant administrators, discipliners, those in charge of keeping things orderly—wouldn't have time in only half a school day to make a decision about how to react. This was in case their reaction was to veto the restraining order and take down the notices. Margalo argued, convincingly, that after two-and-a-half days of waiting impatiently to learn what was going on, and then half a day of knowing about it and wanting to take part, the students would be putting pressure on the school to let the restraining order stand. Probably many parents would agree, since parents could get pretty worked up over injustices and victimizations at school.

After Lunch A on Wednesday they put up their notices wherever they thought a notice would be seen—in the glass window of the library, beside the entrance to the gym, on the Guidance Department's student-interest bulletin board, on the glass front of the locked case that displayed all the sports trophies ever won by any of the teams, by the doors to both faculty lounges and, finally, one on each of their own locker doors. They posted their restraining orders and then they waited for whatever would happen next.

The first thing that happened was people everywhere, in

all the corridors, in all the classrooms, anticipating how Sven and his goons would react to this. "This'll teach them" appeared to be the general opinion.

The bad side of that enthusiastic response was, as Tim pointed out and Margalo couldn't disagree, that somebody was bound to tell Sven *et al*, which meant they would lose the element of surprise.

"What do you mean *at all*?" asked Mikey.

"It's Latin," Margalo explained.

"No it isn't."

"*Et al*," Hadrian said. "It means *and everybody else*, in this case, *and Harold and Toby*."

"I hate Latin," Mikey said.

"No you don't," Margalo told her, irritatingly. "You just don't know anything about it."

"*De gustibus non est disputandum*," said Tim, but then he ruined it by laughing. Tim wasn't the kind of person who could keep a straight face very long.

"What-Ever," Mikey said. "You're right about losing the element of surprise."

"But surprise only lasts a couple of minutes anyway," Margalo pointed out. "And this way, instead of surprise they'll feel dread, which is more what we want, isn't it?"

In a mood of unusual solidarity, not only the people at Mikey and Margalo's lunch table, but almost all ninth graders too, were feeling pretty good about themselves. They were pretty sure no other ninth-grade class—with the help of some tenth graders and to the envy of the upper classes—had ever done anything like this. They thought they might have discovered an anti-bullying technique that would work anywhere. They wondered if maybe some TV station might hear about it and come interview them. "Ronnie and Shawn should be our spokespeople," was the general opinion, which went on to recommend, "Better keep Hadrian off camera. He's too weird."

The restraining order—"Not within 200 yards!"—was the talk of the school on Wednesday. High school was like a terrarium, an enclosed ecological system where the introduction of any new element immediately affected the whole. People measured off two hundred yards—"Two football fields, dummy"—and considered what action might be taken against anyone who violated the order. Everybody was eager for Sven and his stooges (Harold had been renamed Stooge One, and Toby Stooge Two, but Sven was always and only Sven) to show up so they could enforce the order.

On Thursday morning loudspeakers in the homerooms cracked out their usual announcements, reminders of the special schedule in effect on the Wednesday before Thanksgiving break, of the performances of *A Midsummer Night's Dream* over the first weekend in December, of a Senior Class Prom Committee meeting, and more, before it summoned the day's assortment of malefactors to Mr. Robredo's office. Hadrian Klenk's was the first name on this list. He was instructed to go immediately to see the assistant principal, and so he did, leaving homeroom early and arriving back in the middle of English. It wasn't until Lunch A that he could report in.

"You'd think they'd make their own soups," Hadrian said, settling his tray down on the table across from Mikey and Margalo, who were themselves enjoying (Mikey) a baguette sandwich with ham and brie, and eating (Margalo) a leftover leg of chicken, with a bread and jam sandwich on the side. "I'll trade my grilled cheese for part of your baguette," he offered Mikey with—for Hadrian—unusual assertiveness.

She smiled, *How dumb do you think I am? Because I'm not that dumb.* "You aren't going to be one of those people who undergoes a personality transformation when your life improves, are you? Like an overnight screen sensation," she said, thinking of Shawn Macavity's swift rise to popularity last year.

"I don't think that's a real danger," Hadrian said. "I mean, I'm just an excuse here, aren't I? It has nothing to do with me personally. I tried to explain that to Mr. Robredo, and I think he understood. It took a while," Hadrian said. He added, "Because at first he blamed *me* for the restraining order."

"Oh," said Margalo, who hadn't thought this would happen.

"Better you than me," was Jace's response.

"What did you tell him?" Cassie asked. "How'd you get out of it?"

"I didn't tell him anything," Hadrian said. "Not at first, anyway."

"He threatened you?" Tim wondered.

"Why would he do that? What would he threaten me about?" Hadrian was puzzled. "He thinks it's a good idea. Although I did get the impression that not everybody agrees with him. I mean, the Principal might not because of the possibility of negative publicity, and—"

"He *likes* it?" Tim asked, surprised.

"So I told him it wasn't really my idea. Because—It wasn't my idea, so why should I get the credit? I told him it was you, Mikey, and you too, Margalo. He said he didn't know you but I was lucky to have two friends like you." He looked at them with an eager, intelligent expression, like some scientist checking out his thesis with a microscope.

Mikey looked at Margalo. What was she supposed to say to this?

"Us too," said Cassie. "Me and Tim and Felix did all the work. Did you tell him that?"

"What about me?" asked Jace. "I did the sketch of Sven. Everybody says it's great. Peter Paul says it's the best of the three."

For a moment Cassie couldn't think of any response. Then she could. "Like I care. Like this is all about *you*. Which it isn't," she pointed out. "It's about Hadrian and our restraining order."

❖

The effect of the restraining order was immediate; that is to say, nothing happened. Friday passed entirely without incident, however much people were hoping otherwise, or expecting otherwise. The trio kept to themselves as much as they could, and when the necessity of classes separated them, they kept their heads down and their mouths shut.

The mood at Lunch A on Friday was jubilant.

By the next Monday, Sven had withdrawn from school. Toby held out until Tuesday. Toby was going to finish out the year in Iowa, where his mother had a sister, and maybe he'd stay there for his senior year too. Sven, rumor reported happily, was heading off to a military school after Christmas, and until then he was grounded. Sven's parents had been infuriated throughout this whole process, by the police, by the suspension, by what had happened to their son—although what exactly they meant by that phrase was not clear. They decided he needed more discipline. This left Harold alone, and alone, Harold became Harold the Harmless.

Hadrian could now, they all felt, walk the halls in safety, although they all did understand that, for Hadrian, safety was a relative term. Hadrian would always—always in school, at least—have less security than most. But he now had a lot more than before, almost as much as everybody else—which, they sensed, probably wasn't as much as they thought they had. In any case, Hadrian was happy with the results of the restraining order.

"I guess you'll really be giving thanks this year," Tim remarked, and Hadrian agreed.

❖

As if that weren't enough, on the Monday *after* Thanksgiving, John Lawrence was absent from school, which meant that Hadrian, as his understudy, played Bottom during rehearsal. This rehearsal took place in the auditorium, on the stage, where Ms. Hendriks had moved them to give her cast time to get used to an actual theatrical setting. They were rehearsing the awakening scene, which began with people asleep all over the stage. As the scene went on, they woke up and spoke their lines and exited, until only Bottom was left. Until then Hadrian's acting had been limited to the occasional well-timed snore, which nobody had much noticed, although it made Ms. Hendriks smile to herself. As the last remaining actors went offstage, Hadrian acted Bottom waking up.

Ms. Hendriks had stood up from her seat at the center of the front row to end that rehearsal, but Hadrian started to speak. His voice was as thick and confused as if he really had been deep in an enchanted sleep. "'When my cue comes, call me.'"

At the sound of this voice Ms. Hendriks fell absolutely still, listening.

Hadrian stumbled a little, looking around him for friends who had fled long ago, then he seemed to move a few steps closer to consciousness as he came a few steps closer to the front of the stage.

Ms. Hendriks was all attention.

Margalo almost laughed out loud from the pleasure of this,

of Hadrian acting, of the teacher realizing how talented Hadrian was. This was exactly what she had predicted would happen, and there was the pleasure of Shakespeare's lines, too, the way Hadrian spoke them.

Hadrian had the part memorized, and he went smoothly on, with Bottom's unique logic. This kind of verbal befuddlement drove John Lawrence crazy, but Hadrian had no problem with it. "'The eye of man hath not heard, the ear of man hath not seen,'" he said, as if he was speaking perfect sense. In fact, as Hadrian said it, it did. Of course it did. It was Shakespeare.

"'It shall be called "Bottom's Dream,"'" Hadrian announced, his face so bright with ignorant self-satisfaction that he could have been Louis Caselli. "'Because it hath no bottom,'" he concluded.

Ms. Hendriks applauded softly.

The other actors hadn't noticed any of this. Having moved offstage, they were rooting around in the pile of knapsacks and jackets to find their own, ready for the bell to ring to mark the end of the day. Only Margalo had stayed in her seat to watch.

"Hadrian," Ms. Hendriks said. "That was . . . You were Bottom himself."

"I wasn't sure about the pacing in the middle," Hadrian admitted, standing at the edge of the stage and looking down at the teacher.

This admission caused her to look at him even more closely.

"I mean whether speeding up to increase the comedy would undermine the significance."

Ms. Hendriks nodded. "Yes, I see the problem," she said. "Well," she said, and took a breath. "It's too late for me to give you the part."

"That doesn't matter," Hadrian told her, and standing there—a scrawny, underage ninth grader again, but perfectly happy—seemed to mean what he said.

The teacher ran her hand through her hair, and her engagement ring glinted, and she frowned. "It might, if I want to keep my job."

"You *should* keep it," Hadrian told her. "You're really good."

She thanked him for the compliment, assuring him, "I definitely want to. But . . . I wonder how written in stone that school policy is. Which reminds me," she said, once again the teacher talking to the student, "Congratulations on your restraining order."

"Oh, that was Mikey, and Margalo too," Hadrian said.

"And a lot of other people," Margalo added.

"Well, congratulations all around, then," Ms. Hendriks said. Now that she realized that Margalo also had witnessed Hadrian acting Bottom and was unsurprised, she looked at Margalo more carefully. But all she asked was, "Mikey? Mikey who?"

After a week of intense rehearsing, which culminated in a dress rehearsal Thursday that ran from three thirty until nine thirty, including a break for pizza delivery, Drama Club performed *A Midsummer Night's Dream* on Friday and Saturday evening. The auditorium was packed both nights. Some people came twice to see the play, and everybody—everybody in the cast, everybody in the audience—said it was the best Shakespeare production the school had given in years. After the excitement and satisfaction of all that applause, after the presentation by Sally and Richard of an armload of roses to Ms. Hendriks, and the admiring and appreciative speech by the Principal, after the question of whether the handsome, dark-eyed, youngish man who sat at the center of the first row was The Fiancé, and the reluctance—now that it was over—to stop saying their lines, after all of that it was Monday morning again.

Richard and Sally were not in school the Monday after the play. Carl Dane explained it to Margalo. "They always take a day off after a play. They go to the city or something like that," he said, with an ambiguous expression, as if to say, *Who knows what they get up to? Who cares?*

The mood in the cafeteria during Lunch A that Monday was jittery—excited about the upcoming holidays, but actually, now that the play had happened, worried about the next big school event, which was midyear exams in early January, just a few days after school reopened. Not everybody felt anxious about exams, of course. Not Mikey and Margalo, and not Felix, either, since he seemed genuinely uninterested in grades. In fact, he wasn't ever sure what his grades were. "I think I'm passing," he would say. "I'm pretty sure I am."

"Why are we talking about exams?" Mikey asked.

"The exam schedule is posted," Tim explained. "Teachers are starting to review material."

"But we're only one third of the way through the school year. What are they doing talking about midyear exams now? Are they that bad at Math?"

Cassie told them, "Peter Paul doesn't believe in exams. The art exam is your portfolio from the semester's work."

"It won't be a semester. It's three weeks short. A semester is half a year," Mikey pointed out.

"From *semi*," explained Margalo, deliberately avoiding looking at Mikey, as if she wasn't saying this to get Mikey going. "Which is Latin for *half*."

"Even in Latin their math is wrong," Mikey concluded. For some reason this particular derangement of numerical rules really griped her, more even than the constant intrusion of Latin into her life.

"Actually," Hadrian said, then cleared his throat, getting ready to emit information. "Actually," he said again, "it's from the Greek *semester*, which became Latin *semestris*, meaning a period of six months."

They digested this Hadrian-like interruption, and not even Mikey—who felt somehow proved right by it—could think of anything to add.

After a while Cassie recommenced. "They tried to make

Peter Paul give real exams, on papers. You know? But he refused to, and he said if they made it a requirement, he'd write an exam where all you had to know was your own name, and everybody would get an A."

Casey looked up from *A Prayer for Owen Meany*. "Do you think he really said that?"

"Sure."

"Or thought of it later and wished he'd thought of it at the time, wished it so much that now he thinks he actually did," Casey wondered.

Towards the middle of that Lunch A, as if she had eaten in a hurry to be able to come join up with them, Tanisha Harris sat down at their table, beside Hadrian and across from Mikey and Margalo. "Hey," she greeted them, looking up and down both sides of the table. "Hey, everybody. Listen, Margalo? Mikey? That was great, what you did."

There was a moment's hesitation. Great about the play? Had there been a particularly stunning tennis victory? What *had* gone on in the last week, besides the play, or before that, before Thanksgiving? Then the penny dropped.

"Yeah," Hadrian agreed. "It was."

"It was me, too," Cassie said.

"And me," Jace said.

"It was all of us," Tim reminded them. "And not just us, it was people in the school, too. It was everyone, pretty much. Otherwise it wouldn't have worked."

"And it did work, which is the important thing," Tan said.

They thought she would get up then, to return to the table where the African-American students tended to eat lunch together, but she didn't. She leaned back, pulled her bright blue knit sweater down over the top of her flowered corduroy skirt, and looked around at them. They all waited to see what it was she was thinking, to get her smiling like that, until Mikey couldn't stand it any longer. "What is *wrong* with you?" she demanded.

Tan grinned. "I just think it's great," she said.

At which point Ronnie Caselli pulled up a chair taken from one table over, to sit down beside Tan. "I'm glad to catch you two together," she announced, but before anybody at the table could ask her to which two she was referring, she went on, making it clear. "You *have* to come to basketball tryouts today. I don't know why you dropped out of Track," she said to Tan, "but it wouldn't be right if you don't play basketball. You're really tall," she explained, "and athletic. We could be on JV together, because what I hear is that there aren't very many sophomore girls playing basketball because they don't have much chance to get on the varsity."

Ronnie was taking a breath to start off on another persuasive point, when Tan said, "Okay."

"Okay? That easily? What's happened?"

"Now are you going to try to talk me out of it?" Tan teased, and Ronnie laughed and shook her head, absolutely and positively No. Her long, heavy hair flowed from side to side like a curtain.

She turned to Mikey. "What about you?"

"Basketball? I don't know, Ronnie, but I guess if—Margalo, is there a winter play too that you'll be working on?"

"Besides, Margalo has a job, starting after New Year's," Ronnie reported. "Don't you?"

Margalo, already nodding away like some big-headed bobble toy, just kept on nodding, enjoying their surprise.

"Dishwashing," Ronnie announced. "It's a friend of my father's who owns the restaurant. Well, he's co-owner. She applied for the job, and he knows I'm in ninth grade, so he asked Dad about her, and Dad asked me. So I know she got it."

Mikey, who had heard all about it the night before, wasn't interested in re-hearing all about it. She announced to Ronnie, "I'll play. Basketball. Even though I'm not tall, and I'm not African American," she added because she thought Ronnie should have asked her first.

"You make up for those deficiencies," Ronnie said, causing Cassie and Tim to laugh and the others to smile private agreement. Then, "Good," Ronnie said, ready to rise and return to her own seat on the other side of the cafeteria, when Rhonda Ransom approached them. Rhonda stopped just behind Felix's shoulder. She smiled down at Tim and Felix, flipping her hair back over her shoulder before—reluctantly—turning her attention to Mikey and Margalo and, most important, Ronnie.

"Did anyone tell you that Toby and Sven have both withdrawn from school?" Rhonda asked Ronnie.

"Really?" asked Cassie, sarcasm dripping like horror-film blood from every letter of the word. "Are you sure?"

Rhonda reassured Cassie, who clearly had to be socially so far on the outskirts that it might as well be another country, "Yes, for sure. And nobody's talking to Harold. He's real depressed," she reported without sympathy. "I bet Hadrian's glad."

"I guess," Hadrian answered. "Sure."

"So," Rhonda wrapped up, "Have a great vacation everyone, and good luck on exams. Good luck or a good cheat sheet," she said, adding a current student joke. "Although I guess Hadrian doesn't need either one."

"I guess," Hadrian said again.

"Neither do I," Mikey pointed out.

Rhonda's mouth made a little O at that announcement. She looked at Ronnie for silent agreement about Mikey, and then she seemed to think of something. "Are you going to be at The Gables on New Year's Eve too? Will I see you there? Chet's getting together a table—do you want me to see if I can get him to seat you with us? Who's your date?" Rhonda beamed down on them, the Queen of England, the Queen of everything, or at least of high school.

Ronnie was a nice person, and she changed the subject. "We haven't even had Christmas yet. I haven't even started my Christmas shopping, and I have two papers due before vacation."

"I'm getting Chet a sweater," Rhonda confided. "Turtleneck, it'll look great on him. Gotta run. See you New Year's? Ronnie, I mean. Think about it?"

After a short silence, "Some things never change," Tan remarked.

"Except," Ronnie said, sounding worried, "I didn't know Chet had asked Rhonda for New Year's. That's not what I heard," she explained, then added, "Oh well, probably I heard wrong. You know how gossip is."

"Fortunately no," Cassie said, and Ronnie laughed.

"But you will come to basketball? You could try out too, Cassie," she offered, then rose, saying, "See you," with a little wave of the hand as she left them.

Then they turned on Margalo to start asking questions, like "How hard was it to get work papers?" and "How many hours a week?" and drawing conclusions like, "You're not going to have any free time at all."

Margalo was pleased to see that they were all a little jealous of her. She didn't blame them.

II

Margalo in Winter

— 8 —

Heartbreak Alert!

Margalo saw it as soon as she looked at Ms. Hendriks, during the first Drama Club meeting after the vacation: There was no engagement ring on her left hand.

Where had it gone? Margalo tried to figure out if the teacher might be wearing a chain around her neck, tucked under the loose sweater. She didn't think so, although the high neck of the sweater kept her from being positive. She looked for the ring on Ms. Hendrik's right hand, but that, too, was bare.

For the first time, Margalo wished she knew someone besides Hadrian in Drama well enough to ask what they knew about this ringlessness. She couldn't ask Ms. Hendriks. You didn't ask teachers things about their private lives; you had to wait until they let something slip, or somebody happened to find something out and tell people.

Margalo hoped that if the engagement was over, it was Ms. Hendriks who had decided to end it. She had never been dumped, herself, never having been picked up and carried along by any boy, but she knew something about unrequited love or, more precisely, unrequited crush. The key word was unrequited. Unrequited was no fun.

She didn't even think of raising the question of the Drama teacher's possible dis-engagement with Mikey. Moreover, Mikey didn't give her the chance. These days, all Mikey wanted to talk about was basketball. Sometimes Margalo didn't know what she was going to do with these athletic interests of Mikey's. She would have just turned off her attention, the way she occasionally did during classes, but every now and then, trapped in the ranting and rattling-on, like a diamond trying to escape from its lump of coal, there appeared one of Mikey's really interesting ideas. You could count on Mikey for individual thought, Margalo knew that. So she had to listen to tireless complaining about a coach who only wanted people to feel good about themselves and enjoy playing the game. "That's no way to build a winning team," Mikey said.

"Maybe it doesn't matter to her if the team wins," Margalo said, and then, in the deep, solemn voice that movie newscasters use to announce some disaster or another, usually from outer space, she recited: "It matters not if you win or lose, but how you play the game."

"I know, but if you don't play to win you're not playing the game right."

"Yeah, but in the long run what does any game matter?"

"Put it that way," answered Mikey with relentless logic, "and nothing matters, so why are you so worried about going to college, or getting a job and saving money, or even being a good dishwasher in your restaurant?"

This, Margalo had thought about. You couldn't be alive in the present world and not think about it. "Because I only get one chance to have my own one life, and it's stupid to waste any chances to make it better. Or make myself better at it."

Mikey leaned back in her cafeteria seat, victorious. "That's why it's important to win." But Mikey wasn't stupid and before Margalo had a chance to say it she corrected herself. "To try to win."

By then they were no longer alone at the table, and Tim started grilling Margalo about her job. How much did she get paid an hour? How much was withheld from her paycheck? The only jobs he'd ever had had been working for his parents, like painting the porch railing or clearing out the garage. Was it different when you had a real boss?

"Baby-sitting has bosses," Margalo told him. "And since my parents don't pay us for doing stuff at home, I don't know."

"Do the guys in the kitchen sexually harass you?" Jace wanted to know.

Margalo just smiled. Actually she almost laughed out loud. She didn't know how to explain it to them, it was so far outside of their experience at school or even on sports teams.

"Angie—he's the cook—he runs the kitchen? Angie says nobody messes with his dishwashers, and everybody in the kitchen does exactly what he says. Nobody crosses Angie. Because the cook in a restaurant is like the absolute dictator—in the kitchen that is."

"Why would he say that about dishwashers?" Cassie wondered. "Does he have his eye on you for himself?"

Then Margalo did laugh. They just didn't have any idea. "Nothing like that. It's because dishwashing is such a scut job. If he can get somebody to do it, and do it well, and be reliable, he wants to keep them happy."

"You're going to be banking a lot more money," Tim said. "But when do you get a chance to go to the bank?"

At that question, Mikey could enter the conversation. "We walk downtown every other Friday after school, and then Steven gives us a ride home. He stays on a few minutes late at work, waiting for us."

"You are so organized about your life," Tim said to Margalo, with obvious admiration.

Of course she was flattered. She might not have the usual-sized normal streak in her, but she still had one. "Yeah, well, thanks," she said, for some reason not able to look directly at Tim.

Mikey, whose normal streak was about a half a millimeter wide, asked, "What are you thanking *him* for?"

Luckily for Tim, at that moment Derrie approached their table to ask Casey and Margalo, "Did either of you by any chance pick up my blue cardigan from gym class? I left it on the bleachers."

Neither of them had.

"I just got it, for Christmas, from my grandmother, and it was, you know, cashmere? Did you see it? I haven't even written her a thank-you note."

"It's two weeks after Christmas and you haven't finished thank-you notes yet?"

"You write thank-you notes?"

Derrie left, almost in tears, and Tim remarked, "Doesn't she know any better than to leave a good sweater out in the open?"

However, watching Derrie as she walked away, Margalo glimpsed Rhonda Ransom, and that glimpse made her look again. Rhonda looked *terrible*, terrible in a new way, entirely different from her usual ninth-grade sex-bombshell terrible. "What's wrong with Rhonda?"

"What isn't wrong with Rhonda?" Mikey asked without looking up.

Casey, who could move on the fringes of the more popular groups of girls, knew. "Chet dumped her. After Christmas, I think, just before New Year's; so she didn't have a date New Year's Eve, which made it even worse. Chet told her she was getting too serious and she needed to chill out. He's been dating a sophomore—she's cute, and on the honor roll too. Candy something, DeAngelo?"

"But Candy's too smart to fall for Chet Parker," Felix protested.

"Not noticeably," Tim told his friend. "You know, just because a girl is smart, that doesn't mean she can't make stupid choices."

"What I've heard," Cassie offered, "is that when her about-to-be ex-boyfriend told Rhonda he wanted to go out with someone who sometimes said something interesting. . . . You know what she told him?"

They didn't, and waited to hear.

"She told him, 'You should have taken out Margalo.'"

"Margalo?"

"Why Margalo?"

"All *he* did was smirk. Chet's a good smirker. He didn't even ask Margalo Who? He just smirked and said, 'Maybe that's good advice. Maybe I will.'" Cassie grinned around at all of them.

"I'd like to see him try," said Mikey. "Wouldn't you?"

"No," Margalo answered, and even Mikey got the joke of that.

But Rhonda was a misery. Her eyes were red with constant weeping, her long blond hair was lank and dull, her sweaters droopy. The rumor on the first Friday after vacation—by Mikey's private countdown, number fourteen (only twenty-two to go!)—was that she and Chet had been having sex, and then the next Monday the rumor was that Rhonda was pregnant, which certainly explained her unrelenting unhappiness.

Mikey and Margalo, who had for years enjoyed their fully-reciprocated dislike of Rhonda Ransom, didn't know how to deal with this information. Even for Rhonda Ransom this seemed like more than she deserved. A little heartbreak, a little humiliation, *that* they greeted happily. But this . . . Who did Chet Parker think he was, anyway?

Fortunately, Rhonda could assure Heather, who could assure Derrie, who could spread the glad tidings, that she wasn't pregnant. "Which means," Margalo pointed out to Mikey, "that she could have been."

Tim fumed. "How could her mother not let her take sex ed and then let her date Chet Parker?"

"Parents don't know," Cassie said. "They don't want to know."

"I don't *want* them to know," said Jace.

"We should think about this like a mystery story," Margalo advised. "Why Mrs. Ransom would do that. You know, *cui bonum*. Who benefits," she translated.

"I knew that," Mikey claimed. Then, being a painfully honest person—although usually it was somebody else who felt the pain—she added, "Anyway, I might have known it. I bet I've seen it somewhere. Besides, the point is, does anybody benefit? If Rhonda doesn't know anything about contraception and," she drew the logical conclusion, "gets pregnant."

They thought about this, considering everybody involved, whether directly or indirectly.

"Unless Rhonda would be, like, a warning to everybody else? The example of what can happen," Casey suggested.

"Or unless you hated her," Mikey decided. "But even I

don't hate her that much, do we, Margalo? Do you think her mother hates her? I'd hate being her mother."

Cassie had her own idea: "People who want babies to adopt?"

They made their slow way across January, with basketball and Drama Club to look forward to at the end of each day. On the Friday the school year was sixteen weeks old, "Half over!" Mikey announced, then went on to complain, "The JV has only four games and one tournament, which is only JV and doesn't count for much. Only four games. How can we learn to play like a team?"

"You never play like a team," remarked Ronnie, who with Tanisha Harris was sitting with them. During the basketball season Ronnie and Tan sometimes ate lunch at Mikey's table.

Teachers had had to get exams corrected and grades handed in the previous Wednesday, so they learned that day what their first-semester grades were, and by lunchtime every ninth grader had heard that Louis Caselli was in serious trouble. Seriously serious trouble, like on academic probation and scheduled for a conference with Mr. Robredo first thing Monday morning. Louis had passed only one of his five courses, and that one was wood shop, in which his grade had gone down to a C. But still, Louis went strutting around the cafeteria during Lunch A as if he'd just scored the winning basket in a game.

According to Ronnie, the family was furious at Louis, who

kept promising his father that he could bring all his grades up, easy. "But I don't know if Uncle Eddie believes him anymore."

"I never do," Mikey said happily. "Do you think he'll be held back?"

"That wouldn't be until next year," Margalo said.

"We can't figure out *what's* wrong with him," Ronnie admitted.

Mikey and Margalo were both on honor roll, although not high honor roll, as Hadrian was. Tim was impressed, and told Margalo so.

"You're always being impressed by Margalo," Mikey accused him. "What's up?"

This remark caused Tanisha to ask as she accompanied Margalo out of the cafeteria after lunch, "What's with Mikey? Doesn't she know anything about boy-girl relationships?"

First Margalo denied it. "Tim's not having a boy-girl relationship with me." Then she added, "Mikey had that crush on Shawn last year—"

"Don't remind me!"

"And she had a secret admirer, too."

"A what? She never said."

"He used to call her up, and they'd talk. They never met in person, and he stopped this summer, but . . . It's not that she doesn't know about relationships, it's just . . . Mikey. But do you really think Tim thinks he's having a relationship with

127

me?" she asked. Not that *she* thought she was having one with *him*. But not that she'd mind if he did think it.

Mikey went to basketball, and Margalo to Drama. In March, Drama Club was putting on a production of *Our Town*, and as with the December production, they started out talking about the play. But this time they concentrated on the staging, with its unconventional sets, and on the way Thornton Wilder broke the usual rules that separated the audience from the actors. He even had a character named Stage Manager, who was like an overvoice for everything and everybody in the play, who talked directly to the audience. Thornton Wilder even put actors in the audience, pretending to be theatergoers who quarreled with the Stage Manager. *Our Town* wasn't like any other play they'd read, or performed, any of them, ever. It was also pretty old-fashioned, and they weren't sure about that. Ms. Hendriks was sure about it and excited to be presenting it. She was still not wearing her diamond ring.

Just before the bell rang to dismiss them that Friday, Sally King finally raised her hand and asked the question they almost all—you could never tell with Hadrian—had been wondering about. "Ms. Hendriks? We don't know, if you're still, like, engaged?"

Ms. Hendriks looked at her left hand, as if she had forgotten it was ringless. "Oh. No. No, I'm not, I'm afraid. We've decided not to get married. So I gave him back the ring."

"Why?" Sally asked.

Ms. Hendriks elected to talk about the ring, not the failed romance. "Because we're no longer engaged."

"But I always thought, the ring belongs to the girl," Sally said.

"That didn't seem fair to me," Ms. Hendriks said.

Sally continued explaining it to the teacher. "Like the wife gets the silver and china and glassware, too, if they get divorced. You should make him give it back to you."

"Look out, Richard," a low voice said, and people laughed. Sally's cheeks turned pink, but she pretended not to have heard.

"Well." Ms. Hendriks smiled. "That's moot anyway, since he's moved to Florida."

"But you came here to be with him," Sally insisted. "That's why you took this job. You should never have let him have the ring back. You changed your whole life for him and now look what's happened."

"Well," said Ms. Hendriks, with a quick glance up at the clock. "I found a job I really like. That happened too." Then she changed the subject before Sally could add any more insistences. "We don't have as much rehearsal time for this production as we did in the fall, so I hope you're already thinking about what parts you want to read for. Tryouts will be early next week. Can you be ready?"

They could. Sally wondered if the Stage Manager had to be a man, and Richard reminded her that there was a young couple—"George and Emily, they're who the play is about"—and that Sally had promised him that after *A Midsummer Night's Dream* they could do a couple. "Besides, we're seniors, this is our last chance to star together, because the spring play's a musical and you can't sing," he reminded her.

"Or dance," added Sherry Lansing, at which Margalo leaned over to Hadrian where they sat at the rear, near the pile of knapsacks and sweaters and coats by the teacher's desk, to whisper, "What do you bet Sherry can dance? And she probably sings all right too."

But Hadrian had his attention on his copy of the play. "Am I too short to play the Stage Manager?" he asked her. "What do you think? I don't think it matters, do you?"

It was during that week of tryouts, the last week in January, that Tanisha Harris took Margalo aside, Mikey following, as they left lunch A on Wednesday. "I've been wanting to talk to you," she said, "but there wasn't time." Monday had been a snow day and Tuesday a late-opening day; in fact, the tryouts were now scheduled for Wednesday and Thursday, which concerned Margalo because Ms. Hendriks had promised them she would have a cast list for them on Friday. Margalo was thinking about if there was anything she could do to help Hadrian get a part, so she just nodded her head at whatever Tan had said. Then Tan got her full attention. "I need your advice," she said. "You can't tell anyone."

Taking someone aside in high school for a private conversation usually meant withdrawing to the second-floor girls' bathroom, the smokers' bathroom, or outside, but in winter outside wasn't an option. Tan, however, elected to have her private conversation in the middle of the main corridor, which ran from the cafeteria, past the library and main offices, out to the gym entrance. Margalo walked on one side of her, Mikey on the other. Margalo, like Tan, wore tights and a calf-length skirt, with a cotton sweater, while Mikey wore her usual jeans-and-a-T, with a cable-knit sweater over that in honor of cold weather. Margalo and Tan wore dull greens and blues and smoky pinks; Mikey wore bright red, and she had to hurry along to keep up with their longer-legged strides.

Mikey was just about to say something about who should be walking in the middle (her), when Tan announced, "You have to help me."

Mikey looked across Tan to Margalo, to whom this was probably directed. *Hunh?*

Margalo looked at Mikey, *What?*

Mikey's instinctive response to feeling off-balance and at a disadvantage was a strong offence. "You're not trying very hard in basketball. How can we get a winning JV team without you?"

Tan didn't bother answering that question. "I was going to ask you . . . ," she began. But then she stopped.

She stopped talking and she stopped walking.

They stopped with her, letting people move around and past them.

131

Tan said, "I need advice. Loretta said it would be smart to ask you, especially Margalo. After the restraining order."

"What about me?" Mikey demanded but then—after a look at the expression on Margalo's face—said no more. But what made this Loretta think Mikey wasn't as smart as Margalo, and who was she, anyway?

"Who's Loretta, anyway?" Mikey demanded.

"A junior," Margalo said.

"A friend," Tan said. Then she changed her mind—about what?—and said, "No, never mind. I don't think . . ." She fell silent and started walking again. They went along beside her.

"You've been weird all year," Mikey observed.

At that Tan gave them the same glad toothy grin they'd first seen in fifth grade, the smile of a girl who knew what she wanted and knew she could count on herself to work hard to try and get it. In fifth grade it was volleyball, after that it had been basketball and good grades. Now what was it?

"What's wrong with you?" Mikey asked impatiently.

"William," Tan answered, saying the name as if it had a sweet and delicious flavor, like a nugget of dark chocolate that had melted on her tongue.

Mikey looked at Margalo, *Hunh?* (again), and Margalo answered with her same baffled unspoken question, *What?*

Tan was striding along, looking like she was heading to the library.

"William?" Mikey asked. "William who?"

"William your brother?" Margalo asked.

"I'm in love with William," Tan said.

"But he's your brother!" Mikey objected.

"Since last summer," Tan said. "We're all adopted, don't you remember?"

"You said that didn't make any difference," Mikey reminded her. "In sixth grade, you *said*."

"But now it does, doesn't it?" asked Margalo, thinking hard.

"And I don't know what to do about it," Tan answered.

"Isn't he much older? Out of college?" Margalo asked.

"He's going to work in Oslo for at least two years. Oslo in Norway."

"I *know* where Oslo is," Mikey said.

"So what can I do?"

"Forget about him," Mikey advised.

"I've tried. I can't."

"Of course you can," Mikey said.

"I know," Tan admitted, and added with that grin again, "But I don't want to. Because . . . Because what if he loves me back?" Just the hope of the chance of that made her voice sing.

"Does he?" Margalo wondered.

"He might. I don't know. He never . . . But he wouldn't now because I'm much too young."

Mikey had suggestions. "Get a job. Work at a sport. Try for honor roll. Have you ever played tennis? You could be good at tennis, Tan, you're a natural athlete, that would take your mind off William."

"He *should* love me back," Tan told Margalo. "What can I do?"

"Let me think," Margalo said.

"There's nothing to think *about*," Mikey told them.

By then, they had arrived at their lockers and stopped to get the books they needed for the afternoon's classes. Mikey decided, "You have to give it up. Because what if he *doesn't* love you back?"

"Give me some time," Margalo asked, and Tan agreed. She left them then, with a quick backwards wave of the hand.

Mikey looked at Margalo, *Hunh?* for the third time, and Margalo shrugged and shook her head. *Who knows?* They watched Tan mix herself in with the moving throng of students.

"People aren't going to start bringing us their problems, are they?" asked Mikey. "Because I could get pretty tired of that pretty quickly."

Margalo agreed—sort of. But only sort of, because she liked the kind of thinking she got to do, working on other people's problems.

"I may already be tired of it," Mikey decided.

Ms. Hendriks had told them that she would announce the cast of *Our Town* that Friday, the last Friday in January, and despite the delay in tryouts, she kept her word.

Sally and Richard, of course, got the roles of George Gibbs and Emily Webb, the young couple, whose story lay at the center of the play, surrounded by the typical inhabitants of a small New England village—doctor and editor, choirmaster and policeman, and their wives and children. It was an old-fashioned play, with its three acts taking place in 1901, 1904 and 1913, before the start of the First World War. But unlike Shakespeare, the language was easy to understand. Moreover, there were so many parts that most people who tried out got one, making it the usual crew of actors—plus one.

Hadrian Klenk was the plus one, to the surprise of everyone except Margalo. Ms. Hendriks assigned him the role of Stage Manager. The Stage Manager was always onstage, an actor, but an actor who talked to the audience, not to the other actors, unless he was taking some small part in a scene. The Stage Manager had to be a good enough actor to act not being an actor, like being a good enough singer to be able to sing off-key on purpose. The Stage Manager was like a wise old teacher, explaining the world to his classes. It was a really big part, and people didn't think it was fair for Hadrian to get it. They didn't feel *that* sorry for him, not anymore.

Carl Dane voiced their objections. "He's a ninth grader, and can he even act?"

Ms. Hendriks smiled, confident. "Hadrian can act."

"But I thought you said there was a school policy," Carl said.

"Sometimes, people make exceptions."

"I bet she didn't even tell them," Carl muttered to John Lawrence. "I bet she doesn't have permission."

Ms. Hendriks didn't pretend not to have heard this. "I don't believe I need permission to cast my own productions."

An uncomfortable silence fell on the room. This might be *her* first year, but most of them had been in high school longer and knew better. But because now they felt a little sorry for her—she didn't know how things went, and with her engagement broken too, and also because she had given them such a satisfying good time with *A Midsummer Night's Dream*—they didn't say any more. She'd find out soon enough.

"You'll see," Ms. Hendriks told them. "Won't they, Hadrian?"

But Hadrian was studying his sneakers, carefully considering how the laces ran through their holes and then crossed, time after time, before emerging into a knot. He wasn't about to be distracted from this important question—How did shoelaces work, exactly?—to meet the glances of this roomful of people, most of whom were probably wishing he wasn't there, getting in their way, keeping them from having things the way they wanted.

"I want to warn you. We'll have to do some weeks of hard work if you want this production to come up to the standard you set for yourselves with Shakespeare," Ms. Hendriks told them.

That reminder, those memories, made everyone feel better.

"Our performance dates are the twelfth and thirteenth of March," she said.

"Not Friday the thirteenth," Richard said, relieved.

"Is the little fellow superstitious?" Sally mocked.

"*You're* the one who won't walk under ladders." He looked around to assure everyone, "It's true."

"It's Friday the twelfth, so not a problem in any case," Ms. Hendriks said. "Shall we start the read-through? Actors? Are you ready? Anybody who isn't an actor can leave now, if you don't want to stay and listen."

At the end of the day Mikey and Margalo joined up for a bank run. They walked away from the large school building and into the busier streets of town. They passed in front of store windows, but neither one of them looked at the clothing or the designer foods, the books or the video posters, and certainly not the jewelry. When you had only one class together, and lunch, you took advantage of any other time you could find for talking. They were not distracted by windowfuls of things to want, or by the traffic, or by the people they were sharing the sidewalk with.

"There's your restaurant," Mikey said as they passed the big window. "How much are you depositing?"

Both Margalo and Mikey kept a running total of Margalo's bank account, and they both checked in weekly for the value of shares in the mutual fund Mikey's stepfather had advised Margalo to buy, in five-hundred-dollar chunks. It wasn't a great year for the market, but Jackson had forewarned them about that.

"Two hundred and nineteen dollars."

"Not bad."

"Not bad at all."

At the bank Margalo pulled open the heavy glass door, and Mikey followed her inside. This was an old-fashioned bank, with marble on the floor and marble countertops, behind which the tellers stood. At the center of the room there was a high table with slots holding deposit slips and withdrawal slips for various kinds of accounts. Margalo went right up to that table. Mikey came to stand beside her.

With its air as quiet as a library's—a money library not a book one—Mikey found the bank relaxing. She was conservative in her bank tastes. None of these drive-through windows or ATM machines for her. She looked around, at the Friday-evening customers, at the tellers all in a row, at the closed doors with names and titles painted on them in gold, and at the two guards, dressed almost like policemen, who were also looking around at everybody.

Beside her Margalo selected a deposit slip and filled it out.

"You're almost ready to make another investment," Mikey observed.

"Almost," Margalo agreed. She had finished the form, so she hauled her knapsack up onto the tabletop and started taking her books and notebooks out of it, getting down to the bottom, where she kept her makeup kit and her wallet. Doing her banking, Margalo looked organized and businesslike, partly because she dressed not at all like a high school student (which made sense, since she dressed herself not out of the mall teenage stores, but out of the Next-to-New, a store for grown-ups) and partly because of the way she acted—confident, focused, efficient.

Margalo got down to her wallet, lifted it out and opened it. She always counted out her money one last time to be sure she had the correct number written on the deposit slip. But this week she didn't take any thick wad of bills out. This week, she opened her wallet and then she just looked into it.

"Mikey?" she asked.

"What's wrong?"

"It's gone."

"The two hundred and nineteen dollars?"

Margalo looked at Mikey with a dazed expression on her face, like someone trying to see through thick fog or somebody else's glasses. All of the rest of Margalo was motionless. All around them the bank noises went on, hushed voices, muted footsteps, rustling papers.

"It can't be," Mikey decided. She reached down into the knapsack to find the bills, where they must have fallen out of the wallet.

Margalo didn't object, but she predicted, "It's not there."

"What do you think you did with it?" Mikey asked.

"I put it into my wallet this morning. No, first I counted it, then I put it into my wallet, then I did what I always do, I put the wallet into the bottom of the knapsack. And I did what I always do on a Friday when I'm making a deposit, I kept the knapsack with me all day."

"You didn't leave it in your locker?"

"I just said."

"You didn't leave it, like, on a bathroom shelf while you were in a stall?"

"I said."

"So you must have dropped the bills out when you were taking out books for class," Mikey decided.

"But I didn't." Margalo took a breath. "I don't. They were *in* the wallet."

"And besides, if you *had* dropped them, somebody would have noticed it," Mikey agreed. "They'd have told you." A lot of people knew Margalo's banking patterns, the same way they knew about all the baby-sitting jobs she had and this dishwashing work too. Everybody knew Margalo was already saving for college.

Mikey didn't want to say out loud what she was thinking, so she didn't. She didn't want it to be true and as long as she didn't say it out loud, it wouldn't be. She checked the facts. "The knapsack was never out of your sight all day?"

Margalo was thinking the same thing and she also didn't want it to be true, so she postponed the inevitable by answering Mikey's question. "No, never except for Drama, but we all put our stuff by Ms. Hendrik's desk, which is right there in the corner of the drama room, and everybody's always around, you know? So I couldn't have lost it there."

"Except you must have," Mikey said.

Margalo replaced her wallet in her knapsack and carefully set the makeup kit in with it. Then she put in her books and notebooks, the pens and pencils, her face expressionless.

"What about when you were changing books at your locker?" Mikey suddenly thought. "We should go back and look around the lockers."

Margalo crumpled up the deposit slip and dropped it into a wastebasket under the high table. Then she turned and walked across the marble floor, going back out through the heavy glass door. On the street, she turned to Mikey and made herself say it. "I was robbed."

And Mikey had to say it. "You were robbed."

"Somebody went into my knapsack," Margalo said.

"And took the money out of your wallet," Mikey agreed.

"And then put the wallet and everything back in so I wouldn't realize," Margalo said. She felt bad in so many different ways—bad and angry, bad and depressed, bad and disillusioned—that she felt like she never wanted to see anybody in Drama again. Ever.

They thought about it all for a minute, walking side by side. Then, "What are we going to do?" Mikey asked.

"We can't tell Aurora," Margalo answered. "This kind of stuff really gets her down when she hears about it. Aurora has a hard enough time with the news, she doesn't need to hear about some ratfink high school student stealing my money. Stealing is just the way things are," Margalo said. "Like cheating on tests, or like those opponents you thought were cheating in tennis last fall."

"They definitely were," and Mikey smiled, not a nice smile. "For all the good it did them."

"Everybody does it, I guess."

"Not me, I don't," Mikey reminded her. "Or you."

"No," Margalo agreed. "We just get stolen from and cheated on."

"Maybe. Okay, obviously. But I don't like it and I'm not going along with it."

"Hunh," Margalo said. What else could you say to a statement like that? A statement contrary to fact, contrary to reality. She agreed with the spirit of it, and she wished Mikey luck, and she thought that if anybody could say that and mean it and do it, that somebody was Mikey Elsinger, but still, really—"Hunh," she said again. She didn't have the energy or the interest to say more.

"And neither are you," Mikey decided.

— 9 —

What's a Girl to Do?

Give up, what else? That was Margalo's conclusion.

Mikey, being Mikey, disagreed. "They can't get away with this," she said on the phone that night, and all weekend, too, more and more angrily, and she never noticed Margalo's response, which grew more and more discouraged with each repetition, "But they did, Mikey. Somebody did."

Monday morning, first thing, Mikey demanded, "What's first?"

Margalo shook her head, hanging her long green wool coat on the hook in her locker, tucking its hem under neatly. "Nothing," she said, still facing the inside of her locker. "What is there to do?"

"You're the one with all the ideas," Mikey told her.

Margalo turned around and tucked her hair behind her

143

ears, slowly. She squared her shoulders, ready to head on into the day. She told Mikey, "It's February."

Mikey wouldn't get that, but Margalo didn't need to be understood, not by anyone. She knew what she meant, and what she meant was that February was the long low point of the year, and the only good thing about it was that it was shorter than any other month.

Short as it was, on the other hand, February seemed to last forever, an endless, gray, cold stretch of time, like a snowfield you're going to have to cross but there's no destination in sight and you know that you might not make it across alive, or like an ocean and all you can do is swim, hoping that you're heading towards March, but you could be swimming in circles. It was February inside Margalo, as well as outside in the year. She felt alone from everybody.

"Isn't a whole weekend long enough to spend feeling sorry for yourself?" Mikey demanded.

Luckily, they had to go off to homeroom, so Margalo could escape Mikey's nagging, because how she felt—and she had been noticing this, thinking about it, getting the right words for it—was she felt stupid, and she felt ashamed.

At that, Margalo turned and ran to catch up with Mikey, her knapsack thumping against her hip. "Don't tell anyone."

"Why not?"

"Just don't. Promise?"

"Why do I have to promise?"

"Just promise," Margalo asked her.

"Okay, okay, don't get hysterical."

Margalo turned back, moving among the students heading for their homerooms on this side of the central library. Hers was on the far side, so she was going against traffic, which suited her just fine.

Usually Margalo felt pleasantly superior to the other people in school, and in the world, too. Except for Mikey, of course, and in certain specific ways people like Hadrian and Tan, Ronnie Caselli even. Usually Margalo's judgment of other people was that they meant well, although they were pretty hapless and not as smart as they thought they were. Usually she felt like people couldn't hurt her, even if they wanted to.

Now, however . . . This being robbed had really gotten to her. And why should the person who got robbed feel like she must have done something wrong? And who would have done this, anyway? Everybody knew how she was working to save for college, so whoever took her money knew exactly what they were taking—money she had worked for, money she needed. They had to know that, and they just took it.

If people were going to just take things from her, and be able to get away with it, and take things from one another, too, and not just thing-things, either, but abstract things too, like ideas or self-confidence or even safety. . . . Margalo wanted to go home. She wanted to be at the kitchen table, where Aurora would be doing some GED homework, reading and taking notes, or studying for a test, or maybe writing a paper. She could sit with her mother and read. Margalo had never been homesick at school before.

Somebody tapped her on the shoulder from behind, hard. She clutched her knapsack to her chest, not knowing who it might be or what they wanted. Or maybe it wouldn't be anybody, just somebody playing tricks on her. And if they were, what could she do about it?

"Margalo!" It was Mikey's voice. Mikey was breathing a little fast from her run down the hallway to catch Margalo and get back before the bell rang. "I was calling you!" She glared at Margalo. "What's *wrong* with you?"

Mikey's anger and that question dumped down over Margalo like a bucket of cold water. Because that was exactly the question, What was wrong with Margalo? And the answer was: Nothing. What was wrong was wrong with *them*, with whoever had gone into her knapsack and robbed her. It was pretty stupid, to let somebody else make her doubt her ability to take care of herself. *That* was what was stupid, not being robbed. Being robbed was only what could happen.

All at once Margalo felt better. She felt better, and she was getting angry, too. She wasn't going to let them get away with doing this to her.

"What!" she asked Mikey angrily. "What is it?"

"I wanted to say that I promise and I'll keep my word, but it really stinks, and maybe because you're so smart about people it makes sense to you, but I don't even *want* it to make sense to me. It's your money and they can't just take it."

"Yeah but they did," Margalo said again. Only this time she felt a grim, determined smile move onto her face. "Give me some time to think, Mikey."

"You have to strike while the trail is hot."

"The trail's already cold. Friday it was hot. Give me a little time to figure this out."

Mikey smiled. *That's what I wanted to hear.* "He'll be sorry, whoever it was."

"Or she," Margalo corrected, but Mikey was already jogging away down the corridor, dodging approaching students like a football quarterback heading for the end zone, her heavy braid bouncing up and down on her back.

Margalo went on into her homeroom where, when she saw Derrie, she remembered and asked, "Did you ever find your sweater?"

"Are you kidding? *And* I had to pretend when I wrote my grandmother that I still had it? *And* my mother had to replace it? So I guess it isn't entirely bad, since I still ended up with the same sweater. But I'm not going to be wearing it to school again."

At lunch that day Mikey and Margalo ignored the rest of the people at the table, who, it could be said, didn't notice, except perhaps for Tim, and perhaps also for Hadrian. Mikey had made herself a wrap for lunch, with slices of both dark- an light-meat roasted chicken, a sun-dried tomato spread, paper-thin slices of onion and a generous serving of dark

147

green arugula leaves. Margalo looked at Mikey's sandwich and then at her own, peanut-butter-and-grape-jelly on supermarket whole wheat again. She looked back at Mikey's sandwich. "It would make me feel better if you traded half your sandwich," she offered.

Mikey smiled, *Gotcha!*

"Never mind." Margalo felt herself sinking back toward the gray February mood in which she had spent the weekend.

But Mikey reached into her brown lunch bag to pull out a second wrap, sealed in plastic, and smiled again. *Gotcha! Again!* "Now you *have* to feel better."

"I already do," Margalo admitted. "I've decided to talk to Ms. Hendriks."

"Why her and not Aurora? Or you could ask my dad."

They spoke quietly, angled towards each other, ignoring Hadrian's curious glances and not answering Tim when he tried to distract Margalo by asking, "Am I the only person who finds February just . . . dismal?"

Margalo kept her focus. "No parents. You know how crazy Aurora got when someone kept emptying Stevie's lunch box in kindergarten."

"Well," Mikey said. "I don't blame her. I mean, when the only way you can keep your five-year-old's lunch from being stolen by some other five-year-old is to lock it in the teacher's desk, things are pretty bad."

"Well," Margalo said, "things can get pretty bad."

"Well," Mikey said, "maybe. But I don't intend to be helpless. Do you?"

"Not if I can help it," Margalo said. And waited.

It took Mikey—whose sense of humor wasn't a lively one—a few seconds to process the joke, and then all she did was smile. *I guess that's funny.* Then, "Do you have any idea who did it?" she asked.

"No," Margalo admitted.

"Suspicions?"

"I suspect everybody," Margalo said. She thought. "And it really could be any one of them, although probably not Ms. Hendriks. Or Hadrian, either."

At the sound of his name, even spoken in a low voice, Hadrian's head turned to them. They continued to ignore him.

"How many does that leave?"

Margalo counted in her head. "Twelve? Twenty? I'd have to go over who was reading." She thought some more and added, "Most of the other people in Drama are upperclassmen and I don't know any upperclassmen."

"Yeah, but people aren't that hard to figure out. They just want what they want and try to get it. Like taking your money. Which looks complicated to you trying to figure it out but it isn't a bit complicated to the person who took it, I bet. I mean, it's not as if you make a big secret out of going to the bank."

"Why should I have to? No, I'm serious. There are too

149

many bad things that you can imagine happening if you start to think like that."

"You read too many books."

"I plan to spend my life living it, not worrying about it. *Carpe diem*," Margalo added.

"Latin."

Margalo didn't say anything.

Mikey didn't say anything.

Margalo was starting to feel positively cheered up. Irritating Mikey often had that effect on her. "It isn't as if this is the first time somebody's had something stolen. The faculty must have ways to deal with it," she decided.

So after the bell had ended Drama, Margalo approached Ms. Hendriks. The teacher was standing behind her desk, studying the legal pad on which she had taken her day's notes. She was dressed in her usual loose tunic top and loose trousers. "Yes?" Then, coming out of her distraction, she smiled. "Margalo, good, I meant to ask you. I hope you're willing to be the stage manager for this production? The actual stage manager, I mean, not Hadrian's part. Or would you rather be assistant director?"

Margalo had no trouble with that decision. "Assistant director. But—"

"Good. I meant to ask you on Friday but it slipped my mind. I hope you didn't think I didn't plan to use you."

"No, but—"

"Because you seem comfortable carrying authority. That's what makes you so effective backstage, you know."

Margalo didn't know, and she was interested to hear it, but "Ms. Hendriks," she insisted, "I want to ask you—"

Worry flashed across Ms. Hendriks's pretty face, like the movement of a bird seen out of the corner of your eye, gone almost before you noticed it and wondered, *Was there something?* before you named it, *Only a bird*, by which time it was long gone. She asked quickly, "Is something wrong? Not Hadrian, is it?"

"About last Friday," Margalo said. "Somebody stole money from my wallet last Friday. At rehearsal."

Reassured about Hadrian, Ms. Hendriks was immediately sympathetic. "Oh, dear. Oh, Margalo. I *am* sorry." Then she reminded Margalo, "You shouldn't leave your wallet where people can see it."

"I didn't. It was in my knapsack. At the bottom."

"You shouldn't leave your knapsack out."

"I left it in the pile here."

"But why did you bring money to school with you?"

"To take to the bank on the way home. Because most banking hours I'm in school," Margalo explained.

"Of course. That wasn't very bright of me. I'm very sorry about this, Margalo, I really am, but what do you expect me to do?"

"I thought—You could tell me how to get my money back."

"So you know who took it."

"No."

"Are you absolutely sure that you had the money in your wallet? Absolutely, positively sure of it? Because . . . You know, Margalo, we all make mistakes. It would be too bad to get people all upset over something that you weren't absolutely positive happened."

"I'm positive," Margalo said.

"Because," Ms. Hendriks went on, as if Margalo hadn't spoken, "a dramatic production is like . . . like a very delicate ecosystem. We don't want to disturb it. Besides, how can you know it happened here?"

"I know," Margalo said.

Ms. Hendriks studied her for a long minute. "I'm truly sorry this happened, Margalo. I wish I could help, I really do, but I don't see how. Unless I could give you the money myself, which—believe me—I can't afford."

Margalo knew a useless conversation when she was having it. And she knew how to get out of it. "I was just wondering."

Ms. Hendriks decided, "It could just as easily have happened at any time, all day long, anywhere. A school day is so busy, you students have so many different things going on."

"I have to catch the Activities bus," Margalo said. She knew where her knapsack had been all day Friday—right beside her, right at her feet, except during rehearsal. When Margalo was at the classroom door, the teacher asked from behind her, "You aren't going to talk about this, are you? Because I'd rather you didn't. You have every reason to be upset, but will you give me a chance to think about it before you do anything? Please?"

"All right," Margalo agreed. But why did Ms. Hendriks look so relieved to hear that?

It couldn't be that a teacher was stealing from students, could it? If they wanted to rob someone, you'd think teachers would be smart enough to pick richer students than Margalo.

Margalo waited through the whole first week of February to find out what Ms. Hendriks would recommend, or say, or do, but the teacher never mentioned the subject, not to Margalo privately nor to the Drama group as a whole. It was as if she had forgotten, and maybe she had; but she didn't seem to be the kind of teacher who forgot things. And Margalo didn't forget.

Neither did Mikey, who reminded Margalo at least twice a day, "I'm keeping my promise and I'm getting tired of it."

In short, all week nothing happened, nothing pertaining to Margalo's problem, that is. Other things happened, of course. The JV basketball team played a game to a tie, causing a day's jubilation among ninth graders. Another event was Cassie arriving at the lunch table carrying a piece of art to show them before she handed it in to Peter Paul. "He thinks I've lost my touch," she reported. "So look at this, it's my Valentine's Day assignment."

Everybody recognized immediately that she'd painted a

portrait of Rhonda Ransom in the old Americana style of Norman Rockwell. In the portrait Rhonda stood still in a crowded school hallway, with people walking around her. Rhonda was weeping, but nobody was paying any attention to that. It wasn't that people were ignoring her, they just weren't interested. "The assignment was 'Love,'" Cassie told them. She pointed at one of the figures walking away. "That's Chet."

"How am I supposed to know that?" Mikey demanded.

"You aren't," Cassie said.

"Then why bother putting him in?" Mikey demanded.

"The artist paints for himself, not for his audience," said Cassie.

"Does that mean you're an artist?" Mikey asked. "Because if you are, why would you paint a picture of Rhonda Ransom crying?"

Cassie just groaned.

"But who cares about Norman Rockwell anymore?" Jace asked. He showed them what he had painted—a chunk of raw meat with tubes coming out from its top and bottom, a vaguely triangular-shaped chunk of meat set on a plate. The plate looked like it was tilting, and the meat looked like it was about to start sliding off. But not yet. "I call it *Love–1*," he told them.

"That's a tennis score," Mikey announced.

Cassie groaned again.

"Are you feeling sick?" Mikey asked, her lips pulled up in a *Don't mess with me* smile.

"Getting there," Cassie said. "And that picture isn't helping," she told Jace.

The only other interesting event of that first week in February was another Louis Caselli academic crisis. In an effort to force Louis to do homework, Miss Marshall, his English teacher, had announced that Louis was not welcome back into the class until he had done the reading. Then, when Louis *had* done the reading, he would have to answer questions about the story, questions asked by his classmates. Anybody who wanted to could ask a question. The questions could be as difficult and tricky as anyone wanted to make them. Louis would have to answer at least 60 percent to be allowed to return.

"Not fair," was Louis's first reaction, but then he figured out, "I might never have to go to another English class all year. That's not bad," and he strutted around the cafeteria and hallways as if he was the greatest thing the world had ever seen, the envy of all. Because he was on academic probation, he couldn't play basketball, but, "Who cares?" he asked, and ignored people who said, "That's a lucky thing for us."

In high school you had to get pretty good at ignoring what people were saying about you. In that regard Louis Caselli was doing very well in high school. He ignored what people said about him, and what they said *to* him as well, trying to give him good advice. In that regard, in fact, nobody was doing as well in ninth grade as Louis Caselli. "You're just a bunch of wusses," he told his friends. "They're not going to throw me

155

out. They can't, not if I don't actually *do* something. And then it's only suspension, which means I'd get to stay home all day. They never hold people back. They don't want us around any longer than they have to keep us, and besides, it looks bad on their records if people fail. I'm easy," Louis assured them, as if that had been in doubt. "We know," was the answer, spoken in ironic or sarcastic tones by his friends, in amusement by people who enjoyed watching Louis Caselli crash and burn, and without surprise by Mikey and Margalo. But the school made Miss Marshall go back on her threat and allow Louis back in class even though he hadn't done the reading or answered the class's questions. "Bummer," Louis said, strutting off to English again.

The most unexpected event of the week was an announcement during Lunch A on Thursday—and then again during Lunch B, also Lunch C—by the Principal himself, in his own voice. Someone had taken Mr. Radley's grade book out of his desk, and his attendance book too. "Those records are irreplaceable," intoned the solemn voice of the Principal.

"Who cares?" people mumbled, not loudly enough to be identified by the faculty on lunch duty. Suggestions were made as to who might have taken the teacher's record books, with Louis Caselli the miscreant of choice for most people. "If those records are so important, why didn't he make copies?" people muttered. Another reaction, very low voiced, was, "If it'd been me who did it? I'd have taken it *before* midyear grades were handed in."

But you could see that the teachers took this seriously. You could see them being much more anxious about their big gray-and-blue notebooks, one filled with their own class lists and grades, the other with their homeroom's attendance records. Teachers who carried briefcases went around looking smug; they always knew where their record books were.

The authorities might have been upset about the theft of record books, but as far as Margalo could determine, they didn't care about the theft of her money, and that *did* gripe her. As Margalo reported to Mikey at Friday lunch, "Mrs. Hendricks is ignoring me. I think she's pretending it never happened."

"Why would she do that?"

"The play," Margalo said. "For some reason, or maybe it's just the kind of person she is? Whatever, she really wants this production to be good. It's as if she was going after a Tony or an Emmy. It's like . . . It's like you and every tennis match you play."

"But it's only a school play," Mikey pointed out.

"But those are only tennis matches."

"But tennis is different."

"Everything is different to the people who care about it. If it's what you care about, it's important."

Mikey had a sudden question. "What about you? What do you have that you think is so important?"

"I'm looking for it," Margalo answered so quickly that

Mikey almost wondered if she'd been waiting for that particular question. Or if she'd been thinking about it to herself already. "At the moment it's getting a college degree."

Mikey worked that out. "For which you are working and saving the money that was stolen from you."

"Exactly."

They ate for a few, thoughtful minutes.

Finally, "Without Ms. Hendriks to back you up, nobody is going to do anything, are they?" Mikey asked. "Students are used to getting things stolen. Nobody ever does anything about it."

Margalo was having an idea. She laid it out for Mikey step by step, like a Math problem. "If *I* care about something being stolen from me, probably most people care too. They care, but they feel like they can't do anything so they don't care because why bother?"

"You can always do something."

Margalo ignored the interruption. "So it's being discouraged that makes people accept things? So probably, if I talk to the cast members, they *would* care." She pictured it, telling them, all the shocked faces. She imagined the sympathetic comments: "Somebody did? That stinks! How much? That's terrible!" Margalo didn't much like the thought of all that sympathy. Also, she was pretty sure that person after person would respond just that way, one after another, as she told them, including the person who had stolen her money.

But what if she talked to them all together, all at once, in a group? Then, if somebody had noticed something, as people talked about it, that person might remember what he'd seen, or she'd seen. In a group, people might just speak up. Because in a group, the guilty party would be a minority of one. She wondered if she could pick out that one person, out of the whole group.

"I'm going to talk to them, all together," she told Mikey.

"She won't let you."

"How can she stop me? Once I've started."

This was the kind of approach Mikey got. "Good idea."

"I think maybe."

"When will you do it?"

"Today, when she calls everybody together for a wrap-up. Fridays she always ends with a recap of the week's work. I think she doesn't want people losing interest over the weekend, so she pumps them up on Friday. Teachers act like they think school is all there is going on in your life. Sometimes I wonder if they think school goes on forever."

"For them it has," Mikey realized, and added, without any sympathy, "Too bad for them."

Margalo's idea didn't look so smart to her that afternoon as she sat listening to the end of Ms. Hendriks's pep talk. "We've got only five weeks to get ready," said Ms. Hendriks. The teacher was clearly on edge about this play, much more than with the December production, although *A Midsummer Night's Dream* had been a much harder play to do successfully, in Margalo's opinion.

"As soon as we can we're going to be rehearsing in costume and onstage so you'll all be one hundred percent comfortable. I noticed that last time some of you didn't really relax until the second performance," Ms. Hendriks said. "Warn your mothers about the extra laundry and ask them to take extra care with it. Especially—Sally? Alice? Those dresses you wear, and the shawl, Alice, it's very old, and valuable. Tell your mothers."

Sally, who was as usual sitting as close as she could get to Richard, didn't respond, but Alice did. "I do my own laundry, Ms. Hendriks."

"Well, yes, but be careful. Maybe your mother could wash the shawl?"

"I've done my own laundry since seventh grade," Alice said. "My mother works."

"Yes, all right, but please, remember, it has to dry flat. It's crocheted."

"Why would it get dirty, anyway?" somebody asked. "It's a shawl, not a shirt."

"My mom's not going to be happy about this," somebody predicted.

"If there are any problems, please, call me, or have your parents call me. I'm happy to be called at home if it'll help the play," Ms. Hendriks said, then, "All right, that's everything. What *is* it, Margalo?"

Margalo stood up. "Yes." She waited for people to turn around to look at her before saying, "I have an announcement."

Stupid, that's no way to begin.

160

"I mean, I want to tell everybody—and ask—Last Friday, during rehearsal—"

Ms. Hendriks sighed. "*Mar*galo."

"I was robbed. Of two weeks' earnings, which I was going to take to the bank and deposit in my savings account."

Two things stopped her from traveling on down that road to the town of Pity Me. The first was bored voices, asking, "Who cares?" And saying, "I wasn't even here, it has nothing to do with me." The second was her own opinion that while it was easy to get people to feel sorry for you, pity didn't last long, or do much good. So she stuck to the facts. "The money was in my wallet at the bottom of my knapsack. Hard to get to. I want to ask the people who were here Friday if you noticed anything, if you'd tell me."

That said, she sat down again, quickly, before anybody felt like they had to respond right away. But nobody wanted to say anything, not anything public. There was a kind of low murmuring, people making whispered comments to the person next to them, the way people do when they hear something that makes them uncomfortable.

But the only person who should be uncomfortable was the person who robbed her, Margalo thought, before she remembered how easy it was to feel guilty if you thought somebody might suspect you, even if you knew you were innocent. She was sort of waiting, as the room emptied, for someone to come up to her and tell her something. What they might tell her, she didn't have any guess about, but that there was something to be told she was certain. However, not one person said anything. In fact, they pretty much avoided her.

Margalo guessed that answered the question of who cared. Nobody cared.

Only Hadrian approached her. "I'm sorry," he said. "I hope it wasn't a lot of money, although"—and he laughed a little uneasy laugh—"everything's relative. What are you going to do about it?"

"I thought," Margalo admitted, "that I *had* done something by making the announcement. But I didn't find out anything."

"Probably they're not interested," Hadrian diagnosed. "It's only stealing, and that happens all the time. Stealing's not something that makes people outraged. Not like my collarbone, which people could feel good about getting outraged about."

"It should be," Margalo said.

"Ought does not imply Is," announced Hadrian Klenk.

Margalo just stared at him. What an interesting idea. And what an interesting way of expressing it.

"So, what *are* you going to do?" he asked. "Because—if you didn't mind, if you wanted—I could help."

— 10 —

Detective Margalo on the Case

By Lunch A on Monday most people had heard about Margalo's being robbed. They hadn't heard it on the loudspeakers but from one another, as members of Drama Club reported—in one way or another, none of them admiring—to their friends about Margalo's making a speech about it. "Weird," was the general opinion, whether weird and pitiful, or weird and stupid, or even weird but bold.

"It's lousy what some people will do," Tim said to Margalo at lunch. "You'd think—I mean, we're all kids, we're all in the same high school, we should hang together."

Margalo quoted Hadrian. "Ought does not imply Is."

"I know," Tim agreed, "but still . . . I'm sorry about this, Margalo."

She shrugged. "Yeah. Me too."

"What do you expect?" asked Cassie.

163

Jace explained Cassie's mood. "She went to Peter Paul because she thought her semester grade was a mistake. But he meant to give her a C." Jace's mouth turned up slightly, just at the corners, and his voice had a little serves-her-right in it.

"C minus, if we have to talk about my Art grade, Mr. I-got-an-A. He's decided he was wrong about me having talent."

Tim asked Margalo, "So, has anybody said anything to you about it?"

"No."

"Nobody will, you can bet on that," Cassie announced. "I don't know why I'm still in school."

Jace explained it to her. "You're not sixteen. Your parents won't let you drop out."

"They can't stop me. Nobody can stop me from doing what I really want to do."

"I'm still sorry," Tim said. "I wish there was something you could do. Maybe you should dust your wallet with fingerprint powder?"

"Put a mousetrap in your knapsack?" Felix offered.

"Don't bring money to school," Casey suggested.

Jace had the most practical idea. "You should steal it back."

"From who? If I don't know who took it."

"It doesn't matter who, just get even."

Margalo had an entirely different kind of idea, but she was keeping it to herself. Or rather, to herself and Mikey, who she took off to the library for some quiet conversation, leaving the table before anyone else had finished their lunch.

Or rather, to herself and Mikey and Hadrian, since he trailed along behind them into the big, well-lighted room, following them to a table tucked back among the stacks and as far as you could get from the busy computer area. "Hey," he said, dropping his knapsack onto the ground beside a chair and looking expectantly at them, like a clever little dog, a Jack Russell or a corgi. "I'm here to help. I told you Friday I would," he reminded Margalo.

"Then sit down," Margalo said, and she began. "Okay, here it is. We're smart, we can figure this out, that's what I think. So I plan to solve this crime, and I want your help. I'm pretty sure that if we think about it in the right way, we can figure it out. The standard detecting approach is Who, What, Where, When, and Why, right?"

Margalo opened her ring binder and took out a sheet of paper. "We know What," she said, "that's the money. And we know When and Where." She was writing down the questions and their answers as she reviewed the situation for Hadrian and Mikey. Hadrian listened patiently. Mikey did not; she humphed, and shifted restlessly in her chair. "As to Why, there are any number of reasons. Greed, for kicks, to supply a habit, some kind of initiation test for some kind of secret club or gang."

"I never heard of any secret clubs or gangs," Mikey objected.

They just gave her the beady eyes.

Hadrian said, "Precisely Why obviously depends on precisely Who."

"Which makes Who the place to start," Margalo said. "That's the same conclusion I reached, so that'll be our first step. I'll make a list of everyone I can think of who was there that Friday, and you look at it. Between us we should be able to remember everyone."

"What about me?" Mikey asked, but the bell rang and the other two were already gathering up their knapsacks.

"Tomorrow morning, before homeroom, here," Margalo directed.

"Who put you in charge?" Mikey objected, but it was too late. Nobody had time to wait around and quarrel.

The next morning, in the twelve minutes before homeroom, they met up again in the library. Margalo set down on the table in front of them a sheet of paper that held a list of names, starting off with Ms. Hendriks and going on for— Mikey counted—twenty-four more. "I don't know any of these people," she announced.

"Yes you do," Margalo told her.

"Other than Hadrian, I mean, but you already know I know him."

"You have to know Richard and Sally, they're that couple. Seniors. She played Puck. He has a ponytail—which he's going to have to cut for *Our Town*. They dress out of Gap, they're a Gap couple. She's taller than him, and blond, not pretty but really striking, she has terrific eyebrows."

Mikey didn't know where Margalo got the interest or the

energy to notice all of that about anybody. But, "Are they the ones who hold hands everywhere? They block traffic kissing in the middle of the halls?"

"That's them. And John Lawrence, he's the boy cheerleader, you've at least heard of him."

Hadrian was reading down the list and nodding his head. "I think that's everyone."

"Yeah, but Margalo, even if I know some of these people by sight, I don't *know* them. So how will this help me help you figure out who robbed you? Why don't you ask Tim? He probably knows them, being on the paper, being a sophomore and the kind of person who takes people to brunch."

"Tim took you to brunch?" Hadrian asked. "When?"

"Last weekend."

"She has to do brunch for her dates," Mikey added. "Because of her work hours."

"Is he your boyfriend?" Hadrian asked Margalo.

Mikey answered for her. "The world wonders."

Margalo just smiled an irritating, mysterious smile. "We agreed, no date *post mortems*." Before Mikey had time to do more than groan, Margalo went on, insisting, "We made a deal. You know you hate that kind of girly giggly talk."

"I never giggle."

"But I'll tell you this much, I had eggs Benedict. Have you ever had eggs Benedict?"

"Of course I have. My mother's boyfriends used to like taking us out for brunch. I've had eggs Benedict lots of times,"

Mikey answered, feeling a little better. She just didn't want to be entirely left out, that was all.

"Hollandaise is one of the trickiest sauces because of how easily it can separate," Hadrian explained to Margalo and looked to Mikey for confirmation. "Isn't that right?"

"There are ways to fix it," she told him. "You don't cook, do you?"

"No," he laughed, his high seventh-grade-kid laugh. "That would about finish me off, if I did. Being a brain is barely okay, because I'm a dork, but being a cook, too . . . It's all right for you because you're female, and you, too, Margalo—if you want to be cooks. But I'd never get away with it."

"If I was a boy, I'd get away with it," Mikey declared.

Hadrian nodded agreement. "But you're not like other people. Neither are you, Margalo, but nobody can miss it about you, Mikey, whereas you *want* them to miss it about you," he observed to Margalo, then went back to studying the list of names.

Margalo took out a second sheet of paper, which she had divided into sections, each with a title—Stage Manager, Joe and Doc, Howie and Doc, Howie and Mrs. Gibbs, Doc and Mrs. Gibbs. Hadrian studied this new material. Margalo studied the original list of names. Mikey studied nothing and felt left out.

"I get it," Hadrian said as Margalo started filling names into the boxes. "You're making one of those time/opportunity charts. Who had the opportunity to go into your wallet because they weren't in the scene we were reading."

"To rule people out," Margalo agreed. "If they were reading, or if I'm sure I didn't see them leave the room or move around."

"I have no idea what you're talking about," Mikey complained. "I might as well leave." But she didn't move.

Hadrian said, "You're making it way too complicated."

"No she isn't," Mikey said.

Margalo was more open-minded. "You're right! I *am*!" She put a check beside Richard's name and another beside Sally's. "I'm sure I saw them, they went out of the room together, I figured to the bathroom but when they came back they were . . . You know, her cheeks were pink and— Anyway, I was pretty sure they'd been necking, gone somewhere private to neck. Or something. The way . . . You know, their eyes were all shiny and they had secret smiles they'd exchange, you know what I mean, Hadrian. Don't you?"

"I know too," Mikey claimed. "I bet they did it. Don't you think, Hadrian?"

Hadrian pointed at various names, his finger landing here and there like a wasp working on a puddle of melted ice cream. "You should do me next," he said.

"Why you?" asked Mikey. "You didn't do it, did you?"

"If I did—"

"But you didn't," Mikey told him.

"If I did," Hadrian repeated stolidly, "it wouldn't be for the money, it would be for—the game of it, to see if I could get away with it. And if I'd done it for the game of it, helping in your investigation would make it an even better game."

"Psychologically I can see that," Margalo said thoughtfully.

"So can I," Mikey said. "But it's pretty stupid, because you didn't do it."

"I *could* have," Hadrian argued. "Because between this scene"—his wasp finger landed on one ice cream puddle—"and that one"—another puddle—"I don't have any lines, so I could very easily have slipped away. You might not have noticed me, and neither would Ms. Hendriks. She was too busy monitoring other people, listening to their voices, making notes. That's how come it's easy for Sally and Richard to sneak out . . ." His cheeks turned pink at even thinking about necking in front of two girls. He couldn't say any of the words for it. "So it's easy to slip away, and it wouldn't take more than one or two minutes, tops, to get into Margalo's knapsack and find her wallet. Even hidden at the bottom it wouldn't take long. I could easily have done it," he said, pointing again. This time his finger landed on the second sheet. "Here."

Mikey demanded, "How did you know it was on the bottom?"

Hadrian just smiled.

Margalo was grinning away too. Detecting was sort of fun. If you forgot about your own stolen money, it was a lot of fun.

170

"And how did you know Margalo even had any money anyway?" Mikey demanded.

Hadrian kept on smiling.

"Looking goofy doesn't prove anything," Mikey told him. She could detect as well as anybody else, whatever everybody else might think.

"It's probability," Hadrian said. "I happen to know you go to the bank on Friday, but even if I didn't, I'd guess. Margalo works, she has jobs, everybody knows that, and lots of people know she's saving for college. She can only get to the bank late on Friday—unless her bank is open Saturday morning, I guess—but probabilities are that it's Friday afternoon she'd do her banking. Probabilities are that she'd bring the money with her to school, since she doesn't have a license, or a car, or enough time to get home on the late bus and get back downtown. So probably she has it with her. And Margalo's smart, so she wouldn't just drop her wallet in at the top of the knapsack, especially since she'd be taking things out of it all day, and putting things in, books, papers, pencils. Anybody who thought about it, and wanted to see if there was money to be stolen, would take a look in Margalo's knapsack on Friday, if they could get in there without anyone seeing."

"All right then, *did* you?" Mikey asked. "But Hadrian, if you did, it makes no sense for you to tell us. Especially given your motive." She thought. "Your alleged motive. So I don't believe you."

Hadrian smiled again, Mr. Mysterioso.

"And you can stop that smiling," Mikey told him.

He did.

Margalo had been thinking too. She had practiced remembering everything from that afternoon. She could play it like a movie inside of her head, start to finish, first bell to last. "Ms. Hendriks had you up on the platform with her. So you would have had to be there all the time because the Stage Manager is always onstage, even when he's off to the side just watching the action. If you'd moved off entirely, Ms. Hendriks would have noticed and said something. Even if she didn't watch you every minute, she would have noticed right away if you weren't where you were supposed to be." Margalo thought about what she'd said.

Mikey turned to Hadrian. "That's another proof it wasn't you."

Hadrian kept on trying. "Unless I did it some other time. Like during lunch."

Did Hadrian *want* them to think he was the thief? Mikey lost patience. "Since you didn't do it, when else you might have done it if you had isn't worth wasting our time figuring out."

Margalo said, "There is no other time. The knapsack was either right at my feet or hanging off my shoulder, I'm certain of that."

"Well then," Hadrian said. "You've proved it. It wasn't me."

"We already knew that!" Mikey cried.

"So who do you want to do next?" Hadrian asked. "Because now that you've ruled me out, I can help. You wouldn't want the guilty person to be the person helping you figure out who did it," he told them.

Even Mikey was laughing by then.

When they met up after a hasty lunch, Margalo set her papers out on the table again, and they all studied them. She had added a third sheet, for people who had been ruled out. Only five names were on that list: Hadrian, Ms. Hendriks, Richard and Sally, and Sherry Lansing, who had been absent. But Hadrian could add a couple of names to that list. "Gilda Kulka left right away—she said a dentist appointment—and Sue and Leland left early, they weren't in the first act."

"And Tracey and Bill went out with Sue and Leland, all four together, as soon as the cast list was announced. They were complaining about the parts they'd gotten," Margalo remembered. She made the changes and they took a fresh look at the papers.

To Mikey it looked like a kaleidoscope of names, arranged and rearranged, only much more boring than a kaleidoscope because they were using letters not colors.

"I don't know," Margalo said. "I suppose I could ask everybody to tell me everything they remember about that time, and I could make a map of the information."

"Contradictions might show up," Hadrian said.

"It's already too confusing," Mikey objected.

"Whoever did it would lie," Margalo said.

"That would create the contradictions," Hadrian said. "Although they say that nobody is an accurate eyewitness. Everybody thinks they remember what really happened, what they really saw, but usually they don't. But nobody sees that in themselves. Everybody thinks their own version is the right one."

"Mine usually is," Mikey pointed out.

"So we'd end up with a lot of contradictions and they probably wouldn't be useful," Margalo concluded.

"If you ask me, this whole approach isn't useful," Mikey observed.

"All right then, what would you do?"

"I'd figure out who I thought had done it—which I've already done," Mikey said, and she pointed at Richard's and Sally's names. "Then I'd accuse them."

"They're ruled out. They were always together," Hadrian reminded her.

Margalo was willing to consider any option. "If I did accuse people, I might get lucky. Or I bet I could tell from the way they deny it who's lying." She thought about it and the more she thought about it, the more she liked the possibility. "Nobody would expect me to do that, and if people aren't expecting something then you catch them off guard."

"And when they're off guard they'll spill the beans," Mikey agreed.

Hadrian had his doubts, but he didn't express them in words. He expressed them in hums and little short grunts.

"Start with Richard and Sally," Mikey suggested. "It's always the person you think couldn't possibly have done it."

"They're people, not a person," Margalo pointed out. "And this isn't some TV mystery. It's high school."

"Besides, I don't see how anybody *could* have gone into your knapsack without me noticing. I was onstage the whole time," Hadrian reminded them.

"You had lines to read," Margalo reminded him. "Or . . . somebody could have said he was going to the bathroom and picked up my knapsack as he left the room. You could easily not have noticed that. And then brought it back into the room and dumped it back on the pile."

"So you think it was a guy who did it?" Mikey asked. "But girls could make good thieves, just as good as boys, maybe better because you don't ever suspect them. I bet Sally did it."

"Why her?"

"I don't like the way she looks. Anybody who looks like that—all right, all right, but you shouldn't rule out the girls," she advised Margalo.

Margalo was gathering together her papers, which she ripped in half, then ripped in half again. "I'm ruling out this approach. That's all I'm ruling out right now."

For the next couple of days Margalo thought hard. She thought about what she knew about people, and she thought about how to find out what you needed to know from them, if they didn't think they knew it, or if they didn't want you to know it. During the February vacation week the cast of *Our Town* was scheduled to continue rehearsals. Only Nate Emery's and Ann Witherspoon's families had travel plans for that week, which was lucky for Ms. Hendriks, since after the vacation they would move into the auditorium. It was unsettling to be on a real stage, as they had all discovered in the fall, so the first days after that move they would all get worse at whatever they were trying to do. They needed every minute of classroom rehearsal they could fit in before then, to minimize that damage. Ms. Hendriks had scheduled rehearsals from Tuesday through Friday of the vacation week. People grumbled happily about this. It showed that drama was a serious activity, as serious as any sport.

Margalo used the long Presidents' Day weekend to plan her approach—and to work at the restaurant, and to baby-sit, and to have brunch with Tim again (this time she ordered an omelet, with cheese and spinach), and to spend most of Monday at Mikey's house, with Mr. Elsinger and his girlfriend, Katherine, and Katherine's two little boys, until Mr. Elsinger and Katherine took the little boys out for a movie and a pizza dinner, leaving Margalo and Mikey to amuse themselves.

They amused themselves by making a batch of brownies and watching a few classic space movies, *ET*, *Starman*, and *The Last Starfighter*, interrupted only by a stir-fry dinner. Margalo talked over her plan with Mikey, who entirely

176

approved. "It was my idea," Mikey reminded her. "I could do it for you. Because you're too subtle about things."

"What would you do? How would you do it?"

"The only way. I'd go up to Richard and get right in his face."

"Why Richard?"

"That ponytail is a giveaway."

Margalo put a forkful of stir-fry into her mouth, watching Mikey, not saying a word.

"I'd look him in the eye and tell him, 'I know you stole the money.' Then he'd confess." She considered what she had said, and added, "Or not."

"Or he'd lie," Margalo pointed out.

"Probably the guilty person would lie," Mikey agreed. "So I'd need to be more subtle," Mikey said, and saved face with a smile, *I knew that all along*.

"You could come with me. You'd have to sit through rehearsal, but it might work better with you lurking behind me, like a silent threat."

"What *are* you going to say?"

"I'm working that out."

"You could practice on me," Mikey offered.

"That's a good idea," Margalo said.

"You don't have to sound so surprised," Mikey said, and then asked, because she couldn't stand not knowing, "Which idea did you mean?"

After practicing with Mikey—"Hey, if you had an extra

177

couple of hundred dollars, what would you buy?" "Do you ever wonder how it would feel to be stealing something and worrying about getting caught? What do you think it would feel like?" "Do you think you have the nerve to steal anything?"—Margalo decided that she would start with the easy people.

What she meant by easy was: Not strong characters, maybe shy or insecure, usually female, certainly not seniors, and if possible not juniors. What she meant was: People whom it would be easier to push off balance and get informational answers out of. She decided to start with Lisa Mikkel.

Lisa was a junior, but one of those mousy people who in class and in the halls and at parties, too, look like they don't want to be noticed, with her hesitating smile and hands that always held on to one another behind her back as she shifted from one foot to the other, with her way of wearing whatever everybody else was wearing—jeans, khakis, Ts, sweaters—but in muted colors, so that you could never remember just what it was Lisa Mikkel looked like. Onstage Lisa was transformed into a tomboyish person, fresh and quick and confident, but offstage she kept to herself. This made her a good person to start off with and also easy to get on her own.

Margalo spent Tuesday observing individual people and reviewing her plan of approach, so on Wednesday she felt ready to try it. She sat quietly down beside Lisa—who was off to the side of the Drama classroom, alone, doing some

French homework, her knapsack beside her and her note-book and book opened on her lap. Margalo hunkered down beside Lisa and said, quietly but clearly, "I know about it." She kept her eyes on the platform, as if watching what was going on up there with Richard and Sally and Ms. Hendriks.

Margalo felt Lisa freeze, and she turned her head to see. Lisa looked like a rabbit in the headlights, or a chipmunk. Then she started talking, in a whisper, never lifting her eyes from the page of French verbs. "You aren't going to tell people, are you? Everyone knows that's not the kind of person I am. It wasn't me, I just—I was with a bad crowd last year. Otherwise I never would have. Because they made me, because I'm not the kind of person who—You won't tell, will you?" she asked, and then did look at Margalo out of watery eyes.

Half of Margalo was trying to figure out how to find out precisely what Lisa had done, and the other half was dismayed at having dug up a secret she didn't even know was there and couldn't see any use in knowing. From what Lisa had said, Margalo could make a good guess at what had gone on—one of the usual messes for teenagers, probably shoplifting or drugs, scary, and bad enough, but definitely not life threatening. But the secret Lisa was hiding wasn't the secret of Margalo's money, which was too bad, since Lisa hid her secrets so badly.

On Thursday, Margalo sat down next to Gilda Kulka, a

sophomore who had a small part as a baseball player in the second act. In these productions, there were always some male roles played by girls, since there were always more girls than boys signed up for Drama. Gilda had dark, dark hair and wore bright red lipstick; she liked vests with spangles and little bits of mirror on them; she claimed to have Russian great-great-grandparents of royal Romanov blood who had fled from that revolution to Paris first, then to America. Gilda had a loud laugh and thick, muscular legs and a giant crush on Carl Dane, proving once again that opposites attract. Although as far as Margalo could tell, Carl wasn't attracted to Gilda's opposition.

Margalo sat down on the floor beside Gilda, whose full attention was on this rehearsal of Act III. Carl had his big scene in Act III. "I know about it," Margalo said into Gilda's ear with the same tone of voice that had worked so well with Lisa.

Gilda turned and looked right at Margalo. "What? What did you say?"

Somehow, when repeated, the line wasn't as threatening as when she said it just once, and saying it directly into the face of the person she was accusing didn't feel like the right approach, but Margalo saw no way to avoid this. "I know about it," she repeated, looking right back at Gilda.

There was a microsecond's hesitation, and then Gilda faced back to the stage and laughed her loud laugh, as if Margalo had just made a joke.

"People, please," said Ms. Hendriks without turning to see just who was responsible for the disturbance.

Gilda looked back at Margalo, no longer laughing, and said in a low voice of her own, "Look, I'll be friends with you. It's a good offer. I get invited to parties, so . . . There's no point in telling people about it, you know. Nobody cares, and my parents already know. Is that what you want? For me to act like your friend? I'm cool with that."

Margalo just nodded her head. What could Gilda possibly be hiding?

"So give me a call, any time. You have my number? We're in the book. We're the only Kulkas, so there's no problem. So that's that? You're sure?"

Margalo kept on nodding. This wasn't working out the way she had thought it would. She decided that she must be doing it wrong, somehow.

To work out the weakness in her approach, she walked out of Friday's rehearsal beside Hadrian that afternoon, and as they went down the corridor to the main entrance, Margalo said casually, "You know, I do know about it."

"How'd you figure it out?"

Margalo didn't hesitate. Hesitation could blow the cover off a good bluff. "When I thought about it, it just made sense."

"Did you tell Mikey? Does she know? I only made the calls for a couple of months, no more than three. She said she wasn't afraid I was a stalker. I thought she liked our conversations."

Margalo stopped in her tracks. The hallways were almost empty so there was no one around to overhear them. "You're Mikey's secret admirer?"

Hadrian's cheeks were pink. "You said it made sense."

Now that she knew it, it did make sense, but, "Why did you do it?"

"To talk to her. Mikey's not easy to talk to, in case you haven't noticed. Wait," he said. "Does that mean you *hadn't* figured it out? Then what did you mean? Why did you say that?"

"I'm trying to get someone to confess," Margalo explained.

Hadrian's cheeks flushed even darker and he blinked his eyes. Margalo thought she might know what he was thinking and, in case she was right, hastened to reassure him, "I keep not finding out what I need to know," she told him. "I was just practicing with another way to say it. All I want to know is who robbed me."

"You already know I didn't. We proved it."

"I was trying to figure out where I'm going wrong when I ask."

"You should have told me."

"Anyway, it doesn't work," she said, and started walking along, thinking.

They walked a few steps in silence. Then Hadrian said, "I guess I understand. Are you going to tell Mikey?" and he answered his own question, "Of course."

Margalo shrugged, not paying much attention. She had other, more important, things on her mind.

Over the weekend Margalo decided she was not going to be discouraged, not yet anyway. She could be discouraged later, when she had run out of options. But as soon as she gave up on the idea of accusing people herself, she came up with the idea of giving people a chance to accuse one another.

When school reopened after vacation, Margalo hoped it was a good time for a fresh start. She hadn't had a chance to tell Mikey her new detecting idea yet, or about Hadrian, and she was looking forward to lobbing those two grenades before homeroom on Monday morning. But before she could do that, Tanisha Harris rushed up, announcing, "All right. I've been waiting and waiting. You said you'd think about it."

Margalo remembered: William. She had forgotten. Other things had taken over her attention. But she had her pride, and she wanted to seem as if she had spent the time considering Tan's situation, looking at the problem from all sides, thinking about all the possible contingencies. She didn't want to be found out forgetting. She started out with a safe conclusion. "It doesn't look too hopeful to me."

"What doesn't?" asked Mikey, and for once Margalo was grateful for the way Mikey just butted into conversations. "Look hopeful."

"I mean with Oslo and all," Margalo said, starting to remember details.

"William," Mikey announced. "You already know what I think."

"Not without some idea of what's going on in *his* head," Margalo concluded.

Tan offered, "He calls me his killer little sister."

"Killer's okay," Mikey decided, "but little's trouble."

"As far as I can see," Margalo said, her mind now focused and informed, "there isn't much you can do. You could tell him how you feel—"

"No," Tan said. "That would be . . . No."

"In person or in a letter. To see how he reacted."

"He'd be polite. He'd be kind. William's really nice, he wouldn't laugh at me or anything. But . . . I couldn't do that. I wouldn't know what to say, it would be . . ." She was shaking her head. "There are too many girls after him already."

"Or you can wait, wait and hope that—someday—"

"How long? How long do you think?"

"What is *wrong* with everyone?" Mikey demanded.

"Out of high school," Margalo advised, "and what about college? Can you wait that long?"

"The question is, will William wait that long," Tanisha said. "Is that all you can think of that I can do?"

"That and the usual—you know, find out what his interests are and learn as much as you can about them, keep yourself looking good, be around whenever he is, wherever, observe the girls he likes, to figure out what he likes in a girl, let him know you're sexy without putting any moves on him."

"How do you know all this?" Mikey demanded, but before Margalo or Tan could respond, she changed her mind.

"Don't tell me. I don't want to hear about it. No wonder the divorce rate is so high, that's all I have to say."

"Okay," Tan said, talking to Margalo, ignoring Mikey. "I hear you. Maybe that's what I'll do. Or maybe I *should* tell him?"

"I wouldn't," Margalo said.

"I would," Mikey said.

Tan grinned then. "That answers that question," she said, and walked away.

Then there was no time to tell Mikey anything because the homeroom bell rang and separated them.

There was also no time during lunch because Ms. Hendriks asked Margalo to meet with her to go over, for almost the last time, the list of props. Margalo could only explain to Mikey, "It's the play. The play's the week after next, there are only three rehearsal weeks left," before she rushed away. So she never got to hear what Mikey thought of her new idea.

This was something of a relief, but also a little worrying, since Mikey could be counted on to plunk her finger right down on whatever was weak or false in an idea. That was one of Mikey's most irritating habits, sticking her fingers in like that.

By rehearsal, after school, when they had all gathered together in the auditorium, knapsacks and jackets in a long jumble at the foot of the stage, Margalo had given a name to this approach: Operation Stirring Things Up. Stirring things up would be easy because the first week of rehearsals in the auditorium had everybody jumpy. Even Ms. Hendriks upped her anxiety level when they were in the actual place where they were actually going to perform. All week Margalo carried out operations.

To do this, she moved around among the actors who, when they weren't onstage, clustered into groups in the first few central rows of the auditorium—except, of course, for Richard and Sally, who either withdrew together to a dark rear side aisle or were in the front row, watching one or the other performing his or her scenes. The actors got used to having Margalo come up to them, or slip into a seat behind them, and join in their conversation or ask their opinion about a line.

Margalo joined a group and stirred things up. How she stirred, with what spoon, in what direction, depended on the group. With Sue Kind and her boyfriend, Leland Potts, who liked to hang out with another of Drama's steady couples, Tracey Walker and Bill Terramino, she talked about the props they would need for their scenes and where those props would be set out, adding, "That's if nobody walks off with the baseball stuff. John Baker was saying how short the baseball team is on equipment and how Leland was griping about that last year. You don't think there's any danger someone will take our props, do you, Leland?" she asked as Sue jumped to his defense, "Leland wasn't griping. It's just that if you have old, cracked bats, it's hard to learn how to hit well." To which

Tracey responded, "Bill never talked about bad bats. Did you, Bill?" At which Bill grunted and glared at Tracey, who glared right back at him. "What? What is it? I can't even *talk* about the baseball team?"

To John Baker and John Lawrence, sitting with Ann Witherspoon, who was, as usual, working on a homework assignment and not wasting time, she raised the question of Missy Selig's hinting that maybe John Lawrence wasn't as trustworthy as he might be, the kind of person who asked somebody out but never called her up to confirm, and never showed up, either, which meant that when Margalo got to Missy and Sally and Gilda, who were talking about Chet Parker's new love interest, another ninth grader this time, who had stolen him away from Candy DeAngelo after he'd promised Candy she was his one and only, she could report that, "John Lawrence was wondering if Missy was the kind of person who might steal. Or I thought that's what he was hinting. That's what it sounded to me like he was hinting at, and you know, sometimes a guilty person will point the finger at someone else. So do you think John Lawrence could have done it?"

All during that school week Margalo stirred things up and waited to see what would float to the surface, suspecting everybody she talked to and every reaction she noticed. She stirred and prodded and poked. She watched and wondered and waited. But she didn't find out anything. At the end of all this detective work she'd found out that Ronnie Caselli was

187

Chet Parker's new girlfriend and that some business had donated a whole new set of practice bats to the baseball team, but she had no more idea of who had taken her money than she had had at the first moment she realized it was gone.

And, she realized as the rehearsal drew to a close the last Friday in February, she was out of ideas, too.

She told Mikey about this on the bus home. It took a couple of tries to get Mikey's attention. At first Mikey was interested in reminding Margalo that this was the end of week twenty-one of the school year, which meant there were only fifteen weeks to go. Then she needed to remind Margalo that in March—which was the month it would be when they got to school the next Monday—tennis started up again. "Mid-March. The fifteenth," Mikey said. "Nobody but me has been playing all winter, so I'll be able to knock off the last of the people on the tennis ladder. And that means I'll play varsity," she announced, in case Margalo couldn't follow this logic.

"That's good," Margalo said, not paying attention either.

"You don't sound impressed. You should be impressed."

Margalo turned to look at Mikey. "I'm never going to be able to figure out who took my money," she explained.

"You always think up something else," Mikey told her.

Margalo shook her head and looked out the window again. The sky was low and gray, but the temperature wasn't cold enough for snow, so it would be rain. On cold, rainy Friday nights in February a lot of people wanted to eat out, so there would be a massive pile of dishes to wash and—worse—a massive pile of pots to scour clean. "I just have to accept that it's happened," she said, looking out the window. "Like bad weather. Nobody can help me and I can't figure out how to detect it. I'm not much of a detective."

"I guess not. But neither am I."

"Is that supposed to make me feel better?" Margalo demanded even though—for some reason—it did.

— 11 —

Our Town's in Trouble

Not that Margalo cared, but rehearsals went really badly that week. Monday, Tuesday, Wednesday, Thursday and Friday—every day they had a bad rehearsal. People arrived late, spoke their lines carelessly, wandered around the stage as if they'd never blocked out any of the scenes, and, no matter what Ms. Hendriks said, didn't get themselves focused, wouldn't stop talking in the auditorium seats while other scenes were rehearsed, and didn't care.

Hadrian was the exception, of course, and even Margalo found herself thinking it was sort of a pain the way Hadrian kept being so much better than the rest of them. By Friday every one of them could think only of how glad they were that the next two days were a weekend, when there wouldn't be rehearsals.

A number of the actors were hoping to come down with

some communicable disease that would keep them home from performances. "Hadrian knows everybody's lines, he can be a one-man show." Margalo didn't feel quite that strongly, but she was certainly looking forward to the weekend as she sat taking notes on a long yellow legal pad while the teacher, having tried to rehearse the final scenes of *Our Town*, was offering useful advice to her uncooperative actors. Margalo's notes varied from "Alice, a more relaxed and gossipy tone" to "Indirect lighting too dim" and included probably insoluble difficulties like "Set for Act III static."

Ms. Hendriks sat on the edge of the stage, with Margalo at her side; the cast sat in the first rows of seats, facing them. At that point Ms. Hendriks was talking to individual actors. "Carl," she said, "you have to remember that you're a man who killed himself. Who hung himself. Imagine that. Imagine actually tying the rope—"

"Let's not."

"Then throwing the rope over a tree limb, climbing up on a chair to put your head—"

"Ick."

"I get it, okay? I *get* it."

"I saw this movie—"

"So that," Ms. Hendriks continued, "when you say that human life is 'ignorance and blindness,' you really mean it. You mean exactly and precisely that. You have to really mean it, because if you're wrong—Think about it, Carl, what if it turns out you've killed yourself over something you got wrong?"

191

"I wouldn't want to have to figure that out," Carl said. "I'd be afraid to even *think* it. Because then I would have—Yeah, I see what you mean, Ms. Hendriks. I guess this isn't such a dorky play after all," he remarked, speaking to no one in particular and everyone in general.

That caused an uncomfortable silence to settle down over them all like a collapsed parachute, crowding out everything except what nobody wanted to say out loud. People shifted their legs, looked at their watches, turned to look at the clock on the wall, didn't look at the teacher.

After a moment's thought Ms. Hendriks stood up and waved her hand, gesturing to Margalo to go sit among the students.

Margalo moved to the side and to the rear; she sat alone. She was just as glad not to have to look at the mostly empty auditorium. Like everybody else involved with this production, she was aware that a week from that day—a week!—an audience would occupy all those seats, an audience where only some of the people were their parents and other relatives, because the rest would be people from school, people they had to see every day in the hallways and the cafeteria and the classrooms. So if they blew it with this play—or if someone thought they were blowing it, or if someone decided the play was weird or dumb—when you already felt like maybe a jerk for daring to try to act . . .

A stage meant real risks of real embarrassment. Margalo knew that for *Our Town* to work, they all had to have confidence in the play, and they also had to trust the teacher, but especially they had to trust one another, and she personally didn't trust—except Hadrian—anybody. So Margalo wasn't surprised that Ms. Hendriks took advantage of this opening to try to improve things by asking Carl, "Can you clarify for me what you mean by dorky?"

Carl, being a senior and about to leave the school forever, was willing to speak straightforwardly, if he had to. "What I mean is that it's . . . so old-fashioned, I mean—and so *serious*. It's like it's trying too hard. It's too obvious, you know? Everything in it is so *ob*vious."

When one person had spoken, others were willing to join in.

"The characters are stereotypes."

"People aren't that way, really. Do you personally know anyone who's so—I dunno, so uninformed and wants to be so nice to everybody as Emily? I mean—I dunno, she's just too good. Nobody's that innocent and good, not anymore at least, if they ever were."

"They never were."

"The worst thing they do in this play is gossip. What's so bad about gossip?"

"And the costumes? Seriously dorky."

Ms. Hendriks took all of this in, then, "It won the Pulitzer Prize," she reminded them.

"Yeah, we know, but . . . That doesn't make it good for now."

"Maybe you need to be better actors than we are to make a play like this look good."

"And have better lighting, and our acoustics aren't—"

"I mean, what does this play have to do with me? It's nothing to do with my life."

"And it acts like there's no sex in the world."

"They get married and she dies having a baby, so there has to have been sex. Dunnh."

"You know what I mean."

They did. He meant: Everybody who has anything to do with this play could look like a total loser.

"People aren't like that, Ms. Hendriks," somebody concluded. They liked the teacher, and they felt bad for her because her boyfriend had broken the engagement, so they explained it tactfully, so as not to upset her with the news.

"Real people are greedy, and afraid. It's fear and greed that are people's main motivations, everybody knows that, everybody says, I think even Freud. They go together, and it's not just about money."

Ms. Hendriks made a connection. "This has to do with the theft of Margalo's money, doesn't it? But I'm sure Margalo has forgotten all about her money by now. Haven't you?" she asked Margalo.

Margalo knew what the right answer to that question was. She was scratching crisscrossing lines on her yellow pad and thinking—not about the money but about how she was all alone here, how she was the only person on her side.

It wasn't a feeling she liked.

But she had also been thinking that this was what usually

happened to Mikey. Right or wrong, Mikey tended to be the only person on her side. Even when other people agreed with her, Mikey stood alone. Somehow. Margalo was thinking about that, wondering if it was maybe because Mikey was so ready to fight for things.

"Margalo?" Ms. Hendriks asked again. "You have forgotten all about that money, haven't you?"

The trouble was, Margalo *did* think it was important, being robbed, robbers getting away with it. Besides, she knew this was only school. If nothing else, school was a good testing ground for finding out who you were and who you wanted to be. It was a place where the prizes weren't very big, but neither were the penalties. If you couldn't go after what you really wanted in school, you probably never would. So, "No," she said. "I haven't forgotten."

There came the windy sounds of many exasperated sighs and a few whispers. "What is *wrong* with her?" "Doesn't she care about us?" "Doesn't she care about the play?"

Nothing, Margalo could have answered, taking the questions in order, No, Yes but not that much.

"But can't you *see*, Margalo, how bad your attitude is for all of us?" Ms. Hendriks asked.

"What about how bad being robbed has been for me?" Margalo asked the teacher.

"You're saying you're the only important one in the room? More important than the rest of us? Put together?"

"Talk about selfish."

That was about more than Margalo was willing to put up with, even if everybody hated her for all of the next four years. Three, actually, she reminded herself. Three years and fourteen weeks, that was all that was left of high school: She could make it. She said, "You might think about whether it's good for anybody, or even the whole school, when everybody takes it for granted that people will rip you off."

"Oh, come off it."

"Get real."

"Who cares?"

"I think I do," said a deep voice from the other side of the auditorium. The deep voice was none they'd ever heard before, not in this class; it was the voice of somebody braver and wiser than the rest, somebody grown up and experienced, trustworthy and strong, Abraham Lincoln or Gandhi.

Everybody turned around to see who it was, but it was only Hadrian. He cleared his throat, and stood up, and suddenly nobody was quite sure just exactly what this Hadrian Klenk person was like. "Margalo," Hadrian said, like a lawyer in a courtroom. "Tell me about that money. How much was it?"

Margalo looked across over the raised faces to meet Hadrian's eyes. "Two hundred and nineteen dollars."

"That's all? I get more than twice that from my grandmother every Christmas."

"Well aren't you the hotshot rich kid."

Ms. Hendriks tried again. "Isn't that enough, people? It's time to stop all this, isn't it?"

"Yeah, isn't it time Margalo just accepted what happened?"

Part of Margalo wanted to do that for the sake of this teacher who really loved drama and probably needed to keep her job. But still, "I'm not giving up," Margalo said to Ms. Hendriks.

"Stopping doing something isn't necessarily the same as giving up," Ms. Hendriks told her.

Hadrian's deep voice overrode them all. "Tell me about this two hundred and nineteen dollars," he said.

He seemed taller, taller than when he entered the auditorium, taller than he looked onstage. Instead of being younger than anybody else in the room, suddenly it seemed as if Hadrian was older. Even his hair—even though it still stuck up in cowlicks, as anybody could see—*seemed* to be thick and well cut, like a TV lawyer.

Because Hadrian could act.

Margalo had known that since last spring's eighth-grade play, but now she really knew it, knew it in her bones. She told this taller, older actor Hadrian the truth:

"Whoever robbed me took my money, as if it didn't belong to me, as if I hadn't earned it and saved it up. But it was my money, that I earned by working, and they knew it. It was my money that I need for college—and they knew that, too. Whoever it is, even if he can get away with it, I'm not going to stop trying to figure out who it is. And I'm not going to forget about it either." She shrugged, thought, and added, "Even if everybody says I should and wants me to."

"I never said you should."

"We never said we want you to."

"What's *wrong* with you, Margalo? How awful do you think we are?"

"Except somebody *has* been that awful, hasn't he?"

Ms. Hendriks knew when she had lost. "That's all for today," she announced, even though it was way early. "Monday I'd like to see some real effort, from everybody. Have a good weekend. Rest up. Drill your lines," Ms. Hendriks said, but as if that was something she didn't have much hope for.

Margalo was the first to leave the room.

Hadrian caught up with her before she turned the corner. She'd heard footsteps running after but hadn't turned to look. She'd expected Ms. Hendriks, telling her not to bother coming to rehearsal Monday, or ever again, since she was single-handedly ruining the whole production. If not Ms. Hendriks, she'd expected one of the junior girls, talking about school spirit and consideration for others and the unfairness of blaming everybody for what one person did. She didn't at all expect Hadrian Klenk, since he had already done her a huge favor by giving her the chance to say what she was truly thinking. What more could he do?

"Wait, Margalo," Hadrian said.

"Thanks," she said, not stopping. "That was—thanks."

They walked along side by side. He came only about up to her neck, and she couldn't believe how *tall* he'd looked just minutes earlier. "You can act," she told him. "I mean, you can really act, not like a high school actor."

"I think maybe," he agreed, his cheeks turning a pleased pink. "My parents want me to be a computer genius, so it'll be a disappointment to them. There's no security in acting," he explained.

Actually, Margalo thought his parents could be right. Hadrian Klenk was short and sort of funny looking, and he had one of those superior intelligences that you can't miss. He was much better computer-genius-multimillionaire material than leading-man material.

Mikey waited for Margalo by the main entrance to the building, inside for warmth on this chilly March afternoon. They were going to the bank, of course. The week after she'd been robbed, Margalo had started right off saving again. "Maybe they can take my money, but they can't make me change my program," she told Mikey. As soon as he saw, Hadrian veered away towards the lockers, even though he was already carrying both his knapsack and his jacket. "See you," Hadrian said.

"Isn't your mother going to be waiting?"

"She called and said she'd be a few minutes late."

"That's not true."

Hadrian shrugged. He didn't care if she knew he was lying. "Mikey's angry at me."

"About what?"

"Those phone calls I made last year."

Margalo looked him square in the eye. "I didn't even tell her yet." That surprised him, but she went on before he could get too hopeful. "I'm going to today. I've known since fifth grade you had a crush on Mikey."

Hadrian answered, "It's not you I'm worried about."

"Then why don't you apologize to her and get it over with?"

Hadrian shook his head. He shrugged his skinny shoulders. He backed away from her.

More than a little exasperated at his idiocy, Margalo just went on ahead to join up with Mikey, who asked her, "How much are you putting in the bank today?"

"Two hundred and seventy-two, plus change, and that gives me over seven hundred, which means that after today I can invest another five hundred."

"You don't sound particularly interested."

Margalo shrugged. She didn't know that she *was* particularly interested. They left the building, in step, and started down along the sidewalk into town. After a few minutes Margalo said, "It turns out it was Hadrian who kept calling you up last spring. Remember?"

For a few steps Mikey didn't say anything, then, "That was him? The guy on the phone last year? My anonymous caller was Hadrian Klenk? My secret admirer?" Each time she said it, she sounded more outraged.

"I always said Hadrian had a crush on you."

"Then why did he stop calling?"

"How would I know?"

"You could have asked him. So it was Hadrian? Who'd

have guessed it?" Mikey said. She gave a couple of sec
more thought to this unforeseen development and concluded, "Bummer."

"He said you liked talking to him."

"I kind of did," Mikey said. "But I liked it better when I
didn't know it was Hadrian Klenk." Then she added, admiration in her voice, "You solved the mystery."

"Not the one I was trying to solve."

They walked a little farther in silence, past the restaurant
where Margalo would work that evening, where a man smoking in the narrow alley waved to Margalo. He wore a stained
white apron wrapped around his waist. Margalo waved back.

"Who's that?" asked Mikey.

"Angie. The cook." Margalo fell silent again.

Mikey knew she wasn't the most perceptive person around,
but she thought she could figure out what was turning
Margalo so quiet. "I can't think of any way to find out who
stole your money," she said. "I've been trying."

"I can't either, and I'm supposed to be good at this. And
now Ms. Hendriks thinks I should forget about it, to help the
play, and everyone agrees with her. Or almost everyone. The
play's not going well."

Mikey had never heard Margalo sound so dispirited, or
defeated, either, not in all of the—she did the math quickly—
four and a half years she had known her. Not even in seventh
grade. This started to get her angry. "They can't do this to you."

"Hadrian can really act," Margalo said then.

Mikey couldn't work that out. *"Non sequitur,"* she objected.

"That's Latin!" Margalo protested.

"Meaning, it doesn't follow, it's not logically connected," Mikey told her.

"Sometimes you are really irritating," Margalo said.

Mikey had thought of something she *could* do. "I'm cooking breakfast tomorrow. I'll tell Aurora."

— 12 —

Mikey the Fist

Mikey thought of herself—when she did think about herself—as like a rock that got thrown at things, to knock them out. Bad things, of course, and admittedly a self-propelled rock, but that comparison sounded about right. Or maybe she was like a punch that got thrown, or maybe she was like a tennis racket used to send the ball off on a winning shot. *Pow!*

The fist was most like it, she decided. Unless she was . . . not a knife, knives were too small and sneaky. She was a sword, one of those gleaming, sharp blades heroes wielded. The only story she had really liked when she was little was the one about the Gordion Knot. The Gordion Knot was so complex and thick, so complicated and intertwined, that even the wisest men couldn't unravel it. They all came to try, and they all failed. It was a puzzle that nobody could solve. Then along came Alexander the Great. He walked around it, studying it, figuring it out. Then he raised his sword and cut right through it. *Slash!* And that was the end of the Gordion Knot.

Slash! Pow! That was what Mikey was like, that was what she did. And that was what she was going to do about Margalo's money. She was going to go in there and—*Pow! Slash!*—take care of things.

How she didn't know. All she knew was that nobody should be able to get away with telling Margalo to forget about something because it didn't matter to *them.* Nobody should be able to get away with making Margalo feel as bad as Margalo was feeling, so bad that she wasn't even thinking of ways to get even. Usually Margalo was a thinking machine, but not now. Usually Mikey counted on Margalo, but now Margalo needed to count on Mikey. Mikey had no idea what she was going to do, but she sure planned to do something.

The first something was to sit Margalo down and get her talking, because Margalo talking led right to Margalo thinking. That meant a pre–first something, which was Saturday breakfast at Margalo's house. And that meant a pre-pre–first something, which was telephoning Aurora to see what supplies she didn't have. Mikey was already so impatient at all this pre-planning that she almost bagged the entire operation. But this was Margalo, so she didn't.

Because it was Friday, Mikey's father was taking Katherine out for dinner, just the two of them. He entered the kitchen at seven, showered and shaved, wearing a pair of dress slacks and a tweed jacket. "You look good," Mikey told him.

He came over to where she was chopping onion and garlic for a marinara sauce and put his arm around her. "I'm happy. I like being happy," he added, unnecessarily. Then he asked, "What would you think if I got married? I mean, you and me, if we married Katherine. I mean, if Katherine wants to marry me, if Bobby and Phil don't object."

Mikey decided not to ask his advice about Margalo. Besides, at her age she should be able to take care of things herself. She put her arm around her father's rib cage, since he was too tall for her to put it around his shoulders, and told him, "I'd put my money on her saying yes." But what kind of a world was it when she was trying to allay her father's self-doubts about proposing marriage to a woman who was obviously crazy nuts about him?

Although, she preferred his doubts to her mother's confident, been-there-done-that, know-it-all-already attitude. Although, since her mother was happy with Jackson and her father seemed happy about Katherine, it looked like both approaches could work.

As soon as her father's car had pulled away she called Margalo's house. Of course it was Margalo's younger stepsister who answered. "Mikey?" Esther always knew it was Mikey calling. Unless she answered every phone call that way, saying "Mikey?" instead of "Hello?" "Margalo's not here," Esther said. "She's got a job. Dishwashing."

"I *know* that. I want to talk to Aurora."

"Do you want to hear about my Science project?" Esther asked. "And I have a friend for a sleepover. Georgie."

"A boy?" Mikey asked. You could never predict how Aurora and Steven felt about things, except that a lot of the time it wasn't the same way most other people felt.

"I knew you'd think that," Esther giggled.

"Tell Aurora I want to talk to her."

"Georgie's a girl." Esther settled in to tell Mikey all about it. Another disadvantage to having somebody think you were wonderful was the way they assumed that if they admired you, you had to like them back and just as much. "She's my second best—"

"Esther," Mikey warned.

"She's good in Math," Esther offered.

"Save it," Mikey advised.

Esther had been admiring Mikey for years, so she knew when to give up. "Are you coming over tomorrow morning? You can meet Georgie. I'll get Aurora."

Mikey was beginning to wish she'd made this phone call after she'd eaten dinner. But Aurora was efficient on the phone. She almost never chattered, and when she did she preferred to chatter with her children or her husband, not somebody on the phone. "I'll make pancakes," Mikey told her.

"We like pancakes." Not only did Aurora not chatter on the phone, she also didn't cook. Her usual breakfasts consisted of cold cereal and frozen juice. "But not with things in them. No berries. No chocolate chips."

"Do you have flour and milk?"

"Hang on, I'll—Yes, we do."

"Sugar?" With Aurora's kitchen, you had to make sure.

"I think so—Yes."

"Good," Mikey said.

"That's it?" Mikey could hear that Aurora was smiling. For some reason Mikey had always amused Aurora, which Mikey didn't get, but she didn't mind it either.

"I'm bringing syrup," Mikey told her, "and butter, and eggs."

"See you in the morning then," Aurora said, still smiling away.

"Early," Mikey said, and hung up.

When Mikey Elsinger said early, she meant early. It was seven o'clock on a clear, cold morning when she walked her bike down the narrow cement path to Margalo's back door, carrying a knapsack filled with eggs, butter and syrup.

In the kitchen she found Stevie about to serve himself and his little sister bowls of cold cereal. Lily sat in her bumper seat at the table, waiting for the meal to be set in front of her. Lily was the youngest child and she knew how to get herself taken care of.

Stevie had climbed up on a chair to reach into the cupboard. He turned around when Mikey knocked, climbed down to let her in, and then—intent on his breakfast—climbed back up onto the chair.

"Stop!" Mikey cried.

Both of their faces turned to her. Their hair was sleep-rumpled and they had big trusting eyes, like some dogs do. Stevie had furry slippers on his small feet, Lily wore a faded blue cotton nightgown with yellow chickens printed on it and her feet were bare—When they turned and stared at her, not afraid, not even alarmed, made curious, not cross and confused, by unexpected events, Mikey could see why people liked having little children around.

"Hi Mikey."

"Hey Mikey."

"Pancakes," Mikey announced.

"Only me and her are up," Stevie reported.

"Then you'll have to set the table," Mikey told him. She began preparing the batter, meanwhile heating the heavy iron frying pan that was the nearest thing Aurora had to a griddle and putting the tin of maple syrup into a pan of water over a low flame. When everything was ready to go, Mikey sent Lily off to wake up Margalo. Then she sat down at the table across from Stevie. They stared at each other, until he announced, "I like pancakes."

"I know."

"I like our syrup better than yours."

"No you don't."

"Yes I do."

"No you don't. Mine's better."

Actually, Mikey enjoyed the kind of stupid conversation

208

you could have with little kids, especially boys. She was getting a lot of practice in with Katherine's sons.

"Nunnh-unnh."

"Then I guess you don't want any of it today," Mikey said. She watched him work his way through that, trying to find a way to have his family pride and eat real maple syrup on his pancakes at the same time.

"I have to have what you brought. Because you brought it," he explained.

Esther, of course, burst out of bed and down the stairs to the kitchen when she heard that Mikey was there. "You didn't let me help," she complained. "You keep saying you'll teach me how to cook and you keep not letting me help." A small, pale girl in checked red-and-blue pajamas trailed in, Georgie, it had to be. "This is Mikey," Esther told her. "She's my sister's friend, not yours."

Mikey turned to the stove and started dropping pancake batter into the pan. She knew that Margalo would be the last one down.

But Margalo wasn't the last one down when she entered, her hair still a little wet and definitely stringy from a shower. Aurora and Steven were the last to come to the table, and they didn't come in talking the way they usually did. Aurora had a book in her hand, her finger marking her place, and Steven had his chin stuck out. When they entered, everybody at the table got quiet. The silent parents took seats side by side.

Mikey set a second platter of pancakes on the table and exchanged a look with Margalo. As far back as Mikey could remember, Aurora had never fought with anyone, never sulked at anyone, and, though she sometimes raised her voice, never yelled. And as far as she'd seen, Steven had never taken advantage of that. In fact, he always looked at Aurora as if she was more fun than anybody else—except maybe the children. As if he'd rather look at her than anybody, even some movie star. Mikey didn't think she could stand it if Margalo's parents started having what they called marital difficulties. She counted on Aurora and Steven.

"I have a big test on Monday," Aurora said, to nobody in particular.

Mikey refilled the jug with warm syrup and put it beside Aurora. She moved the butter plate from where it had come to a halt between Esther and Georgie, setting it down between Aurora and Steven.

"History," Aurora added. This was not good news.

"Tests are hard," Esther announced to no one in particular, and Stevie added, "I hate spelling tests." Margalo offered, "Can I help you study?" but Steven stepped in quickly, "I want to do that." Lily took advantage of the lack of attention to start feeding herself chunks of sticky, syrupy, buttery pancake with her fingers. Then things got back to normal, with everybody talking about nobody needing forks and spoons in olden days, and nobody thanking Mikey for cooking breakfast. Mikey didn't care about that. She cared about going off with Margalo while other people washed dishes, to get Margalo thinking again so Mikey could get to work on this theft problem. "Let's go for a walk," Mikey suggested.

Once they had left the house and were out on the sidewalk, they wasted no time deciding where to go—it was always the same place, the playground of their old elementary school, a mile and a half away—and they wasted no time talking about schoolwork, or gossiping. They walked along, side by side, shoulder to shoulder, and got started.

First they checked in. "My father is proposing to her," Mikey reported. "She'll say yes, I'm pretty sure."

"Good. But what if they have another baby?"

Mikey tried to imagine that. She couldn't. She tried to think of a worst-case scenario—triplets? All-boy triplets? All-girl triplets?—and she realized, "There probably wouldn't more than one pregnancy before I'll have graduated from high school, so it won't make much difference to me. But what about Steven and Aurora? Is something wrong? Because they were weird this morning."

"Steven is worried that if Aurora gets her GED she'll go on and take college courses," Margalo reported. "At least, I think that's what's wrong, because he only has a high school diploma. But if Aurora wants to work with children, she'll have to have at least some college training. I think he's afraid she'll get too educated for him. And then she won't . . . admire him anymore."

"Do you think that will happen?"

"I don't know what I think exactly, but I hope she gets the high school diploma. And she'd be really good working with children, so I guess I'm hoping for college, too. Mostly," Margalo admitted, "I hope Steven is the kind of man who can still love someone who has more education than he does. Howard and Esther's father had a master's degree, so Aurora knows what she's missing. She knew it when she married Steven. Aurora's pretty smart," Margalo said, and stared right at Mikey.

"I know that," Mikey said. "She always liked me, didn't she?"

"You aren't going to start trying to make jokes, are you?"

"Probably not," Mikey said.

"Although it *was* funny," Margalo admitted.

"Do you think I *should* start?" Mikey asked.

"Is that another one?" Margalo asked back.

They were walking fast.

Mikey had waited as long as she could. "What about Drama? What about being robbed? What are you going to do now?"

They had walked past the houses and were now walking around the outside of the high fence that protected the school playground. That was their walk, down to the elementary school and back again. It was already half over.

Margalo shook her head. "The only thing that I didn't try was one of those reconstructions, reenactments, you know? But by now—"

"I can help," Mikey said. "We'll gather everybody together in the Drama room and have them all do and say the exact things they did at the time. *Now* what's so funny?"

"You think the thief will reenact robbing me?" Margalo asked.

Well, that *was* pretty funny. But, "Maybe," Mikey said. "It would make things a lot easier if they did. Or forgot and gave themselves away. Richard and Sally aren't all that smart, are they?"

"Forget Richard and Sally. Forget the whole thing, in fact. That's what I'm going to have to do and it won't help me if you keep on . . . not forgetting it."

"But that's not right."

"Nothing about the whole thing is right." Margalo upped her walking pace, in a hurry to have this conversation over with.

And that also wasn't right. It wasn't like Margalo and it was all wrong. Maybe Mikey would keep quiet for now, to Margalo, but she wasn't going to keep quiet in her head. But now she changed the subject. "I have a plan. For our lives, I mean. I think we should go into business together. After school. After college, I mean, and I may go for an MBA, although maybe not right away. I mean," she clarified it, in case Margalo missed her point, "I plan for us to stick together even after high school."

Margalo had an idea of what was worrying Mikey. It had to do with all the things that made friendships fade away, like boyfriends and differing activities in school, like differences in families and different interests, and wishing the other person had made different choices from the choices she had made, and didn't play tennis or didn't have a job. It worried her, too. "That would be all right by me," she said, trying to imagine being an adult in business with a grown-up Mikey, remembering having been a kid in business with her. "I might want to have an MBA too, though. Because I'd want to be an equal partner, not with you as my boss."

They stopped walking, turned to face each other.

"Deal," Mikey said, and held out her hand.

"Deal," Margalo said, and they shook on it, like doubles partners at the end of a good match, or like two pirates about to set off together after riches on the high seas.

"So I'll be at rehearsal on Monday," Mikey announced. She had no plan, but any plan she decided on was going to require her to hang out with the Drama group, and rehearsal was where she was going to find them all, these days.

"Why?" Margalo asked.

Mikey had to tell the truth because she couldn't think fast enough to think up a good-enough lie. "I don't know." Then she thought to say, "Solidarity."

On Monday, Mikey had a little trouble tracking down Drama Club. It was almost as if someone didn't want her to find it. The Drama classroom was empty and dark, its door locked. Mikey had to go to the office and ask the secretary to hear

214

that rehearsals had moved to the auditorium. "But it's rather late for someone to be in the building. Do you have a hall pass? Are you going home with someone in the play? Do you have a note from your mother? Are you one of the lighting crew?" the secretary asked, the questions coming too fast for Mikey to even start thinking of how she wanted to answer them. "Could you tell Ms. Hendriks to *please* be more organized about hall passes?" the secretary asked, and Mikey got in a quick "Sure."

When she entered the auditorium, Hadrian was standing alone on the wide stage. Students were scattered around in the front rows—Richard and Sally off to the far side of the third row, with their heads close together, Mikey noticed, grateful that it was their heads and not their lips. Margalo and the teacher were sitting alone together at the center of the first row. They were both looking up at Hadrian.

Onstage Hadrian looked older and taller; he sounded older and taller too. He was wearing his usual khakis, belted up high, and his usual shirt, but for some reason he had a tie loosened around his throat. Every now and then, as he went through his lines, he fiddled with the tie, almost as if he was a man getting dressed up to go to work, or dressing down after his day's labors.

"Try taking a couple of steps towards rear center stage on that line," Ms. Hendriks instructed Hadrian. He nodded, then repeated his lines—which Mikey recognized as coming from the very start of the play. "'Up here,'" said Hadrian as he moved towards center stage, indicating with a large gesture of his arm some invisible line across the stage, "'is Main Street.'"

"That's good," Ms. Hendriks said. "That's just what I meant. Keep moving, now."

"'Way back there,'"—another gesture towards something offstage—"'is the railway station; tracks,'"—he turned, gesturing—"'go that way.'"

The way Hadrian was pointing, and acting as if he could see something where he was looking, Mikey could almost actually see what he was talking about, in a distance that stretched beyond the walls of the auditorium. For a minute she believed in this town Hadrian was talking about, even though she had held the book in her hand and read the words of the play in it and knew it was imaginary. Margalo was right about Hadrian. He could act.

Sometimes it was pretty tiresome how right Margalo always was.

Still not knowing what she planned to do, Mikey went on down the dimly lit aisle and slipped into a row, sidling along until she was behind a group of boys and girls. They turned their heads to see who it was, then turned back to face front, not interested. Some of them had schoolbooks open on their laps, a couple were writing in notebooks, a couple studied their copies of the play. When they spoke, they kept their voices low.

Mikey decided to play this like a tennis match, waiting to see what the opponent would send across the net to her. Once she knew that, she would know how she wanted to respond. She leaned forward in her seat and eavesdropped. They were talking about a couple of new releases, their senior research papers, and how Chet Parker was still dating Ronnie Caselli—"That ninth grader, the beautiful one, it's been almost a month." This topic led them to plans for a restaurant dinner before the prom. (The prom? The prom wasn't until May and they were already talking about it? What was *wrong* with these people?) Every now and then one or another of the girls would slap her book, saying, "I just *can't*."—Can't get this scene right, can't do this problem, can't decide whether to buy the CD or not. The boys were talking about how the pre-season games looked, what kinds of summer jobs they wanted, seriously cool CDs, and one or two grumbled, or boasted, "I'm going to have to just bluff my way through the scene."

After several minutes of eavesdropping Mikey leaned even farther forward to say—speaking to no one in particular, just speaking between two heads to anyone close enough to hear—"I don't know what to think about Margalo being robbed. What do *you* think about it?"

"We don't," said Ann Witherspoon, a junior who planned to apply to Berkeley and so didn't encourage trouble. "We think about the play."

"Like how different the world then was from the way it is now, and why we're putting so much work into something so irrelevant," said Carl Dane.

Mikey had heard from Margalo what people were saying, and she had her own idea about that, so this was a shot she could make a good return on. "You're all wrong," she told Carl. "You're not getting it."

He turned his head to ask, "Oh yeah?"

"Oh yeah," Mikey assured him, and smiled back, a *Look out, Buster* smile. "Because you know how sometimes things seem simple but they're really not? Like when Agassi's game is on, he makes it look easy to make those shots. But if you think it really is easy, you're missing the best of his play."

From the row in front John Baker said, "I can dig that." He turned to Missy, beside him, to ask, "Can you dig that?"

"You mean like that Picasso drawing of the dove of peace?" asked Ann. "I guess, if you put it that way—"

"Put it that way," Mikey advised. Now that she had their attention, she asked again, "So what about Margalo's money?" a hard shot straight down the center, to see what kind of a return that would draw.

"Look, Mikey," they began.

"How do you know who I am?"

"Word gets around," said Carl, sounding sarcastic.

"We're sorry she got robbed and all, but—you know— what was she doing bringing all that money to school? And leaving it in her knapsack?"

"You mean it's her fault?" Mikey demanded.

Ms. Hendriks turned around to shush them, and Margalo saw Mikey but was too occupied to greet her. Hadrian saw her too. Mikey lowered her voice. "You think it's her own fault if she got robbed? So, what is it? If you run over a dog it's the dog's fault for being there?"

"If it ran out in the street," someone pointed out.

"So if Hadrian gets his collarbone broken by the Three Stooges, it's his own fault for—For what? Being in school? Being so smart he skipped grades? No, wait, I get it, he shouldn't have been in the hallway where they could see him."

"I didn't mean that. But Mikey, I didn't do it, what do you want me to do about it?"

"It's not like we can fingerprint her wallet."

"After all this time."

"And the money's long gone by now, so what's the point?"

"It's not like we even know who did it."

"So what do you want from us?"

When they asked like that, Mikey discovered that she had an answer. "Pay her back."

"What?"

"Why?"

"Well," Ann said thoughtfully, "you know, if I'd been robbed, I'd feel better if people cared. It would show we cared if we did that."

"Yeah, but I don't happen to have two hundred dollars to give away," John Baker pointed out.

"People!" called Ms. Hendriks, clapping her hands sharply together. "May I ask you to please, please keep it down?

You've got Hadrian so distracted he can't remember half his lines."

"Hadrian? Forget a line? I wish," Carl murmured after the teacher had turned her back again.

Ann whispered, "But John, you have ten dollars, don't you? Or five? I mean, I've got ten I could spare easy, and there are enough of us in the cast . . . we *could* do it. No, I'm serious. Because, personally, I'll feel better if we do, because . . . I don't like anybody being robbed, do you? And we're all supposed to be so tight, in a play."

"Yeah, but do you think enough people will chip in?"

"We could ask. Ms. Hendriks, too, she'd probably put in a fifty—"

"Teachers don't have fifties."

"—just to save the play."

"But why should I pay for something I didn't do?" John Baker asked.

"Because," Mikey told him, "it's the only thing you *can* do."

"Besides," whispered Ann, "what if it was you who was robbed?"

"I don't leave stealable stuff around in Drama," he assured her. "Not anymore."

"Exactly," Ann said, and waited.

"How much are you going to put in?" John Baker asked Carl Dane.

Mikey's work was done. She leaned back in the seat and

took a look at the stage. Hadrian was still alone there, but now he had come to the edge and was kneeling down to talk to Ms. Hendriks, and a couple of times he looked up to where Mikey was sitting, almost directly in front of him. Mikey waved, but he didn't respond. Finally Ms. Hendriks shooed him offstage, calling, "Alice? Missy? Let's do your Act I scene now."

Hadrian, meanwhile, disappeared behind the curtains. Mikey watched for where he would emerge. But he didn't come out, not from either side of the stage.

Probably he was scurrying around backstage, hiding behind some flats or something. She didn't know why he should be scurrying away from her, and she planned to let him know that as soon as he came out. It wasn't as if she was about to stuff him into trash cans or anything. She'd thought he was someone who liked her, or at least someone who didn't mind her. Especially if he was her secret-admirer telephone caller from last year.

Mikey was feeling pretty relaxed and good about herself. She had the feeling that, beginning with her brilliant Andre Agassi comparison, she had entered the zone. If this was tennis, and she was playing in the zone, what she would do next would be to go on the attack. She would head for the net and try to force an error. Mikey slid on over to the aisle and strode up it until she came to row three. There she went in to sit right up next to Sally.

"Who—?" Sally said.

Richard kept his arm tight around his girlfriend's shoulder. "Can't you tell when you're not wanted?" He leaned forward a little bit so Mikey could see past Sally's head to his unfriendly face.

Sally's was the question Mikey chose to answer. "I'm Margalo's friend. In fact"—she smiled at the two of them, *You don't want to hear this, but you can't stop me*—"I was with her when she discovered she'd been robbed."

She waited, in case either one of them had something to say. Like, for example, "You mean after I stole her two hundred and nineteen dollars?" But they just looked at her as if she was seriously weird. Neither one of them spoke.

Their silence surprised her. She'd have thought Richard at least would say something, like "So what?" Without their saying something, Mikey couldn't think of what came next. She just sat there staring back at them, waiting, like a player who has made a weak net shot watching the ball sit up high, watching the opponent draw his racket back to fire off a shot right past her. She was cross at herself. She should have had something ready to say next. But what could it have been? Maybe—

"Where was that, exactly?" Sally asked, politely curious. "On the bus?"

Why would Sally want to pretend to be interested in where Margalo was when she found out she'd been robbed? This was making no sense to Mikey, but in tennis terms it was a returnable shot so she said, "At the bank. She'd already filled out the deposit slip." And why *not* go for a put-away? "Personally? My theory? I think you did it."

"Me?" asked Richard, and, "Me?" asked Sally. They looked at each other, little private smiles dancing up at the corners of their mouths.

"Who do you think you are—Columbo?" Richard said, mocking.

"No, she's Jessica Fletcher. You know, Richard, in *Murder, She Wrote*."

"You watch that?"

"My grandmother does," Sally explained.

"If you want an alibi," Richard told Mikey, smirking, "at the time of the crime me and Sally were in a place we know. A private place. We were *together*. Do you want to know more?" He raised and lowered his eyebrows at her, and Sally giggled, burying her face against his shoulder, protesting, "Richard! You're terrible!"

Mikey got up then, but before she went away she leaned towards them to ask—angling the ball over so close to the net nobody could possibly get to it—"Did I say, I think you could have been in it *together*?"

That was her exit line. Where *had* Hadrian scurried away to, anyway? She was already going to be in trouble for being late to basketball so she'd have to ask Margalo about it on the way home.

But Margalo derailed that conversation by starting out, "Ms. Hendriks doesn't want you at any more rehearsals. She said that no nonparticipants should be present, but she really meant you." After that they had to talk about abuses of power, if this was one, and democratic rights, if the auditorium was a public place, open to everyone, and then if students had any democratic rights. So Mikey just had to act on her own.

She telephoned Hadrian after supper. This, when she thought about it, really served him right, since it was his own phone calls last year that had gotten him into whatever trouble he thought he was in with her. She dialed the number she found in the phone book, the only Klenk listed, and when a woman answered, she asked for Hadrian.

The woman said, but not to her, "It's for Hadrian."

"A phone call for Hadrian?" said a man's voice.

"It's a girl, I think."

"A girl's calling for Hadrian?" the man said.

"You get him," the woman said. Then, "Hello? He'll be here in a minute. You hold on."

Mikey held on.

After a few long seconds the woman said, "Are you there? Did you hold on?"

"Yes," Mikey told her. Was it possible that Hadrian was the most normal person in his family?

"I couldn't hear you breathing."

Mikey waited some more, until finally the woman asked, "Are you still there? Because here he is."

After muffled conversation—which sounded like, "Give it

to me," and, "I was just holding her on the phone for you"—
"Hello?" came Hadrian's cautious voice.

Mikey had decided to give him a taste of his own medicine.
"So I want to talk to you tomorrow morning, before homeroom, in the library. You don't have to worry. You won't be
alone with me," she said, and hung up before he could say
anything. Hadrian Klenk wasn't the only person who could
ambush people on the phone.

Then Mikey spent a few minutes just sitting there, smiling
at the telephone, thinking over her day's work. She was
entirely pleased with herself, until she realized that the one
person who would really admire what she'd done was the one
person she couldn't tell about it. Not about *all* of it, anyway,
only about the Hadrian part. But that was something, and
she picked up the phone to punch number one on speed dial,
Margalo's number.

— 13 —

Settling Accounts

When Mikey and Margalo got to the library the next morning, Hadrian was waiting for them.

Because the library was supposed to be the symbolic center of the school, the architect who designed the building put it in the geographic center. The librarian worked behind a large, curved countertop, and spreading out around his desk, like rays of a sun in a little kid's drawing, were the stacks of books and racks of newspapers and magazines. The library had computers, also, and a media room and—wherever they could be fit in—tables, at one of which Hadrian Klenk sat, the prisoner at the defendant's table in a courtroom, looking nervous, just waiting, his hands folded on the table in front of him.

He didn't look taller, older, or wise that morning. Not a bit of it. He looked like a nervous kid.

Mikey and Margalo marched up to him.

Hadrian had already waited and worried more than he could stand. He started right in talking, before they had even sat down. "I'm sorry," he said to Mikey. "And I'm sorry to you, too, Margalo. I just made that first phone call, I don't know why. Because sometimes I just want to go ahead and do what I want to do instead of backing off? So I called, and it was fun, so I called again—and I got better and better at it. But I didn't mean to . . ." His voice faded off, as if he couldn't even imagine what it was that would make them feel more kindly towards him if they knew he had never meant to do it.

Mikey and Margalo sat down facing Hadrian, and they looked at each other at the end of this little speech. Mikey spoke first.

"Don't be a jerk. I liked talking to you."

"You did?"

"And it was a mystery."

"You really did?"

Margalo affirmed it. "She did. We called you her secret admirer."

Hadrian's cheeks turned bright pink. All he could say was, "I'm sorry."

"Sorry for what this time?" asked Mikey, but Margalo cut in, "Having a secret admirer is good for someone's ego."

"Even Mikey?" Margalo was the person Hadrian asked about this.

"Yes," Margalo said. "Even Mikey."

Mikey had had enough of this subject. "I've been evicted from rehearsals," she told Hadrian.

"But I'll be fine now," Hadrian said. "I'll tell Ms. Hendriks. If you want to come to rehearsals, then I think you should be able to."

"It wasn't just disturbing *you*," Margalo said. "Mikey was asking questions."

"About your money. Did you figure out anything?"

The way Hadrian was looking at Mikey, she didn't know *what* he was thinking, so she asked him outright, "Are you still my secret admirer? Because whatever Margalo says, I don't think I want one."

Hadrian blushed again. "I used to be, in sixth grade, and fifth, too, maybe seventh, but—you know, maybe I could be gay, because a lot of actors are."

"That's stupid," Mikey responded, but Margalo could only gape across the library table at this squirty little ninth-grade wimpoid dork who had just been bold enough to say what he had just said. "Aren't you scared by having an idea like that?" she finally asked.

"No," answered Hadrian. "Why should I be afraid of an idea in my own head? It's the ideas in other people's heads that are scary."

"And it's not as if you're handsome," said Mikey, who never noticed when she wasn't following a conversation.

"I could get handsome," Hadrian pointed out. "After high

school a lot of actors do. Or there's Dustin Hoffman, he's not handsome. I think it's a reasonable ambition."

The bell rang then, and they stood up to head off for homeroom. "I'm glad we had this talk," Hadrian said to Mikey first and then to Margalo, in a voice deeper than the one they'd just been hearing come out of him. He reached across the table to shake their hands, as if he were a multimillionaire investor agreeing to back their fledgling company. Without hesitation, they both reached out to shake, and it wasn't until they were out in the hallway that they realized how Hadrian had stolen their scene away from them, and had the last word, too.

Mikey glared at Margalo, who just said, "I *told* you he could act."

Actually, Margalo was relieved that Mikey wasn't going to be present at these final rehearsals. Ms. Hendriks was right, Mikey did make things even worse, and they couldn't afford for that to happen. The play had enough problems without adding Mikey to them.

As she entered the auditorium, John Baker and John Lawrence stepped out from the dim shadows behind the last row of seats. "Margalo," they said, low voiced, motioning her to join them. Then all they did was offer her a business-size envelope, sealed shut, no address, no stamp.

"What is it?" She didn't take it. Probably it was a petition asking her to drop Drama. If it was, she thought, probably she'd do just that.

229

John Baker said, "It's for you."

John Lawrence said, "It's from all of us. Well, almost all."

"We signed it."

"Because we wish your money hadn't been stolen."

"Just take it."

So she did and they went down together to join the others, who were sitting in the front rows waiting to be called to perform. Ms. Hendriks was asking, "Margalo? Has anyone seen Margalo?" so Margalo just jammed the envelope into the pocket of her skirt and ran up the side steps onto the stage, dreading the day's rehearsal.

But the rehearsal went well—went really well, in fact. Actors got their lines right and moved comfortably around the stage. When Ms. Hendriks stopped a scene to do it again and better, they listened to her, tried the changes, and did better. Every now and then Ms. Hendriks looked at Margalo with raised, inquiring eyebrows, but Margalo just shook her head. She had no idea. At the end Ms. Hendriks said only, "Good work, people. I *knew* you could do it. You're going to be *something* by Friday."

"Yeah, yeah," was the mumble. "So you say." But all at once they were feeling pretty good about their chances.

It wasn't until after rehearsal, when people had picked up the knapsacks and sweaters that had been piled at the front of the auditorium and gone off home, that Margalo remembered the envelope in her pocket. She pulled it out and looked at it.

"Do you know what this is?" she asked Hadrian, who had waited with her.

"If it came from John and John I do," he said. "Open it."

Margalo ripped the envelope open as they walked up the main aisle and out through the big doors into the broad hallway. Inside the envelope were thick sheets of paper, folded up. She unfolded them.

But it wasn't sheets of paper. It was one sheet of paper folded around ten bills, ten twenty-dollar bills.

There was no message on the paper, just signatures. And the signatures weren't even real people, except probably each actor had signed for his or her own role. Margalo counted, twenty-three signatures.

Odd because there were twenty-four parts in the play.

But one of the signatures was Ms. Jeanette Hendriks.

Margalo just stood still where she was, right outside the auditorium doors, right in the hallway. She had the money in one hand and the signed paper in the other. She stared at the paper.

"What's the matter?" Hadrian asked. "We didn't think you'd mind."

"I don't," Margalo said. "Not a bit. The opposite, in fact," she realized. In fact, it was suddenly almost as if no one had ever stolen any money from her at all.

Not that she didn't know they had. And not that she wasn't still nineteen dollars short. But somehow, if everybody cared enough to all chip in something to get her money back to her, even though twenty-three of them hadn't been responsible, twenty-four counting Ms. Hendriks, then Margalo didn't feel so bad. Not about being robbed and not about what people were like.

"This is . . . ," she said to Hadrian, but she was smiling too broadly to say more.

He backed away, probably afraid she might hug him.

And maybe that wasn't so stupid, because Margalo certainly felt like hugging someone. She wanted some outlet for this energy of gladness, and relief. "Let's tell Mikey. Come on. I wonder who didn't sign," Margalo said as they headed for the school entrance.

"People who didn't chip in."

"That, I figured out for myself. What I don't know is who that is."

"Richard and Sally," Hadrian told her. At first he didn't notice that she had stopped dead in her tracks again. He didn't notice until he had gone about twelve paces and she wasn't right behind him. He turned around to look for her.

"Margalo?"

"Richard and Sally?"

"Come on," Hadrian urged her, then reported, "They said since they hadn't done it they weren't about to pay for it. Which makes sense but nobody paid any attention to them."

Now Margalo hurried to catch up to him. "Richard and Sally," she announced with satisfaction.

"I *told* you. Twice."

❖

They were seated on the bus, Mikey beside the window, before Margalo showed her the envelope. "What's that?" Mikey asked, not reaching for it, since Margalo so obviously wanted her to.

"Money," Margalo said, deliberately and, she hoped, irritatingly minimalist.

"How much?"

"Two hundred dollars."

"Where'd you get it?"

"In this envelope."

"Where'd you get the envelope?"

"At rehearsal."

Watching Mikey be patient and calm, when what she really wanted to do was take you by the throat and squeeze information out of you like toothpaste from a tube, was more fun than telling her straightaway what she'd learn in the end. Margalo watched Mikey take a deep breath and press her lips tight.

Then Margalo watched Mikey's expression change to her *Gotcha!* smile. "They paid you back," Mikey announced.

Watching Margalo figure out that somebody had gotten ahead of her, then try to figure out a way to get herself up on top of the situation again, always made Mikey feel better. She knew that she'd never—not for years, anyway—be able to tell Margalo all about it, but at least she would take a little of the wind out of Margalo's sails right now.

"I'm beginning to think you're right about Richard and Sally," Margalo said then.

That one Mikey couldn't work out for herself. "Why?"

Margalo explained what had led her to her conclusion. "They're probably getting a good laugh out of everyone else repaying the money and them saying it's not fair so they won't do it."

"I was right!" crowed Mikey.

"Probably," cautioned Margalo.

"They won't get away with it," Mikey assured her.

Margalo disagreed. "They have. They are."

"But now we know."

"Now we *think* we know."

"*Now* is the time to start accusing people," Mikey decided.

Margalo shook her head. "You keep forgetting the play. Today's rehearsal went really well, probably because this money . . . When almost everybody pitches in to do something," Margalo explained, "it's like a team. The cast in a play is like a team. Now they feel like they've done something good together, which is good for the play. I better figure out some kind of thank-you," she concluded, rising as the bus came to her stop.

"Just remember who figured the whole thing out right from the start," Mikey told her.

Margalo spent the first minutes of the Wednesday rehearsal checking on the costumes, making a note of any that needed buttons or hems sewed by the volunteer mothers. Thursday was dress rehearsal and everything should be ready for that, since Friday was the first performance, when everything *had* to be ready. That done, she went out front to watch what Ms. Hendriks was doing onstage. She made a point of thanking everyone she met for contributing to the envelope of money—except, of course, Richard and Sally.

That day's rehearsal went over, and over, the last act of *Our Town*, the graveyard scene, with most of the cast onstage, many seated in chairs that had been set out over half the stage in rows to look like cemetery tombstones. Two of the cast members not onstage when Margalo went out front were Richard and Sally, Sally being the dead character who was going to be left off after her funeral, and Richard playing her widowed young husband. They were sitting together on a side aisle, waiting for their cues. He had his arm around her. She looked up as Margalo passed in front of them, on her way to the side steps onto the stage. "Hey, Margalo," Sally called in a voice so quiet it wouldn't disturb the actors or the director.

Margalo stopped, turned back, approached the two of them. Prime suspects. She wanted to hear what they would say, so she just waited in front of them. Let *them* end the silence.

After a while, "So you got your money back," Sally said.

"Most of it."

Margalo waited some more to see where Sally wanted this conversation to go.

"Nineteen dollars is nothing," Sally eventually told her. Margalo shrugged.

"So why do you think they did it? Took up the collection, I mean," Sally asked. "I already know why we didn't contribute," she said, and now she was the one waiting.

Richard was looking intently at the stage, as if he was seeing the play for the first time and couldn't wait to find out how it ended, as if he had no interest in whatever it was those two girls were talking about, probably boring gossip.

"I think I know that too," Margalo said. "But it doesn't matter," she added quickly, waiting a couple of beats before she said, "I mean, why people contributed or not doesn't matter."

Sally gave her a sharp look. "I'll tell you anyway. It's because I always hate group guilt. Don't we, Richard?"

"Yeah," mumbled Richard. "We're glad you got it back."

"Speak for yourself," Sally said, but she smiled to identify it as a joke.

Which Margalo didn't for one minute believe. But she had told the truth. It didn't matter. She didn't care all that much anymore, now that she was pretty sure she knew who had done it—these two—and now that everybody else had cared enough to try to make it up to her, which meant they *had* really agreed it shouldn't happen. And they were right about that, Margalo thought.

She smiled down at Sally, who was still smiling up at her.

"Confession is good for the soul," she advised, turning away before they could say anything else.

Why should they think they had gotten clean away with it?

At one point in Act III Richard's character, George, was off-stage for two long scenes, while Sally's character, Emily, joined the other dead people in the cemetery and then revisited a day in her life until it made her too unhappy, the way people kept not-seeing everything that life held for them, every minute, and she couldn't stand it, the way people wasted the little time they had to be alive in.

As far as Margalo was concerned, this was the best scene in the play, the scene that people would remember and think about after, and when someone sat down in the seat right next to hers, she barely looked over. Her attention was on all the production details—lighting, props, costumes. In fact, she only gave an annoyed glance at this person, to be sure whoever it was wouldn't start talking to her.

When she did that, she saw that it was Richard, for once on his own. And he wasn't watching Sally, he was looking instead at his knees, on which his two hands rested, each one balled up into a fist, as if he was about to start a round of one-potato, two-potato.

The only thing Margalo could think of to say was, "Richard?"

"It wasn't my idea," he told her, speaking so softly that she had to lean closer to hear him. "I didn't want to, but Sally . . .

Well, you know how it is once Sally gets an idea in her head."

Margalo, who didn't, didn't respond. She just stared at his profile.

"It wasn't anything personal. It was—The idea was that after graduation Sally and me would go and spend a week at the beach, in a motel, just the two of us. We're old enough, we're over eighteen, and the idea was that if we paid for it ourselves, the parents couldn't stop us. So . . . And since everybody knows you go to the bank on Fridays, we thought . . . We thought, why not start with you? So we did, and we got lucky. But then we couldn't do any more. Because—We didn't think you'd say anything because . . . Things get taken all the time. Everybody knows that, but it's way not cool to whine about it."

"I guess I'm not cool," Margalo said.

"We already knew that," Richard assured her. "But we thought—Anyway, everybody's been super careful ever since. You know? And two hundred nineteen dollars isn't nearly enough for a week at the beach, in June, so we got some other stuff instead, and now I don't think we'll get to go anywhere for graduation. Not by ourselves, anyway."

Richard unfisted his hands and flexed the fingers. He sat up straighter in his seat. "You know? You were right. I do feel better. Not that I was feeling bad, just . . . It was sort of like I was waiting to get caught. Sally's the one with guts. She says you can't prove anything, so what can happen to us?" He turned in the seat to look right at her. "You won't try to tell

238

anybody what I said to you, will you? Because what good would that do? Since we already spent the money and you already got it back. And besides, if you do, I'll deny it."

Margalo nodded. "I get that," she said.

"Everything's all right then," Richard said, and he slipped away.

Margalo returned to her job. She would think about all of this later, when she could talk about it to Mikey.

They were bouncing along home on the bus when Margalo acknowledged, "You were absolutely right about Richard and Sally."

"I know," Mikey said, without interest.

"What night are you coming to the play? Saturday will probably be the best performance."

"We can't Saturday, because it's Saturday," and that was, in fact, enough explanation for Margalo. "But what about your dishwashing on Saturdays?" Mikey realized.

"They finally agreed to shift the schedule and give me a night off. Angie didn't want to do it. I almost had to ask you to fill in for me so I wouldn't get fired."

"Not on Saturday," Mikey repeated.

"It's actually going to be good," Margalo said. "The play," she added, since Mikey seemed to be unable to keep track of the conversation. What was wrong with Mikey?

She didn't have to wait long to find out. As soon as nobody had said anything for about half a minute, Mikey announced,

"Tan's going out for Track, not Tennis." She looked out the window at the houses they were rumbling past. "She wouldn't listen to me. She might listen to you."

"Nobody would listen to my opinion about what sport they should take."

"I guess not. I guess, some people, you can't tell them anything. Anyway, at least spring starts next week."

"Spring doesn't start until the twenty-first. That's the week *after* next, Mikey. I thought you were keeping such careful count."

Reminded, Mikey told her, "This week is number twenty-three." She worked it out further. "That means only thirteen to go, which is not a lucky number. What if your play bombs?"

"Not with Hadrian in the lead it won't."

"Yes, but what if it does? I'm definitely going to see it Friday," Mikey said. Then she told Margalo some really good news. "Monday's the start of the spring tennis season." Then she realized, "That makes it spring, so I'm right. Again."

III

Mikey Springs

— 14 —

Getting to the Top

When Mikey arrived on that mid-March Monday, Coach Sandy was posting the tennis ladders on the bulletin board outside her office. They were both a few minutes early for the first practice of the spring season. They were both dressed for tennis, the coach in a short pleated shirt and a Windbreaker, Mikey in shorts and a warm-up jacket. Mikey had her tennis bag, the coach had her clipboard.

Coach Sandy had put all the slips of paper for the girls' ladder into their slots and now she was working on the boys', starting at the top, with Mark Jacobs. Fiona Timmerley was at the top of the girls' ladder, a strong all-court player, a match Mikey was looking forward to. She herself occupied slot six.

Mikey studied the ladder, thinking about when she could schedule her first challenge match. No sooner than Wednesday, that was her guess. Probably there would be some intensive drilling to bring people back to their fall level of play, since as far as she knew she was the only person who had kept on over the winter. So probably people wouldn't accept a challenge before Wednesday or maybe even Thursday. There was time before the team's first match, plenty of time to play her way into the number one position. But she should challenge Deborah today for Thursday. "Exactly when is the team's first match?" she asked.

"Aren't you the eager beaver," the coach answered.

Mikey didn't disagree. "But when?"

"April twelfth, it's a Monday."

Mikey was trying to remember the strengths of Deborah's game; she thought it was at the net, and she didn't remember Deborah being all that effective at net. After Deborah there was Bev, who wore you down with moon balls; but Mikey could run around a court forever—or practically forever— and sooner or later there would be a chance at an overhead. Given a chance at an overhead, Mikey had the point.

"Daydreaming?" the coach asked.

"I'm already on the team." She pointed to her name in position six.

"My guess," said the coach as she slotted Hal Weathersing into his number six position, "is that you have your eye on number one."

Mikey shrugged and bent to pick up her tennis bag.

"That would be a first, a ninth grader and number one girl player," the coach said.

Mikey straightened her out. "It's nothing to do with what grade I'm in. It's about being the best, because I am."

Coach Sandy looked at her, measuring. "You have a lot to learn, Elsinger."

"Except for you, but you're the coach," Mikey said.

Other people were coming up by then to remind themselves where they were on the ladders. About forty people had signed up for tennis, and the squad Coach Sandy would play in matches would be sixteen of them, twelve on the team itself and four alternates. Those who wanted to see if they had a chance to be on the squad jostled in close to the bulletin board. The others, who had no chance, hung back, continuing their conversations.

"Do you think Kellie would ever go to the prom with me? Or does she already have a date?"

"I can't believe I didn't get an A. Mine was the longest report of anybody's."

"Chet Parker's getting a car for graduation, did you hear? And he's letting Ronnie go with him to pick it out."

"It's just the usual—my parents are so convinced the other one is letting me get away with stuff, and my dad can't stand my mom's boyfriend, so yeah, life's not too much fun for me these days."

"Don't let them get you down."

"They never want me to leave the house. I wish they'd just trust me a little."

"Don't let them get you down."

"Did you hear about Rhonda? She's been born again. Check out her hair—and her shoes."

"Are Richard and Sally breaking up? Because what I heard is, he hasn't asked her to the prom yet."

"Maybe I'll go out for Drama next year. I don't have a chance for the tennis team anyway."

"But when else will you get to have a professional—I mean a real professional—for a coach? I mean, you know how we did last year, and there's Mikey now. How good is she really?"

"She can't be as good as she thinks."

Ha! Mikey thought. But maybe she was, and what if she was? She was miles better than any other girl, except for Fiona—and she expected she could beat Fiona without too much trouble. First, however, she had to get herself into the number two position. She figured that wouldn't take more than a week.

Coach Sandy tossed a spanner into that plan right away. "Before we head out to the courts," she said to her assembled players, "I want to announce that there will be no ladder challenges played until next Wednesday. That is, a week from Wednesday. The twenty-fourth. Everybody got that?" She looked right at Mikey, and smiled, to explain, "Nobody would want to have an unfair advantage just because they happened to play all winter, would they?"

Mikey wasn't so sure about that. If you worked and got ahead, did that constitute an unfair advantage? She went up to the coach as they all left the gym to go down to the tennis courts, but Coach Sandy didn't give her the chance to say anything. "Don't get yourself in a dander, Elsinger. I want you playing on my team. You're not the only one who really wants to win."

So Mikey challenged Deborah for the twenty-fourth, or the twenty-fifth if they couldn't be scheduled onto a court first thing. Deborah was a junior, too old, you'd think, to have any illusions about the level of her tennis skills. But her blue eyes teared over when she was challenged, and she said, "I knew it. I've never been on a varsity team, and now— if I'm number six, anyone could challenge me. And I can't re-challenge you for a week." She said this as if she hoped that hearing it would make Mikey not ask for the match.

But if it wasn't Mikey knocking Deborah down the ladder, it would be somebody else, so Mikey offered the only consolation she could think of. "There's next year. Fiona and Chrissie and Bev are all seniors. If you work, you should have a shot at it next year."

"Thanks a lot," Deborah said, and walked away, whipping at the air with her racket, going up to a couple of other juniors to say something that caused them all to look over at Mikey.

Well, she didn't care. She'd never been popular, and it wasn't as if she thought playing good tennis was going to change that.

"But I don't get it," she told Margalo that weekend. "Everybody wanted Martina Hingis to get to be number one, and that was in the whole world. We're just a high school tennis team."

"She was cute," Margalo explained. "She was perky. When she won the Australian, she went running over to the stands to jump up and kiss her mother."

"Can you imagine my mother if I tried something like that on her?" Mikey asked. "They can't stop me," she said.

"Do you think they want to?"

"I think they'd like to."

"You could pretend to be perky and cute. I could help, we'd buy you some clothes, we'd cut your hair and—Have you ever used a curling iron? I could loan you some mascara, too, and what about lipstick? Do you even own a lipstick?"

"Ha, ha," Mikey said. "They can't turn me cute, and they can't stop me either."

Certainly, on the Wednesday, Deborah couldn't stop her; she couldn't even hold serve. The next day Mikey played Bev, who got the ball back, high and soft. Bev did manage to take one game off of Mikey, and it was one of Mikey's service games too, a long deuce game, with Mikey running all over the court trying to get a good shot. Then Mikey netted a backhand overhead and then—this was weird—double-faulted, on a first serve so neatly tucked into the corner that Mikey would have sworn it was in, and then a second serve that went just wide. Since Mikey was still up 5–1 in games, she just won the next one to take the set.

Anne Crehan, on Friday, did hold serve once, when a couple of Mikey's shots went long—"Just barely," Anne called, calls Mikey agreed with—and then a couple of Anne's drop shots took Mikey by surprise before she learned to look out for them. But Anne was the kind of player that as soon as she thinks she's going to lose starts playing badly. Trying too hard for a winner, thinking too much, caring too much. So by the last weekend in March, Mikey was the number three girl player and had challenged Chrissie for Monday, Fiona the day after. Chrissie would be no trouble, Mikey was sure of it.

But she was wrong, as she realized at 3–all on Monday afternoon when time ran out on them. She had broken Chrissie once, and Chrissie had broken back right away, although . . . Mikey wasn't sure. How could she be sure without a camera on the ball? There was that unwritten rule that if you weren't sure the ball was out, you called it in. It was a fair-play rule, and it meant that you could play a match without someone there to make the line calls for you. If you couldn't play without an umpire, you wouldn't be able to play at all, most of the time, unless you were a professional. So this was the kind of rule that actually worked to everybody's advantage. But with Chrissie, if there was any chance that a ball of Mikey's might be out, it was called out. Sometimes, Mikey thought, a ball was called out even when there was no chance at all.

"It's no fun playing like that," she told Margalo on the bus going home. Margalo was already working on her next production, *Oklahoma!* It was a musical, and Mikey had let

Margalo know pretty clearly how she felt about musicals. It was a mild end-of-March day, practically warm. "How can she feel like she's won if she's cheated?"

"Are you sure about it?" Margalo wondered, although she thought, Mikey being Mikey, she would be sure, and she was probably right, too.

"How *can* I be sure? I'm on the other side of the net. I'm watching her, I'm getting set to return whatever her next shot is. I can barely make good calls on my own side of the net, which is why there's this unwritten rule. I'm going to have to figure out how to keep her from doing that," she announced. "Any ideas?"

"Easy—don't give her the chance. I mean, she wouldn't cheat openly, would she?"

"*That* she'd never get away with."

"So are you good enough to keep everything well inside the lines?"

"Of course. But you're right—Maybe I'll just fire everything right down the center, right at her. That'll teach her."

That was what Mikey did when they finished their match on Tuesday. She whipped her ground strokes as hard as she could—and that was pretty hard—either right down the middle or right at Chrissie, and sometimes both. That finished off the set and put her in second place. She challenged Fiona for the next afternoon's practice before she went to report to Coach Sandy's office about the results of that day's match.

"I saw some pretty aggressive play from you," Coach Sandy remarked.

Was this praise or criticism? Mikey couldn't tell.

"I wonder how you'll do against Fiona," the coach said, not as if she cared very much. "Fiona's got some good shots, a nice variety, and she plays a smart game. She's going to give you a match," the coach predicted.

The coach was correct. The match between Mikey Elsinger and Fiona Timmerley took three days to complete. There were deuce games that lasted for eight or ten ad points. There were points that took ten or more shots to complete. Fiona kept Mikey deep in the court with hard, flat shots and low-arcing lobs that she couldn't run down; Mikey followed her serve into the net to draw a put-away or force a low-percentage passing shot. They left the court on Wednesday and Thursday, the set incomplete, both of them tired, exhilarated, and resolute. Mikey was ahead four games to two, with one service break. On Friday she took both games, both of them hard fought, the deuce advantage veering back and forth between the two players, both playing error-free tennis. Mikey won the set, but it had never been a sure thing. "That was good," she said, shaking hands at the net. "I wouldn't mind doing that again."

"Don't I get a week to recover?" Fiona grinned.

A few other team members had stopped to watch them play: Roy Garo, Mark Jacobs, and Hal Weathersing; Tammy Evans, whom Mikey hadn't played with, or noticed, since the fall, hand in hand with another ninth-grade tennis player, Ralph, who was reminding everyone, "I was her doubles partner last year." Mark approached the two girls to say, "Good game."

"Yeah," Mikey agreed.

"Not quite good enough," was Fiona's opinion.

Walking to the bank, Margalo asked, "How were the calls this time?" Mikey's answer was immediate, "Fine, of course." All of the calls had been as good as they could be when you were calling balls for yourselves. The set had been tennis the way it's supposed to be. Then Margalo asked, "What did Coach Sandy have to say about you winning the top spot?" and Mikey realized that the coach hadn't said anything.

"Not that I *want* her to say anything," Mikey said. "Not that I care. But you'd think—"

Margalo had a theory, of course. "Some coaches make it as hard as they can, like drill sergeants? They're particularly hard on the most promising players." They were crossing in front of her restaurant then, and she looked inside to see if there were any early diners, but the big room was empty, the tables set and waiting.

"That *is* Coach Sandy's style," Mikey said. "She really wants to win the regionals this year, and after that probably the state championships, too. She did pretty well last year with her team, and this year they're probably better because they've had a year more of her coaching. And there's me, too."

"Unless she thinks if everybody on the team hates having

a ninth grader at the top of the girls' ladder, they'll all try harder. Play better. If they all really want to bring you down," Margalo suggested.

That made sense to Mikey. In fact, she kind of liked the possibility. She smiled, *Let them try.* In fact, she was feeling pretty good, walking downtown with Margalo on a spring afternoon with a lot of daylight left. "How did Aurora do on that paper you helped her with?" she asked Margalo, to spread some of her good feelings around.

The next Monday, which was the first Monday in April, twenty-six school weeks done and gone, Mikey felt for the first time as if ninth grade might not be so bad after all. She was the number one girl player on the tennis team, which impressed the few people who didn't mind her, and annoyed the majority, who did. If she couldn't be impressive, Mikey was satisfied to be annoying, and besides, she was playing a lot of tennis, six days a week, all spring long, how could she not feel good? Thinking of all spring long, she realized—and announced—"There are only ten weeks left. To the school year," she specified, since most of the people at the lunch table greeted the news with blank faces.

Margalo, who had listened to more of Mikey's counting down than the others, just nodded her head inattentively.

"That means today is day fifty. That means tomorrow will be forty-nine."

When Mikey said that, Margalo could see for the first

time how the numbers rolled relentlessly on, like a truck wheel clicking off each complete rotation, unstoppably counting backwards until they got to zero, year's end, ninth grade over forever. When Margalo got that, she began to share Mikey's pleasure. "And after that forty-eight," she said.

"Well, dunhh," said Cassie.

Mikey looked sternly at Margalo. "You're jumping the gun. What's gun in Latin?"

"There is no word for gun because there weren't any guns then. I'm just counting my chickens."

Casey looked up from her book. "You're counting *Mikey's* chickens."

"Or burning my bridges? Am I burning my bridges before they're hatched?"

"Counting your chickens before they're burned?" Casey offered. "Before they're fried?"

Mikey had a limited interest in this form of foolishness. "Today is fifty," she repeated, "and I'm the number one girl on the tennis team."

"Not bad," Tim said, clapping his hands softly together.

Mikey looked around at all the people gathered there—Tim and Felix, Casey and Cassie and Jace, Hadrian, Margalo. Probably only Margalo would really get it, but she wanted to tell them all. "I tried to challenge Mark Jacobs to a match, but . . ." She hesitated.

"He wouldn't do it, would he?" Cassie crowed. "Isn't that just like those jocks?"

"No," Mikey said. "It's Coach Sandy who won't let me."

"You asked permission?" Jace demanded. "I thought you were smarter than that, Mikey."

"You think Peter Paul's the only adult in the world who makes sense," Cassie told him. "You don't even get it that the guy's a windbag."

"Just because he didn't like your fruit sculpture. Or your textile montage."

"Those were great pieces," Cassie pointed out. "You think so too, you said so."

Jace shrugged. "Maybe I was wrong."

While Cassie struggled with her possible responses—crowing over Jace for admitting an error, or berating him for spinelessness—Margalo got back to the interesting subject. "Why *won't* Coach Sandy let you challenge Mark?"

"She said, That's not the way it's done in tennis. She said, Mark Jacobs wouldn't want to play me anyway."

"Maybe he wouldn't want to because he'd be afraid you'd beat him," said Hadrian loyally.

"Maybe he wouldn't because he's a jerk," Cassie suggested.

"Maybe he just doesn't want to hurt her feelings," Jace suggested, and Tim added, "Or have a bad effect on your self-confidence, because—if you think of it—he's got to think about what's good for the team. Because you're sup-posed to be such a hot player, they need you feeling confi-dent."

"Maybe," said Casey, closing *The Stranger*, which she had

just finished, and laying her hand on top of the slim volume, "Maybe in the long run it doesn't matter. If you play him or if you don't. Why he wouldn't or shouldn't play you. Or even who wins, if you were to play. I mean, what difference will it really make, however it turns out?"

That was too difficult a question for Monday lunch, so except for Felix they pretended that Casey hadn't spoken, since she usually didn't. Felix glanced at her and said, "Deep." Casey glanced at Margalo, but Margalo knew better than to try to discuss existentialism, or nihilism, or maybe just history, at that time of day, in that place. Although she didn't want Casey to think she didn't know just about exactly what the girl meant. "Do you think I should read that?" she asked, and Casey passed the book over to her, saying, "See what you think."

Mikey tried to grab it away, but Margalo held on firmly.

"I can read too," Mikey said, and she might read it, and if she did, probably she'd have some unexpected and interesting ideas, too. But Margalo elected to divert her. "Do you think Coach Sandy's decision is against Title Nine?"

On the bus ride home that day Mikey was still carrying on about inequality in the sports programs. "For another example, the boys' JV basketball got a lot more practice time than the girls'—Tan said the same thing. And their coach played on his college basketball team, at least. Ours is a Biology teacher and all she did was play high school basketball. I don't think she was even on her varsity team. They'd never do that to a boys' team. It's entire inequality."

"That's the way sports are," Margalo said. "Except tennis."

"Absolutely," Mikey agreed. "Another reason for me to get to challenge Mark Jacobs."

The logic of this escaped Margalo.

Grandfather clock Mikey began to toll the days—forty-nine, forty-eight, forty-seven—until they expected the lunchtime announcement, and even anticipated hearing it. "Day forty-six," she could say on Friday, and add to that good news, "End of week twenty-seven. We have a match against Woodrow Wilson on Monday."

"Not Woodrow Wilson personally, I take it," said Jace, grinning around the table.

Mikey was accustomed to being misunderstood. "It's a school," she explained, and even Margalo didn't know if that was meant to be a joke. Mikey was on a roll, and Mikey on a roll might try just about anything.

Walking away from school that day, with the spring late-afternoon light cool and golden, just the two of them together heading down the sidewalk among ordinary people, people of all ages, not just kids and teachers, they didn't say anything for a few minutes, just walked along and looked and listened. Finally, "How much are you depositing today?" Mikey asked.

"Two hundred forty-eight dollars and twenty-five cents. I like getting a regular paycheck."

"Maybe I'll get a job too."

"You'd like working."

"Maybe I'll get a job at your restaurant."

"It's not my restaurant," Margalo said. "So? Did you ask Mark Jacobs what he thought about playing you?"

"I was told not to," Mikey said. And smiled. *Of course I did.*

"What did he say?"

"He said, He wouldn't mind it. He said, It looked like I might be fun to beat." Mikey smiled again. "I said, I was thinking *he'd* be fun to beat, and he said—catch this—he said, It was too bad I was only in ninth grade, I was more entertaining than most girls and he didn't have a date for the prom." Mikey shook her head at the stupidity of some people. She'd cut her boyfriend teeth on Shawn Macavity last year, so she knew most of the flirty tricks boys liked to try on girls. "I said, I was looking for a tennis date, a game, and was he asking me to the prom or just putting out hot air?"

This time she and Margalo grinned at each other. Margalo was as pleased with Mikey as Mikey was with herself—and that was pretty pleased. "So, when will you play him?"

"Probably not for a while, if ever. Mark says he won't sneak around behind Coach Sandy's back, *and* he said I'd have to challenge my way up the boys' ladder to earn the right to challenge him."

"A cop-out."

"Not really. But I told him, He was planning to graduate before I had a chance at him, and he said, That's for sure."

"That's pretty funny," Margalo said.

Mikey tried looking at it from Margalo's angle. "I guess. Yeah, I guess it is."

"Flattering, too," Margalo observed.

"Coach Sandy will probably figure out a way to keep it from happening."

"I thought you liked her."

"It's confusing," Mikey admitted.

"I used to think I knew something about people," Margalo admitted.

"I know," Mikey said. "I used to think you did too." Then she had a cheering thought. "I'm playing my first ever varsity match on Monday. Are you going to come watch me?"

— 15 —

Pretty Bad Stuff

The bright yellow tennis ball landed so close to the end line that Mikey could have called it out.

She wanted to call it out.

If she had called it out, it might have been the correct call.

But she had to call in it because she wasn't sure it was out. "Nice shot," she said, projecting her voice to the girl across the net. It was the tennis team's first match of the year, she was the only underclassman on the Varsity team, and she was playing a singles match against the number one female player of Woodrow Wilson High School, a senior. The girl was also over five ten, which gave her at least six inches on Mikey, an advantage not only in serving but also in speed around the court.

Mikey didn't mind being at a disadvantage. She enjoyed winning against the odds, and on paper she was the underdog in this contest. But her opponent was only big and fast. She had no strokes, she just ran and blasted.

Mikey had been blasting back. Her shots had fallen nice and deep, but too many of them had been called just long, and too many of those on key points. When her shots fell within the lines, Mikey was winning the points—her opponent just blasted wildly back.

This meant that Mikey had to play more cautiously, keep her shots safely in, and draw errors by moving her opponent around the court, from side to side, up and back. But she should have taken this set easily, 8-1 or 8-2. Instead the present score was seven games for Mikey, four for her opponent. Calling this last, doubtful ball in brought the score of the present game to 40–all.

The next point was one Mikey had to win, because not only did the sets in team matches get scored differently (the winner of the first to reach 8 games, with a 9-point tiebreaker at 7–all), but also the games. The games in team matches were played no-ad, which was like sudden death, since at 40–all whoever won the next point won the game. Mikey sent her first serve hard and into the T. "Out!" her opponent called, to Mikey's surprise. The second serve Mikey curved wide to the girl's forehand, and, "Out!" the girl called.

What? Mikey didn't think it was. But you didn't question calls.

That made it seven games for Mikey and five for the opponent. Mikey got ready to receive serve. She practiced the calm inner voice Coach Sandy had taught them. "I used it for years on the tour," she'd told them, not mentioning that it was the Satellite Tour, "before I settled down and got over my ambitions." Coach Sandy knew what she was talking about and she *had* improved Mikey's game a lot. This made it sort of a pity that Mikey's serve seemed to be off today. She had wanted to show her stuff with an easy win.

Now Mikey focused her attention and advised herself in a calm inner voice, "Return low, down the middle, hard." That would either draw an error or get a ball up in the air that she could put away. She advised herself, "Don't try for too much," because she wasn't having an accurate day. Apparently.

The sun was in her eyes, so she adjusted her cap and got ready to receive the first serve. *Hard and down the middle*, she reminded herself, whaling away with her best shot, the two-handed backhand.

Her return went hard, down the middle, and the girl backed up to get a racket on it, sending the tennis ball up into the air for Mikey to put away with an overhead smash that wasn't all that powerful but was perfectly placed.

Love–15.

The next two points went exactly the same way, except one called for a backhand overhead; but Mikey got a good angle on it. Love–40, and three chances to win the set. Mikey was in charge, and that was the way she liked it. In fact, she'd felt in charge of the entire set, but those just-out shots had cost her points.

The next serve that came at her was a smart one for a change, out wide to the backhand, and Mikey—her attention divided between calling the ball (Had it touched the line? Exactly what was she seeing? Was she seeing green all around the ball or not?) and setting up for the return—didn't get a good racket on the ball. Her shot floated up into the air and fell wide.

"Nice serve," Mikey called.

So now the score was 15–40, and Mikey reminded herself, *Hard, down the center.* When the serve came in to her forehand, she hit it hard but a little late so that it went crosscourt. That was a riskier shot, but the ball was in—inches of court showed all around. The set won, Mikey smiled, *One for me.* She shifted her racket to her left hand and approached the net to shake hands.

But her opponent was standing there looking at the line as if she wasn't sure that she'd lost the point, as if she was about to call the ball out.

"That was in," called a woman's voice from the sidelines, beyond the high fence. Coach Sandy had stopped by to see how Mikey's set was going.

"You're sure about that?" the opponent asked.

"No question."

"Well then, I guess you win." The girl held her hand out as she approached the net. "You're really a ninth grader?" They shook hands and the girl ran off, to cheer her teammates playing mixed doubles.

While Mikey was packing up her tennis bag, Coach Sandy came up behind her. "You should have had her eight–one, Elsinger. What went wrong?"

"I was hitting a little long mostly, although some of my shots did go just wide. I wasn't accurate enough," Mikey said.

"You sure about that?" Coach Sandy asked. She had little pale button eyes, and her face was almost always expressionless.

"I netted two, maybe three, but the bulk of my errors were over the lines."

"You *do* remember that the team totals all of its won games to score the match," Coach Sandy said.

Of course Mikey did.

"So winning your set isn't your only objective," Coach Sandy said. "Keeping their scores low matters too."

Mikey knew that. She had been told it many times since the start of the spring tennis season. The coach had taken them over the match scoring system once a day for the first two weeks of practice, which meant ten times. After time two Mikey understood all the differences in game and set scoring, and also about how a team won a match.

"We wanted to deny them those four extra games you let her take from you."

"I get it," Mikey said. "I get it. But it wasn't as if I wasn't trying."

Coach Sandy gave her usual response to that. "Try harder."

Mikey agreed with that way of looking at things, but she pointed out, "I won the set, didn't I?"

Coach Sandy froze, and stared straight at Mikey. "It should have been a walkover and it wasn't. You're supposed to be such a hotshot. Think about how that happened, Elsinger. Because it's not what we want to have happen again."

When the opposing team had climbed onto their bus and driven away, the team gathered outside Coach Sandy's office for her wrap-up speech, the twelve Varsity players waiting patiently for her to finish talking.

"The good news," Coach Sandy said, "is that we won the match." Before anyone could get too excited about that, she went on. "The bad news is—not one of you played anywhere near at the top of your game. You're just lucky Woodrow Wilson wasn't up to much. But you're not that lucky with me so I give you fair warning: I want to see better scores in your sets. Singles and doubles. If I don't see that, I can promise you, you won't continue to play on my team."

She stopped speaking and just looked over her tennis team, making eye contact with each one of them, letting the threat sink in.

Hal Weathersing raised his hand, which surprised the coach, but she said, "Yes?"

"Someone lifted my racket," Hal reported.

"If you'll wait a minute," she snapped.

"It's in your hand," Mark Jacobs pointed out.

"I mean my backup racket, from my tennis bag. I think one of those guys took it home with him because it's almost new."

"I'll look into it," Coach Sandy assured him, then went back to her speech. "When you barely beat a weak opponent, you shouldn't be satisfied with your performance. *I'm* certainly not, so think about that before practice tomorrow. Because you've got two more matches this week, only two, in which to prove to me you're players I can work with. Make a team out of. Make a winning tennis team out of." She turned her back on them and went into her office, her short pleated skirt bouncing from side to side in irritation. She tossed the door shut behind her. They saw her through the big window, putting on her windbreaker, unlocking a drawer to take out her purse.

People moaned and mumbled among themselves, "What's with her?" "How was I supposed to get that serve back? You saw that serve." "I had some really good points—I'd like to hear about those, too." Mikey, as the only underclassman on the team, had no one to moan and mumble with so she just left, heading down the hallway and out the big main door of the gym to meet up with Margalo and catch the bus.

Hadrian Klenk was waiting with Margalo, his knapsack hanging from his hand, looking like his everyday self. Mikey carried her knapsack over one shoulder and her tennis bag over the other. Margalo had her knapsack on her back.

"I won," Mikey greeted them, "but it was closer than it should have been."

"We saw the end of it," Margalo said.

"Do you ever use a slice backhand?" Hadrian asked.

"What do you know about tennis?" Mikey demanded.

"I watch television," he answered.

They walked down the sidewalk, away from the school buildings, Mikey in the middle. Margalo, the heavy knapsack on her back so that her hands were free to tuck her straight brown hair behind her ears, looked across Mikey to confer wordlessly with Hadrian before asking, "What do you mean, closer than it should have been?"

Hadrian cut in, looking across Mikey to Margalo, "Because we thought she made a lot of bad calls."

"A lot of them we're positive were bad," Margalo said.

"Especially your last service game," Hadrian said.

Mikey took that information in. "So I *was* making those serves? Good." Then she took the information in further. "She was cheating?"

"We're pretty sure," Margalo said. "On a lot of them."

"I didn't see you there," Mikey said.

Margalo observed, "You don't notice much when you're playing tennis."

"Focus is important," Mikey told her. Then she took in the information entirely. "She was *cheating*!"

When they arrived at the road, Hadrian left them. "My mother's waiting." He waved at the white Audi parked behind the Activities bus. "But there's no question about it. Ask your coach, she was watching too." He ran off. Mikey and Margalo watched.

"You're sure?" Mikey asked. "Coach Sandy was there for my last service game too?"

"Didn't you say, a couple of times in the sets you played on the tennis ladder, didn't you say you thought they were mis-calling?"

"That's different. A ladder challenge isn't like a real match. It's . . . it's just to make the team, not at all like playing against another school."

Margalo wasn't buying that. "It's exactly the same and you know you think so too."

Mikey didn't argue.

"So what are you going to do about it?"

Mikey didn't know, and she didn't want it to be true, either, so she changed the subject. "How was rehearsal?" she asked.

Margalo let her change it. "It went okay. Hadrian can't sing or dance, not really, but he acts like he can, and he's getting away with it so far."

On the bus she suggested to Mikey, "You could ask your dad."

"I should be able to handle it myself." This time Margalo had the window seat. "I'll ask Coach Sandy, but what I can't figure out," Mikey said, giving voice to what really worried her, "is, if she saw what was going on, like you did, why didn't she say something?"

"Because you were winning anyway?"

"That's what I think. But then she yelled at us because we didn't win by enough. So what's she after?"

"You're the competitive one," Margalo pointed out. "You should be able to figure her out."

"Yeah, but cheating is a fake victory. Do you cheat at solitaire? Because if you do and you win, you know how it feels like you haven't really won?"

"I don't play solitaire."

"But if you *did*."

The next day Mikey walked down to the tennis courts with Coach Sandy, which meant going side by side down the gym hallway carrying the long-handled metal baskets in which the practice balls were stored. Mikey carried two baskets, and her racket in its case over her shoulder. Coach Sandy carried one basket and her clipboard. The coach never brought a tennis racket. When she wanted to demonstrate a stroke or a move, she would take a racket from one of the players. "I'm here to teach you what I know," she explained. "Not to play. What do I need a racket for?" They all understood that her racket—except she probably had several of them—was too valuable a tool to be used with high school players on high school courts. They knew they were lucky to be coached by someone who'd really played the game, played professionally. They believed that she was way too good for this job, and she believed it too.

Coach Sandy moved fast, with energetic steps, her attention on her clipboard. Mikey had to hustle to keep up with her. They went down the long hallway and out the rear doors towards the playing fields—soccer and football and baseball and track. Beyond them were the six tennis courts, surrounded by a high wire fence. Some players had already arrived and were stretching out or running laps around the courts to warm up. From a distance they looked like little-kid-size dolls.

"Coach," Mikey said. "About yesterday. About my match."

Coach Sandy stopped. She turned to study Mikey out of her pale blue eyes. "What about it?" She was taller by a few inches, but they had the same build, stocky, muscles in their arms and legs, and they were both unsmiling types. There was no question in the coach's mind who was the kid and who was the coach.

There was no question in Mikey's mind either, although she wasn't sure just what that difference meant, if it meant as much as Coach Sandy thought it did. The coach sensed this and didn't like it.

"There's a complaint you want to register, Elsinger?" she asked. Never give an inch was her teaching rule. On the offensive was her teaching style.

Mikey actually preferred this directness. "A complaint about bad calls? I sure do."

"Are you ready to make a formal accusation?"

"You were there," Mikey pointed out.

"I'm asking *you*, Elsinger."

In absolute honesty Mikey couldn't be positively sure, not the way you should be to make that kind of an accusation. She said what she was sure of. "There were too many bad calls. My friends—"

"Your friends." The coach dismissed this evidence. "Are they trained linesmen?"

Mikey took a breath. A deep one. "Okay," she said. For a few seconds the coach stared right at her. Mikey, who recognized intimidation when it was being blasted at her, stared back. She smiled, just a little smile, a little bending of the lips. *You think you're scaring me?*

The coach nodded and didn't smile. She turned and started walking again. "You don't believe they were just bad calls." She said this glancing back over her shoulder at Mikey, to show how unimportant it was.

"No," Mikey said, following. "I don't."

"So, what are you going to do?"

"That's why I'm talking to you," Mikey pointed out. The woman might be a good tennis player, but she didn't seem any too swift at making logical connections.

"But I just asked *you*," Coach Sandy said, now with a sideways glance. "I mean, it could be that she was just outplaying you. Maybe you were actually losing those points, did you ever think of that? Maybe you aren't as good as you think."

Until that last statement Mikey had been willing to consider doubting herself. But she knew how good she was, as clearly as she knew how good she wasn't—not yet, anyway. The coach was pushing her for some reason, in some particular direction.

271

Mikey didn't like being pushed, in any direction. "I was winning," she repeated patiently. "I was the better player and I was playing better. I hit harder and I got to net more times. And"—she held up one of the baskets to keep the coach from interrupting her before she was finished—"I won almost all the points I went to net on. Although"—her hand was still raised—"she had a good down-the-line backhand passing shot." The coach opened her mouth but Mikey got in first. "And a pretty good serve out wide."

Then Mikey waited.

"Correct me if I'm wrong, but the score didn't reflect that big a difference between the two of you," the coach said.

"That's what I'm asking you about," Mikey insisted.

Coach Sandy sighed, a teacher with a slow student. "You know, Elsinger, we're not in this for the fun of it. Take a look around you, winning's what it's about."

"And I did win," Mikey repeated patiently.

That stopped Coach Sandy again. They had almost arrived at the courts, and the rest of the players were half-watching them, curious, and half-pretending not to notice them.

"Let me see if I've got this straight. You're asking me what you do if you think someone is cheating on line calls."

Mikey nodded. She waited.

"Seems like a no-brainer to me," the coach said.

Mikey didn't get it. She shook her head, as if to clear it.

"Did you ever hear When in Rome, Elsinger? Ever heard When in Rome, do as the Romans do?"

More Latin, Mikey thought, irritated. Then it came to her. "I should make bad calls too?"

That made Coach Sandy angry. "I never said that. What kind of a sportswoman would I be to say something like that?"

But wasn't that exactly what she'd said?

"Or what kind of a coach," Mikey agreed.

"All I'm saying is, I want winners on my team, people who know how to do what it takes to win. Tennis is a game of figuring out your opponent's weakness and then hitting hard, right at that spot. She was no fool, that girl, she knew exactly how and where to attack you. So think about it. That's my advice to you," and she turned her back on Mikey to call out, "All right, people! We'll start with cross-court drills. Get your feet in gear, people! We've got two matches in the next three days, and I can promise you, you've got a lot of work to do. Jacobs, Masters, Thompson and Elsinger, I want you on Court One. Go—go!"

Mikey reported in to Margalo on the phone that night, before Margalo even had a chance to ask—before, in fact, she even remembered what Mikey had told her she planned to do at practice that afternoon. Mikey wasted no time. You'd think that with so many of their combined children out of the house, Aurora and Steven would have increased the phone limit to ten minutes, or even fifteen, but Mikey didn't voice that complaint, not if she wanted to have time to hear what Margalo had to say about Coach Sandy.

"She blamed me for *not* cheating," Mikey concluded. And waited.

"You must have heard her wrong," Margalo decided.

"When in Rome—she quoted that at me."

Now Margalo was surprised. "She actually said you should cheat?"

"Not exactly actually. It's what she meant, though."

They were both quiet, wasting their time, but neither could think of what to say. Finally, "What are you going to do now?" Margalo asked.

Asked that direct question, Mikey knew the answer. "She can't make me."

"Can you get away with not doing what she says?"

"All I want to do is play good tennis," Mikey answered, and hung up.

Margalo took the receiver away from her ear and looked at it, as if it had a face and a long brown braid. "I'll take that as a yes."

— 16 —

Seriously Bad Stuff

Things were going badly for Mikey. Her set in the away match on Wednesday was as riddled with bad calls as a mobster's car in a movie about the thirties. It was so full of holes made by the bad calls that the few good calls lay bleeding inside, dead bodies. None of them were Mikey's bad calls, although she was tempted. Really tempted. And furious, too, and frustrated, thwarted—the only person angrier than Mikey was Coach Sandy, who didn't even let Mikey get on the bus before she let her have it. "That's it for you and singles, Elsinger."

"You know she was cheating," Mikey argued. Being the object of someone's anger had never troubled her.

"And before you start telling me about how you won didn't you, let *me* tell you that the score was too close for singles. A tiebreaker! What were you thinking of? You don't have enough experience to play singles. I'm putting you on a doubles team. With Chrissie," Coach Sandy added.

Her own anger flamed up through Mikey like some exploding volcano. Her jaw was clenched so hard it hurt, but getting angry felt—as usual—pretty good.

However, she wasn't about to say one word. If she said one word, she didn't know what she might say next, but she was pretty sure whatever she said wouldn't be what Coach Sandy wanted to hear. So Mikey merely smiled. *Don't you wish you knew what I'm not saying?*

Coach Sandy glared at her, a beady blue glare, for a long minute, and Mikey kept on smiling right back, *If you did, you wouldn't like it, not one bit.* The other members of the team moved around them, hefting their tennis bags up the steps onto the bus. Only Hal Weathersing failed to notice all the anger flowing back and forth between them. He took advantage of the silence to say, "Coach? You don't have to worry any more about my racket being stolen, because I forgot my mom took it to be restrung."

Mikey didn't know what the coach was waiting for, but she knew she could outwait the woman; and she wasn't about to say one single word until she had a chance to talk to Margalo. She didn't even know where she would *begin* when she told Margalo about this.

What with Aurora's five-minute rule, it took three phone calls to tell Margalo about the tennis debacle. "You're *kid-*

276

ding," Margalo said whenever Mikey stopped for a breath. "I don't believe she did that," first about the opponent and then about Coach Sandy. "She said *that*?" At the end, the first thing Margalo said was, "That was really smart of you, not saying anything."

"I didn't do it to be smart," Mikey said.

"I know that, and I also know you didn't do it to be safe. I'm just saying."

"So what do you think?"

"I think it stinks," Margalo said. "And it's stupid, too. It's not like anyone is going to get a lot of glory if her tennis team wins a match, or get a lot of money, either. The regionals might be worth cheating on, but—"

"They aren't. And if I'm spending all my time checking to be sure if some ball is in or out, how am I supposed to set up for my shot?" Mikey lapsed into fury again.

"I think," Margalo said, "that you're just supposed to call it out. I think," she added slowly, "that might be Coach Sandy's point."

"That may be what *she* thinks the point is," Mikey muttered. "But what am I going to do?"

"I have no idea," Margalo admitted.

"But you will by tomorrow, won't you?" Mikey answered her own question, "Probably. I hope so, because the only idea I really have for right now is to punch her in the snoot, and even I know that's not a good one. So you can stop laughing," Mikey said, but she was starting to laugh herself, at the satisfying picture in her head of her fist landing right on Coach Sandy's little snub nose. *Smack.*

Mikey took a deep breath and focused her complete attention on the feel of the tennis ball in her left hand and the feel of the handle of her racket in her right hand. Then she exhaled slowly, picturing in her mind where the serve would land. This was a point they had to win in this no-ad scoring system. It was a game they had to win to avoid the risk of a tiebreaker. Her problem was not her serve, which was just fine and occasionally terrific. Her problem was her partner. Chrissie planted herself at net and didn't move, not to right or left, not backwards either. This meant Mikey had to stay back to cover deep service returns, which meant they couldn't take advantage of her own net game to dominate the match.

Also, the opponents had figured out pretty quickly that if they fired a service return right at Chrissie, she would give a little scream and turn her back to the ball. Also, Chrissie was the kind of partner who muttered at the end of a game that a serve that had been called out was actually in. "That serve? It was in," she had muttered to Mikey four times in the set, and once could have been right; but even if she was right, that made no difference when it had been called out and scored out. In fact, the distraction of wondering about calls made it harder to focus.

Mikey was reaching a level of frustration—she *hated* playing a defensive game and she wasn't that good at it anyway— a level of frustration that was higher than she'd ever run into before. *Day forty-one*, she said silently to herself. *End of week nine.* This was her mantra. She let the ball float off her left hand, up into the air, and served.

The return came cross-court to her forehand, and she put it away down the alley to win the game. *Good.*

The leggy redhead across the net looked over at her partner. "Was that serve in?" she asked. "I couldn't—"

"Definitely in," the redhead's partner said. "Nice serve."

Mikey nodded her acceptance of the compliment. Now all she and Chrissie had to do was break the redhead's serve, which they'd already done once, so the girl was starting out demoralized. Chrissie returned the first serve, then stayed planted just inside the baseline, waiting to see first if her own shot was in and after that what the redhead would do with it. Mikey moved on up to the net, too far to the center, in hopes that the redhead would try to go down the line. The girl obliged, a low-percentage shot that Mikey would have gotten to easily and put away if the ball hadn't gone wide.

Mikey assumed position to receive serve and smiled across the net at the redhead. It was not a kind, warm smile, and she didn't intend it to be. She wasn't enjoying this match one bit.

The serve came flat and fast, skimming over the net down along the center line. Mikey had to dive for it and could manage only a weak return, an easy floater for the net person.

"Out!" Chrissie called.

The net player pulled her racket back to let the ball go by her.

279

Mikey transferred her not-kind smile to Chrissie. "The serve was good," she said. "It caught the inside of the line. Your point," she called across the net. "Sorry about the mis-call."

Chrissie objected, "I thought it was deep."

Mikey shook her head. "I'm almost positive it wasn't."

"That's what I mean exactly. That's why I called it out," Chrissie explained.

Since Chrissie seemed to have missed the point, Mikey said, "If the ball's not clearly out, then it's good," and Chrissie approached Mikey, as if for the kind of between-point con-ferring that doubles teams always did, to hiss, "That's not what Coach Sandy says. You can't overcall me like that, Mikey."

Mikey didn't bother arguing about it. It was clear that she could overcall, and she had, and she hoped Chrissie under-stood that she would do it again.

They won the set, but it didn't feel much like a victory to Mikey. It felt like an endurance test. It felt like she didn't care if she won or not, and especially she didn't care if the tennis team made it to the regional championships if this was the way people were going to play.

Mikey and Chrissie went to the net and shook hands with their opponents. Then they left the court side by side, the way partners did. Mikey repeated her silent mantra, *Day forty-one, end of week nine.* And it was the weekend, too; it was Friday. *TGIF.*

Another wave of irritation and frustration washed over her as she remembered that Margalo was working that evening. Maybe she'd see if she could work at the restaurant too. She was thinking about this, thinking that she'd have to work for free in order not to take income away from Margalo, thinking that there was no point in working and not getting paid, thinking maybe it wasn't much of an idea anyway, as she and Chrissie bent over to pack up their tennis bags, when Coach Sandy stormed over. "That's it, Elsinger. You're on the bench."

Mikey straightened up. What? Where did this come from? Coach Sandy, like any other adult, and especially teachers and especially coaches, figured that no answer meant she should lecture on.

"The team follows its coach's instructions," Coach Sandy said. Chrissie stayed hunched over her bag. Coach Sandy continued. "Because the coach knows the game. I'm keeping this simple for you, Elsinger. The team's job—and the job of every player on the team—is to do what you're told. It's like an army, obedience is required."

"This isn't a war," Mikey pointed out.

"Teams function when they work together towards a common goal."

"It's a game," Mikey continued.

"I was doing you a favor, trying to teach you how to be coached," the coach announced. "Now I'm doing the team a favor and getting rid of you."

"You're not doing me any favors trying to get me to cheat," Mikey said. She suspected there might be some other way to phrase it, which Margalo would have thought of, something that would have made the coach stop and think; but Mikey didn't know how to say what she was thinking any other way than straight out. "Or the team, either, without me on it."

Coach Sandy's eyes sparked, and her short, curly, high-lighted hair practically crackled. She beat her hand flat against the side of her pleated skirt. "Get out of my sight," she said to Mikey, and then mumbled, just like a kid grumbling at unfair adult treatment, "These hotshot kids. They think they're such hotshots."

Mikey *could* keep her mouth shut, so that was what she did. She went to the bleachers to watch Mark Jacobs play his singles set, and cheer him on, if cheering him on would help his game. "Good match?" somebody asked her, moving down along the bench to give her room. "Ask Chrissie," she said, and heard Chrissie say, "We won," as if that answered the question.

When she heard about Mikey being benched, Margalo wasted no time on sympathy. "Are you positive your shots are in?"

"No, but . . . but I'm pretty sure they're not out. Mudpies, Margalo, just think about it, you're supposed to be so good at thinking. I have to get myself set up to hit a return shot, and hit a good return shot, hit a winner if I can, *and* I'm supposed to worry about seeing if a close ball is in or out? Nobody can do that," Mikey announced. "Not and play her best. So in tennis you call it good unless you're sure it's out, because we don't have linespeople to call for us. Nobody in the county league makes bad calls like that," she argued, but then, remembering some questions she had had, she repeated with a changed emphasis, "Not like *that*. Probably Coach Sandy's going to tell people I'm benched because I don't have school spirit," she predicted gloomily.

"You don't," Margalo reminded her. They had breakfasted—poached eggs on English muffins, sausage links, home fries—and walked to the elementary school playground. They paid no attention to the boys and girls playing basketball on the asphalt court on a sunny Saturday spring morning. They went straight to the little-kid swings, which offered the pleasing awkwardness of having to bend their legs at the knees to splay them out to the sides, which in turn made swinging difficult. But this wasn't about swinging. It was about tennis.

Mikey settled herself into a low rubber seat. "What would you do about it? If you played tennis and Coach Sandy was your coach and she benched *you*. Because you wouldn't make bad calls."

"What *can* you do? I thought coaches were expected to rule with an iron fist. If the team is winning, that's all anybody cares about."

"So you think I should tell her I'll start cheating? But I can win without doing that."

"You couldn't cheat. Could you?"

283

Mikey doubted it.

"I could," Margalo claimed. "If I wanted to."

"She wants me off the team."

Margalo couldn't argue with that; the evidence certainly pointed in that direction.

"But the team needs me to win. And they know it."

Day forty, Mikey reminded herself, *week eight*. She took a deep breath to announce, before the tennis players could divide up over the courts for Monday's practice session, "I want to say something."

Everybody turned to look at her, then turned to look at Coach Sandy. Some of the boys batted rackets against their calves in either impatience or unused energy. The girls smiled politely. Coach Sandy was not smiling politely, but neither did she look worried. Maybe she didn't know the kind of person Mikey was so she couldn't guess the kind of thing the kind of person Mikey was would do.

Or maybe she wasn't worried because she knew there was nothing to worry about.

It was too late to think about that now, even if Mikey had wanted to. "I want to say that Coach Sandy has benched me. The reason she doesn't want me playing is because of my calls. Because unless I'm sure a ball is out, I call it in," Mikey told them, in case there was someone who didn't already know that.

They didn't seem too interested. Probably they already knew she'd been benched. A couple of people said, "What's

284

your point?" and one asked, barely loud enough to be heard, "Who cares?"

Mikey said, "I'm wondering what you think about that."

Then there was a silence. They looked at one another, not wanting to look at her. Now Mikey began to think maybe she should have talked this over with Margalo, what to say, how to say it. But what other choice was there?

Coach Sandy was the only one looking at Mikey. Everybody else looked embarrassed. But what did they have to be embarrassed about? Mikey was the one speaking out in public.

"Well," said Anne Crehan, "If you're not sure it's out then it still could be. Out, I mean. I mean, it doesn't have to be in just because you're not sure. So, why call it in?"

Mark Jacobs answered this, "Giving your opponent the benefit of the doubt."

What did that mean? Did it mean he was on her side? Or was he on the opposite side and just explaining her point of view?

"It's not as if opponents don't do exactly the same thing," Hal Weathersing said.

Murmurs of agreement greeted this point.

"Perhaps I can add a different perspective to the question," Coach Sandy said. "Perhaps if we look at it from the point of view of the team—that being the way a coach is supposed to think—because we don't play just for ourselves, do we? We play for a team."

This discussion was going the wrong way. Mikey tried to get them to see what she meant. "It's cheating," she said. "Or, to be perfectly accurate, sometimes it is."

With that she lost them entirely. She could see it. Too late she figured it out. They all felt a little guilty because, like everybody else, they hadn't been perfect all of their lives, and they wondered about some of their own close calls, as well as remembering—maybe—some deliberately dishonest ones. Mikey tried to change what she'd just said. "I know everybody cheats . . . but—"

"Speak for yourself."

"What do you mean, do you mean I cheat?"

"Who *cares*? Let's play."

Mikey overrode them all. "But I don't want that to be my policy. Do you?"

"What makes you so sure I cheat?" demanded Chrissie.

Mikey could only smile. *You're not asking seriously, are you?*

But others also began protesting. Who needed some ninth-grade squirt coming in and telling them they were cheaters when they weren't. Were they? "I'm not. Are you?"

"That's not what I mean," Mikey said. "I mean I shouldn't be benched because I won't call what I'm not sure I've seen." She glared at Coach Sandy, who was looking calmly at her, the grown-up in a kid–grown-up confrontation.

"And when did I ask you to do that?" Coach Sandy asked. "I don't believe that is what I asked you to do. I believe I was talking about being a team player, and how a player is foolish not to take the advice of an experienced coach. Rather than turning it into yet another authority conflict," she said.

Mikey ignored her. "Because that's not what a coach is supposed to do. Is it?" she asked the gathered squad of tennis players. Most of them were looking at their sneakers now, as if wondering about the quality of the knots—would they hold up to two hours of play?—or fingering the strung heads of their rackets like Sampras between points. Although, a few people were staring right at her, too surprised to look away, like rabbits in the headlights of an oncoming truck.

Only Mark Jacobs was looking at her as if she was saying something interesting, something he found worth thinking about, something he was thinking about right then.

"A coach is supposed to teach you to play better, and play fair, and play together if you're a doubles team. A coach isn't supposed to care so much about winning."

Coach Sandy answered this. "Get real, Elsinger. In the real world winning is what matters. Winning is all that matters."

"I don't call it winning when I cheat to do it," Mikey said. "And I don't call it coaching when that's what you tell me to do."

"That's it!" Coach Sandy slammed her clipboard down onto the ground. "I have had it up to here with you, Elsinger," with her hand raised flat in front of her eyes. "You are off the team. Off the squad. Out of tennis and my life. Get!" she said. "Go!"

A surprised silence answered her. Mikey looked around. Nobody was going to protest this, she could see. Well, if nobody else was going to argue, she certainly wasn't. If they were too stupid to see, or too chicken to say anything, or—and this was not a pleasant thought—if they all agreed with Coach Sandy, she was not about to want to be on their team. She nodded her head, slowly, once, turned her back, and walked away. She walked at her usual pace, not faster, not slower. Their loss. Their problem.

But she really, really didn't think Coach Sandy should be able to get away with it.

"I know, but what can you do?" Margalo asked Mikey on the phone that night. "It's not as if you can ignore what she said and show up and expect to play."

Mikey had never thought of doing that. Now she wondered if she could. She pictured it to herself, and she didn't see how she could pull it off. "They should fire her."

"Of course they should, but they won't." Margalo had already pointed this out, and more than once.

"I could get her fired."

"Probably not," was Margalo's opinion.

"Remember Louis Caselli in fifth grade?" Mikey reminded Margalo.

"This isn't fifth grade," Margalo reminded her right back. "This isn't another student. This is a teacher, and teachers don't side with students against other teachers. It's like in a business, if you were the CEO of a business, and somebody's secretary—or something like a file clerk, somebody way low down on the ladder—came to tell you that her boss wasn't doing his job right, wasn't talking to customers the right way—"

"You mean I have no clout."

"Partly that. But also, if you think about it compared to a business, you can see why people might not pay any attention to you. Why would they think you know anything? So you have to get people on your side."

"They don't want to be on my side. That's what I was asking them."

"Well then," Margalo said. They were silent for a few seconds. "And besides," she said, "you can still play competitive tennis with the league. You already do that."

"I know," Mikey said. "I know. But still—I'm going to talk to Mr. Wolsowski. He's my adviser."

"Waste of time," Margalo predicted.

"Or maybe Mrs. Burke."

Suddenly Margalo was tired of being negative. "Mrs. Burke gave really sensible advice about STDs and contraceptives," she agreed. "She might know something." Although Margalo couldn't think of what that might be. But they both admired Mrs. Burke, so, "Why not try her?"

"Unless—Is it too late to accuse Coach Sandy of stealing your money?" Mikey asked, her voice getting excited at this prospect. "Richard and Sally never confessed, so who would know? Do you think Hadrian would say he saw her doing it? They'd fire her for stealing, wouldn't they?"

"See you tomorrow," Margalo said, and hung up.

As soon as the phone was back on its stand, it started ringing again. Mikey picked it up. "Margalo?" She wondered what sudden new idea Margalo had had.

"Mikey?" a girl's voice asked.

"Who is this?"

"It's me. It's Ronnie Caselli."

"Ronnie Caselli?"

"Yes."

"Why are you calling me?"

"Margalo's phone was busy. I want to ask—I want to talk to you two tomorrow. Both of you. At lunch, but . . . Can we go somewhere private? Meet me outside, okay? Because you have to help me."

— 17 —

Everybody Can Use a Little Help

Mikey had agreed to meet up with Ronnie during lunch the next day, Tuesday, day thirty-nine, but that was about all the attention she had paid to the phone call. "What do you think it's about?" Margalo had asked when Mikey called to relay Ronnie's request, and Mikey had answered, "I'm going to ask Dad to drive me to school tomorrow, instead of the bus."

"It must be serious for her to want to talk to us," Margalo said.

"That way I can see Mrs. Burke before homeroom," Mikey explained.

Mikey's father didn't mind going half an hour out of his way before work in the morning. What did it matter? A half hour, an hour—He and Mikey had lots to talk about, like how they could add on to their two-bedroom house to make room for the new, larger family, and like what kind of a wedding everyone wanted, and where, and when. Mikey didn't even have to pretend to listen. She just sat there while wave after wave of happiness, tireless as an ocean, washed over her. She was glad for her father, but that didn't distract her from her own concerns.

At school she didn't even stop by her locker before running up the stairs to the second-floor faculty lounge. It was Peter Paul who answered her knock on the door. His bright red t-shirt declared ART MATTERS in black letters, and he looked back over his shoulder to finish what he'd been saying when her knock on the door interrupted him. "You don't expect kids to *know* anything, do you?" Then he turned to fix Mikey with a bored glance (not an Art student) and ask, "Yeah?"

Mikey kept it simple. "Mrs. Burke."

"Lillian Burke? She doesn't mingle with us." Mikey caught the whiff of cigarette smoke—but this was a No Smoking Zone, the whole building! "You could try her classroom," Peter Paul advised, and had the door closed before she had a chance to say anything else, if there had been anything else she needed to say.

"Thanks a lot," Mikey muttered at the door, and as if they had heard her and thought the feeble sarcasm was funny, laughter sounded from within.

Luckily, Mrs. Burke was in her classroom, correcting papers with a red pen. The door was open so Mikey walked alongside the rows of desks up to the front.

Mrs. Burke put down her pen and looked up at her. "Mikey?" Mrs. Burke was a fading person, her hair a fading gold, her eyes a fading hazel, and her body fading into shapelessness. "What is it?"

"Can I ask your advice on something?"

"Nothing personal."

Mikey thought about it and decided that her question qualified. "I've been thrown off the tennis team."

"This sounds personal," Mrs. Burke objected. She might look faded, but she had a crisp mind.

"Because the coach doesn't agree with me about calls."

"Complaining about a teacher is personal, Mikey."

Mikey hastened to explain. "What she doesn't like is that I won't call a ball out if I'm not sure." Now she thought about it, Mikey wasn't sure that Mrs. Burke knew anything about tennis and how it was scored.

"When you complain about how the tennis coach is treating you, that does sound personal, Mikey."

"Except there's a principle involved, about fair play."

Mrs. Burke started rolling up the sleeves of her blouse. She always wore khaki pants and a blouse to work; in cold weather she put on a cable-stitched cardigan sweater over the blouse, but when it was warm, she rolled up her sleeves, to get to work. "The bell's going to ring any minute," she said. "My homeroom will be arriving."

"No, but listen, Mrs. Burke," Mikey said. She tried to think of how to make the teacher understand. "If you threw someone out of your course for—I don't know, copying or being disruptive or—"

Mrs. Burke was shaking her head. "But I can't throw someone out of Science. Teachers can't do that, so the analogy doesn't hold. Classrooms aren't sports teams."

"It's all education, though. Isn't it?" Mikey argued. "It's all school. It's all to teach us, isn't it?"

"You know what I mean," Mrs. Burke argued.

"No, I don't," Mikey said.

"Don't you have an adviser?" Mrs. Burke asked.

Finally Mikey realized: Mrs. Burke wasn't going to talk to her about this. That was what she meant by "nothing personal," no non-Science-class problems.

"I do know what you mean," Mikey said. "But it's wrong."

"That's as may be," Mrs. Burke said. "Was there anything else I can do for you?"

Mikey was tempted. She thought maybe she would just plant herself right there in front of the desk and make Mrs. Burke listen to all the bad stuff that went on in ninth grade, the bullying and stealing and unearned grades—both unearned bad grades and unearned good ones. The teachers playing favorites and kids being cliquey, teachers smoking in a No Smoking Zone and kids smoking in the third-floor bathroom, a cafeteria that served pizza and french fries in the same lunch, just for starters, just off the top of her head. But really, Mrs. Burke was right. Her job was to teach Science, not to fix the world, not even the little world of high school.

So Mikey shook her head, *No, nothing else*, and she left.

She did, however, take the one piece of advice Mrs. Burke had sort of offered. She asked Mr. Wolsowski if she could come see him after last period. "Today?" he wondered. The English class was leaving the room in its usual hurry and he was erasing the board, clearing it for his next class, so she wasn't sure he'd really heard her.

"Today. Two fifteen today," she said.

Mr. Wolsowski had a long face and short hair. He wore a jacket and tie to school, every day. He wore the same style of glasses as his daughter, and also like Casey, he could surprise you. "Today?" he asked again, and Mikey finally got it: He was teasing. "Of course you can," he said then. "That's today, right?"

Actually, what with everything else going on in school, classes were kind of relaxing. Mikey didn't have to think about classes. She was a smart person who did her homework; classes were easy, and sometimes fun if she had an opinion she wanted to tell people about, especially if someone tried arguing with her. Sometimes classes were even interesting. They were certainly easier than hallways and cafeteria, and everything that was going on.

For example, this tennis stuff. For another example, Ronnie. Mikey was not looking forward to lunch and whatever it was that Ronnie was up to. "What could she possibly want with us?" Margalo said when they saw Ronnie coming towards them, long legs in jeans, long hair in a ponytail.

Then they watched her stop, and head off in a different direction.

The day was warm enough for eating outdoors; Ronnie had been carrying some kind of sandwich in her hand; so it wasn't the weather and it wasn't hunger that had diverted her.

"You two—You've gotta tell me what you think of this. I think it's my masterpiece," said the voice of Cassie Davis, and turning their heads at the same time, they understood why Ronnie had turned away. Mikey opened her brown bag to take out a ham and cheese sandwich on rye, with lettuce and tomato, as if nothing Cassie Davis might get up to could interest her much because she was too cool to be curious. But Margalo didn't try to keep the surprise out of her voice. "Cassie?"

Cassie Davis had dyed her hair—and dyed her eyebrows, too—a bright fluorescent pink. She was, for just a few seconds, unrecognizable, because the effect of hair that pink was to grab all the attention. That hair could have been wearing anybody's face underneath it.

"I'm not asking about *this*." Cassie smiled in satisfaction and ran her fingers through her short pink hair. She opened the big art folder that she had set down on the ground beside her feet—she wore yellow clogs—resting it against her legs, shapeless within paint-spattered Dickies overalls, and pulled out a piece of stiff cardboard almost as big as a movie poster. "I'm talking about *this*," Cassie said.

She turned the cardboard around to show them. Bits and

scraps of paper, some with pencil marks, some with colors, plus bits and rough scraps of painted canvas, plus bits and rough scraps of black-and-white photographs—all had been glued onto the cardboard. It looked like pieces of a jigsaw puzzle when they are first dumped out of the box onto the table. Only there was a sort of thick, curved white fence holding them in. A bowl? And the more you looked at it, the more it looked like all of the scraps were swirling around the middle of the picture.

Margalo wasn't sure what to say. "It's very modern," she tried.

"Ha!" responded Cassie, meaning *I knew you'd get it.*

"It looks like it took a lot of work," Margalo said.

"You're right about that."

Mikey, however, knew exactly what she thought and said so. "It looks like a toilet to me," she said, and went on to be specific, "Flushing."

Margalo started to laugh.

"I'm not joking," Mikey told her.

Margalo opened her own lunch bag and jammed a straw into her drink box. "I know you're not. That's pretty clever, Cassie."

Cassie grinned. Even the heavy eye makeup she was wearing couldn't make much of a stand against the bright pink hair. "It's even better than you know. Because I ripped up all the assignments from the fall and winter—those yellow pieces? They're the still life he said was so good. Ha! Some life drawings." She was pointing at different scraps and pieces. "The pencil portraits, remember them? I've titled this *Art I*. Get it? Or maybe I should call it *Freshman Art Class*—which do you think? It's a collage."

"What will Peter Paul say?" Margalo wondered.

"The way he's hated everything I've done since Christmas?" Cassie asked. "He'll hate it. Big deal." She stopped grinning. "I'm never taking another art class in my life."

"I thought you were going to Art School," Mikey said.

Cassie shook her head. "What's the point? If I'm not any good. Like you not playing on the tennis team."

"That's different," Margalo said.

"Why? Because she was thrown off for not doing what she was told? I think my C minus in Art is exactly the same thing. I mean, how can anyone get a C minus in Art? I'm hoping he'll flunk me for the year."

"What about Jace?" Margalo asked. "Is he dropping Art too?"

"Actually"—and Cassie grinned again—"Jace is getting an A. I think Peter Paul is trying to break us up."

"Why would he bother?" asked Mikey.

"If I were painting the way he does? I'd do anything I could think of to keep from having to see how my work stank. Like your tennis coach, Mikey. They take out their failures on us. I'll tell you, I'd wash dishes before I'd teach Art," Cassie declared.

Margalo, who knew what she was talking about, told Cassie, "The benefits aren't as good. Or the pay, or the hours."

Cassie looked down at Margalo and announced, "You're making fun of me. But it's not funny," she said, and packed her flushing toilet collage back into the folder. Then she looked out over the clusters of students trying to improve their tans. "I gotta let Jace see this. He won't know *what* to think. Ha!" and she walked away.

Mikey had time to finish up her sandwich before Ronnie at last approached and sat down on the far side of Margalo. Close up Ronnie didn't look too good. Maybe she was tired, maybe she hadn't paid attention to her makeup? "Hey Margalo," she said, as if she wasn't sure that was the right thing to say. Then she leaned around Margalo, with a smile that stretched her mouth out wide and made her look definitely sad. "Hey Mikey."

They had seen Ronnie looking good in all kinds of situations, looking good happy, looking good weeping, looking good athletic or studious, for so many years that both Margalo and Mikey sat up straight. "What is wrong with you?" Mikey demanded.

Ronnie's big brown eyes filled with tears, and they already looked tired from crying. "You have to help me. I don't know what to . . ." She stopped, gulped, tried again. "I can't tell any—"

"You're not pregnant," Margalo said.

"No, no, that's not—But it's—It's embarrassing."

Usually Mikey didn't have anything much to do with Ronnie Caselli. She didn't dislike Ronnie, but she didn't trust her for much or care very much what she got up to, since their interests seldom coincided. But now Mikey was worried. Because if Ronnie Caselli wasn't on top of the world, who knew what could happen to the rest of them?

"Drugs?" Mikey asked. "Are you sick? Not HIV." Because kids didn't get AIDS, did they? But they did, didn't they? "Cancer? Are your parents getting divorced? C'mon, Ronnie."

"It's Chet," Ronnie murmured. One tear pooled out of her eye and started down her cheek. She wiped it away, with another one of those sad, sad smiles.

It was one of Ronnie's love crises, and who cared about that?

"What's happened?" Margalo asked. Mikey leaned back and took a bite of apple turnover, ready not to be surprised.

But she was. Shocked, in fact, and so was Margalo, even though Margalo's face didn't give that away. Margalo's expression didn't change at all when Ronnie started telling them. What Chet wanted—Well, that wasn't surprising, Mikey guessed, everybody said boys just wanted to have sex—and then what he had threatened to do.

"Rhonda," Margalo said.

"What?" Mikey asked, and then she got it. *Rodents!* Was she going to start feeling sorry for Rhonda Ransom, too? As if she didn't have enough problems in her own life.

"But why would he want to if you don't?" Mikey demanded.

"He's a guy," Ronnie explained. Now that she had stated her problem out loud, she seemed a little more normal, for which Mikey was grateful.

"And it's his Senior Prom," Ronnie added, as if that explained something.

"And if you won't sleep with him," Margalo said, stating it clearly, "he'll tell everyone that you did."

Ronnie nodded. "And then he'll ditch me."

"You mean you haven't already broken up with him?" Mikey demanded.

Margalo asked, "When did all this happen?"

"Yesterday. Last night. We had a study date, at my house because I'm not allowed to go out on school nights."

"He said this in your own house?" Mikey demanded.

"He was whispering," Ronnie explained.

"He can't get away with that," Mikey declared.

"They'll believe him," Ronnie explained to Margalo. "They will, and everybody knows how much I love him."

"You have to stop all this falling in love," Mikey told Ronnie. "It's not like you really are, anyway, because"—she raised her voice to drown out their objections—"if you really are in love, it's not that easy to fall out of it. You've been in love three times that I personally know about, and we're not even friends, and that's just in one year."

"Never mind that," Margalo said. "Who have you told about this?"

"Nobody. He does love me," Ronnie explained.

"Like I believe that," Mikey muttered.

"He says I'm breaking his heart." Ronnie smiled again. She was about to weep again.

"Right," Mikey said, but Margalo, she could see, was thinking about something else, so Mikey reassured Ronnie, "I'll be happy to tell him what I think. And punch him in his baby blues, too."

"You can't," Ronnie said. Her voice was low, urgent. "You can't do that because he'll say it then—about me. And you know everybody will believe him. Because they'll want to believe him about me," she said, and, "Do you think I have to do it with him? I don't want to. I don't want to have sex with anybody, not yet," Ronnie whispered, as if that embarrassed her too. But it was the first smart thing she'd said since she started all this falling in love, as far as Mikey was concerned, so why should it embarrass her?

"Maybe you should tell your parents," Margalo suggested.

"I can't. No, really, I can't. They—They don't know anything about how things are for me. They'd—they'd probably ground me for a whole year or make me change schools. What if they didn't believe me? They don't understand what it's like for me, so whatever they did . . ." Her voice trailed off, and she explained simply, "They're grown-ups."

"Okay, then, what about your adviser?" Margalo suggested.

"The faculty tells everything to anybody, about students. They talk about us, you know they do, especially if you're having problems. Then everybody would know, and then Chet would—"

"Mr. Robredo?" Mikey suggested, but Ronnie looked alarmed and maybe even frightened at that suggestion.

"I *couldn't*," she said. "Really, I just couldn't. Could you?"

"Of course," Mikey maintained, although she wasn't so sure of it. But she wasn't sure she wouldn't, either, and besides, this wasn't a problem she expected to be running into.

"All right," Margalo said, leaning forward and resting her elbows on her knees, to think. "All right, then. I have an idea. To make it work, we'll need Louis's help and you're going to have to—How good a liar are you? Or how good an actress, because you're going to have to pull the wool over Chet's eyes."

"He's a senior," Ronnie protested.

Margalo ignored that. "And we're going to need to get it set up fast, today, right away. So you have to start lying right away. And go put on some makeup, too. People are already wondering what's wrong. The way you're talking privately with us. The way you're looking not at all good."

This was true. Neither Mikey nor Ronnie had noticed it, but they were getting looks from some people. Mikey Elsinger and Margalo Epps were not the kind of girls that someone like Ronnie Caselli had what looked like it might be a private conversation with. Curiosity was building as to what this private conversation might be about.

"I'll tell them . . ." But Ronnie was too upset to think of a believable lie.

Then Margalo asked, "What do you know about Mikey's stepfather?"

"Jackson?" asked Mikey, as if she had a choice of step-fathers. What was Margalo doing asking Ronnie about Jackson? Talk about *non sequiturs.*

"He's from Texas. He's somebody important. Rich," Ronnie added. "Why?"

Margalo said, "Let's say he's a lawyer, and you asked Mikey to get his advice."

"Is he?" Ronnie asked.

"Because you're thinking of bringing a sexual harassment suit against Chet," Margalo said.

"What?" asked Ronnie.

"Brilliant!" cried Mikey. "Why not date rape?"

"That's a serious crime. We don't want to mess around with something like that," Margalo said. "But listen, Ronnie—If Mikey has a stepfather who is a lawyer, and if she asked him about what constituted sexual harassment, and if Chet knew she was doing that for you," Margalo said, setting out the points of her plan. She concluded, "He'll head for cover. He'll be frightened, I'm pretty sure of it." She began her instructions. "If I were you, I'd start by asking Rhonda if Chet sexually harassed her, and then just one or two other girls he's been out with, like that tenth grader between Rhonda and you—"

304

"Candy DeAngelo?"

"Her. Ask her if she's ever been sexually harassed. They'll talk to their friends about your asking that question, you can count on it. You don't have to tell them exactly what happened, you just bring up the subject, like a reporter gathering information. But Louis is key to this plan. You need Louis to talk to people about how your family is thinking about doing what Jackson advises."

"But everybody's furious at Louis for messing up in school, his father especially, so Louis isn't in the mood to help the family. Although he might help *me*," Ronnie said. Just thinking about this plan was reestablishing her self-confidence. "He'd do it to help *me*," she assured Margalo and Mikey. "I'll get him to come talk to you. You stay right here," she said. She rose, already looking better, with some sparkle to her eyes and some straightness in her shoulders. "What's your stepfather's name?" she asked Mikey.

"Jackson. But he's—"

"Don't say it," Margalo advised.

That was irritating, Margalo giving orders like that, but Mikey obeyed. This was one of Margalo's best ideas ever. This was fighting fire with fire, rumor with rumor, taking an eye for an eye, really getting even and maybe even getting ahead. "Do you think it'll work?" she asked Margalo.

That question alarmed Ronnie. "What if it doesn't?"

Margalo just grinned, like a little kid who got excused from taking a spelling test she forgot to study for. "I don't know," she told Mikey. "I just thought it up, I haven't thought it through. But it *could*."

"Hey hey," said a male voice, distracting the three of them. A large male hand emerged from one side of Ronnie's waist, and Chet was standing behind her. "Hey, Babe, I've been looking all over for you." He smiled down at Mikey and Margalo, who remained seated, staring up at him, a little stupefied. *Had he heard what they were saying?*

Stupefied seemed to be what Chet liked. His smile got lazy, sure of itself. "I haven't met these friends of yours, Ronnie."

Ronnie had recovered quickly enough to say, with a toss of her head that made her ponytail brush against his neck, "Margalo Epps. Mikey Elsinger."

Chet *was* handsome, with dark, thick eyebrows, and he did have a great smile, also sky blue eyes and broad shoulders; and he was tall, already over six feet. He ignored Margalo but said to Mikey, "You got tossed off the tennis team. Am I right? Mark was grousing."

Mikey smiled right up at him. "Call me Michelle."

"Michelle? That's your real name, right?"

"Yeah." Mikey continued smiling, *You are in big trouble.* Even she could figure out what Chet was thinking. He was thinking, *There goes another one.* He didn't know anything about Mikey.

"So, what are you girls getting up to?" Chet asked, pulling Ronnie in close to him.

Ronnie looked at Margalo. Mikey looked at Margalo.

Margalo looked at Chet and discovered that she had the answer. "Ronnie wants us to tutor Louis." She looked at Ronnie. "Because her family is so upset about him flunking the year." She looked at Mikey. "Mikey will do the Math"— and then she turned back to Chet—"and I'll do English. If he passes those two, he can make up Science and Social Studies in summer school."

"Why would I agree to tutor Louis?" Mikey demanded, not having yet figured out what Margalo was up to now. "He's stupid and he doesn't want to learn anything. It would be a total waste of my time."

Margalo said to Chet, "I, on the other hand, think we could do it."

"Why doesn't Louis ask them himself, Babe?" Chet asked Ronnie.

"He hates us," Margalo explained.

"You're right about that," Mikey said. "And it's mutual."

"That's going to be part of the fun," Margalo said.

"I don't get it," Chet said.

By now Mikey and Ronnie did. Ronnie said, "I was just about to go find Louis and tell him."

"I'll come with you," Chet said. "I haven't laid eyes on you all morning."

Ronnie looked up into his face with the soft-eyed look he was hoping to see.

"I really miss you when I don't see you all morning, Babe,"

Chet said. "She's made my senior year just great, just about perfect," he said, apparently speaking to Mikey and Margalo, but still looking at Ronnie.

To get the conversation off of this topic, Mikey said, "I don't think Louis *can* get caught up. There's only thirty-nine days left—less, counting the exam period."

"Where's your fighting spirit, Michelle?" teased Chet.

Mikey smiled again. *You're about to find out, you no-good ratfink lunchpail bum.* "He's been flunking Math since the second marking period. That's November."

"I bet we can do it," Margalo argued, keeping the conversation focused. Their only hope to successfully attack Chet was the element of surprise. "I bet when we get through with Louis, he'll pass both English and Math."

Mikey played along. "How much? C'mon, Margalo, put your money where your mouth is. How much will you bet?"

Margalo hesitated, thought about it, looked at Chet as if about to ask his advice, but just as he was about to offer it, she said, "A nickel."

"Done," said Mikey, and she held out her hand. Margalo took it in hers and they shook, like wrestlers at the start of a match only they knew was fixed.

"Tell Louis we want to see him at lunch tomorrow," Margalo said to Ronnie.

"You let them tell you what to do like that, Babe?"

"Let us do the explaining," Margalo advised Ronnie.

— 18 —

But Not Everybody Gets It

Mr. Wolsowski was waiting for Mikey at the end of school, behind the desk in his classroom with its shelves full of books—class sets of novels and dictionaries, anthologies of poetry and essays—and its literary posters—Shakespeare, of course, surrounded by his most famous quotes; a time line showing major world events and when writers lived, from Homer to Toni Morrison; the movie poster for *A Room with a View*. Mr. Wolsowski had his windows wide-open, so he was using one of the dictionaries to weigh down his pile of papers.

Mikey went right up to the desk. Mr. Wolsowski put down his red pen—didn't teachers do anything but grade papers?—and sat forward in his chair. "What's the problem, Mikey?"

Mikey spoke carefully, making sure she was presenting the exact answer to this question. "Coach Sandy. She's the tennis coach."

"Sandy Delorme? But I don't know her at all, I don't—I've heard about her, though, she played pro tennis, didn't she? But Mikey, you're a good tennis player, so how can there be a problem? Didn't Casey tell me—" Something about what Casey had told him made him not finish that sentence.

Mikey continued. "She threw me off the team, and now she's thrown me out of tennis, that's the exact problem. I'm the number one girl on the tennis ladder," Mikey told him, in case he hadn't heard or didn't understand how bizarre what had happened was.

"Why would she do that?"

"Because of my line calls."

"You were cheating? That doesn't sound like you."

Mikey shook her head. "Because I wouldn't call balls out if I wasn't sure."

That got Mr. Wolsowski up out of his seat. He was getting worked up, Mikey could tell, and she took that for a good sign. The teacher went over to an open window and looked out.

"So I'm wondering, what can I do about it?" Mikey asked his back.

He turned around and smiled. But it wasn't the confident, grown-up-about-to-take-charge smile she was hoping for. "I think your real question—here, this afternoon—is, What can *I* do about it? And the unfortunate truth is, I can't do anything. Not really. I don't have firsthand information to take to Mr. Robredo, even if I were convinced it was appropriate for me to go to him. For one thing. I mean, if it were Casey, then I might feel justified, and he might listen, but—Teachers are always hearing things about other teachers. Usually they're not exactly accurate," Mr. Wolsowski said. "Gossip, complaints. Or things get blown out of proportion. Or it's a one-sided version that distorts the facts."

Mikey nodded. She could see that. She hadn't thought of it, but she could see it. "Then, what can *I* do?"

He shook his head, he didn't know. He took off his glasses and polished them with a tissue. "Sports aren't a metaphor for life," he announced, as if she had been trying to convince him that they were. "Especially, team sports aren't."

"But then, maybe tennis is, because you play one against one. Or two against two at the most if it's doubles."

"That's if life's about winning. If the correct metaphor for life is beating somebody else to get a prize only one person can have," Mr. Wolsowski said, polishing away.

"But only one person *can* come in first," Mikey pointed out. "Or one team."

"That only matters if life only has one kind of prize," Mr. Wolsowski said. "Maybe golf works as a metaphor."

"Golf's not a sport," Mikey told him.

He looked at her, surprised. Then he put his glasses back on and looked at her some more. "But it is. Don't underestimate what you don't know anything about, Mikey."

"Okay," Mikey said. She wasn't here to argue with Mr. Wolsowski. She was here to get his help. "What can I do?

About Coach Sandy," she reminded him, in case he had lost track of what they were talking about.

"I honestly don't know. I wish I could help you, I do—"

"I believe you," Mikey assured him.

"But I can't. Have you talked to Mrs. Smallwood?"

"The guidance counselor? She doesn't even know who I am."

"The counselor can deal with things teachers aren't supposed to, or aren't skilled with, or aren't trained in. I'm your academic adviser, and—you know—she *might* know you. This far into the year."

"The year's almost over."

"I know."

"There are only thirty-nine days left. Thirty-nine school days, I mean."

"That, I didn't know. I am sorry not to . . ." His voice drifted off and he started polishing his glasses again.

"Yeah, me too," Mikey said. She stood looking at him, not moving. He went back to his desk and started piling papers into file folders and file folders into a canvas carryall. Mikey kept on waiting.

Mr. Wolsowski looked up from what he was doing. "You know what I think? I think reading is a metaphor for life. Because everybody can do it, and the more you work at it and think about it, the better you are at it, although there are some lucky people who just seem to be born knowing how to do it well. But that's talent, and talent is a different situation.

I'd say," he concluded, "that if sports is a metaphor for any-thing, it's a metaphor for war."

"Not golf," Mikey pointed out.

"Except, people die in wars."

"There can't be one-on-one wars, so not tennis, either," Mikey told him. She waited some more, in case he had some-thing useful to say, something not a metaphor.

He had filled his carryall, and he looked up at her again. "What do you want to have happen?"

"I want her fired," Mikey said. As soon as she said it, she heard how impossible and unlikely that was. So she said, "Thank you, good-bye," and went to the library to get a good start on her homework—since she no longer had to be on the tennis court but still had to wait for the late bus.

On the bus, after she told Margalo about her conversation with Mr. Wolsowski, she asked, "Is there any point in talking to Mrs. Smallwood, do you think?"

"If you're not going to leave any stone unturned," Margalo advised. "Any adult stone, that is." Margalo was feeling that Mikey didn't seem very interested in any thoughts she, Margalo, might have on the subject. And she did have a couple of ideas, including a couple of things that—based on her own experience—Mikey shouldn't even think of trying.

"That means I have to get to school early again tomor-row," Mikey groused. "At least when your money got stolen, that was fun. It was a mystery, at least."

"And this is definitely *not* a mystery. This is just plain and simple human nature."

"Do you think people are inherently bad?"

Margalo thought about that. Were all of the—how many? Seventy?—people on this bus rotten? And the bus driver, her too? Adults too? Was she willing to say that they were all bad? What did she mean by "bad," anyway?

Mikey went on. "Everybody is self-interested, but that's not really bad, is it?"

"Everybody, almost, in the whole world, on television and in the news, even parents, some teachers—everyone tells us this is the way things are, that's the way to win the prizes."

"What prizes do you mean?" asked Mikey, who had already had too many metaphors in her afternoon. "You mean like winning Wimbledon?"

"That's one kind of prize."

"But it's not at all easy to win Wimbledon."

Margalo continued her thinking out loud. "Besides, what's wrong with wanting to have a comfortable life? Or with wanting to be admired for doing something well?"

"Does that mean you agree with Coach Sandy? That I *should* be making bad calls? Deliberately?" Mikey was staring at her, shocked.

Margalo didn't get all that many chances to shock Mikey. "If I did, would you do it?"

"You wouldn't," Mikey decided.

"Anyway, that wasn't at all what I meant. I just meant, maybe what's bad is when you go too far. When, for example, you become a drug dealer to get money, or make a promise you know you can't keep—or don't plan to keep—to get elected, or—"

"Like the tobacco companies."

"You don't think it's just the tobacco companies, do you?"

"Telling lies? Keeping important information a secret? No."

This was all pretty depressing, and it depressed them for a few bouncing blocks. Then Mikey announced, "Nobody can make me live that way."

"Nobody can make anybody do that, mostly," Margalo pointed out. "They just make us *want* to. Or, want to choose to."

"I'm not letting Coach Sandy do it to me."

"Good," Margalo said, and meant that, 100 percent. She didn't know *what* she would do if Mikey started letting people make her do, or want, what they wanted her to do, or want. Or even started to pretend in order to fit in or get to play varsity tennis. Because this was, Margalo knew, her own personal particular danger. And there was another interesting idea.

She asked Mikey, "What do you think your personal particular danger is? The kind of mistake you're likely to make," she explained. "Or the kind of wrong thinking you are vulnerable to?"

"I'm going to see if Mrs. Smallwood will get Coach Sandy fired," Mikey answered.

The next day—Wednesday, April 21, by most reckonings; day thirty-eight on Mikey's personal calendar—Mikey once again came to school early. This time she went to the guidance offices, which were next to the health room. All of the doors on this corridor were open, and Mrs. Smallwood's was the first she came to. Mrs. Smallwood, who was in fact smaller than average, sat behind her desk reading an open file. She wore a blazer and a white shirt, and her narrow office had no room for posters, only a tall bookcase and a tall file cabinet. She looked up when Mikey knocked on the doorframe.

"Have a seat," Mrs. Smallwood said, indicating the two chairs facing her desk. Mrs. Smallwood was an organized-looking person, her hair cut short and tidy, the nails on her folded hands also short and tidy, her features tidy on her face. She smiled understandingly and asked, "Would I be correct in thinking that you are Michelle Elsinger?"

"Mikey," Mikey corrected her. "I hate Michelle, but I want to talk to you about—"

"One minute." The counselor stood up, revealing that below her blazer she was wearing a straight khaki skirt and low heels, making her tidy from head to toe. She went to her filing cabinet and pulled out a drawer to extract a folder. Returning to her seat, she opened the folder and took out a

316

pad of lined paper and a pen. Now she was ready to listen. "What can I do for you?"

"I want to know, if . . . if Coach Sandy threw me off the tennis team and there was no good reason for it, what I can do about it."

"Coach Delorme? There will have been some reason."

"I said no *good* reason. She wants me to call balls out even if I'm not sure they are, that's the reason, because I won't do that. Another reason is I asked her what to do if I thought people were cheating on their calls, and she said, When in Rome."

"Those exact words?"

"When in Rome, do as the Romans do is exactly what she said."

Mrs. Smallwood stared thoughtfully at Mikey. Her eyes were light brown, hazel. Then she started to write on the pad. Mikey waited. After a few lines of writing Mrs. Smallwood put her pen down again. She picked up a pair of glasses and put them on, then leaned back in her chair to stare right into Mikey's eyes.

Hunh? But Mikey looked right back at the guidance counselor, and waited.

"That must make you angry," Mrs. Smallwood said.

"Well, yeah."

"What do you think the other side of the story is, though? Most stories have two sides."

"Stories have as many sides as there are people in them," Mikey pointed out.

"Yes, well, this story has two people in it. You and Coach Delorme. I always like to hear both sides."

Mikey thought she could make a good guess about what was going on in Coach Sandy's mind. "She wants to win, and she thinks if other people are doing it, why shouldn't her team?" She thought a little more, but that was all the mind reading she could manage.

"I understand how serious this is for you," Mrs. Smallwood said sympathetically.

It wasn't understanding that Mikey was looking for. She waited.

"But I hope *you* understand that compared with some of the problems some of your schoolmates have to face, yours is a relatively minor one." At the expression on Mikey's face she specified, "Addictions, abuses, criminal charges—or even social problems, the way a person looks . . ." And at Mikey's expression she proved her point specifically. "Your classmate Hadrian Klenk, for example, last fall, think of what life was like for him."

Mikey pointed out, "But we did something about that. What I want to know is, what can I do about Coach Sandy? What if you told her what I came to tell you, so she'd know that you knew about it?"

"I can't accuse a teacher, not without evidence. I wonder, Mikey—You might not know how many times every day a student will come to me, or to one of the other counselors, with a complaint about a teacher. If I told every teacher every time any student had a complaint . . . I wouldn't have time to do anything else. I wouldn't have time to do any of the important things I need to do, to help people who really need help."

Mikey nodded. She could see that, and she agreed with the counselor's choice of priorities. "I'm not asking you to do anything for me," she said. "Just tell me what—"

"Students complaining about teachers, and *vice versa*," Mrs. Smallwood went on.

Did the whole world know Latin? Mikey was even happier that she was taking Spanish.

"You might be interested in some of the things that have been said about you," Mrs. Smallwood said, tapping the file folder with the fingers of her left hand, where a wedding band glowed gold.

"Why would I?" Mikey demanded impatiently, and then she realized, "Does that mean Coach Sandy has already talked to you? Is that why you already knew who I am?"

Mrs. Smallwood's mouth smiled gently again. "If she has—and I'm not saying that she has, only *if* she has—it would be a breach of confidentiality for me to tell you. I'm sure you can understand how important that confidentiality is. You wouldn't want me telling everybody what you thought of them, would you?"

"They already know," Mikey said.

"Yes. You know, Mikey, that may be your problem."

Mikey repeated it patiently. "Coach Sandy is my problem."

Mrs. Smallwood studied her again, just for half a minute—but half a minute of being studied can feel like a long time. "I think," she finally said, and smiled again, a sad, understanding, disappointed-grandmother smile, "you had better go to homeroom now. Come back when you can see beyond your own nose, Mikey. You have a lot of abilities, we all know that. It would be a pity if you never got to realize the fruit of them."

Mikey considered asking her just what she meant. Was the counselor talking about getting into a good college? Or getting a good job? Or having any friends, or even having a husband and family? Or was she talking about tennis, and if she was, what kind of tennis-fruits was she talking about? It felt like a threat, that compliment about her abilities, or a warning. Maybe Mrs. Smallwood knew something Mikey hadn't thought of—or Margalo, either. But Mrs. Smallwood didn't know much of anything about Mikey, so how could she know enough to either compliment or threaten or warn her? She couldn't.

Neither could she help Mikey. Mikey got up from her seat, turned, and left the little room. This had been a waste of time. She found Margalo at their lockers, reported the conversation, and—there was still a lot left to say—walked beside Margalo to Margalo's homeroom. "I'm tired of talking," Mikey concluded. "I want to *do* something."

"What? What can you do?"

"I don't know."

"Maybe you're going to have to forget about it."

"And let her get away with it?" They had arrived at the door to Margalo's homeroom and stood facing each other.

"*And* we have to talk to Louis Caselli," Margalo reminded her.

Luckily, it was raining and they had to have lunch inside, in a crowded cafeteria where nothing happened without somebody noticing. This meant that the meeting Ronnie had set up between Mikey and Margalo and Louis would take place with maximum publicity—exactly the way they wanted it. In fact, Louis Caselli came up to a table where not only Mikey and Margalo sat, but also Casey and Cassie, Tim, Felix and Hadrian, all ready to listen in on whatever got said.

Louis was short and round like a rooster, with a rooster's bright, greedy eyes. He had put two streaks of color into his hair, running backwards from his forehead, one stripe fluorescent green, the other purple. He wore a yellow Phish t-shirt that listed the stops they made on their world tour, blue-and-red plaid shorts, and sneakers without socks. He strutted up and smirked down at them. "Ronnie says you want to talk to me."

Ronnie had reported to them that Louis was furious that anyone—even if that anyone was someone like Chet Parker, a senior, a football player, and an early-admission acceptee at Duke University, captain of the baseball team and general all-around enviable guy—furious that anyone at all would try to get away with pulling a trick like that on one of the Casellis. He'd told Ronnie he was willing to give Mikey and Margalo a listen.

"Did you bring your books?" Margalo asked.

"What do I need books for?" Louis strutted even while standing still.

"You better sit down," Mikey advised.

Louis did, twirling the chair around so he could cross his arms along its back. "So what's the story?"

The rest of the table was watching. Everybody except Hadrian had a little smile of anticipation (this could turn out good) on their face. Hadrian had an attentive expression, like a scientist looking into his microscope or a therapist listening. Louis, who was always checking up on whoever was watching him, noticed this. "What're you staring at, Dorko?"

Mikey got his attention back on them. "Personally, I'm betting you can't possibly pass English and Math."

"Why would I want to?" asked Louis, maintaining his reputation for cool.

"So you can take Social Studies and Science in summer school," Margalo answered.

"Why would I want to waste my summer going to school?"

"So you can be in tenth grade next year," Mikey explained patiently. She was enjoying this. "I don't think you can do it, but Margalo"—she gestured towards Margalo, as if Louis might not be sure who Margalo was—"disagrees. She thinks you can. We have a bet on it."

322

Louis hesitated, a little confused. This wasn't what he'd thought they wanted to talk to him about. Then he decided— with everybody there listening in the way they were—to continue playing it cool. "My father says I'm not leaving home until I get my high school diploma. Unless I run away, and if I run away, my father says I don't need to bother coming back. Unless I have a diploma. This upsets my mother," Louis told them.

Margalo wanted to wonder out loud if Louis's mother was upset because her little boy might run away or because he might end up living at home indefinitely. But she had a show to put on. "Have you realized that if you flunk this year, you'll end up spending a whole extra year in school?"

"When the rest of us graduate, you'll be left behind," Mikey observed. "*And* I'll have won the bet."

"You mean if I pass Math and English, you lose?" Louis asked her.

Mikey nodded.

"And I win," Margalo added.

"And if I flunk them, you win," Louis said to Mikey.

Mikey nodded.

"And *you* lose," he explained to Margalo. He thought about this. "Yeah, but *I* can't win either way."

They had gathered a certain amount of attention in the lunchroom by then. There was some hope that on a rainy Wednesday, still a long way from the end of the school year, something might be happening. Anything to relieve the tedium.

Margalo said, "Tell me what your class read in English this year," and Mikey said, "Let me see your Math book."

"With all of them listening in?" Louis asked, indicating the others at the table, Cassie and Casey, Tim, Felix and Hadrian.

There were always empty chairs at Mikey and Margalo's lunch table, so the three of them moved away. Louis put his chair at the end, like the father on Thanksgiving, with Mikey on one side and Margalo on the other. He wasn't sure what expression he wanted on his face, so he kept changing it, from grin to frown to boredom.

Mikey opened the Math book and looked at the index.

"What does this have to do with Ronnie? She said—"

Mikey interrupted him. "We did this in seventh grade."

"It's Basic Math Operations," Louis said. "That's the name of the course. It was supposed to be a gut, but it has home-work."

"Never mind that right now," Margalo said. She took out a piece of paper and a pencil, as if ready to write things down, and spoke in a low voice. "About Ronnie."

That topic focused Louis's attention. "Yeah," he said, leaning forward and lowering his own voice. "I told her me and Sal would work the guy over, but she said you had a better idea. Which is why I'm here," he reminded them, in case they had forgotten.

"But you have to actually work with us too," Margalo informed him. "Or Chet'll see through it. Ronnie can't afford to have Chet seeing through it."

"I *know* that. I'm not a total dunce," Louis said. He looked at Mikey. "Whatever Mee-shelle here might think. At least I'm still in school, but I don't notice her on the tennis team anymore." Satisfied, he sat back. "So, what's this great idea of yours? Because if you let Chet weasel out of this—"

Margalo told him. "What if your father and Ronnie's father were talking to a lawyer, who would you tell about that? Talking about bringing a sexual harassment case against Chet, I mean," she added.

"But they're not. Do you think they should? It's a stupid idea anyway, because Ronnie told me she really doesn't want a lot of gossip. In case you can't figure it out, that means she doesn't want any law cases. Don't you ever watch TV?"

"But what if," Margalo asked, "even if they weren't going to do that, Chet *believed* they were? What if he thought Mikey's stepfather was a big-time Texas lawyer who was helping her family with the case?"

Louis considered that. "Boy," he concluded. "I wouldn't like it if some girl said that about me, that I sexually harassed her. Because whether I did or not, people would think I did. Especially if she took me to court." He considered a little longer. "And Chet's a senior." In case they didn't see the importance of that, he explained, "It would ruin his whole senior year if Ronnie did that. Is that what you're thinking?"

They left him to realize it for himself.

"And I bet his hotshot college wouldn't want someone who'd been accused of sexually harassing my cousin. In court.

That's a pretty good idea, Margalo. I have to say. I'll tell my dad. I bet he would do it."

"No, no," Mikey said. "Louis, wait. Because . . ." At a glance from Margalo she skipped the explanation. "The plan is, the plan Ronnie wants is that Chet *believes* that's what's going to happen. A thing doesn't have to happen just because it *might* happen, right? That's where you come in. That's where Ronnie needs your help. You have to tell Sal, but you absolutely can't let him know what Chet really did. Just say something vague about a lawsuit, like you could ask him if he knows what a lawsuit is? You have to tell it as if you don't know anything specific. All you know is that something is going on."

Louis objected, "I thought this was Margalo's idea."

Margalo knew what Mikey was about to say. Mikey was about to say, "How big a jerk are you?" at which question Louis would probably answer, "Not as big as you, Mee-shelle," and then either he would kick Mikey under the table and she would kick him back under the table, or she would shove his Math book right back at him so hard it would take his breath away—because she would aim for his gut, the obvious target. Then Louis would whomp her on the head with the book, or maybe just on the hand, or maybe Louis would get up and leave the table after he said the most cutting, sarcastic thing he could think of. For sure, the Ronnie plan would be ruined. That was the only truly predictable thing that would happen if Mikey said what she was thinking.

So Margalo intervened. "Making the bet was my idea. I can never resist a challenge."

The diversion worked. Louis said, "You really think I could pass English? You're supposed to be such an English genius, but I always said you aren't as smart as everyone says."

"And I always said you aren't as stupid as they say," Margalo answered. "Because nobody could be. So we're even."

Mikey stuck to the main point. "So, you'll talk to Sal?"

"You think Sal will tell Chet?" Louis asked. "Sal's not even a blip on Chet's radar."

"I think Sal will tell a couple of people, and they'll tell a couple of people, and sooner or later—I'm betting sooner," Margalo said, "Chet'll get told. And then Chet will come to ask you about it."

"Cool," Louis said.

"But you won't be able to tell him anything definite because you don't know," Margalo said. "Because it's a big mystery to you, it's just something going on that you can't figure out."

"I get it, I get it," Louis said. He started to rise from his seat, but Mikey stopped him.

"How far has your class gotten in this Math book?" she asked.

"Almost to the end. The intro Algebra chapter is due next week, but—"

"What were your grades?"

"I got a D first semester, a sixty-four. I did okay the first marking period. Then it got to hard stuff—long division, you know, and fractions. And decimals," he remembered, outraged. "And I can never do word problems."

Mikey waited.

"I got my grade up to a fifty-five in the fourth marking period, but he's grading me harder in the fifth. A forty-eight, he says, if I'm lucky. My father got on my case after midyears because—They called him in," another outraged memory. "It's not fair. There's not supposed to be homework in the D-level classes. Is there?"

Mikey told him, "So you need a seventy-seven for the final marking period. And at least a sixty on the exam to pass the year."

"You did that in your head?"

"So first you have to talk to your teacher."

"He hates me."

"And tell him you want to try to pass. Ask him if you can make up old homework assignments. I want to see the chapter one, two, and three assignments on Friday, that's two nights."

"That's only two nights," Lou protested.

"You don't have much time," Mikey pointed out.

"And if anyone asks you what you're doing talking with us, tell them about this," Margalo instructed. "About the bet."

"I already figured that out on my own," Louis said.

"Also, you need to ask your English teacher about extra-credit makeup work," Margalo said.

328

"She hates me."

"Plus, the reading assignments."

"I stink at reading. You *know* that," Louis protested.

"I'll be tutoring you," Margalo pointed out.

Louis couldn't think of how he wanted to respond to that. "How much is the bet for?" he asked her. "You should split your winnings with me."

Margalo just smiled—Mona Lisa, she hoped—and Mikey smiled more like the big, bad wolf. Neither one of them answered Louis, so after a brief wait he got up. "Okay," he said. "Okay. I'm going to find Sal. I'm only doing this because of Ronnie," he told them. "Just to remind you about that fact."

When he was gone, Cassie called down to them from the other end of the table, "What was that about? You don't have crushes on him, do you?"

"Are you looking for a fat lip?" Mikey asked.

"We've got a bet about Louis," Margalo said.

"What bet?" they wanted to know, and when Margalo explained the part of it she wanted people to know about, reactions varied. "You guys don't know a lost cause when you see one, do you?" was one. "How big a bet?" was another, and a third was, "You think I believe that you don't have crushes?"

"Believe it," Margalo advised.

And as if Margalo hadn't been busy enough all day, riding home alone on the late bus she had an idea, an idea so possible that she telephoned Mikey first thing. "I was thinking."

"You're always thinking."

"About what you said Monday. Remember? About accusing Coach Sandy?"

"I already did. Nobody cared."

"But what if you made your accusation a protest? What if you protested, like in the sixties, with signs and placards, like the anti-war protests, like anti-abortion placards, like when people go out on strike, protesting their wages or hours or benefits? What if we protested at tennis games? Or even just at practice?"

"We who?" Mikey wondered.

"You, me, I don't know, Hadrian. Isn't there anybody on the team who agrees with you about this?"

"You and Hadrian are in rehearsal every afternoon."

Margalo hadn't thought of that. That was like a bucket of very cold water poured down over her very hot idea. "Oh."

"I'll have to do it alone," Mikey concluded. "But you have to help me with slogans. I want to start tomorrow, so you call Casey and I'll call Cassie. Cassie can get us into the art room," she explained, then asked, "What's so funny?"

— 19 —

Mikey on the March

On Thursday—the thirty-seventh-to-last day of ninth grade—it was still raining. Mikey and Margalo, plus Cassie Davis, their point person in the Art Department, and Jace tagging along, and also Casey Wolsowski, who happened to overhear their plans, spent their lunch period in the Art Room making posters for Mikey's protest march.

"It can't be a march with just one person," Cassie pointed out.

"It's raining, so it won't be a march at all." Mikey had been looking forward to circling the wire cage enclosing the six tennis courts for the whole length of the practice, not saying a word, just pumping her posters up and down. She planned to have a variety of posters, with a variety of messages. She planned to be as stony faced and unresponsive as those guards at the gates of Buckingham Palace. What she hadn't planned on was rain. "It's raining. In the rain, how will I be able to—"

Margalo interrupted. "Tennis will meet in Coach Sandy's office, won't they? A tactics class, isn't that what you did on other rainy days? So you can stand at that window while she's talking to them."

She was right as usual. So Mikey could go ahead with her protest, but she had to admit to herself that she was a little tired of Margalo being so smart, and so right, and so filled up with ideas. Mikey was just as capable of having ideas. She just didn't usually, and how could she? The way Margalo was always rushing around, waving her ideas in your face like flags, having her ideas first.

That was not a line of thought that was going to take her anywhere forward, so Mikey forgot about it. She set to painting her slogan onto the piece of poster board in fat red capital letters, easy to read: YOU SHOULD CARE. Then she added a couple of exclamation points to build it up: YOU SHOULD CARE!! The red paint was a little runny, making the letters messy. She mopped at them with a paper towel and stood back, studying her poster. It wasn't art, but it went straight to the point. It said exactly what she meant.

Everybody had something to say, and either red or blue paint to say it in, and a sheet of poster board to say it on. Mikey took a second sheet and painted in red, being more careful this time because she didn't actually like the smudged look: BAD CALLS MAKE BAD TENNIS.

Cassie and Jace worked together to paint a pointing finger

attached to a hand, a copy of the famous World War I enlistment poster where the finger points right at the viewer. ARE YOU A CHEAT? they wrote at the bottom.

IMPEACH COACH SANDY! Cassie wrote on another poster, in bold longhand letters, like graffiti on a wall. "What do you think?" she asked Margalo, who asked, "Can you impeach someone who hasn't been elected?"

Casey took that piece of poster board and turned it over to write: "Tennis players of the team, unite! You have nothing to lose but your coach!" There wasn't enough room for capitals, so she had to write it out in lowercase letters, and at the looks on their faces she had to explain, "It's what Karl Marx said." That didn't make anything any clearer, so she added, "'Workers of the world unite, you have nothing to lose but your chains.'"

"Who's Karl Marx?" Mikey asked.

"Are you a Communist?" Margalo wondered.

"He was actually a political philosopher," Casey said. "I like the way it sounds, and anyone who knows the original saying will *really* get it."

"That'll be you and who else?" Cassie asked.

"Me, actually," Jace admitted.

"Communism isn't the big enemy anymore," Mikey reminded them. "Besides, I like it, even if I didn't really get it. But have you noticed?" she asked Margalo. "There's always some big enemy. Why do people always want to have an enemy? The Soviet bloc had us," she pointed out. "It wasn't just us having them."

Cassie said, "You have Coach Sandy."

"I don't have her for an enemy. I just want her fired," Mikey said. "That's different. An enemy you have to keep around, and keep making bigger so that you can keep on fighting against them."

Margalo's poster was finished. She pushed it down the long table for Mikey to see. COACH SANDY 15, it said, and right underneath that, like a scoreboard, FAIR PLAY 1.

Margalo's was the best, no question. It was so good a best that Mikey couldn't even be jealous.

Mikey was leaning against the wall opposite Coach Sandy's office. She had set the posters up against the wall, facing in. Most people ignored her, finishing their own conversations— "Sally finally had to ask Richard to the prom, she got so tired of waiting for him to ask her." "Does it ever burn you how Chet Parker gets the best of everything and now Ronnie Caselli too?" "Do you have the Chemistry homework? Have you done it? Can I see it?" A couple of players greeted her as they went past, going in for the rainy-day tactics class. "You cost us our chance at the regionals, I hope you know." "Are you here to apologize?" Only Mark Jacobs said simply, "Hey, Mikey, how are you?"

Mikey shrugged in answer. She was fine, just fine. It was Coach Sandy they should be worrying about; and a lot of them, now she thought of it, should be worrying about themselves.

Through the wide plate-glass window Mikey watched the squad settle itself facing a blackboard on wheels that stood beside the desk. Some people sat on folding chairs that had been set out, some chose the floor. When they had all gone in and the door had been closed behind them, Mikey picked up her pile of posters and approached the window.

All she could see through it were a couple of rows of backs of heads and the profiles of the people sitting against the side walls, under promotional materials from the big sports companies, pictures of big-name players in full swing, and Coach Sandy standing facing her at the front of the room beside the blackboard, with a piece of chalk in her hand, her short pleated skirt swinging. She saw Mikey standing in the window, stared coldly for a couple of seconds, and then pretended there was no one there.

The coach started talking, and Mikey let her get settled into whatever speech she was making before raising the first poster to the window. With the poster held up in front of her, Mikey couldn't see any reactions. All she could see was the blank white surface of the back, so she stepped off to one side, stretching out her arms to keep the poster level.

The coach had noticed it. How could she miss it? And she had read it. So also had a couple of other people, who shrugged and rolled their eyes at each other. Then the coach went back to pretending nobody was doing anything outside of her window, while people nudged one another and, under pretense of taking out a pencil or a sheet of paper, whispered to one another.

335

Mikey switched from YOU SHOULD CARE!! to BAD CALLS MAKE BAD TENNIS. More heads turned—quickly—to see what was going on and then turned—just as quickly—back to the coach. She had called them sharply to attention, was Mikey's guess. After a few minutes she raised the ARE YOU A CHEAT? poster and saw some heads lowered, as if that was a question they didn't want to be asked. She held that one up for a while, letting Coach Sandy get some good looks at it.

She couldn't hear anything that was being said in the room, although the coach had started to draw Xs connected by arrows on a rectangle on the board, the rectangle divided in half by a line that was probably the net. It looked like she was telling them when to move up to the net in doubles and when to fall back. Mikey raised another poster. This one was Casey's, so while Mikey could see Cassie's IMPEACH COACH SANDY! slogan, the coach herself, and some of the people in the room, read Casey's more literary-historical message urging them to unite.

Mark Jacobs was grinning to himself when he turned back to face the front of the room, but Coach Sandy went to her desk and picked up her phone. Since she wasn't watching them, the people in the room could now look at Mikey, trying to express without words whatever feelings they were having. Not many of the feelings were positive. A lot of them were expressed by a waving of the arm, *Scram, Get lost, Beat it.*

Mikey smiled, *You don't get rid of me that easily,* and held up Margalo's poster. This one she held right in front of her, putting it smack in the middle of the window. She held it up for a long time so they could work it out.

She expected, at any moment, that Coach Sandy would burst through the door. She didn't know what the woman would say to try to make her stop. She had decided that she wouldn't say anything in response. Not one word. She'd just keep holding up her posters, one after the other, for everybody to have to see.

She was waiting to hear the door open. She was waiting to hear her name called, and at last she did.

"Michelle Elsinger?"

But that was a man's voice.

Mikey turned her head and saw Mr. Robredo jogging down the corridor. She turned her head back to stare at the blank back of the poster.

Mr. Robredo?

Mr. Robredo!

As soon as he'd seen her see him, Mr. Robredo stopped jogging and started walking, fast and firm, right up to her. Mikey kept the poster up, but she turned to watch the assistant principal.

When he got up to her, he didn't waste a minute. "Come with me," he said. He didn't sound angry, he just sounded like he expected to be obeyed. "Bring those placards, too." Turning on his heel, he marched abruptly away, back down the corridor. He never even looked to be sure Mikey was following.

Mikey picked up her knapsack and the posters and followed his straight back, keeping eight paces behind, maybe ten. She wasn't about to catch up with him, and she wasn't about to lag too far behind, either. She followed Mr. Robredo up the wide staircase and down the hallway where glass cases displayed various trophies won by various teams at various times in the school's history. She followed him through the broad gym doors and across into the classroom building. She followed him past the closed doors of empty classrooms. She followed him into his office.

There he let her step past him before shutting the door behind her. "Sit," he told her, and turning to a tall file cabinet, he pulled out a long drawer and from that pulled out a single file folder.

Mikey's chair was alone on its side of the desk, like the criminal's chair in a police interrogation scene.

Mr. Robredo sat down in his chair and opened the file.

The only sound in the room was the rustling of papers as he read. Mikey looked around her. The walls were completely covered, by bookcases, file cabinets, and posters—Habitat for Humanity, Oxfam, HIV/AIDS in Africa, FINCA, Heifer Project.

Then, since she didn't feel like sitting around doing nothing, she leaned down and took out the notebook in which she was making a list of math skills Louis Caselli would have to have mastered in order to do the makeup homework assignments and pass the unit tests so he could have a chance of passing his final exam with a high enough grade to enable him to pass Math for the year. The basic math operations, and fractions, decimals—she needed to check him on those; then there was the problem of word problems. If people who were bad at Math—even Margalo, who always got A's in English—had trouble with word problems, she could just imagine what a hash Louis would make of them.

Although, that word-problem problem was odd, since Margalo never had trouble with poems, and those struck Mikey as merely giant word problems, just without the convenience of numbers to help figure them out.

Mr. Robredo cleared his throat. Mikey looked up, all attention.

"Michelle," he said. He was looking right at her, his expression serious. "This—"

"Mikey," she interrupted. Then she explained, "Call me Mikey." Then, since he was waiting, she added, "Please."

He nodded, satisfied with how the discussion was going. "May I see those placards?"

She passed them to him, one at a time. He read them, one at a time, and passed them back to her. Then he rose to come around to the front of the desk and lean back against it. She couldn't tell if this was a more threatening posture or a friendlier one. She pushed her chair back a little.

"Did you do all of this yourself?" he asked.

The question took Mikey by surprise and she hesitated.

"Why?" Because she wasn't about to rat on her friends, if that was what he was after.

Mr. Robredo was relaxed, half sitting on his desk, calm, in control of the situation. "Because they sound like different minds to me. If they were all yours, I'd want to know that about you."

Mikey wished she *had* done them all, had thought of them all herself. But she had to tell him, "It was other people too."

He nodded. He'd been proved right.

"Just exactly what is the problem here?" he asked.

"I got thrown off the tennis team."

"I know that," he said, indicating with his hand the open file behind him. "And I know why."

"It's not true," Mikey said.

"What's not true?"

"What she said."

"What did she say?"

Mikey had to admit, "I don't know. But not the truth, I bet."

"What is the truth? According to you."

He already knew that from reading the posters, but Mikey answered his question anyway. "Because I wouldn't cheat on calls. All right, not exactly cheat, but—Do you play tennis?"

He shook his head.

Mikey waited for a while, and when he didn't add anything, she asked, "What sports do you play?"

"Tai chi," he said, and something in her face made him

340

smile before he added, "In school I played baseball and soccer. I swim."

Well, he was in good shape. He wasn't muscular and he wasn't a big man, but he wasn't flabby at all, not like a lot of men who work in schools, teachers and administrators. Mikey tried to explain, "Tennis is different. Because you don't have referees or umpires or anything. The players call lines themselves. Even if it's a close call."

He nodded, listening.

"And if I want to get to a ball and get a good shot off of it, I have to focus on the ball itself, but I'm watching it so I can hit it, not so I can call it in or out. So whenever it's close, the way it's traditionally done in tennis, when it's close it's called in. In fact, it's easier that way."

He nodded and waited.

Mikey couldn't believe he couldn't work out the rest for himself. "She got angry at me for doing that in a match."

"Tell me something. Do the other players on the team also make their calls in the traditional way?"

Mikey wasn't about to rat on the people on the tennis squad either. "I'm talking about matches," she said. "Sometimes I've had opponents make bad calls."

"You're sure of that?"

Now Mikey was the one nodding and waiting. She had completed her case.

"So Coach Delorme asked you to cheat?"

Mikey had to admit, "Not in so many words. But that was

341

what she meant." She didn't know if he believed her or not, but she was guessing probably not. Adults, in schools, tended to stick together and stick up for one another.

"Coach Delorme reported"—he indicated the file behind him again—"that you refuse to take instruction. Your insubordination is having a bad effect on the team."

Mikey smiled, *What else do you expect her to say?*

"There haven't been any other complaints about her," Mr. Robredo pointed out. "The opposite, in fact."

Mikey could see where this conversation was going. *Day thirty-seven*, she said silently to herself. It was almost down to only seven more weeks of school.

"So I'm wondering if we aren't dealing with a personality conflict here," Mr. Robredo said.

"We certainly are," she agreed, and that surprised him. He didn't look like someone easy to surprise, and it cheered her up to be the one to do it.

"Can I take it, then, that there will be no more of these placards?" he asked her.

Mikey shrugged and gathered them together into a pile. She picked up her knapsack. It wasn't as if the tennis team had risen up to support her. It wasn't as if the school wanted to do anything about Coach Sandy. It wasn't as if she couldn't figure that out for herself. "Okay," she said, and walked to the door. There she turned around to see if he had anything else to say, but he didn't, so she left.

❖

Margalo was as glum as Mikey on the Late Activities bus. "Robredo, hunh?" was all she had to say when Mikey reported in. "Was it bad?" was all she asked.

Mikey *was* pleased to be able to report, "He's not as tall as he looks." Then she waited, but Margalo was seated next to the window, looking out. Then, "Chet doesn't look worried," Margalo reported.

"Maybe he hasn't heard?"

"This is high school. He's heard. Maybe he's bluffing?"

Mikey had a nasty idea. "Maybe he doesn't believe it."

Margalo had an equally bad one. "Maybe he doesn't care?"

"Maybe he knows nobody cares."

They were both looking out the window at the gray, rainy afternoon.

Finally Margalo asked, "So, what about tennis?"

Mikey shook her head. "I can't think of anything else."

Margalo sympathized. "I can't either."

"But you're the idea person," Mikey protested. "You *have* to have an idea."

— 20 —

Brainstorm Alert!

Mikey didn't exactly think of it. She woke up with it. When she opened her eyes in the morning, the idea was in her head and she knew how good it was. As good as anything Margalo had ever thought of. Mikey hadn't felt as pleased with herself, or as eager for whatever was going to happen next, since the day she moved into the top spot on Coach Sandy's tennis ladder.

Part of her gladness was the idea itself, but the other part—the biggest part—was that she'd had it by herself. It was her own idea and no help from Margalo.

She waited impatiently for Margalo to arrive at school that Friday morning—day thirty-six, a great day for Mikey and a beautiful end-of-April day too—so she could present her idea. When she saw Margalo coming down the hallway towards her, she started smiling. *Just wait until you hear this.*

Margalo was swishing along in some skirt with flowers on

it. She was grinning right back at Mikey, as if she already knew what Mikey planned to show off to her with. Well, maybe she did. Sometimes Margalo was so smart about people even Mikey was surprised.

"Listen to who—," Margalo said. Mikey said, "Wait till—" Neither one of them said *You go first.*

Mikey said, "You hear—," and Margalo said, "Called—"

Mikey shoved her idea ahead, keeping it short, simple. "Linespeople. To call lines at matches."

"But that's brilliant!" Margalo exclaimed.

"It is, isn't it?"

"Absolutely."

Both at the same time, they reached out to shake hands on it, like Stanley and Livingstone finally meeting up in the jungles of Africa.

Mikey already had her books for her morning classes, so they went to Margalo's locker.

"Who are you going to ask to do it?" Margalo asked as she worked her combination lock. (L1-R5-L6-R4, as Mikey happened to know, the year of Shakespeare's birth, just the kind of combination Margalo would choose. She herself used the first primes and reversed the order, so it was L7-R5-L3-R2, much easier to remember.)

If Margalo thought Mikey hadn't already thought about who to ask, she was wrong. Mikey could make plans as well as have ideas. "You and Hadrian," she said. "We'll have to pick which sets to call, because they play on all six courts, but—"

345

"Hadrian and I have rehearsals."

"But that leaves only me! You need a minimum of two people to call lines, one for each side of the court." Nevertheless, Mikey wasn't about to give up her idea. "All right, it'll be hard, but if I'm always on the receiver's side, I can do it," she decided. An idea this good should never be given up on.

"What if—"

The homeroom bell interrupted Margalo, and Mikey was still solving her problem out loud. "Plus, I'll have to figure out which matches are likely to be the crucial ones."

"What is *wrong* with you?" Margalo demanded. But they had to head off, and Mikey had no time to answer.

Besides, how can you respond to that kind of question?

By lunchtime Mikey had thought of how. She joined Margalo in the sunshine, sitting on the low brick wall, and unpacked her lunch bag onto her lap, asking at the same time, "What do you *think* is so wrong with me? Because I don't agree."

"Two things," Margalo said. "One is you're so self-involved you didn't even ask about what I wanted to tell you, and two is the way you only think of one answer."

"One's all there is. That's what makes it the answer."

"Wrong—that's what makes it *an* answer. Look." She passed Mikey a sheet of paper with names written on it, the last two, Hadrian and Margalo, in parentheses. Margalo bit off a mouthful of sandwich—it looked like supermarket packaged sliced ham—so Mikey had to wait until she had swallowed to say, "I thought you had rehearsals."

"Sometimes we can get away early."

"Do you really think all of these people would be willing to help *me*?" Mikey asked, because whatever was *wrong* with her, it wasn't being so dim she couldn't figure out what the list was for. Neither, however, was it being unaware of how people felt about her.

"A lot of them, maybe, would want to help. Ronnie, for example—and Louis owes us. Louis would bring in Sal. Cassie liked doing the posters. She likes being an activist, and Jace—well, Jace might not, it depends on how he and Cassie are getting along that day. But Casey might if she thinks it's a good cause."

"It's a good cause."

"And I bet Tim will, so probably Felix, too, and that's already eight."

"Nine with me."

"Eight without Jace."

"Tanisha," Mikey announced, and Margalo nodded. Encouraged, Mikey suggested, "Derrie? Annaliese? Do you think Shawn Macavity, because it's sort of a spotlight position?"

"You can always ask," Margalo answered, "but I wouldn't."

"We don't have to call the lines on every court," Mikey decided. "I'm going to have to explain things, how to make the calls, how the games are scored."

"When is the next match?" Margalo asked.

"Tuesday."

"So we have the weekend."

"We should start asking people right away," Mikey said. "What do you think, together or separately?"

"Together," Margalo decided. "It'll be harder to say no to both of us."

That settled, Mikey set about proving that she wasn't self-involved by asking, "What did you want to tell me this morning?"

"Nothing about tennis."

"Then, let's get going," Mikey said.

They moved off in search of whoever they saw first.

Many students were eating lunch outside on this warm Friday. They were all over the place, sitting in rows on the low wall, sitting in clusters on the grass. Upperclassmen had claimed the seven picnic tables the school had set out for good weather. The school had also set out half a dozen faculty members, who stood drinking water out of bottles in the shade of the trees that had been planted when the school was new, twelve years earlier.

Mikey sighted Tan, having a picnic lunch on the grass with Loretta, just the two of them. Both wore jeans and short-sleeved tees, with sandals that displayed bright red toenails. They sat cross-legged, facing each other, involved in a serious discussion. What were they talking about? Margalo wondered, but Mikey hunkered down on her heels beside Tan and said, "I need you to help me out."

"I told you, I don't have any interest in tennis."

"Excuse me, we were having a conversation," Loretta said.

"It's a favor," Margalo said.

"A private conversation, wasn't it, Tan?" Loretta said.

"Here's my idea," Mikey said before the conversation could veer off course. She explained about teaching people how to call the lines during tennis matches.

This being high school, word had already spread about her being dropped from the team and why, although there were many different versions of that going around, ranging from Coach Sandy being jealous of Mikey's ability (the way some teachers are made uneasy by intelligent students) to Mikey being jealous of Coach Sandy's successes (the way some students need to feel as if teachers can't do anything and don't know anything either).

"Yes, sure. I'll do it," Tan said immediately, but Loretta was an upperclassman, more cautious, more experienced. "You know they're not going to like it," she warned Mikey.

"Especially Coach Sandy," Mikey agreed cheerfully.

Loretta's warnings continued. "I don't think you know what you're getting into."

Margalo answered that. "I don't think they know what *they're* getting into."

"I don't think you want to get mixed up in this, Tan," advised Loretta.

Tan, however, had gotten mixed up in things with Mikey and Margalo since fifth grade, sometimes on the same side, sometimes not. "But I do," she said. "It'll be fun. A lot more

349

fun than sitting around waiting to get older. And Mikey's in the right about this," Tan said.

"Suit yourselves," Loretta said.

"I do," Mikey said, and, "We will," Margalo said, and they went off to see who else they could find.

Ronnie found *them*. Mikey and Margalo were in front of the library on their way to see who was in the cafeteria when Ronnie caught up with them from behind. She put one arm around each of their shoulders—a little awkwardly because Margalo was a lot taller and Mikey so much shorter. "You two!" she said. "I owe you!"

They all stopped, making an inconvenient little island of three in the center of the hallway. People moved around them. If it hadn't been Ronnie Caselli, there would have been some audible complaints and maybe even some shoving. But it was Ronnie, so there weren't.

"How can I thank you?" Ronnie asked, glowing with happiness.

In their experience, when Ronnie glowed with happiness it had to do with falling in love with someone. Mikey looked at Margalo. Margalo looked at Mikey. If Ronnie was in the process of falling in love with someone, she'd be pretty useless as a line caller. But Mikey answered her question anyway: "You can be one of the people who calls lines in the tennis match on Tuesday."

Ronnie's arms fell back to her sides. "What?"

"You asked how you could thank us," Mikey reminded her. "You said you owe us."

"I know, but—"

"Let me explain," Margalo said. She reminded Ronnie about what had happened to Mikey in tennis and explained how if lines were called by impartial people, it would be fairer for everybody.

"But do you have permission?" Ronnie wondered.

"Why would they object?" Margalo asked. She didn't answer the exact question, on the principle that it was always preferable to avoid an outright lie. Mikey had already said, "Why would I need permission?" but Ronnie usually listened to Margalo, not Mikey.

"Well, okay, I guess," Ronnie said. "Who else is doing it?"

"So far, Tan," Margalo said.

Ronnie smiled then, radiant with white teeth and self-confidence. "I could ask Chet."

"Chet?" Mikey echoed, appalled.

Margalo told her: "That's what I wanted to tell you. Ronnie called me last night. Chet's backed off. He apologized."

"Not Chet," Mikey said.

"It's not like we're going together anymore," Ronnie explained quickly. "Although he'd like to, and he's asked me out for Saturday. Lunch," she told them. "Only lunch, so I said I would. He says he's really sorry, he didn't mean it the way it sounded, but he doesn't blame me for being upset. In fact, he admires me for it, he says." She looked happily from

Margalo to Mikey and back again. "He's pretty scared. That was a great plan you guys came up with."

"I don't want Chet calling lines with me," Mikey told Ronnie. "I mean it," she said, to make sure she had gotten through.

"Well, all right, but . . . He says he'll do whatever I want, and I think I'm going to have him take me to the Prom."

"You're still dating him?" Margalo asked.

"No, of course not. What do you think of me? Chet knows I'm not, but other people don't. I really, really want to go to the Senior Prom. I'll be the only freshman there," Ronnie explained. Then she looked at Mikey and back at Margalo and admitted, "I know it's shallow. But what do you want me to say?"

Mikey kept to the point. "I'll call you about when we're meeting to learn line calls."

"I'm busy Saturday lunch."

Cassie and Casey and Jace and Felix were together in the cafeteria at the usual table. Tim was with them and so was Hadrian. Mikey and Margalo took chairs at opposite ends of the group and at opposite sides of the table. They hadn't planned this in advance, but they worked it out that way so that they could send the conversation back and forth between them, like a tennis ball.

"Mikey has an idea," Margalo said, and the heads turned to her to hear what she was saying.

"Listen to this," Mikey said, and the heads turned to look at her. "What if we had people calling the lines in our tennis matches, like the pros do?"

"Good idea," said Tim.

"Who?" Casey asked, and, "Us," Margalo answered. The heads turned to look at her.

"But we have rehearsals," Hadrian said, dismayed, and, "Not on Saturdays and not always," Margalo assured him. "Sometimes we can leave early."

"Plus"—the heads turned to look at Mikey—"Tanisha Harris."

"Mikey"—the heads turned back to Margalo—"can teach everybody how to do it."

"Yeah, but it's not like they'll give us permission," Jace pointed out.

"It's not like I'm asking for permission," Mikey answered. The heads turned.

"Also"—and Margalo waited until the heads turned back to her—"it's not like they'd want to make a big scene to stop us, I don't think."

"You can count me in," Cassie offered, and she was echoed by everybody at the table.

Tim was obviously impressed. "I don't know where you two get your ideas."

Cassie knew this. "Ideas are easy. Ideas are all over the place. You see something and it gives you ideas."

"Yeah, like I see one of those Victoria's Secret catalogs and it gives me lots of ideas," Jace joked.

"We know," said Cassie, not joining in the laughter. "We've seen your artwork."

"Yeah, but who's the one Peter Paul's saying has the talent to get into art school?" Jace asked her back, and when Cassie answered, "Who wants to go to art school?" Margalo wondered if competitiveness was going to accomplish what common sense, infidelity, boredom and constant quarreling had not yet been able to—that is, cause Jace and Cassie to end their long-term (since the start of eighth grade) romance.

Tim said, "If I have to write an op-ed piece, the topic is by far the hardest part for me."

"This one popped into my head while I was asleep," Mikey admitted.

"That's your unconscious," Casey explained.

"What would I want with an unconscious?" asked Mikey.

Margalo's curiosity had been aroused by Tim's question, and she told them, "To have an idea, I think about where I want to end up, and then my mind goes backwards to find a way to end up there. You know?"

They were so engrossed in this conversation that they were all startled when Brenda Means leaned over between Tim and Felix to ask, "Tim? I'm not interrupting, am I?"

Brenda also wrote for the paper, humorous poems with clever rhymes, about love or the weather, sometimes about styles, of dress or talk or food, sometimes about families, sisters and brothers, parents and grandparents, pets.

Brenda said, "I'm wondering if—I was working on a poem, in the newspaper room . . . But it's not there now, and I was wondering if you already picked it up? Because it's not finished."

Tim shook his head. "What was it about?"

"Oh, spring and a girl whose boyfriend is on the baseball team. I called it *Run Home*."

"When did you leave it there?"

"Yesterday. I just forgot about it, and—When I went back just now, because the deadline's coming up—as you know . . ." She shrugged. "I guess someone must have thrown it out."

"Don't you make notes? Don't you have a draft?" Tim asked.

"No, I just . . . write. Well, maybe, it was on the table, probably somebody just picked it up with some other papers of theirs and didn't even notice. I'll ask around."

"Let me know if it turns up, okay?"

She looked puzzled but agreed, "Okay, sure."

After Brenda left, Tim turned to Felix and said, "Remember that really good new writer I told you about? Her poem? It sounds just like Brenda's."

"I remember."

"But it was Cathy Johnson who submitted it."

"You think she stole it? She's on the paper, isn't she?"

"A proofreader. But without notes, or without a draft, how can Brenda ever prove it's hers?"

"What can you do? Accuse Cathy? Throw her off the paper? Because that's plagiarism, isn't it? Or does plagiarism have to be copied from something published?"

"I'll have to talk to Stuart. He can ask Miss Marshall, that's what advisers are for. We're not printing it, that's for sure, so we'll need something for that space. But about Cathy? I don't even want to—Why would someone do that?"

"How could someone think she'd get away with doing that?" Mikey asked. "When the paper came out, Brenda would know, everyone would know. So, we meet tomorrow morning to learn how to call lines? Here at school? At nine?"

Cassie objected. "Saturday mornings I sleep late."

"I'll call you to make sure you're up," Mikey promised. "Meet me at the courts, behind the gym. Let's go, Margalo. The more people I have, the more courts we can cover." She rose and Margalo followed her, out of the cafeteria and partway down the hall before they realized they didn't know where they were going next.

They met up with Louis accidentally. He was thundering down the broad cement staircase, with Sal at his side and Danny Schake right behind them. Louis pretended he didn't see them, pretending he was engrossed in whatever Sal was telling Danny, but Mikey planted herself right in front of him and he had to stop. He stood on the lowest step, glaring down at them.

Sal and Danny moved on a little ways, then they stopped too. They were curious, since everybody knew how little these three liked one another and for how long. But everybody also knew about the weird bet Mikey and Margalo had going, about getting Louis to pass Math and English, so who knew what might happen next? Sal and Danny were hoping that something might happen, something that might even end up with people getting in trouble, or at least getting into a fight.

Louis took the offensive. "I have until after school. You said, you both said. I'm going to do the work in my free periods."

Mikey and Margalo just waited.

"It's not like you're doing me some big favor," Louis said, with a glance over at his cousin and their friend to be sure they could see how unwilling a participant he was in this encounter.

"Actually," Margalo said, "we want you to do *us* a favor."

"You owe us," Mikey pointed out. "You owe us two, three if you count Math separate from English. If you can count as high as that."

Louis's face got satisfyingly red, maybe embarrassment, maybe fury, they didn't care. Either one was equally desirable.

"I did what you asked about Chet," he reminded them in a low voice.

"That was for Ronnie," Margalo pointed out, adding, "And for your whole family."

"For Ronnie's reputation," Mikey specified.

"I'm your bet," Louis argued.

"Lou-ie! We're waiting," Danny called.

Sal said, "Whatsa matter, man? You need help?"

Louis shook his head at them and said to Margalo, "I gotta go."

"You know," Margalo said, "if you were tutoring someone in something he didn't know much about, you could teach him the wrong things. Couldn't you, Mikey?"

Mikey had never thought of that. "You could." Already she could think of two ways to do that to Louis.

"You could teach him incorrect spelling and bad grammar," Margalo suggested.

"Hey," Louis protested. Then he thought of the argument. "You'd lose the bet," he reminded Margalo.

"I'd win," Mikey said.

"*And* you'd be in a different class from us forever," Margalo said.

"All *right*," Louis said. "So, what is this big favor?" he asked, but as if he couldn't care less about it. He turned and waved a hand in circles in the air, to show how they were talking on and on and wouldn't stop, so his friends could see he was cool.

Mikey started to explain. "I was thrown—"

"I already know that and I don't blame her. I wouldn't want you on any team of mine."

"Yes you would," Mikey said. "If you wanted to win."

"I'd never want to win that bad," Louis said.

"Badly," Margalo said. "Grammar," she said in answer to the expression on his face.

"All I'm trying to do is get even," Mikey said.

"Get even with a teacher? With a coach?" Louis wasn't beyond that temptation. "Let's get Sal over too. Or is it only me you want?" He seemed to think this might be the case.

"Hey, Sal," Mikey called quickly. "You too, Danny. Louis needs you."

They slouched over, cool, and she explained the idea, and

Margalo explained why they would have to learn something about how to do it, which meant learning something about how the games were played.

"Yeah, but," Sal said, looking at Louis for confirmation, "I heard—We all heard you got benched. Insubordination. I thought that was why you walked out on the tennis team."

Mikey shook her head. "Not true. Not even close to true."

"Maybe a little close," Margalo allowed. "Maybe in the same neighborhood?"

"Maybe a neighborhood in the same city, if the city's Tokyo," Mikey said.

"The thing is," Sal explained to Danny, "she doesn't lie."

"Yeah," Louis agreed. "She bites and kicks and punches—"

"I never bit anybody."

"But she doesn't lie," Louis concluded, a TV newscaster reporting the latest bad news.

"So, what *did* happen?" asked Danny, who because he had met Mikey and Margalo only in ninth grade, and then mostly by hearsay, didn't have a long history of hostilities to keep him from asking for their side of the story.

"She wanted me to call anything close in my favor," Mikey said.

"Well, dunnh," Louis commented.

"Even if I wasn't sure," Mikey said. "In tennis if it's not out for sure, you're supposed to call it in."

"She actually said that? Told you to cheat?" Sal asked.

Mikey had to admit, "Not exactly, but essentially."

"So you're going to fix things so that can't happen," Danny said. "I can dig it."

"But it only makes sense to call in your own favor," Louis pointed out.

"Yeah, sure, I'll do it," Danny said. "Coaches think they can get away with anything."

"Coaches know what they're doing, man. Doesn't everybody cheat a little? If they can?" Louis asked.

Sal said, "Lou? What do you think, are you gonna help them?"

"Ronnie is too," Margalo offered. "And Tan, Tim, Felix, Jace—"

It wasn't an entirely geeky group, which gave Louis the opening to say, "Yeah, man, I guess."

"I'll get Ronnie to call you about when we meet to learn how," Mikey told Sal, and at last the three boys were free to walk away. They took their opportunity.

"Sometimes," Margalo said, "I almost feel sorry for Louis."

"I always do," Mikey agreed.

"No, I mean *really* sorry for him."

"That's why it's important to keep him on his toes," Mikey agreed. "He needs pins stuck in him, like, once a week, otherwise he'll really do himself permanent harm."

"Yeah, but I thought we hated him."

"That's one of the things I don't like about ninth grade," Mikey said. They had been standing close to the pale cement wall, letting people pass them to go up the staircase or pass them after coming down the staircase. Nobody noticed them.

Everybody was too busy doing whatever interested them to pay much attention to anybody else. "It's not as simple to hate somebody as it used to be."

The bell rang, separating them for the afternoon.

The biggest surprise of the day was Ira Pliotes, who came up to Mikey as they were both entering Math class to ask, "Can you use me to call lines?"

"How'd you hear?" Mikey demanded, angry. "Coach Sandy's going to find out, and she'll try to stop me."

Since fifth grade Ira had grown tallish and thinnish, but his ears still stuck out more than ears should, and he was still a nice person. If he hadn't been such an all-rounder—a good student, but not a brain; a pretty good athlete in both soccer and baseball; okay looking, but not outstandingly cute— other boys would probably have made fun of his ears, and the girls would have followed their lead. But Ira seemed to know how to get people liking him. Mikey pretty much respected him: Ira went his own way and thought his own thoughts; he was just normal, but Ira's normal included sometimes disagreeing with other people's normal.

Now he took Mikey's complaint seriously and thought about it. "Probably nobody will tell her," he decided. "I wouldn't. I wouldn't tell any of the coaches about it."

That reminded Mikey. "Aren't you on the baseball squad? Don't you have practice after school?"

"It's JV and I'm about the fourth-string third baseman, so

361

I don't have to be there if there's a tennis match. I've got good vision, Mikey. I'd do a good job."

"I *know* that," Mikey told him, irritated. She could appreciate nice, but sometimes it *was* annoying. "Okay, then," she said. "Tomorrow morning at nine, at the courts."

"Thanks," Ira said, and went on to take his seat.

Mikey took hers—Thanks? What was Ira doing thanking her? She couldn't wait to see Margalo's face when she reported that Ira Pliotes had asked to be one of her line callers.

Mikey figured she had had about all the surprises any day could offer, but there was one more waiting for her beside her locker, its long blond hair now cut short and held to the side by a plain black barrette, its shoes dark blue canvas slip-ons. "Rhonda?" Mikey asked it.

"Yes," Rhonda admitted. She smoothed down the front of her skirt. "I have to catch the bus, but . . . I heard."

"Heard what?" Mikey also had a bus to catch, and Margalo to run down before that. She opened her locker. "Don't believe everything you hear," she advised Rhonda.

"I want to say, I'm sorry for always being so . . . mean to you," Rhonda mumbled, looking about at Mikey's waist. Since Mikey was wearing jeans and an un-tucked-in t-shirt, Mikey was pretty sure her outfit wasn't being admired.

"Okay," Mikey said. She didn't care if Rhonda was mean to her or not, as long as she didn't have to spend any time with her.

"But I'd like to help."

Mikey turned to face her, her arms full of books, to say *Please*, *No*, when Rhonda went on, "But I can't because I can't agree with what you're doing. Rebelling. Trying to break things down. I don't agree with that, Mikey. I never have. And you've always done it and you never got in enough trouble, especially about the squirrel." Rhonda was getting wound up now. Her eyes filled with tears at the remembered injustice.

"That was Margalo." Mikey felt better. This was Rhonda being her old self. She didn't look like her old self, but Mikey knew, You can't judge a book by its cover.

"I don't know what's going to come of you," Rhonda said, her tone of voice revealing the hope that whatever it was would not be anything good.

"Neither do I." Neither did anyone, did they?

"But I would like to help you," said Rhonda the New. But did she mean help in general? Or help in this particular case?

"I don't need help," Mikey said.

"You already have enough people?" Then, in another flash of her old self, she asked, "Don't you and Margalo worry about getting all these people into trouble?"

"Nope," Mikey said, which was the truth, and then, not wanting to give up a chance to give Rhonda a chance to practice having good and generous thoughts, she added, "Margalo can't do it anyway because of the play."

— 21 —

Who's Calling the Shots?

Tuesday was a good day for tennis—warm but not hot, windless, and the overcast sky meant no late-afternoon sun in your eyes. The six tennis courts out behind the gym had two teams warming up on them, one in orange shirts and black shorts, the other in maroon shirts and blue shorts. Beside Courts One and Two there were bleachers, only three tiers high, but tennis never drew much of a crowd. If you wanted to watch the play on Courts Three, Four, Five or Six, you had to stand at one or the other end behind high wire fencing.

Mikey had gathered her linespeople behind the bleachers. Even if anybody had been looking to see if anyone was getting up to anything, her linespeople would have been hard to spot. Since the coaches were busy giving their players last-minute instructions, and since the stands seemed to be unusually crowded—maybe half-full already and people still arriving—nobody paid any attention to the cluster of ninth and tenth graders behind the bleachers.

They all wore khaki trousers—in a couple of cases khaki skirts—and white shirts. Mikey looked around at them and felt weird.

She felt weird because she was going to be on the courts but not playing. Also because she was used to being the person in a group of people who was going off in her own direction, alone, but on this occasion she was the leader, with followers. And really, even if she hated to admit it, she felt weird because Margalo wasn't there to let her know as things went along how they were going.

Not that Margalo wasn't involved. They had discussed who to pair with whom and how to use twelve people to cover each of the four courts they could monitor. "Don't put Louis with you," Margalo had advised. "You bring out the worst in him. You could put him with Tim, he thinks tenth graders are cool. Or Ira, Ira's good with anybody. And if you put Sal with Tan, she'll keep him calm, or Danny with Ronnie because he's got a crush on her, and—What do you think? Keep Cassie and Jace apart? But Casey and Felix would be okay together." They had also talked about when the linespeople should make their entrance. That is, when it would be too late for Coach Sandy to send them away but early enough to allow the players to get used to their presence before the actual matches started.

Now, here, without Margalo, Mikey was going to have to

decide what to say to her people to be sure they wouldn't change their minds on her before they even started, or even quit after they'd begun. She had decided what they should wear and what hand signals they should use and how much about the game and the lines they needed to know; but it seemed to her that everything was about to start happening and she didn't know if she could count on them or not.

She told them, "Remember, if you're not sure it's out, then it's in."

"Even against our own players?" Louis asked, not for the first time.

"Absolutely," Mikey said, so uneasy that she wasn't even impatient with him.

And that was something else unpleasantly weird. She wasn't nervous and excited, the way she was before a match. She was nervous and uneasy—no fun at all.

"Remember," she said. "Only *Out* gets called out loud."

"How many times are you going to tell us this?" grumbled Cassie.

"You never call *In*," Mikey persisted.

"You're like some Hitler dictator," Cassie kept on. "Isn't she, Jace?"

This was more than Mikey could be patient for, and she felt a welcome anger. "You want to leave, Cassie? Because now's the time if you do."

"*I* want to leave," Louis volunteered.

"You don't have the choice," Mikey told him.

"I don't need to be told the same stuff over and over," said Cassie.

"What, are you saying the rest of us *do* need to be told?" demanded Jace.

Ira turned to Cassie and asked with what sounded like genuine curiosity, "Do you two always quarrel like this?"

"You have a problem with that?" Cassie answered.

Whistles blew, the signal that the coaches were gathering their teams back together.

"Dad says we should be ready to get in trouble," Casey warned everybody.

"You told your father?"

"Of course, but—Dad and I have a deal. Unless somebody's in physical danger—or psychological danger too—neither one of us will disclose what the other has told him. Or her. You can trust him," Casey assured them. "Personally, I'm ready to get in trouble over this."

"I'm already in enough trouble," Louis pointed out, and, "Me too, actually," Felix said. "I've been doing a lot of class cutting."

Casey explained this to them. "He's working in the darkroom."

"I had an idea," Felix said, and his face lit up. "An unofficial yearbook. You know, all the things they don't want going into the official yearbook?"

"I'm writing the captions," Casey said. "We're using pseudonyms."

Mikey got them back on track. "Okay. Okay. It's time. You all know where to go and what to do."

"Besides," Louis observed, not unhappily, "if anyone gets in trouble, it should be Mikey."

Mikey smiled grimly. *Trouble? Bring it on, I'm ready.* "Let's go," she said, and led them out from behind the bleachers, out onto the courts. Because of the audience seated on the bleachers, she and Margalo had decided they didn't have to worry about bad calls on Courts One and Two, so Mikey led her linespeople down to the gates between Courts Three and Four, leaving a set of three people at each of those courts, and then went with her remaining five people to the gate between Courts Five and Six.

That was where Coach Sandy caught up with her. "Stop right there, Elsinger. What do you think you're doing? You're off the team."

Mikey smiled and held out her empty hands. *Look, Coach, no racket.*

"So what are you doing on the court?" Coach Sandy stood back to let the girls who would be playing on those courts go past her, and as they passed, she advised her players, "Cover the alleys. Go down the middle. Rush the net," before she turned back to Mikey. "Well?"

"We're going to call the lines," Mikey said. "We want to help out," she said loudly.

Whatever Coach Sandy was thinking of saying in response to this got stifled by the approach of the opposing coach.

"Sandy, you really are a wonder," the other coach said. It was a man, about the age of Mikey's dad, long legged, tanned, wearing white shorts and an orange Windbreaker. "I wish I could assemble some linespeople so my players could concentrate on playing. I wish I could get my school more enthusiastic, too, about tennis. You've got a real crowd here."

Both Mikey and Coach Sandy turned their heads to look down the line of fencing and see that the bleachers now had a lot of students sitting on them, with a few mothers huddled together at one end of the bottom row. All of the students were backing the home team.

"I do, don't I?" said Coach Sandy suspiciously, with another evil eye for Mikey.

"I wish I knew how you did it," the other coach said. Then, "Good luck to all of them," he said. "Let the games begin!" he called, and blew on his whistle.

Mikey ran to take up her position, chosen for maximum visibility of her half of the court. The opposing team had won the toss and were serving first. Chrissie would receive serve, and Mikey knew exactly the serve she would have tried against Chrissie—out wide to the forehand to draw a cross-court response that the net person could put away.

That was exactly what this server did and exactly what happened. Mikey didn't even begin to think about how much she would rather be playing in this game than calling lines for it. She didn't let herself wish she was in Chrissie's place against this intelligent opponent. She concentrated on calling the lines.

Vaguely, as if from a distance, she heard calls being made on other courts.

Margalo slipped out of the rehearsal a few minutes early so she could get to the tennis courts in time to see how the line calling was going. She almost ran, down the hallway and across to the gym entrance, then through the gym, down the stairs and out the rear to the tennis courts. The first three courts were still being played on when she got there. Each of those courts had four linespeople on it. She heard occasional calls, *Out*, and the servers calling out the scores, *fifteen–thirty, forty–love*.

Margalo went up to the side of the bleachers and asked one of the team members sitting there, "How's it going?"

"Mark won his singles, but Fiona lost hers, but we took two of the doubles sets, so it's not too bad," she was told.

"It could still go either way," somebody added.

"You're that friend of Mikey's."

"Yes," Margalo said.

"Can you get her to come back on the team?"

"Jerk, it's not up to her. It's up to Coach Sandy."

"But Coach Sandy has it in for her."

"I don't think she'll give up."

"Who, Coach Sandy?"

"No, dummy. Coach Sandy would give up in a minute if Mikey would let her save face. It's Mikey who won't. It doesn't help that she's right."

370

"You mean Mikey is?"

"Exactly."

Margalo moved on. She had heard enough, and it was pretty much what she expected to hear. Coach Sandy was standing behind the fence, watching over the game being played on the middle court, clapping loudly for good shots and calling out encouragement.

Mikey was crouched down on the service line to make her calls, and Jace was at the right rear, watching the sidelines and the end line. The air was full of the *thwap* sound of the tennis ball hitting the sweet spot on the racket.

Margalo thought tennis was like most sports, not all that interesting to watch unless Mikey was playing. So she spent her time looking around, trying to match up kids and parents, enjoying the temper tantrum one of the opposing players let himself have when he double-faulted. It wasn't even set point, and he still slammed his racket down onto the court as if it was set point—set point and more, match point at the U.S. Open on national TV.

Because she wasn't watching the matches very carefully, Margalo was one of the first to notice Mr. Robredo emerge from the gym. As far as you could tell from looking at him, Mr. Robredo was here to see how the games were going and to support the tennis team. He went to stand next to Coach Sandy, every now and then saying something to her. He was wearing a suit and tie, she was wearing a short blue pleated skirt and a maroon shirt. From the rear they looked built to the same model, both compact, carrying no extra weight, both with short, practical hairstyles, both of them adults dressed for their jobs.

Margalo turned her attention to Ronnie, calling lines for a boys' doubles match on Court One. "Out!" Ronnie called, and when the player protested—"You can't be serious!"—she turned her smile on him. "It really was out."

He stopped arguing, stopped even feeling bad about having lost the point. *Nothing like a pretty face and a good body to help things go along smoothly*, Margalo thought, grinning to herself. She looked for Mikey, to repeat that observation to her.

Mikey was coming off the court, with Jace and Tan and Sal following her, while the players were shaking hands over the net. As the linespeople emerged, Mark Jacobs stood up in the bleachers beside Margalo and called, "It was great to have you guys calling the lines. Good going," he said, and he started clapping.

Others joined in, and once enough others were doing it, everybody clapped. Beside the fence, Mr. Robredo slapped his palms together—clap, clap, clap—and smiled as the linespeople clustered together, some more embarrassed than others, while one (Louis Caselli) was visibly delighted, holding his hands up over his head like a victorious boxer. Beside Mr. Robredo, Coach Sandy smiled as if she had bitten into a lemon and discovered that all the enamel had worn off her teeth. She put her hands reluctantly together—was there something nasty on one of them? Something she didn't want to spread onto the other?—and took them apart without looking at them, as if unwilling to see what she might find.

It didn't take long for people to clap themselves out and then look at their watches. Everybody started drifting away. The coach gathered her team together for the *post mortem*, looking back over her shoulder with a firm, coachly nod when Mr. Robredo said, "So that's ten tomorrow morning, Sandy? My office?"

"I'll be there," she said, going off with her players.

Margalo approached Mikey just as Mr. Robredo's voice grabbed at her. "Mikey," he said.

Mikey looked at Margalo, *Uh-oh*. Then she aimed her smile at the assistant principal, lots of teeth showing. *Yeah, but I already did it, so what can you do?*

After a flicked glance from Mr. Robredo's dark eyes Margalo turned away, as if watching the tennis team make its exit down past Court One; but she stayed close enough to hear what he said.

He said, very calmly, "You're not going to do that again, Mikey."

Of course Margalo turned around to see how Mikey would take that.

Mikey had pulled her long braid over her shoulder, twisting it, thinking. Margalo stepped back towards the two of them. "Because . . . ?" Margalo asked Mr. Robredo, as if he was an actor who had forgotten his line and she was cuing him.

Mr. Robredo looked at her, looked at Mikey, then looked back at her. "Because I have just told her not to," he answered. Then he looked at Mikey's face and revised his statement slightly. "Asked her not to."

Mikey nodded and shrugged. She guessed this was about what she expected.

Margalo stood beside Mikey and told Mr. Robredo, "I'm Margalo Epps. I'm Mikey's friend who helped organize this."

"Well," Mr. Robredo said, "it was a good job of work you two did. But that's going to have to be an end of it. Understood, Mikey?"

Mikey nodded and shrugged and pressed her lips together. *So what? Who cares?*

Margalo knew pretty much just what she felt like: Bad.

Powerless, helpless, and solitary bad. Rock-bottom, why-bother, just-let-me-out-of-here bad. Rotten, stinky, useless bad. Bad without any smallest flicker of angry in it.

Defeated.

— 22 —

Ask the Parents

Neither one needed to explain to the other how they were feeling as they climbed up onto the bus and slouched down the aisle to an empty seat. They had done everything they could think of and it hadn't made any difference. They bounced along, not talking, not looking out windows, just bouncing. Finally Mikey spoke. "Want to have dinner at my house?"

"Why not?"

"Don't fall all over yourself being grateful," Mikey advised.

"Why should I be grateful?" Margalo demanded.

Mikey, being Mikey, thought Margalo was really asking. "One, because the food will be good. Two, because Katherine will be there, it's Tuesday, and you like her. Three, because maybe you'll pick up a cooking tip. And four, the most important, because if you go home with that face on, Aurora will worm everything out of you, which I don't want her to do. I mean, it's not like you're the one Robredo put out of action."

"It might be smart to ask Aurora's advice, or Steven's, if you still don't want to tell your father," Margalo observed.

"I should be able to take care of this myself," Mikey said, repeating what she'd said several times already; and Margalo didn't disagree. "We're in ninth grade, we're not little kids. Are you going to come to dinner or not? Dad can drive you home after, when he takes Katherine."

Margalo considered. "I guess," she said. "But I'm not feeling too bouncy."

Mikey, who was feeling bad enough for two people already, tried to distract herself by thinking about what they would serve for dinner. Asparagus, and maybe she'd make some buttered bread crumbs to go on top. Katherine watched her weight, so she'd probably scrape them off, but she'd appreciate the extra touch. Katherine appreciated things.

Thinking about what to cook made Mikey feel better. Not a lot, but some. And some was welcome, because she didn't like to think about that tennis coach, and the team that let their coach tell them to act that way, and the school that didn't want anything to change, even for the more honest.

Or maybe she should top the asparagus with some chopped-up hard-boiled egg?

By the time Mikey and Margalo banged in through the kitchen doorway, dropping their knapsacks onto the space on the floor beside it which was kept clear for just that purpose, Mikey's father was already home and cooking, with Katherine at the table watching and chatting. Margalo went straight through to the living room to call Aurora, who said, "Of course," of course. Then Margalo returned to the kitchen, to sit with Katherine at the table and watch the Elsingers at work together. Mr. Elsinger prepared chicken breasts, while Mikey did the potatoes and salad and snapped ends off the asparagus. Katherine greeted Margalo, "I brought a pie."

Katherine was short and round and cheerful. She worked in Mr. Elsinger's office, which was where he had met her; she was divorced and had two young sons. She didn't seem to mind being a divorced single mother, maybe because she had a good job, or maybe because she'd had a bad marriage, or maybe because she was an upbeat person by nature. It had taken Mikey a while to get used to Katherine. On Aurora's advice Margalo had just gone along with whatever Mikey was saying at the time, agreeing with her every step of the way, through anxiety, curiosity and doubt, to acceptance and now genuine liking. Katherine had just been herself through all of this, and by now they all felt pretty comfortable together, and pretty friendly, too.

"It's an apple pie," Katherine told Margalo. "Not home-made, which is lucky for you. How have you been, Margalo? And how's your mother's GED course going?" Katherine was always interested in what was going on in Margalo's life, and Mikey's, too. Not personal things or private things, just

377

things you'd talked to her about earlier, things that interested you. "And do you still like the dishwashing?"

"I like having a job," Margalo allowed.

"A paycheck," Katherine agreed. "How do you get along with the people there?"

"They don't pay much attention to me."

"But I bet you pay attention to them."

"They're interesting," Margalo said. "They're not high school kids, and they talk as if I'm not there at all."

Katherine smiled broadly, and her cheeks got rounder and her eyes got smaller. "Learning any new words?"

"New expressions mostly," Margalo said. It cheered her up to talk about work, and she was glad she'd accepted Mikey's invitation.

They ate at the dining-room table, in its corner of the living-dining-family room. Before Katherine they had eaten at the small kitchen table, serving themselves from pots and pans on the stove top; now there were place mats and colorful cotton napkins and serving dishes passed around. For dinner they had sautéed chicken breasts with a lemon-caper sauce, steamed asparagus spears served plain, and little new red potatoes. There was also a tossed salad with Mikey's special dressing. Mr. Elsinger and Katherine had glasses of ice water. Mikey and Margalo had glasses of milk.

Seated, they spread their napkins across their laps and looked around at one another. "This certainly looks good, Anders," Katherine said. Mikey and Margalo agreed.

"Let's hope it is," said Mr. Elsinger, his usual response. "Who wants to start the chicken?"

Margalo had seen Mikey's father depressed and unselfconfident, then she had seen him lonely but all right, and now she was seeing him in contented high spirits. Over the years Mikey's parents had done a lot more changing than Margalo's had. Only recently had her parents surprised her, or rather, had Aurora begun making unexpected choices, causing Steven to react uncharacteristically. But having practiced with the Elsingers, especially during their about-to-decide-to-be-divorced period, Margalo could be calm about her own family, where it was only a matter of people—well, only one person, actually—getting on with a new direction in her life and the rest of them adjusting.

"This sauce smells good," said Mikey, who always started a meal by lowering her face down over her plate and inhaling.

"How was your tennis game?" Mr. Elsinger asked, serving himself potatoes and not looking at Mikey.

Margalo did.

Mikey looked back at Margalo and shrugged, just a little.

"Did you play doubles again?" asked Katherine, who had seen this quick look-exchange and now glanced with raised, inquiring eyebrows at Mr. Elsinger, having a look-exchange of her own. "Or has the coach put you back into singles?"

Sometimes the sideways ways adults went about getting information just made Margalo want to laugh. She grinned at Mikey. *So? Are you going to tell them?*

"Actually," Mikey said, "I didn't play."

"Why not? Are you injured?"

"Actually," Mikey said, "I'm not on the team anymore."

"Why not? I thought—You're at the top of that tennis ladder, aren't you? Didn't you tell us you'd beaten the final girl? You did, her name was Fiona, I remember because it's an unusual name."

"Actually, the coach threw me off the team."

Now Mikey had their full attention. They had stopped eating. "But why?" asked her father, and, "Whatever happened?" Katherine echoed.

So Mikey told her father what had been going on. She told him about the calls and about Coach Sandy's instructions, about being benched and having a one-person protest, then about arranging to call the lines. "With a bunch of other people. You know."

Mr. Elsinger was shaking his head and his eyes were wide. "How would I know? This is the first I've heard of it."

Mikey went on. "That was today, but Mr. Robredo—he's the assistant principal. He said we can't do it again."

"Because . . . ?" Mr. Elsinger asked.

"Dunno," Mikey said, and returned to her dinner. "He just said."

"Margalo, do you know why?"

"Not really. Except—You know how it is, in a school, if somebody is rocking the boat. Probably maybe in any society or business," Margalo added. "Boat-rockers get asked not to do it."

"Are you in trouble in school now?" Mr. Elsinger asked.

"I don't think so," Mikey told him, then turned to ask Margalo, "Do you think I am?"

"I was there," Margalo explained to the adults.

"She was trying to take some of the credit away from me," Mikey said, and Katherine laughed out loud.

"Do you want me to talk to the school?" Mr. Elsinger asked Mikey. "I could call this—you said his name was Robredo?"

"It wouldn't change anything," Mikey said.

Katherine had been thinking. She had bright blond hair, probably not natural, and bright blue eyes, and she always wore eye makeup and lipstick, so she looked like someone who might never think about anything. But that was a false appearance. Now she asked, "What were you after, with this protest and this line-calling? What is it you want to have happen as a result?"

An easy question. "I want Coach Sandy fired."

There was a short silence, until everybody laughed. Everybody except Mikey, who did, however, grin a little and add, "Well, you asked me what I want."

"And I agree with you," Katherine said. "Well I do," she said to Mr. Elsinger. "And if I can't say what I think at what's going to be my own dinner table . . ." She didn't need to finish that sentence.

"Ask me why you'll never be President and CEO of the company," Mr. Elsinger said, not sounding upset. "Even as smart as you are, and as well-liked, and as good at the job."

"Ask me if I care," she said, then turned her attention back to Mikey. "But if we admit that you can't get the woman fired?"

Mikey nodded her head. She knew she couldn't.

"What would you settle for?"

"I never thought about that."

"Think about it," Katherine advised. "What's your bottom line here?"

"To play on the team?" suggested Margalo. A new way to think about problems always got her interest.

"And have everybody make good calls, no matter what any other team does."

"That doesn't sound unreasonable," Mr. Elsinger said.

"And Coach Sandy should apologize to me," Mikey finished.

"I agree," Katherine said. "But is that a requirement?"

Mikey considered this. "Yes," she decided. "Because what if people think I just changed my mind about the calls or got talked out of it, like when you settle out of court. It's a little suspicious when people do that."

"Often they do it to save the expense of a trial," Mr. Elsinger pointed out.

"I know, but—"

"Or to avoid the risk of losing everything if the trial doesn't go well, if the other lawyer outlawyers yours," Katherine said. "It's reasonable to choose a sure thing over a risk."

"I know that, too," Mikey said. "But if you really believe you're right, you shouldn't settle. Should you?"

"No matter how much money the settlement is?" Katherine asked.

Mikey shook her head. No, no matter how much. "Because if it's about money, then you might as well never have started the case."

"Besides," Margalo pointed out, "even if you do get a big cash award in a trial, don't the lawyers take an awful lot of it? And aren't those awards often overturned on appeal, because there are usually appeals. So you might not get anything if you were in it for the money."

This argument improved Katherine's already happy mood. "You two," she said, "I hope you're the wave of the future."

Privately Margalo agreed with her, but she had to admit, "I don't think we are. At least not at school we aren't. Unless it's a very distant future."

Katherine doubted this but said nothing. Mr. Elsinger expressed it in his usual unassertive way, as a question. "Do you think a wave of the future—Do you think it always knows what it is?"

"I think I can't figure out what anybody's talking about," Mikey announced. "Except me, and I'm talking about how I'm not going to be playing on the tennis team for four years, which isn't such a terrific topic, if you ask me."

"There's still the county league," Mr. Elsinger said.

"You can teach my boys to play," Katherine suggested, and

her face lit up at the possibility. "It would help everything if you did that, Mikey."

Mikey looked at her father. He smiled reassuringly.

Katherine ignored this. "Seriously, it would. The boys aren't stupid, and they're worried about having a new sister, and an older one. They're not worried about a second dad, they know about fathers. Your father doesn't worry them, but you do sometimes. But if you were teaching them tennis—"

"We get along fine," Mikey reassured her.

"I know that, but . . . You're always beating them. If you think about it, you win at Go Fish and Candy Land and War and when you run races of any kind, even when they have a head start. But what if you were helping them to learn how to do something?"

Mikey didn't mind helping the boys, and she also realized, "It would be good for my game, I bet. Sure, I'll try, if they want. But what will I do at school instead? I'm not going out for track," she told them, as if they had been trying for hours to persuade her to do that.

"You'll do regular gym, like me," Margalo suggested.

Suddenly Mikey scraped her chair backwards from the table and threw her napkin—hard—down on the floor. "I hate giving up!" she yelled, loud as a siren. She looked around at them all, bent to retrieve her napkin, drew her chair back in, and popped an asparagus spear into her mouth, apparently satisfied with the effect.

"But who said anything about giving up?" asked Katherine.

"You know the story about that book that won the Pulitzer?" Mr. Elsinger asked.

"*Confederacy of Dunces*? You should tell them," Katherine said to Mr. Elsinger.

"If you want to hear it?" Mr. Elsinger asked Mikey and Margalo.

"If you want to tell it so badly," Mikey said, and, "Yes," said Margalo.

"It has to do with giving up. That's what made me think of it, because this young man, in his twenties, I think, he'd written a novel. A huge, long book, and original, too, unlike almost everything else. Publishers rejected it."

"Well," Katherine offered, "I don't blame them."

"That isn't the issue." Mr. Elsinger had the floor. "Eventually the young man killed himself. From what I remember, it was a very long time that he kept sending it out and getting it back, and it was just too discouraging for him."

"You aren't worried that I'll kill myself, are you?" Mikey asked.

"I never thought of that. Do I have to think about it?" her father asked, ready to put some worrying energy into the question if it needed the attention.

"Just finish the story, Anders," Katherine advised.

"His mother, the writer's mother, after his death she sent the manuscript to a well-known Southern writer—Did I say the young man was Southern? He was. Anyway, this other famous writer, he really liked the book. He liked it so much he took it to his publisher and persuaded them to publish it. And it won the Pulitzer Prize. *A Confederacy of Dunces*, that's the name."

"So what are you telling us?" Margalo asked. She knew it was Mikey's father's conversation with his daughter, but she was too interested to take a backseat.

"That he didn't have to give up," Mikey said.

"Although it could be that his suicide made a good marketing point for the book when it came out," Mr. Elsinger said, thinking out loud.

Margalo nodded. She could see what he meant. "Not that any of it made any difference to him," she said. "Since he was dead. Which is a pretty important point."

Mr. Elsinger nodded.

"If it had been me, I'd have written another book," Katherine said. "It's just . . . *boring* if you don't keep trying."

"That's what I mean, why throw your cards down on the table and quit the game?" Mr. Elsinger agreed.

"You just always do what you *can* do," Katherine said. "Don't you think? You just keep on doing what you can— until . . . something changes? And sometimes it has to be you that changes, don't you think?"

Now they were talking just to each other, and Margalo looked at Mikey to see how she was taking this. Mikey didn't seem to find anything odd in this personal communication between her father and his . . . fiancée now, wasn't she? In fact, Mikey joined in.

"Like getting divorced," she announced.

Both of the adults turned their heads and stared at her.

"I don't mean to say that getting thrown off the tennis team is that serious. I just mean *like*, similar to. When something bad happens, like marriages going bad. What people do about it—that's all I meant."

Margalo reassured the two adults. "She's glad you're getting married."

They turned to stare at her then.

"Honest," Margalo assured them. "We really *are* talking about the tennis team. About Mikey being thrown off the tennis team. That's all."

But Mr. Elsinger—who, after all, had been in therapy with Mikey and knew how important talking frankly was—said, "Except I sort of was talking about my divorce, because I did give up on the marriage. But I gave up on your mother, not on love."

There was a silence, during which two of the people at the table—Margalo and Katherine—were a little uncomfortable.

Mikey said, "I'm not about to stop playing tennis, Dad."

"Good," Katherine said. "Now, I think I'll clear the table and serve dessert. Anders? You can help me. You girls sit. You've had a hard day. Save your strength for the dishes."

Mikey and Margalo remained alone at the table. They didn't say anything and they didn't need to, since they both were thinking the same thing: *Not me, it's not going to happen to me, I'm not turning into any weird grown-up.*

It took a little longer than necessary for Mr. Elsinger and Katherine to come out of the kitchen, bringing dessert plates, the apple pie, and a pint of vanilla ice cream, too, because Mr. Elsinger liked his desserts à la mode. Their cheeks were a little pink and their eyes were a little shiny, reminding Margalo of Sally and Richard coming back into the Drama room. At that thought she decided to concentrate on thinking about dessert.

For a while they ate without saying anything much. "Good pie," said three of them, and, "Good ice cream," said the fourth, everybody being particularly polite, the way people do when they want to make sure nobody at the table is upset with anybody else. Finally Mikey said, "I could look for a job. Like Margalo. Do you think they'd hire me at your restaurant?"

"You don't dislike the work?" asked Katherine.

"Just the pots and pans. And the cooking trays. But you know what I really like washing? The dough hook, it's about three feet long, and it's thick, heavy, really solid. It's like I'm washing a modern-art statue, the way it curves." She described the curve with her hands. "And it's really heavy."

"I know what you mean," Mr. Elsinger said. "I feel the same way about mowing the grass. In my hands," and he held up his hands to show her what he meant—which actually made sense to Margalo.

Mikey stuck to her point. "Would they hire me?"

"They might because it gets busier during the summer, when more people want to eat at restaurants."

"Also, I think I'll start coming to your rehearsals."

"Why would you do that?"

"To help out."

"I don't need help. Also, it's not the kind of thing you're good at."

"Maybe I can prove Richard and Sally stole your money."

"Nobody is interested in my money. Nobody cares who did it."

"What happened with your money?" Mr. Elsinger asked, and at the same time Katherine asked, "What money are you talking about?"

"I care," Mikey said.

"Except maybe Hadrian," Margalo said.

"Is anybody going to answer our question?" Mr. Elsinger demanded. So Margalo told them that sad story, from the beginning (at the bank, discovering she'd been robbed), through the middle (asking for advice, then help, then trying to solve the mystery on her own and finding out things she didn't want to know), to the end (when she got the envelope with two hundred dollars, but with nobody being held responsible).

"Aurora must have been in a tizzy," said Mr. Elsinger.

So Margalo had to explain that she hadn't told her parents, and why, and that she didn't want to. It wasn't that important, she said, and besides, what could they do now except feel bad? "Like you are," Margalo pointed out.

This caused another thoughtful silence. They had finished

eating, so all they could do was poke forks around on their dessert plates, scraping up the last sweet crumbs, the last moist lickings.

"Then you *will* tell your restaurant I want to apply for a job?" Mikey asked Margalo.

Mr. Elsinger asked, "Is that it? Is that everything we should know about?"

Mikey and Margalo decided without any consultation to spare Mr. Elsinger and Katherine Ronnie's story. Ronnie's story was the kind that would *really* get parents going.

"Of course not," Mikey said, and, "There's lots more," Margalo offered.

"Don't you remember ninth grade?" Mr. Elsinger asked Katherine. He reached over to take her hand. "There was always something else in ninth grade."

"Don't remind me," she said, clutching his hand with both of hers at the memory.

When Mr. Elsinger had left her off, before taking Katherine home, Margalo went slowly around the side of the house to her back door, taking a couple of minutes on her own in the mild early darkness of a spring night. At this time of year eight-thirty held the promise of summer nights, with the sun setting later and later, and the dark coming on more slowly. Through the open window to the bedroom she shared with Esther came a faint sound of music—some new band, she couldn't keep up with Esther's music fads. A country-and-western song from the neighbor's house dueled with Esther's band. Light from the kitchen windows lit the narrow sidewalk. She thought she could hear the TV and tried to remember what Steven liked to watch on Tuesdays, but then she wasn't sure she could hear it after all.

Through the glass pane of the back door, she saw exactly what she expected, her mother working at the wooden table under a bright fluorescent light while one of the cats walked back and forth across the yellow legal pad on which Aurora wrote. Aurora's hair was held back from her face by clips, and she wore a sweatshirt, probably with jeans. Her feet were up on the chair next to her and Margalo guessed that she was in her stocking feet, dressed for studying.

Aurora had a mug, probably coffee with lots of milk and sugar, on the table in front of her. She was concentrating, just as Margalo expected.

What Margalo didn't expect was to see Steven sitting with his back to the door, bent over his own open book. Steven also wore a sweatshirt and jeans, and the feet she could see the soles of as he leaned forward to read also wore only socks. Neither of them was paying any attention to the other. The little kids had been put to bed; older kids still living at home were upstairs doing homework, except for Margalo, who was with Mikey, as far as Aurora and Steven knew. This was the time of day they had to themselves.

Margalo was sorry to interrupt them, but what was Steven doing in the kitchen and not watching TV? She didn't plan to interrupt them for long. She had homework of her own to do. When she opened the door, Aurora looked up at her and Steven swiveled around on his seat to say, "You're later than we thought."

"We didn't worry," Aurora said, by which Margalo knew that they had.

But since all three of them understood that it had been one of those groundless parental fear occasions—they had known where she was, and with whom, and how she was getting home; they had known better—Margalo just explained, "Mikey got thrown off the tennis team, so she organized a group of people to call the lines—because the reason she got thrown off was the coach wanted her to call everything in her own favor, and she wouldn't do that, not if she wasn't sure. But the assistant principal told her not to do it again, call lines during a match, and she was pretty discouraged."

Aurora nodded. It all made sense to her. She could understand that this might keep Margalo a little later than planned. "Mikey doesn't have much patience with cheating."

"Is it really cheating?" asked Steven. "Or just giving yourself the benefit of the doubt?"

"Oh, it's cheating," Margalo assured him. She pulled out a chair and sat down, just for a minute. She kept her knapsack at her side so they would know she wasn't going to stay long. "I was there, I saw. Other schools do it too."

"Well," said Steven sarcastically, "I must say, that makes me feel a whole lot better."

Margalo laughed. Somehow, that evening, grown-ups were cheering her up about things. And Margalo knew that if she told Aurora and Steven about being robbed, they would react in just the right way, with sympathy and outrage and offers of help. But they had too much to think about already, especially since there was nothing more anybody could do about it, and she had her money back too.

During the car ride home Margalo had thought about what Katherine asked Mikey. She had decided that what she had really wanted was her money back and a public acknowledgment of guilt. What she had been happy enough to settle for was getting the money back.

"I think I'll have a glass of milk," Steven said.

"I'll get it," Margalo said. "But don't you want a beer?"

"Not tonight. I'm studying. I need my wits about me."

"What're you studying?" Margalo asked.

It was Aurora who answered. "Electricity, because he can fix everything. So why shouldn't he get an electrician's license?"

Steven grinned, as if he was a little embarrassed. Then he said to Margalo, "You heard the lady. Why shouldn't I? I can't have your mother getting too smart for me, can I?"

"No danger of that," said Aurora.

Margalo gave Steven his glass of milk, and he thanked her, then asked, "Does Mikey play baseball? Because you know what they say, there's no use hitting your head against a stone wall. When I come up against a stone wall, I never hit my head against it. I try an end run, or I try to burrow under it," he said, waving his hands in the direction of his textbook as his show-and-tell. "Mikey's a natural athlete, and she's pretty fast, I'd think a shortstop."

"She has league tennis and the county team in the summer," Margalo said.

"She's too competitive to get through the rest of the school year without playing something," Steven announced. "As I happen to know, being a pretty competitive person myself."

"Which in this case," said Aurora, "is a good thing for all of us."

"You know," Aurora added, "sometimes you realize that one phase of your life is over and it's time to start another. Like closing down Café ME."

Margalo nodded, agreeing but not wanting to talk about it. "How long will it take you to get your license?" she asked Steven. She had thought he was perfectly happy driving his delivery truck. She'd thought he'd do that for the rest of his life.

"A couple of years, studying part-time like I'll be doing. But it's interesting, unlike that stuff your mother has to learn, so I'll get there in the end. Picture me, tunneling under that high stone wall."

"They called them sappers," Margalo told him.

"Hunh?"

"The soldiers who dug tunnels under fortifications."

"Oh," he said.

"It's a weird word," Margalo said.

"Nnnhh." He looked down at his book, a hint. Aurora was

already back at her writing. So Margalo went upstairs to her room.

"Radio off!" she greeted Esther, who plugged in her headphones and put them over her ears. The music ceased. Margalo dropped her knapsack onto her bed and went out to the telephone in the hall.

Esther followed Margalo out of the bedroom, her arm stretched out behind her to hold the headphones, which were still attached to the radio, although now unattached to her head, emitting tinny bursts of noise. "Are you calling Mikey? I want to tell her something. Isn't it too late to call? Isn't it after eight-thirty? Did Aurora say you could?"

The best way to handle Esther was to ignore her, so that's what Margalo did. She dialed the number, pretty sure that Mr. Elsinger would not yet have returned. First he would walk Katherine's baby-sitter home. Then he would return to Katherine's house and see that the boys were all right, maybe even wish them good night if they were awake. *Then* he'd go home, not hanging around at Katherine's because he knew Mikey was alone. So Margalo thought she had time to tell Mikey what she'd just realized.

"Hello?" Mikey answered.

"They're all telling us the same thing," Margalo said.

"Who all?" Because Mikey had no doubt who this was calling her. "What same thing?"

"I'll tell you in the morning, but I wanted to say right now, you shouldn't give up."

"Okay," Mikey said. "If you don't either."

"You'll have to read the script for *Oklahoma!*" Margalo warned her.

"You'll have to take me to work with you, to the restaurant," Mikey said. "To let them meet me."

"We'll figure something out," Margalo said, and, "I know," Mikey agreed, and it was as if they had reached out elastic-man arms over the mile and a half between them, to shake on it.

"Yeah, but what?" demanded Mikey. "*What* will we figure out?"

"The world," Margalo announced. "Our lives. People."

"How to get rid of Coach Sandy," Mikey decided.

— 23 —

Failure and Other Educational Experiences

At lunch the next day Mikey announced that it was day thirty-three, and Cassie was off on a rant against the world and the people in it, the school, the students, the teachers, and the administration. You name it, it was rotten. They had occupied one of the picnic tables, and the noontime weather was ignoring, or maybe even contradicting, Cassie's low opinion of how things were. It was the kind of spring day that made you feel that life was good and you could be glad to be alive. Unless you were Cassie.

"When Mikey refuses to cheat, she gets thrown off the team. And when she figures out a way to make sure the line calls are fair—"

"As fair as they can be," Mikey said, being precise.

"What happens? Do they praise us? Do they thank us? No, what happens is Robredo comes down on us like a ton of bricks. He tells Mikey not to do it again. Or else."

"He didn't say *or else*," Mikey pointed out.

"And look at what happened to Margalo and how much help she got," Cassie went on.

Mikey had something to tell them all. "He didn't say *or else*, and you know what? Even if he had, I'm going to go ahead and call lines on Friday."

"I'm with you," said Cassie without hesitation.

"Me too," said Felix, "and you will too, won't you, Casey? Tim? We can have dinner, after, downtown. We could eat at your restaurant!" he announced to Margalo, as if he was giving her a present.

"And I could wash your dishes!" she announced back.

"Well, I can't risk it," Jace said. When they all turned to him, he explained, "I'm up for a juried high school exhibit, in the main library, in the city. It's a big deal. I can't afford to be on Robredo's hit list. Or Peter Paul's, either."

"That's right," Tim said. "I'm sorry, Mikey, but I'm up for associate editor of the newspaper."

"And now I think of it," Cassie said, "I'm not so sure I *should*. It would be hypocritical, acting as if I thought anything would make anything any better."

Mikey rose to move off. "A bad call is a bad call, and I'm not going to do nothing about it."

"You know what? You're absolutely right," Cassie said. "Count me in!"

Mikey didn't answer what she was thinking, which was

that she wasn't about to count on Cassie for anything. "We need to see Louis," she reminded Margalo.

Louis wasn't hanging around outside with a bunch of boys, being raucous, and he wasn't in the cafeteria with a bunch of boys, being raucous, and he also wasn't in the library working on English or Math. They found Louis behind the school building standing among a bunch of boys, being stupid and smoking.

What he was smoking, and what any of the rest of them were smoking, Mikey and Margalo didn't care about. Frankly. What people got up to was their own business, as long as it didn't interfere with Mikey's life or Margalo's. They had enough to do dealing with their own lives. They didn't need to worry about other people messing up.

"Louis," Margalo greeted him. "We need to talk to you."

"Yeah, well, I don't need to talk to you," Louis responded, and grinned around at his friends. *One for me.*

"Yes, you do," Margalo said.

Mikey was already walking away.

Margalo thought it out. If she embarrassed Louis, he'd just get stubborn, or if she threatened him or made him feel like he looked stupid. Louis wanted to feel like he was looking cool, looking good. "Somebody wants me to tell you something," Margalo told him, Miss Mysterioso.

"Woo-woo-Lou!" one of the boys said.

Louis grinned happily.

"In private." Margalo smiled just the smallest smile, switching to Miss Mona Lisa.

"It's not Mikey, is it?" Louis wanted everyone to know he wasn't that desperate. He bent over to pick up his knapsack. "Not any of your scaggy friends."

"You'll be surprised," Margalo promised, Miss Flirtorama.

Louis's eyes lit up then, as if he actually believed what she was pretending to be hinting. Could he have forgotten the tutoring bet they had? Could he have forgotten that he was about to fail ninth grade and have to repeat the year? "Who is it?" he asked.

Margalo shook her head, she couldn't say.

"Maybe I won't go with you unless you say who," Louis said, setting his knapsack back down on the ground, taking a deep pull on his cigarette, letting the smoke out from his nose slowly.

What did he think he was, a dragon?

But Margalo was fascinated by this conversation because she was just figuring out that Louis Caselli didn't think more than five minutes ahead. It was as if she had been given that fairy-tale gift of understanding the speech of animals, only this gift was that she could see into Louis Caselli's brain and watch what was going on. There wasn't much to see when his memory range was about five minutes, and his forward-thinking distance the same—Otherwise why was he smoking? And why wasn't he doing the homework they'd assigned him?

Then Margalo got it: All Louis Caselli had in his life to

feel good about was what his friends thought of him. That was it, everything, the whole enchilada. Louis would *hate* losing face, and he was afraid of it too.

"I promised," lied Margalo, wide-eyed with fake sincerity. "I can't tell anyone but you, Louis." And at that little victory for his coolness Louis shrugged, pinched the end of his cigarette to put it out, and then put it into his t-shirt pocket for later consumption.

"A man's gotta do what a man's gotta do," he said, and followed Margalo off to where Mikey awaited.

They took him into the library, where none of his friends were liable to see him, and sat him down at one of the small tables behind the stacks. Louis leaned back in his chair. "So. Who's the chick?"

"Get real," Margalo advised him. And this was the best advice anyone could offer Louis, if he could just figure out how to take it. But that wasn't her present problem. The present problem—the thing they *could* do something about and were going to do something about—was English for her and Math for Mikey.

"You mean you were lying?" Louis glared and crossed his arms over his chest. "Were you in on it?" he asked Mikey.

"Probably," Mikey said.

"Yeah, well, I knew all along," Louis assured them. "You didn't fool me for one minute. So, what do you really want? I thought—Now Ronnie's going to the prom with Chet, did she tell you?—I thought everything was fixed."

"*You're* not fixed. Our bet is still on," Mikey reminded him.

"And we can't risk Chet figuring out that he was scammed," Margalo added.

"Oh. Okay, but . . . I thought I didn't have to do anything until Friday. Today's Wednesday, in case you forgot. You *said* Friday."

"We changed our minds," announced Margalo. She added a one-page essay to his assignments, at which he grumbled, "As if I didn't have anything better to do." Then, "Mikey? Your turn," she said.

"Isn't one subject enough?"

"No," Mikey answered. "The plan for Math is you review the basic operations, then take the unit tests, one after the other. Mr. Radley said he'd take the unit tests into consideration as makeup work—if you pass them—but they have to be taken under his supervision—"

"He *wants* to flunk me."

Mikey didn't blame the teacher if he did. She'd want to flunk Louis too, a student who never did his homework, never tried to learn, cracked disruptive jokes in class and generally seemed to like being a buffoon.

Buffoon, that was Louis exactly. She started to write it down for Margalo so Margalo could enjoy it too. *B-u-f*—two *f*s or one? She'd never been much of a speller. One, she decided—*o-o-n*.

"Precisely," Margalo murmured, adding a second F.

"I'm pretty sure you can't pass," Mikey told Louis. "But

402

I've got a bet to win here and I want to win fair and square."

"Maybe I don't care," Louis asked. "What's in it for me?"

"Summer school," Margalo told him.

"I'm going to kill Ronnie."

"That's a good idea," Mikey said. "You'll like jail."

"Didn't you tell your father you were going to pass?" Margalo asked him, a guess, but a confident one. "At least enough to be able to do summer school for the remaining credits?"

"How'd you know that? Did Ronnie tell you?"

Margalo nodded. This would count as a white lie, wouldn't it?

"How else was I going to get him off my back?" Louis demanded, but then he realized, "All right. All right, you don't have to be such a pair of nags."

"Tomorrow, here, same time," Margalo told him.

"With the work completely done," Mikey said.

"Yeah, yeah," Louis grumbled, getting up and—after carefully looking to be sure no one was observing him—stepping from behind the stacks. He strutted out into the hallway.

Mikey remembered then, and she ran after him, ignoring the way he was trying to ignore her. "Louis? Wait up."

"Bug off!"

"No, I wanted to ask, will you call lines again on Friday?" Mikey was talking at the round back of his head, but her question stopped him. He wheeled around to tell her, publicly and loudly, "Look, I'm in enough trouble already without you trying to add to it." He looked around to be sure everybody noticed this, him shoving Mikey Elsinger off his back. "So count me out. O-u-t, out. And stop trying to get me thrown out of school."

They found Ronnie in the girls' bathroom, talking shopping with a couple of upperclassmen. "I looked there," Ronnie was saying, "but—you know—it's only a prom. It's not, like, it's not a wedding or something. Those dresses were ex-*pen*-sive. And they didn't look any better on."

"Yeah," one of the seniors answered, "but you could wear a paper bag and look good."

"No, seriously," Ronnie said. She sounded like she was apologizing for her looks, and maybe she was. "I found mine at T.J. Maxx. They had a great selection. You can probably wear deep colors like burgundy or forest green or—have you ever tried on gold? Hey, hi, Margalo. Hi, Mikey. What do you want?"

The upperclassmen picked up their books and left, continuing to talk about prom dresses. Ronnie smiled in the mirror at Mikey and Margalo. "Aren't you pleased?" she asked.

Happiness always looked good on Ronnie. Mikey glanced briefly at Ronnie's reflected face, then her own, and then Margalo's. Mikey was round faced, and her nose was sort of stubby, and her eyes were sort of small, and her eyebrows—which she privately liked—were sort of too straight and thick. The kind of prettiness Ronnie had was in her bones. Margalo had strong bones shaping her face, but her face was more square than oval, her mouth more wide than full, her eyes not so dark or deep and all those small differences made a big difference in the total effect.

"Pleased about what?" Margalo asked. She met Mikey's eyes in the mirror and crossed hers, which Ronnie, studying her lipstick, didn't notice.

"It's thanks to you I'm going to the prom. And don't think I'll forget that."

"Actually, it was Chet I was hoping would never forget it," Margalo remarked.

"Can you call lines on Friday?" Mikey asked.

"But I thought . . ." Ronnie turned away from the mirror to remind Mikey, "Mr. Robredo said not to do it anymore."

"I know. But . . . I'm going to do it anyway." At Ronnie's doubtful expression Mikey added, "You just said you wouldn't forget."

"But Mikey"—Ronnie turned to Margalo, who was someone who would understand—"I have an appointment right after school on Friday to try an updo." She lifted her heavy, dark hair up off the back of her neck to show them. "To see how it will look with my dress, and if I like it, that's the way we'll have it done Prom Saturday. Because that's in only three and a half weeks," she told them, her eyes in their pleased excitement shining as darkly as her hair. "Less than that, really."

"What's in less than three and a half weeks?" asked Tan,

who had burst into the bathroom, but before Ronnie could answer she said to Mikey and Margalo, "I want to talk to you two."

In the mirror the warm dark brown of Tanisha's skin, together with her height, her long neck and short, curly hair, her strong features—full lips, square chin, large black eyes—made her just as satisfying to look at as Ronnie. Mikey wished they would *both* go away so she could talk with Margalo about this, about what made people attractive to look at. She knew, for instance, that she had thick, heavy hair, and that was good; but what about her face?

"I'm leaving," Ronnie said, not offended. "Guess who's going to be Chet Parker's date for the prom, Tan."

Tan couldn't be made jealous about this achievement, nor was she any more interested than to say, "Funny. I heard you were taking him to court."

"That was all a misunderstanding." Ronnie gave a conspiratorial smile in the mirror to Margalo first, then Mikey, before she said, turning and exiting, "Sorry about the line calling, Mikey."

"What about line calling?" Tan asked when they were alone.

Margalo was disappointed. She'd hoped Tan wanted to talk to them about something more interesting than the line calling.

"I'm going to keep on doing it," Mikey answered. "Will you help?"

"Maybe," Tan said. Then, "I'm going to Oslo!" she announced, and waited for their reactions.

"Norway?" Mikey asked.

"You aren't running away, are you?" Margalo asked.

"The whole family is going, this summer, because William will be there—"

"I remember," both Mikey and Margalo said.

"And that means I'll see him," Tan concluded.

"Yeah, but what difference will that make?" Mikey asked.

"It's just going to make you feel worse," Margalo predicted.

"That doesn't matter if I can see him," Tan told them. "I can't wait!"

Mikey knew what was really important. "So will you call lines? It'll make the time pass more quickly."

The next day, Thursday, Louis had almost made it into the cafeteria when they grabbed him. "We're going to the library," Margalo said, on one side of him, and from the other side Mikey told him, "You better have that work done."

"Hey!" Louis protested.

Margalo could see the gears working: Did he want to push them away and make it a rejection scene? That would mean he'd flunk ninth grade for sure. But did he want to be seen going off with Mikey Elsinger and Margalo Epps? Definitely not cool. Did he have a chance of its not being noticed? Only if he kept his mouth shut, which would mean running a brief risk of looking un-cool, but maybe he could get away with that. "Hey," he protested again, but he walked a little faster and a little ahead of them. After all, who could blame him if Mikey Elsinger and Margalo Epps were walking along the hallway in the same direction he happened to be walking in?

Louis didn't say anything until they had entered the library, where nobody who mattered would see who he was with and talking to. Margalo led him to a table and sat him down. They had their plan ready. Margalo would go first, trying to explain to Louis how to take notes on a short story. While Margalo did that, Mikey would look over the problems Louis had done, drilling the four most basic math operations. In the next two weeks Mikey intended for Louis to have taken—and passed—all the unit tests of the first semester.

But as soon as they were seated, with Louis in the middle, and Margalo had taken out her notebook, Louis started to make difficulties. "What about my lunch?"

"You don't need it," Mikey answered.

"You're one to talk," Louis said. He watched her circling errors on his Math paper and protested, "I worked hard on that!"

"You can get something after," Margalo said. "They leave it set up for second lunch."

"But everything good will be gone," Louis complained.

"Too bad," Mikey said.

"And besides, see?" Louis indicated the paper Mikey was marking on, and the paper in front of him covered with scratched-out words and sentences. "I couldn't write that essay," he told Margalo. "And I didn't even want to." He leaned back, crossed his arms over his chest, and glared.

Margalo took a breath and looked at Mikey. "Okay," she said to Mikey, and, "Okay," again to herself. "Take out a sheet of clean paper, Louis, and write down first the title and author."

"You already know that," Louis groused.

"After that write 'I won't complain' a hundred times," Mikey muttered.

"Next make a list of all of the characters," Margalo continued. "With the most important ones first, then"—she held up a hand to stop him from speaking—"a list of all the different places where the story happens, in order. I have to go to the bathroom. Come on, Mikey," she said.

Louis smirked. "What is it with girls never going to the bathroom by themselves?" At the look on Mikey's face he added, "Everybody says that."

"Just do it," Margalo ordered him. "Mikey!" she urged, since Mikey was still sitting there, looking up at her, not moving.

Mikey had her role to play in this scene, so she followed. But as soon as Margalo was out in the hallway, she stopped. "I thought you had to go to the bathroom," Mikey protested.

"Remember Dumbo?" Margalo answered.

"Dumbo? Are you having a nervous breakdown? Are you worried about your play?"

"The movie. You remember, the elephant with big ears."

"You want me to rent a video of *Dumbo* for you?" Mikey guessed. This was weird, even for Margalo, whose mind was a natural bungee-jumper.

Margalo shook her head impatiently.

"It's playing downtown and you want to go?" Mikey guessed. "You want me to go, and take Stevie and Lily?" What was this, twenty questions? "Is it bigger than a bread box?"

"No, don't be so . . ."

Stupid, Margalo was going to say *stupid*, and Mikey wasn't about to take that, even from Margalo, because if there was one thing she knew she wasn't, it was stupid. She was about to tell Margalo just that, when Margalo went on.

"I mean, remember Dumbo's magic feather?"

"The one the crows gave him?"

"Exactly."

"But it wasn't magic," Mikey pointed out, trying to figure out where Margalo's wavelength was so she could get on it. "You didn't do any funny drug stuff, did you?"

"Mikey!" Margalo protested, exasperated. "Just listen. Louis needs a magic feather."

"Oh, of course." Mikey knocked on her head with her knuckles. "Silly me. I can loan him mine."

"Not literally, not a real feather. But . . . what if he really believed he could do this work? Learn this material. What if he really believed he could do well enough to pass the exams?"

"He'd have to be even stupider than I think he is if he can't. But he doesn't work."

"That's because he's afraid it's too hard. He's afraid that even if he works, he'll fail, and then he'll look seriously like a loser, if he's trying. But he's not abnormally stupid. He might not even be stupid at all once he gets out of school," Margalo said. "So I think we ought to try a magic feather. Not literally," she said again. "But I mean, what if we can persuade him that he can do it?"

"But he *can*. We already know that."

"So could Dumbo," Margalo pointed out.

"Oh," Mikey said. "Oh, okay. Okay. I get it, but . . . What's this non-literal feather going to be?"

"I think we should tell him we think he can."

"He'd believe us?"

"He'd want to believe us."

"But he still won't do the work."

"He will if he thinks it's easy."

Mikey worked it out. "And if we convince him he can do it, he'll be convinced it'll be easy—because if it wasn't, he wouldn't be able to do it—so he'll do it."

Margalo smiled as if Mikey was a student who had been having trouble learning and finally got it, as pleased as any teacher.

Mikey returned that smile, *You are very close to a punch in the snoot*, and Margalo stepped back a little. "Let me do the talking," she said.

"With pleasure," Mikey said.

But when they had seated themselves again, and Margalo had taken the sheet of paper Louis had shoved across at her, Mikey had an idea. She charged in.

"You shouldn't have made all these mistakes," she said to Louis, indicating the Math homework.

He shrugged. He could care less. Getting him through these courses was *their* job.

Mikey waved the imaginary feather. "You're too smart to make this kind of mistake in long division."

"Yeah. Right," Louis answered.

"So do the first three problems again," Mikey told him. She copied them onto a clean sheet of paper.

"I already did them and got them wrong."

"You couldn't have been paying attention. What is it, were you watching television at the same time? Because nobody as good at weaseling out of situations as you are would make those mistakes, unless he was trying to watch television and do homework at the same time."

"I didn't want to miss the game. Jeez, Mee-shelle, I thought you were such a sports person." But Louis took the paper, and maybe took the bait, too, because he looked carefully at her corrections. The thing about non-literal magic feathers was that you couldn't see Dumbo wrapping his trunk around them and starting to flap his ears. You could only hope.

Margalo was glaring at her, but Mikey didn't care. Her idea was: Louis would probably believe her before he'd believe Margalo, because he knew for sure how much Mikey had never thought much of him. Whereas Margalo was always harder to figure out.

When Louis had finished the three problems and shoved the paper across the table to Mikey, Margalo looked up from the papers he had shoved at her and said, "This is exactly what I meant. Exactly right. Now, think about who is in each of these scenes—"

"Do nonhumans count?" Louis asked. "Like, what about that deer the ants eat, is the deer a character in the scene?"

"You're getting ahead of me."

"I am?"

"Can you slow down a little?"

"Sure," Louis announced. "But I'm including the ants as characters," he told her. "And the deer, no matter what you say, and I can prove it too. Because they're there." He jabbed his finger onto his paper with lists on it.

"These problems are all correct." Mikey passed his paper back to him.

"You don't sound surprised."

"Why should I be surprised?"

"I told you he was smart enough," Margalo said to Mikey, as if Louis was invisible.

"I never said he wasn't," Mikey played along. "I just said he wasn't going to do the work."

"I don't have time to sit here and listen to you two arguing," Louis said to them. "I've got better things to do than—

Can we just get to work? Because if you think I'm going to go without any lunch, you've got another think coming."

So they all got a chance to have lunch. When Mikey and Margalo sat down at their table, Cassie announced that, after all, she did want to help with calling the lines at the next day's match. "Because even if it's not going to change anything, sometimes the only thing worth doing is the right thing. The same time as Tuesday? The same outfit?"

"Yes," Mikey said. And then—because if she hadn't, it would have been breaking a habit she'd gotten used to, as unnerving as forgetting to brush your teeth—she added, "Today's day thirty-two."

"But I'm not calling any away matches. I'm not spending hours trapped on a bus filled with people having school spirit."

"That's up to you," Mikey said.

"Robredo's going to be chewing nails over this," Cassie added.

Mikey reassured her, "It's totally my responsibility."

"Believe me, I've already figured that out." Cassie grinned.

Then, passing Mikey in the hallway on the way to class, Tan turned back to say, "I'll be there for the lines tomorrow." So the numbers were mounting.

Her anxiety should be mounting too, Mikey knew, since she had no idea what Mr. Robredo would do when she directly and personally disobeyed *him*. She would guess suspension, if she had to make a guess. She didn't mind suspension. If she didn't have to be at school, she could go downtown to Margalo's restaurant and apply for a job, so it wouldn't be entirely wasted time. But there was missing the work with Louis, for one problem, and for a bigger problem there was whether she would go ahead and call the lines for a third time when she got back to school from however many days of suspension Mr. Robredo gave to her.

Mikey thought probably she would.

Margalo had a slightly different point of view. "It's turning into a no-win situation, like the cold war. All it can do is escalate," she said to Mikey at lunch on Friday.

"Day thirty-one, it's already day thirty-one," Mikey answered. "The year is really almost over."

"Or it's like Thomas More in *A Man for All Seasons*," said Hadrian. "They cut off his head because he wouldn't compromise his principles."

"What kind of principles would be worth getting your head cut off over?" Jace wondered.

"Religious," Hadrian told him. "Personal integrity. Afterwards they mounted his head on a stake on the walls of the Tower of London."

"Ick," was Tim's response, but Cassie said, "Like the hands in a Grünewald crucifixion," and Casey's opinion was, "That's barbaric. Like hanging criminals in cages and letting them starve to death, then letting the bodies rot in the cages until they're only bones."

"Or putting them into jails," Felix suggested.

Hadrian continued, "Che Guevara. Martin Luther King Jr. Think of Jesus Christ. People frequently die for their principles. And Socrates."

Margalo pointed out, "Mikey's not going to get assassinated for arranging to have the lines called in a tennis match."

"I know that," Cassie said. "But there's the ninth-grade equivalent."

"Suspension," Mikey supplied. "I guess they could expel me, and then I guess I'd have to move to Texas to go to school."

"A bad idea," Margalo said, promising, "We could stop them from expelling you, somehow. We could stage a sit-in or take them to court."

Casey reminded them, "My father is one of them, don't forget. He's not going to agree to expel Mikey about this."

"Yeah, but what can one *teacher* do?"

Casey continued, "They're not bad. They really do want us to learn and graduate and succeed in life."

"Some of them can be pretty bad," Cassie maintained. "In it for the power, for example. Or the ego trip. Peter Paul," she named one.

Jace quarreled with that. "You just have it in for him because he thinks—"

"Thinks what?" Cassie demanded. "What does he think? That I'm boring? Talentless? Or does he just think I'm female, which is about as low as you can get on the Art ladder."

"Maybe he just doesn't think you're any good," Jace said.

"Well, it's mutual," muttered Cassie. "Not that it matters anymore."

Mikey ignored the sweethearts. "This is just making an athletic event go more smoothly. It's just calling lines for a single match, or a few matches. It's not—"

"Don't you dare say it's not important," Margalo warned her.

When Mikey led her group out onto the tennis courts that afternoon, there were only five of them, Cassie having met up with Mikey at the end of the last class of the day to say that it wasn't that she didn't agree, but she didn't want to become an activist, she didn't want to start being a member of any group, she didn't want people thinking they knew what she would do. Mikey nodded and rearranged in her own mind the disposition of her small group for maximum effectiveness. But as the five of them crossed in front of the bleachers, Cassie ran up to join them. "If an artist can't do what her conscience tells her, she might as well go to work for some Wall Street brokerage house."

Mikey just nodded and readjusted her readjustment. She repeated the instructions of Tuesday, again giving them in a loud enough voice so everybody—the home players and the visitors—would hear. "Remember, if you're not sure it's out, you call it in." Then she assigned linespeople to the courts on which singles would be played, since line calls interfered most with those games, where the players lacked partners to correct or corroborate a call. This Harry Truman High School team had some objections. "Hey," they protested, and, "Hey, man," and, "What're you doing?"

"We'll call the lines," Mikey explained.

"But, hey, that's not fair. I mean, you'll call in favor of your own team."

"If you don't trust us, lend us some of your squad to call too."

There was discussion about this, then six of the Harry Truman players came forward, and Mikey mixed everybody up and distributed them around the courts. She gave her instruction again: "If it's not clearly out, if there's any doubt, call it in."

"But hey, what if it might be out?"

"If you're not sure, it's not."

"Who're you, the tennis mafia?"

Mikey liked that idea, but before she could think of a good response, Coach Sandy came storming up.

"Have you permanently unplugged your memory banks, Elsinger?" Coach Sandy asked. "Off the courts. Now. And take your little friends with you."

Mikey would never have just ignored her. That would have been rude, and Mikey wasn't out to be rude. She was out to be rebellious, maybe, or disobedient; or you could put it another way and say she was out to ensure fair play. You could say that there were just two different points of view here. But that didn't mean Mikey couldn't be polite. So she turned around to face the coach and answer her. "No."

Then she turned back to her work. "Ira, take the far line of court two, and you"—pointing at an Asian girl with very short dark hair and sweatpants under her tennis shorts—"take the sidelines and the service line."

"I'm warning you, Mikey," Coach Sandy said.

Mikey turned around to respond politely, "I know."

"Your choice," the coach said, and stormed off back the way she had come, towards the gym.

Mikey figured it wouldn't be all that long before Mr. Robredo was out there, and she wondered how that conversation would go, because he was big enough to lift her up bodily and carry her off if he wanted to.

Or, she thought, picturing it, he could just crowd her off, stepping closer, driving her like cattle. In which case she would have to run, run around the courts, and he would have to run after her if he wanted to catch her.

She had no good guess about how fast he was.

But that would seriously disrupt the games, which was the opposite of what she wanted to do. She hoped that when Mr. Robredo got there, the conversation would give her a clue about what to say, how to behave. Because she didn't have any ideas of her own. Meanwhile, she hustled over to the court where Mark Jacobs was playing singles.

"Good to see you guys back here," he greeted them. "Are you ready?" he asked his opponent. "Are all of you ready?" he asked the linespeople. "Then, let's do it. You spin your racket, I'm calling up."

The racket showed down, so Mark got in place to receive the first serve. The match had begun.

When Margalo and Hadrian arrived at the courts after rehearsal, four games were still in progress.

Mikey was calling the lines on Court One, a girls' singles game. Margalo went over to the players' bench to ask about scores, but instead, looking around, realizing, she asked, "Where's Coach Sandy?"

The two boys and one girl sitting there didn't take their eyes off the court in front of them. "Dunno. She went off a while ago. Move, will you? I can't see."

Hadrian had taken advantage of the change of sides to offer his services and Margalo's to Mikey, who just pointed to Court Four and said, "When they have a changeover." But those doubles players didn't want the lines called. "We're fine, we're in the groove," they said. So Margalo and Hadrian went to sit on the second row of bleachers and watch as the sets were played out.

One court after another emptied its players and line callers out, and people milled around, watching whatever games were still in progress. Mr. Robredo arrived for the end of the match, showing administrative interest in the sports program, introducing himself to the coach of the opposing team and standing beside her to watch the final game of the final set, with Mikey, Ira, and two strangers calling the lines. At the end, "Good game," Mr. Robredo said, then turned to the players sitting on the bleachers to say, "Good playing, everyone. Thanks for the match," he said, shaking the hand of the opposing coach, and then—putting a hand out to grab Mikey's shoulder as she tried to get past him, going fast, as if he wasn't there—"I want to talk to you."

"Absolutely," Mikey said. "In a minute," she said, and turned to finish her own job, telling everybody, "Good work."

Mr. Robredo added his thanks, then told them, "You will be doing this for our last two home matches, won't you? I'm counting on it." At the expressions on their faces, *Trapped!* he warned, "Otherwise it would look like you had some hidden agenda here. Is there a hidden agenda?"

They shook their heads No, they wouldn't think of it. Sure, they'd call the last two home matches.

"I've been thinking, it probably should be the responsibility of the tennis squad to call lines. As of next year," Mr. Robredo added.

Margalo had moved closer to Mikey, showing solidarity. Hadrian had stayed back, showing insecurity. Hadrian wasn't accustomed to dealing confrontationally with the authorities. But he didn't scurry off, Margalo noticed, which she noticed the other tennis players and linespeople doing now, gathering up sweaters and knapsacks.

"Mikey," said Mr. Robredo. He sounded disappointed but calm. "I told you."

Mikey nodded.

"I should not, however, be surprised," he continued. "And I'm not."

Mikey nodded again.

"I want you to show up for practice on Monday," he said then. "Ready to play, will you do that?"

"All right," Mikey said, "but—"

"No questions," Mr. Robredo said.

Mikey stopped talking.

"You're lucky I'm not suspending you," he reminded her.

Mikey didn't nod.

And Mr. Robredo—after waiting briefly for a reaction—asked her, "How many weeks is it?"

This was unexpected. Mikey hesitated, then, "Six," she told him. "As of Monday."

"That's thirty days," Mr. Robredo said.

"Yes," Mikey agreed.

Margalo was having a pretty good time watching this conversation. She was having a pretty hard time not laughing.

"Although," Mr. Robredo said thoughtfully, "if you factor in that the last week is only four days because one is an in-service day for teachers so they can get their exams corrected and final grades calculated, and if you remember that there are three exam days and that attendance on the final day of school is optional, for those who want to find out right away what grades they're getting—Adjusting for that, it's effectively only five weeks as of Monday. Which is twenty-five days. How are you handling Memorial Day?" With that question he turned on his heel and strode away.

— 24 —

Back to Normal—Wherever That Is

On Monday, Mikey and Margalo finished quickly with Louis, praised his work—which was, in fact, perfectly acceptable—and then negotiated a Wednesday deadline for his next assignments. Louis fled the library feeling as if he had won a great victory and maybe even pulled the wool over their eyes. "You think you're so smart but you're not as smart as you think," was his parting blow.

They didn't try to contradict him and have the last word. They had their own purpose for Louis, which came under the heading of They Said It Couldn't Be Done. "Do you think he'll pass these courses?" Margalo asked Mikey.

"If he doesn't pass Math he'll hear from me. I don't know about English."

"Miss Marshall is being generous, letting him make up

assignments from the fall and winter. I tried to warn her not to expect him to thank her."

"How about answering the question?" Mikey asked.

"Well, yes, he could pass English. He *should*."

They were satisfied and entirely pleased with themselves as they went outside to eat lunch in the sunlight. Most of the school felt the same way that early May day, so all the tables were occupied, and the wall, too. They had to sit cross-legged on a cement sidewalk, sandwiches and fruit, cookies and cake, boxes of juice and milk set out on paper napkins in front of them.

"This is week six," Mikey announced. "Day thirty. It's really getting on down there. According to the way Mr. Robredo counts"—she liked remembering this—"it's actually week five. Day twenty-five. Actually, day twenty-four, because of Memorial Day."

"He's right, you know. Exam period isn't like school." Margalo was having peanut-butter-and-jelly for about the twelfth straight day, and she was pretty tired of it.

"I brought you a piece of cake." Mikey passed over a thick wedge of chocolate cake with chocolate icing and a pink candy rose.

"Is this a birthday cake?"

"It was Katherine's birthday Saturday."

"She had a party? Why didn't you ask me?"

"You were baby-sitting."

"You could have asked anyway."

"There were balloons and hats, even though it was only us." Mikey had an entirely thick sandwich, thick slices of wheat bread with thick slabs of white cheese and chunky golden chutney. "Presents, too. The boys each gave her a water pistol."

"She wanted two water pistols?"

"No, *they* did. We gave her an electric juicer, one of the small ones, for orange juice and grapefruit juice. She always drinks juice at breakfast and now she can have really fresh juice, which is always better than packaged."

"That's not an awfully personal present for your fiancée," Margalo observed.

"I think Dad has something else. Something private. Maybe a watch?"

Margalo gave Mikey the beady eye, *Who do you think you are deceiving?* then she made her countersuggestion. "A nightgown." Something in Mikey's face made her counter-countersuggest, "Probably a watch, that's a traditional important gift, or maybe books she'll like. A cookbook?"

"I *know* they're doing it," Mikey said. "Having sex. I'm not stupid, I just—I think it's private to them."

Margalo wouldn't quarrel about that. "Agreed. One hundred percent agreed. And I don't want them speculating about *my* private life either."

"You don't have one, do you?"

"Sooner or later we probably will," Margalo said. "We're not entirely abnormal."

426

"I don't think we're abnormal at all. I think we're what normal should be. We're what normal *is*. It's everybody else that's getting it wrong."

Margalo gathered up her papers, crumpled them into a ball, dropped them into her paper bag. "Maybe. But everybody thinks it's us that's wrong." She rose to her feet.

Mikey got up too. "But what do *they* know? They think school is going to last all the rest of our lives. *They'll* be surprised."

On that cheerful thought they went to the girls' bathroom, before the afternoon classes started. Most of the stalls were empty this late into lunch. But Ronnie and a couple of friends were occupying the mirrors, applying lipstick and mascara and combs. When Mikey and Margalo emerged from their stalls, only Ronnie was left. "I wanted to say . . . ," she started, then stopped, distracted.

They waited. She was giving herself a final check in the mirror, and something about her mouth wasn't right apparently. When she saw them in the mirror watching her, she smiled, *I know*, and said, "Uncle Eddie told my father that Louis got a C on a makeup Math test, and Louis told him—told Uncle Eddie, that's his father—that he'd pass English, easy."

Margalo corrected both errors at the same time. "Not easily."

"Which is really great," Ronnie said. "You really . . . you really helped me, and my whole family, too. So I was wondering"—a final lifting of hair to resettle it onto her shoul-

ders finished the job, and she turned around to face them—
"how I could repay you. So I was thinking, I might be able
to—Would you like me to get you a couple of dates for the
prom?"

"The prom?"

"*Your* prom?"

"The Senior *prom*?"

Ronnie smiled and nodded, the queen tendering a favor to
her loyal knights.

"That's crazy!"

"What's wrong with you?"

Ronnie's smile faded and her nodding ceased.

Then, "No!" Mikey cried, and, "No," said Margalo
equally emphatically, although she did add, "But thank you
anyway."

Mikey had more to say. "That's the worst idea you've had
as long as I've known you, Ronnie Caselli, and it's been a
while. It's been a while and it includes some real stinkers."

"You don't have to start insulting—" Ronnie said. "All
right," she said, and swung away from the mirror, huffing out
of the room. But she stopped with the door open to tell them,
"It wasn't going to be easy, you know."

Mikey and Margalo were left looking at each other in the
long mirror, their expressions doubled by being reflected.
Mikey looked to Margalo like someone who just got hit
across the head with a ladder, in that old movie joke.
Margalo looked to Mikey like someone who just drove past

a bad accident and was trying not to remember what she'd seen. They looked shocked and dismayed, both of them.

"What's happened to her?" mirror Mikey demanded of mirror Margalo.

But Margalo had already moved on to a more interesting idea. She looked now at her own face, now at Mikey's. "We're not particularly pretty, are we."

"You're closer than me," Mikey answered, which was true.

Margalo shook her head. Mikey wasn't getting it. "No, I mean . . . Actually I prefer to look the way I look. Don't you? I mean, don't you prefer the way *you* look? I *like* my face."

Mikey agreed. "I'd rather look at mine than hers any day."

"Is that weird?"

"I don't think there's anything weird about liking my own face better than anyone else's," Mikey announced. "Including yours," she said, picking up her knapsack. "I think that's the way it should be. Normal."

Margalo had turned to look right at Mikey, who was looking right at her now. She didn't need to say what she was thinking because Mikey was thinking pretty much exactly the same: *We agree on the important things*. "Shake," Margalo said, and they did, like two people at the end of a long journey, two people who have been lost together, hungry together, sleepless, cross and embarrassed together, not to mention invigorated and excited together, exposed together to unfamiliar people and languages and food, and now they have arrived.

❖

As ordered, at the end of the day Mikey went to the gym and changed into tennis clothes. She did not look into the coach's office as she went by it, but she did stop in front of the bulletin board where the tennis ladders were posted, to confirm a dark suspicion.

She was right. She'd been dropped right back to the bottom of the girls' ladder. Which wasn't fair, and it wasn't right, either. She should be at least in the top four. She *should* be number one, since that was the position she'd earned and nobody had won it away from her.

And she'd been about to get started working her way up the boys' tennis ladder.

She'd have to get this straightened out with Coach Sandy, but she thought she'd wait until the end of practice to mention it. That decided, she hefted her tennis bag over her shoulder and went out to the courts.

The team had gathered on the bleachers, where Mr. Robredo stood waiting for everyone to arrive. He wore his usual suit and tie, but he had changed into tennis shoes, for coaching. When Mikey arrived, he broke the silence, which had been lying over everybody like a wet blanket. "All right, people," he said.

Then he had to stop and wait for four more players, who were running up to sit down on the bottom row of the bleachers and look around at everybody, confused, puzzled, worried.

Mr. Robredo asked, "Is everyone here now? Mark, can you tell me?"

Mark Jacobs stood up to count heads. "Cissie Streeter isn't here," he reported.

"She's not in school today," Mr. Robredo answered, and then he began again. "All right, people. I'll be running today's practice, but as of tomorrow your new coach will be Mr. Elliot."

There came a deep silence as people took in that information. There were a few murmurs. "Say what?" "Isn't he a shop teacher?" and a few "Oh no's." It was Mark who raised a hand to ask, "But isn't he a track coach? Isn't he high jump?"

"People," Mr. Robredo warned them, and they fell silent again.

"All right. Now. I trust you to know how a practice should go," Mr. Robredo said. "Don't disappoint me," he instructed them.

They set up cross-court forehand and backhand drills, after which they would practice approach shots and net play, and by then they could get themselves sorted out onto the courts to play games, switching around teams and players, so that everybody would have a turn to play forehand and backhand, as well as to serve and to receive. Mikey kept a low profile. Mark Jacobs, leading them onto the courts for the first drill, had said to her, "It's good to have you back. But . . ." He didn't finish the thought, which was okay by her, since she could probably finish it for him.

It wasn't just Mark Jacobs with whom Mikey was unpopular.

431

It turned out, as the drills and the games went on, that of the whole team Mark Jacobs disliked her least.

"You didn't have to make such a big deal out of it," they said.

"Why didn't you just say something to us and let us take care of the calls ourselves?"

Mikey didn't bother responding to that.

"I was learning a lot from Coach Sandy."

"What is she doing now?" Mikey asked, trying to change the subject as they changed drill setups.

"What's it to you?" they said.

"I heard she's just switching jobs with Mr. Elliot."

"Has the man ever played tennis in his life?"

"And I heard that the people who don't make the team will have to call lines. Thanks a lot, Mikey."

They were blaming Mikey for losing their coach and for adding to their responsibilities, and they were right. She *was* the one who had done it. She'd had a little help from Coach Sandy herself, but still, Mikey felt she did deserve most of the credit.

However, she knew this wasn't a good time to point out to people that she should be on the top, not the bottom, of the tennis ladder. Her real problem was going to be scheduling the sets to win her way back up. But then she had an idea that cheered her up—Maybe a lot of them would just default?

They had arranged for Steven to drive them home that Monday so that Mikey could apply for a dishwashing job. As

432

they walked away from the school, Mikey reported, "She put me right back to the bottom of the tennis ladder," to which Margalo responded with advice about the interview. "Angie only cares about if you're strong enough—to do the work, to lift the pans—and if you will show up on schedule. If you're motivated to work. He doesn't care what you think. Not about anything, including cooking."

"What's Angie got to do with it? He's not the owner, is he?"

"The cook runs the kitchen. I mean really runs it, runs everything to do with the kitchen. He's the general, or more like a dictator. He yells at anybody he wants to, and I should warn you, he doesn't care if he's right or not. I mean, he *really* doesn't care about being fair. He just wants things done the way he wants them done, so the food we serve will be as good as he wants it to be. He'll tell you that's what he's paid for, the food. Not for employee satisfaction."

Margalo looked at Mikey, wondering if there was anything she should add. There was. "He'll tell you that over and over. He likes telling people that."

"But he doesn't have anything to do with the dishwashing part of it."

"I said the cook runs everything. That means he's responsible for everything, including clean dishes. Angie can fire me anytime he wants to."

"Did he hire you?"

433

"Him and the owner, Mr. Talle, he's the one Ronnie's father knows. Mr. Talle manages the front of the house." To the expression on Mikey's face she answered, "That's the restaurant part of the business. I should warn you, neither one of them thinks much of teenagers."

They had arrived at the restaurant and through the plate-glass window saw that three tables were already occupied, ten customers, all of them older, white haired and gray haired and bald. One couple, a group of three, and a group of five had been seated in the dimly lit dining room, with water and wine already on the tables and candles lit. "We better get going," Margalo said. "Dinner service has started, and Angie . . ." She hurried into a narrow alley and entered the brick building by a side door, beside which four outsize garbage cans rested in a rack.

The first thing Mikey noticed was how bright the kitchen was; the second, how hot. The brightness came from overhead lighting, and the heat from the two ovens and the one pizza oven, all three along the back wall. A side wall was lined with workstations and gas burners, over which pots and pans hung within easy reach. The wall opposite that was lined with what looked like glass-doored refrigerators, and between them, down the center of the room, was a long, wide steel-topped counter with two sinks fitted into it. The room was crowded with light and the noise of many meals being prepared and the odor of meat mixed with sauces and spices.

A big double swinging door led to the restaurant itself, and a doorless opening next to the refrigerators led who knew where. Somewhere that nobody in the kitchen wanted to see.

In front of the ovens, standing with his back to them, stood a tall, skinny man. He wore an apron wrapped around his waist; his black t-shirt sported a Grateful Dead emblem; his dark hair was shaved short. He was cleavering away at red and green peppers like some robot. Chop-chop-chop-chop, chop-chop-chop. He scraped the slim slices of red and green off to one side with the blade of the cleaver and began again. Chop-chop-chop-chop, chop-chop-chop. Mikey moved so she could see his hands. His fingers backed nimbly away from the approaching blade, but she still expected to see the occasional fingertip fall off into the pepper pile. She couldn't take the tension of waiting for that to happen, so she looked away.

Two younger men worked at the gas burners and at the counter, one with a frying pan, the other with a row of plates set out in front of him, on some of which he was arranging salad greens from a large stainless steel bowl. Nobody was talking.

This kitchen was definitely a workplace.

The aproned man scraped the entire mound of peppers into another stainless steel bowl, looked briefly at Margalo, more briefly at Mikey, and called out, "Where are you on that five-top?" to which the man with the frying pan answered, "Three minutes for the chicken," and the tall man said, "I'm putting the pasta in now get out of here Margalo you don't work Mondays." "Salads plated for the three-top," the third man said, and the tall man added, "And take your friend with you."

"Behind you," said the salad man.

Margalo pulled Mikey up close to the counter. Behind them a refrigerator door opened, then thunked closed again.

"It's Mikey," Margalo said. "Mikey, this is Angie."

"I said *go*," he said.

"You said to bring her by," Margalo said.

"Not *now*." He looked up, irritated, impatient. "I didn't say bring her by on Monday just when things are starting to get busy. In ten minutes." He hacked off a chunk of dough, which he shaped into a rough circle. Or maybe a rough square, Mikey couldn't tell. "Get out of my way," he said.

They weren't in the way, but they got out anyway.

Margalo took Mikey into the room behind the refrigerators. This was a much smaller space, so crowded with racks of dishes and bowls, pans, pots, stacks of metal trays, and plastic containers holding glasses, that Mikey barely noticed the two deep stainless steel sinks, each one large enough to hold a seated adult—maybe because the steel counter beside them was piled so high with pots and pans, mixing bowls, flat metal cooking trays, and deep plastic storage buckets, all waiting to be washed, rinsed, and set out on the drying racks.

Bent over the sink was a brown-haired boy. He didn't turn around to greet them. He might not even have heard them over the sound of water running into the sink he had his arms buried in. He might not even have been a boy—he was just someone slim and young looking, with long hair in a ponytail and wearing jeans, his apron looped over the back of his (or her) neck and tied at his (or her) waist.

Mikey did notice a heavy machine just inside the doorway. Almost as tall as her shoulder, the machine's one thick leg ended at a broad foot. It held out two heavy metal arms as if offering to give someone a hug. Set within the arms was a deep metal bowl. A large, thick, curved hook descended into the bowl from a cylinder that made up the robot head of the machine, where, she figured, the motor must be housed. "What is that?" she asked.

"The Hobart," Margalo answered in an offhand display of knowledge as irritating as Latin quotes. "Isn't the hook beautiful?"

"Beautiful?" Mikey took a few seconds to study it, considering the question. "No."

"You two—out!" Angie had come in behind them. "Now!" he specified, crowding past them to pull down a wide stainless steel bowl.

They waited for Angie in the alley, standing away from the garbage cans, leaning against an older-model Subaru wagon, from which position they could look back into the busy kitchen. It was a mild May evening, the kind of evening that made you feel you should slow down and just enjoy being where you were, wherever that was.

"Monday's usually pretty quiet," Margalo said. "Anyway, that's what they tell me."

"Coach Sandy will be a terrible track coach," Mikey said. "At least she knows how to play tennis."

"Maybe knowing she knew so much is what got her into trouble. Maybe thinking she was superior was her problem."

"Yeah, but she *was* superior. I never said she wasn't a good tennis coach, because she was. And Mr. Elliot doesn't know anything. It'll be like not having any coach at all."

"You got your wish about Coach Sandy. Almost."

"It doesn't feel like I won."

"Neither of us won," Margalo agreed.

They were silent for a minute, watching the three aproned figures move in and out of their line of sight, thinking. Then they looked at each other, having almost the exact same thought at almost the exact same time. "Yeah, but we came close."

"What're you two beauties cooking up?" Angie asked as he stepped out the kitchen door. He lit a cigarette.

"You smoke?" Mikey demanded. "In a kitchen?"

"I'm not in a kitchen," he said, staring at her, exhaling. "You're not one of those crusader do-gooder types, are you?"

Mikey wanted to deny it, on principle, and she wanted to claim it, in the spirit of perversity. So she kept quiet.

This was the response he seemed to want, maybe because it made him think he'd shut her up and won an argument. "So, you want to wash dishes."

"I want a job," Mikey corrected.

"You vouching for her?" he asked Margalo.

"No, I just brought her here to waste your time."

"There speaks the queen of sarcasm," Angie commented to Mikey. "Are you sarcastic too?"

Mikey thought about that. Then, "No," she said.

"Okay, then, you're hired," he said.

This Angie was definitely not like a teacher or a parent. He was a whole new kind of grown-up. "Margalo will train you Saturday. You can cover for her when she's off doing her Steven Spielberg imitation. That's in a couple of weekends, right? After that it'll be summer and we'll be busy, no time off. Do you have a Social Security number? You have to get yourself a Social Security number."

"Of course I have one, what do you think?"

"I think you told me you aren't sarcastic," and he grinned at her, *One point for me.* "Did your friend tell you about August?"

Mikey looked at Margalo, who, as far as she could see, didn't know anything about August.

"August is your one-month vacation. Vacation without pay," Angie told them. "Any problem with that?"

The opposite, Mikey thought, but did not say. She was scheduled for her three-week Texas visit with her mother and Jackson in August, and she wanted to have Margalo with her again, so August off suited her perfectly. But there was no reason to tell Angie this.

Margalo could see that Angie wanted to explain himself, so, "Do you close in August?" she asked.

Angie grinned, another point for him when she asked. "You kidding? That's our best month." Then, as if he couldn't stop himself, he told them, "I've got a couple of nephews, they fly in from Milan to get the American experience, language. They work here Augusts, where I can keep an eye on them, keep them out of trouble. You know how kids are. Teenagers. Magnets for trouble. Keep 'em busy, keep 'em working, that's my technique with teenagers."

Mikey and Margalo waited, saying nothing.

"So get out of here, the both of you," Angie said. "See you Friday at the usual?" he said to Margalo, then, "And you come in with her Saturday afternoon. What's your name?"

"Mikey. Elsinger."

"Mikey. Be here by noon, Mikey. The rule in my kitchen is, on time or early if you want to still have a job when you get here." He lit another cigarette, and they left.

Back out on the sidewalk, they passed the restaurant window on their way to meet Steven at his office. A few more tables had been occupied while they were out back. Two waiters were visible, taking orders, serving water and wine. Everybody at the three original tables was eating. Mikey and Margalo did not linger to watch all this. They walked quickly along, their shadows stretched out on the sidewalk ahead of them.

"Do you think we could wait tables?" Mikey asked. "Eventually, I mean."

"Waiters make good money, although I thought you'd

rather be a sous chef. That was my idea," Margalo said. "That I'd wait tables and you'd cook."

"You've got it all worked out," Mikey observed. "Do you think it'll turn out the way you plan?"

Margalo shrugged. "It *could*. And why not try?"

"Absolutely," Mikey agreed. "You know . . . ," she said hesitantly. Then stopped speaking.

Margalo waited for a few steps, until, "Know what?" she asked, irritated—and curious, too, about whatever it was that could make Mikey hesitate.

"He's not like a teacher. Angie."

"Of course not. He's a boss."

"This could be fun," Mikey said.

Margalo thought about that. "This could be work."

"Work can be fun," Mikey said, going for the last word.

"*Non sequitur.*"

"Latin."

That closed the subject.

Mikey opened a new one. "I should have asked you to Katherine's birthday. Next year I will. Do you want to be asked to the little boys' parties too?"

"You know," Margalo said, "you could take Latin, too. Next year."

"I'm happy with Spanish. You could take Spanish."

"Maybe I will," Margalo decided. "Maybe I'll take two languages."

"First we have to finish getting through this year," Mikey reminded her.

"We practically already have. I think we're going to be all right in high school, don't you?"

"Why shouldn't we?" Mikey asked, and answered herself, "No reason. I'm sort of looking forward to college."

"And after that our whole lives," Margalo agreed. "Do you think we'll stay friends our whole lives?"

"It would be smart of us if we do."

"They could put it on our tombstones, 'Friends From Fifth Grade to Death.'"

"You're having a tombstone? You're not being cremated?"

"Actually, I was thinking of never dying." Margalo had never admitted that to anyone before, not even Mikey, so she added, "Is that weird, or what?"

"It's normal," Mikey declared. "Absolutely normal, just like us."

They walked on together.